JAMES AND NATASHA

James and Natasha

Kathryn Balteff

James and Natasha is a work of fiction. All names, characters, dialogue, business organizations, places, events, and incidents, either are products of the author's imagination or are used fictionally, and are not to be construed as real. Where real-life landmarks and landscapes appear, the situations, incidents, and dialogue concerning these elements are entirely fictional and are not intended to depict actual events or to change the entirely fictional nature of the work. In all respects, any resemblance to persons either living or dead is entirely coincidental.

No part of this book may be reproduced in any manner whatsoever without written permission except in the case of brief quotations embodied in critical articles and reviews.
For information address:
Winter Woods Publishing, LLC
Attn: Permissions, 808 W Bay Rd, Gouldsboro, ME 04607

Any use of this publication to train generative artificial intelligence ("AI") technologies is expressly prohibited. The author and publisher reserve all rights to license uses of this work for generative AI training and development of machine language learning models.

Library of Congress Control Number:
2026902758

ISBN: 979-8-9944-955-0-6
eISBN: 979-8-9944955-1-3

Copyright © 2026 by Kathryn Balteff
All rights reserved

Published in the United States by Winter Woods Publishing, a division of Winter Woods Publishing, LLC, Maine.
First Printing, 2026

For My Big Old Bear
Always and Forever

One

James sat alone on the pink granite bench overlooking the sea. Rolling waves pushed onto the rocky shore breaking against ragged, worn edges of ancient stone. Salted spray reached skyward, then fell, caressing dark, exposed shoulders of satin basalt before slipping back into the silver-gray sea mirroring the late afternoon sky. Again. And again.

The gentle slap of water against lobster boat hulls moored on their buoys in the deep cove, an occasional muted cry of a gull, and echoes of whispery puffs of a breeze high in the firs on the reach floated along the undulating water. Every now and then, a fisherman's punt tied to the wharf lightly bumped into another adding a hollow, percussive thump to the August melody of the shore.

It was the accompaniment of his life—always had been. He gazed past the reach, seeing nothing. Thick forearms rested on his thighs. Fisherman's hands, rough and worn from years of working the water and hauling traps were clasped tightly together above his knees as if he was praying. At first glance, a passerby might mistake the older man in his rumpled gray work pants, T-shirt, and ragged sun-faded baseball cap for a stone sculpture attached to the unforgiving bench.

He'd been this way for the past hour or so with nothing to turn his attention anywhere else. He'd have stayed the same, except that a sudden movement off to his right, above and almost behind him, caught his sight in the mostly still, drab, late afternoon. He turned his head toward the motion expecting to see a wheeling gull diving for dinner or the chevron pattern on the under-wings of an osprey swooping down low toward the harbor from its nest atop the fieldstone chimney of the old Billings House. Instead, a whorl of colors was careening toward him. It took a couple of seconds to register that the object was a young girl steaming down the hill on a bike so fast that James immediately felt certain she would continue straight onto the wharf, then soar into the harbor ending up ass-over-teakettle where the road ran out and the world began.

He tensed. Placing his burly, weathered palms against the rugged, granite seat, he pushed himself off the bench. He'd have to move fast. He was certain the child was going to hit the water before he'd be able to reach her. But just as he started forward, the girl jammed her heels back on the bike's brakes, locking them. Small clouds of dust bounced away behind her as she launched herself from the pedals toward the rocky beach. The bike slid helplessly sideways, banana seat nose down in the sandy dirt by the side of the road, cross-eyed handlebars upside down, askew. Frayed purple and white tassels fluttered down into the dust. The front wheel wobbled in the air with rhythmic, protesting squeaks that continued long after the child bounded to the edge of the largest outcropping at the shore.

She took her stand there—all toffee tanned arms and legs in her faded blue-jean shorts and red T-shirt, shoulders up to her ears, fists clenched tight at her sides. She turned, staring across the water toward the reach, drawing herself up, head high and proud. Long dark hair moved in shiny kelp-like waves down her back.

Her stance immediately reminded him of his wife, Anna, when she was ready to take him to task for something that was most likely his fault. He could almost feel the vibration of the girl's anger. Whoever this little person was, she looked to be a handful and then some—just like his Anna. The comparison amused James. The wrinkles around his eyes deepened with his smile. He relaxed, backed up, and lowered himself back to sitting on his perch.

James continued to watch the child as she watched the sea. She wasn't familiar to him. He didn't think she belonged to one of the summer people. If she did, she wouldn't have been down here by herself, and she certainly wouldn't be riding a ratty, old bike out of the musty corner of someone's bait shed. This time of year, there were only a handful of annual summer residents left in Balsam Cove. Most of those families had been coming to town for years, and he knew just about all of them by face, if not by name. With only four hundred or so full-time residents in the village, he figured he'd have seen her long before now if she lived in town. It also seemed unlikely that she was part of any group of tourists that stopped for lunch or to poke around in the three shops in town as they passed through on their way to other places.

He massaged his chin with his right hand wondering where she belonged. Then he scratched at his cheek through his peppered beard thinking of how he would describe the youngster to Anna when he got home. This little soldier was ready for battle with an unseen enemy—so much angry energy for such a young being.

No. He wouldn't be able to tell Anna anything. He shook his head trying to clear the dark mist that seeped into him. He swallowed and peered again past the reach to the horizon where the smoky gray sea met the woolen sky. He wished he could get in his boat and go until he got there, until that sodden mist ate him up whole, and he would disappear too. Maybe his Anna was out there now. She wasn't of the land anymore.

She was gone. There would be no more telling her stories, no lights on to guide him home, no dinner waiting, no welcoming smile. No nothing. It had been weeks now, yet he still expected her in all the familiar places at all the familiar times. Now there was only emptiness and silence wherever he went.

He couldn't understand how this could have been allowed to happen. It wasn't right. To him she was the best of everything. She was gentle, giving, and kind. She was tough and gritty too, but not in any harsh way. She had a wicked sense of humor and was almost always smiling. He didn't think there was a soul in town that wouldn't agree with him on any of those points. She also harbored a mercurial, temperamental streak that, truth be told, James often could be accused of deliberately egging on. It never lasted long. But how he loved to see the stubborn set of her chin and the lightning in her eyes when she got riled up. In the end, she gave back as good as she got. Soon the brief storm would pass, and she'd be back to her bright, sunny self. Besides, making up over their silly spats was the best.

Anna was a member of the choir, and the ladies auxiliary, at the tiny Methodist Church in town that she attended whenever she was able. She volunteered or organized everything that church did to help in the community. She baked for every bake sale and knit mittens for the mitten tree in the library each winter. She sewed costumes for the kids' pageants long after their own children were grown and moved away. She'd help anyone who needed it, whether they asked for it or not.

He used to tease her that she was one of the pillars that held that old church up. She'd shake her head and laugh saying the church held her up, not the other way around. Early on she'd tried to get him to go with her to services. After a few years, she stopped asking. She'd dress the kids and herself up, give him a kiss, and say, "You know where to find us," leaving him at home as they walked up the road toward the white clapboard steeple. He attended baptisms, weddings, funerals, Christmas pageants, even a bean supper here and there, but he hated getting trussed up to attend Sunday service. He told her he talked to God every day out on the Cathedral of the Sea. He didn't need some stuffy building to have faith. She just smiled and let him be.

Now he didn't know what to believe. He couldn't fathom how God had let her suffer. Heaven couldn't need her more than he, and she was no match for hell. So where did that leave her? Where had she left him?

His breath caught—another sucker punch to his chest. She hadn't even told him she was sick until it was so late. Too late. No one had known. She'd let him stay his course until the night the ambulance had to come when she fell in the kitchen. James found her surrounded by jagged shards of her favorite china serving bowl, tears streaming down her face in pain and frustration, her legs abandoning her.

She was admitted to the hospital. There were blood tests, x-rays, scans, a biopsy, then more tests.

The children were called.

Sophia came home.

Thomas did not.

The doctor arrived with news no one wanted to hear. He told them the cancer had started in her bones, but it had taken over her body. It was everywhere. There were no options. No miracle treatments. No hope. It was too late before they even knew it was there.

They moved her from the hospital to the nearest hospice facility thirty-five miles away. Taking her home was never an option. The doctors said they'd try to keep her comfortable with medications. Comfortable? Like hell. What a lie.

Friends took over their day-to-day living chores at home. They kept the house, fed the cat, and brought food—more food than anyone could eat. Fellow lobstermen hauled his traps and sold the catch for him. The remaining church ladies organized a benefit to help with the medical bills. People came and went and went and came. The pain medicine made her sick. Her pain made him want to cry. He could do nothing except sit beside her bed and hold her hand. And so he did.

She stayed with him barely a month more, disappearing a little each day, until she was so thin and pale she became almost transparent, like the late summer jellyfish that washed up on the beach.

One night as he sat dozing in a chair beside her in the murky predawn, she woke him, squeezing his hand. She whispered, "Stay safe, Love," like she'd always done in the silver slivers of mornings before he left out to haul. He raised her hand to his lips to kiss it in reply, but she slipped past him and was gone.

When he went back to their home that day in the drear, late June fog, her damn cat ran right out the door and was gone too. Now, here he was . . . sitting on an old stone bench watching the falling tide and some strange child the wind blew in.

He glanced back to the rocky beach. The girl's stance had changed. She was in a pile on the rock, knees pulled to her chest, head leaning forward toward the horizon. He couldn't see her face, but he could tell she was weeping. He thought of his own daughter, and how he hated it when she cried; how tears had fallen silently from her lowered face onto her mother's still body; how he had done nothing to make it better. His jaw tightened. He never knew what to say—what to do. Anna was the one who'd always known how to handle things.

The child on the rocks stood up, turned, and wiped at her face. James looked to the other side of the harbor, studying the punts securely moored to the wharf. He didn't want the girl to know he'd seen her. He didn't want to feel he had to acknowledge her if she saw him. But neither worry mattered, because when he turned his head again she was grabbing her bike out of the dirt with no indication that she even knew he was there. She slung herself over the seat and began pedaling toward the hill like the devil was after her.

"Well, I'll be," he mused.

He reached for the brim of his baseball cap, picked it up off his silver-gray hair and placed it right back on, like it had been sitting the wrong way on his head. The kid had spunk. There was no way she could pedal that bike up that hill. No way at all. Still, he admired her trying.

He shifted slightly, just enough to see how this was going to go. About twenty feet up the hill she stood up on the pedals, trying to force the wheels to keep moving. The effort was obvious, though clearly not enough. In one fluid motion, she swung herself off the bike and began walking it up the hill, shoulders stiff and unyielding.

James sighed. *Oh, to be young again; what determination and energy.*

In his mind Anna's voice rang out. "James Edward, why on earth are you just sitting there? Get moving! You have things to do!"

He turned, half expecting to see his wife standing behind him, hands on hips, chin jutting toward him in mock, righteous anger. But the only thing at the head of the walking path along the shore was the hedge of faded pink beach roses.

James closed his eyes and rubbed his forehead with back of his hand. He shook his head. "OK, OK," he muttered. "I'm moving." He rose from the bench and began trudging home, up the same hill the mystery child had disappeared over moments before.

Two

James pushed the white, wooden screen door open with his right foot. Half in, half out, he leaned over and placed a stoneware cereal bowl full of cat kibble outside to the left of the door, same as he'd done every other night for the past month. For days, after the cat first ran off, he had searched the whole damn town. He'd asked everyone he ran across if they'd seen it. He'd walked down each road in the village peering in every corner. He'd checked obvious places he saw other strays, like down at the lobster co-op where they hung out waiting for bits of baitfish they could steal. All he found was frustration and guilt.

Anna would have ridden up one side of him and down the other for letting the cat out. The freeloading furball had first shown up on the doorstep about a year ago when James left to haul one morning. She sashayed in through the door, staring up at him like *he* was the intruder. James turned right around to try to catch it to throw it back out, but Anna shooed him off telling him she'd handle it.

When he got home that night the cat was fast asleep on a kitchen chair. It never went outside again—until now. Anna had coddled the mooching barnacle with treats, toys, and gourmet cat food. She'd even sewn up a plush, pink fleece bed to put on the cat's favorite sunny windowsill. Wherever Anna was in the house you'd find the lounging feline close by. In the rare times that Anna sat down, it immediately jumped up into her lap, turned around a couple times, and settled in for a nap. Anna had talked to that cat like it was a dearest old friend. James sometimes teased her that she loved the stray more than she loved him. She'd just laughed and said it was sad he was jealous of a cat.

He figured most likely a fox had gotten it by now. Since late spring there had been a female and her kits roaming around the edge of town. A small cat would be a tempting meal for them. Still, he left food out every night hoping it might show back up. Each morning there was nothing left in the dish. A fox probably ate that too, but James couldn't take the chance on his wife's cat somewhere out there starving to death. Anna would never forgive him.

James felt a flash of anger. Goddamned cat anyway! He pivoted sharply to go in, letting the door slam defiantly behind him. Anna would have scolded him for that too. He kicked off his tan deck shoes right inside the door and made his way across the kitchen, thinking he'd turn the kettle on to make tea. Halfway across the room he turned back. He picked up his shoes, then placed them neatly on the mat to the left of Anna's faded, floral slippers. He stared down at them sitting on the mat. Side by side. Both a little older, scuffed, and worn.

That's how it was supposed to be. Us. Everything. Comfortable. Older together.

He shook his head and sighed as he walked over to the stove where he turned on the gas under the kettle. He pulled a Red Rose tea bag from the box sitting beside the stove and plopped it into his waiting mug.

Sophia and Thomas had bought him the mug, at least five years back, when they were both still in high school. The years had faded the Patriot's logo, and there was a hairline crack on the top of the handle. Still, it was his favorite. He distinctly remembered watching the kids come in the door together the Saturday afternoon they gifted it to him. Of all the presents they ever gave him this was the best, because it was for no particular holiday or any other reason except that they'd thought of him.

Memories. James stared at the flame under the kettle. *Is that it? Is that all I'll have now?*

He shook his head, disgusted. "And apparently feeling sorry for myself," he muttered. "Now what?"

The only reply was James's stomach growling. He realized he hadn't eaten anything since morning. That one burnt English muffin with blueberry jam was long gone. Luckily, the fridge and freezer were still full of food. He opened the fridge door and immediately stepped back, accosted by the rank odor of something way past its prime.

Well, at least it doesn't smell as bad as bait. He leaned back in to move things around the shelves looking for the offender.

He rummaged by the butter dish, leftover lasagna in a Tupperware container from the day before, and a tidy row of yogurts — the kind Anna ate one of every morning.

Then he found it. A small, tan plastic bowl covered in plastic wrap. James peered suspiciously into it. Whatever was in there had to be the problem.

He walked over to the wastebasket and peeled back the wrapping. A bunch of green-black stems and mush appeared. Broccoli! He flipped the entire bowl into the trash. There was no keeping any of it. The trash would have to be taken out, and that stench would stay with him all night. So much for feeling hungry. Tea would have to do.

The kettle began making the comforting, crackling sounds of heating up. Steam curled up from the spout. James poured the near-boiling water over the tea bag, set the kettle back on the stove, then ambled mug in hand toward his chair in the living room.

The TV was already on, tuned to the national news. A reporter's voice rumbled in the background while scenes from war on the other side of the world flashed across the screen: bombed-out buildings and vehicles, flames and black smoke roiling in the air, people huddled in shelters. As James sat down, a high-pitched whistle behind his head began screaming. He jumped up, splashes of hot tea barely staying inside the mug.

"Holy hell! I forgot to turn off that thing—again!" He placed the mug on the end table and hustled back to the kitchen, and turned off the burner. The screaming whistle stopped. "I swear one of these days

I'm gonna end up burning this place down. Thank God that thing yells."

He made his way back and settled into his chair just as the newscaster began a story about the rise of mass shootings. James shook his head. "What is happening to the world? I can't even," he muttered.

With no ball game to watch, he flipped through the satellite channels, settling on a rerun of *The Andy Griffith Show*. He took a sip of the cooling tea and reclined his chair.

He woke at eight o'clock when the opening music for yet another half hour with Opie, Andy, and Aunt Bea began.

"Time for bed," he said to the walls.

He pushed the recliner closed, heaved himself out, and grabbed the now cold mug of tea on his way to the kitchen. He stood for a long while at the sink, watching the light dim over the harbor. The clouds had cleared. The tide was almost completely out. Through the open window he watched the water gently lapping against the exposed rocks shining with the lowering sun's reflection. He remembered how Anna's voice sounded like that ebb and flow of a gentle sea. His throat tightened. He lowered his head.

He loved listening to her. She'd read him all kinds of stuff about art, science, nature, and things he had no interest in. But he didn't care. He just listened. She accused him of not hearing her, of not paying attention to the stories. He'd tell her that he could listen to her read the packaging on toilet paper and it'd be fine by him. She'd roll those blue-green mermaid eyes and stomp off into her kitchen pretending to be mad, but smiling all the way. He missed her voice. He missed those eyes. Those eyes saw him. Those eyes knew everything about him.

He didn't move from the window until the sun was well behind the trees. The sea darkened in the dusk. He heard the tide turn . . . a sacred stillness. Then the waves began rolling in again past the reach.

James crossed over to the kitchen island. He picked up his phone to check the forecast. Tomorrow would be a good day to haul. He tried to call his new sternman, Bustah, but it went straight to voicemail. God, he hated that! Why couldn't people just answer their phones?

It would be a harder day out there if Bustah didn't show. Every captain valued skilled hands when hauling to help make the operation go smoothly. Once a trap was brought up on the winch and perched on the rail, it got opened and cleared out. Most anything that wasn't a lobster went back to the sea. The lobsters were measured. Any too big, too small, or v-notched tail females got thrown back. If an egg-bearing female that wasn't v-notched came up in the trap she got her own brand new tail marks before she was thrown back to make more baby bugs. Finally, the trap was freshly baited and returned to the ocean floor to entice more lobster into it. All this took place in a matter of minutes as the boat kept moving slowly forward. This went on over and over, all day.

A good sternman also helped with boat chores, setting up bait bags, mending traps and lines and more. James could do it alone. He'd been lobstering since he was a kid. But it meant leaving the wheelhouse to haul up each trap, and some days that was just about more time- consuming than it was worth. Still, if he had to, he'd go it alone. Lobster fishing was James's life, as it was his father's, and his father's before him. He couldn't imagine any other. It was all he knew.

A tone sounded at the end of the recorded phone greeting. James cleared his throat. "Hey Bustah, James here. Be on the dock at three-thirty sharp."

He wasn't a big fan of his cell phone, but he had to admit it was good for some things. He could see the weather radar whenever he wanted or check the scores of ball games. Anna had bought this newer model for him after his flip phone fell out of his pocket into the water one day when he leaned over to snag a buoy. He'd managed to keep this one out of the drink so far, plus Anna had put it in a God-awful expensive case to keep it safe from anything James might do to break it.

When they got the new phone, she'd tried to teach him all the things it could do, but he told her he didn't want it to do anything except tell him the weather and call people—if they'd answer their damn phones. He was kind of addicted to checking the Sox scores on it too, not that he'd ever admit it. He checked to see if the phone needed charging, decided it was fine, and put it back on the countertop.

He frowned, frustration deepening the ridges in his face. He really hoped Bustah would be there in the morning. It was harder than hell to find anyone, much less someone willing to show up on time, ready to work. The job never got any easier. Plus the pay only got worse as expenses rose, and the wholesale price of lobster sank lower.

His last sternman had signed on with a different captain when Anna got sick and James's boat had stayed for weeks on its mooring in Heron Bay, the harbor at the base of the hill below James's and Anna's home. James didn't fault him for that. The youngster needed to make a living. He'd been with James for a few seasons. He was reliable as sternmen go, besides not showing up a couple times after a rough night at the pub and, of course, the day his baby had been born. All in all, they worked well together until James wasn't hauling for that bit. Loyalty tended to fly with the wind when rent was due and the pantry was bare. Last he heard, the boy was fishing with another old-timer out of Beals a few miles up the coast.

Like most fishermen who had sons, James had hoped that his own boy would work the water with him someday. But lobstering was not what it once was, and he really did want better for his son. Besides, as Anna had pointed out many times to him, the water was not in Thomas like it was in James. So, as much as he would have loved to pass on his knowledge and love for the sea and all she holds to his son, James never pushed Thomas after the first couple times he approached the idea without anything coming of it. The boy had expressed zero interest. Anna was right; they were different men. Completely different.

Thomas had been artistic, right from the start. He had a talent for drawing, but the things he drew were nothing like James knew from his world. Thomas drew geometric figures, harsh lines, shapes James couldn't make out to be anything. They weren't like the soft, undulating surfaces of the land, boats, traps, or the sea. Anna called it Modern Art. James didn't know what to call it. He knew what he'd like to say, but Anna would have told him that just because he didn't understand it didn't make it wrong. So he'd just nod his head and say something like, "Very nice, Son," whenever he was expected to comment.

Anna tried to explain the ideas and meanings behind the drawings, but gave up in disgust when James said he still didn't get it. She accused him of shutting it all out because it was different. They'd left it alone after that.

Thomas left for art school in Portland a month after he graduated from high school. Then he'd earned an art internship in Boston, and later he took a job at that museum. It seemed to his father like he'd been gone a long time.

Thomas was a city man now. He was an assistant curator at The Institute of Contemporary Art in Boston. James was proud of Thomas's success and told anyone who would listen all about it. His buddies loved to give him a hard time over that. Once in a while someone would haul up some unidentifiable piece of something in a trap, and you could bet they'd get right on the radio ribbing James as to how they had discovered a piece of Modern Art for Tommy at "The Institute." James took it all in stride. It didn't make him happy, but there was no use being put out over it. He never told Anna about any of it. She would have gone off like a rocket and been hurt to boot. He told her plenty of other stories about the other fishermen, things he saw out on the water, happenings down on the dock. Still, he was smart enough to know some things are better left unsaid.

As far as James understood, Thomas's duties varied. He might be setting up exhibits, keeping track of artworks, researching anything and everything having to do with his job, but always working long hours. Sometimes he traveled to other museums to lend a hand or to move art pieces to his museum in Boston. Anna had explained all this when James asked her exactly what did their son do at his job? James could have asked Thomas himself, but they'd become distant. This bothered James more than he cared to admit. Thomas worked hard and seemed happy. Maybe that was enough.

Thomas came back home a couple of times a year to visit. He arrived for Christmas and sometimes Thanksgiving, but he never stayed more than a day or two. A year or so ago, he'd brought home a girl with purple hair who toted around an ever-present, over-sized sketch pad. Whenever anyone spoke to her she toyed with a silver ball that pierced her upper left ear and answered in a voice so soft that James thought it sounded like humming. He was secretly horrified that Thomas might marry the girl, and they'd have children with purple Mohawks and eyebrow piercings who were scared of their own shadows. James was pleasant when he was around them, but he made himself mostly absent, escaping to the shed in the backyard to repair traps. He just knew if he stayed near the youngsters too long, he'd end up saying the wrong thing. That could've been disastrous. After the pair left to go back to Boston, Anna told James she was proud of his restraint. He'd just kissed her forehead and left it at that, never telling her his fear that the "purple girl" would become the mother of their future grandchildren. A couple weeks later, while they were chatting in the kitchen after dinner, Anna told him the girl had moved on.

"Tommy called today. Marielle, the gal he brought here last time, broke up with him. He said she told him he was 'uninspiring.'"

"Thank God for small miracles," James muttered, taking a sip of lukewarm tea from his mug. He was leaning against the side of the Frigidaire watching while she washed the dinner dishes.

She laughed softly, not looking up. Anna's laugh always reminded him of the tinkling wind chimes that had hung on his grandmother's porch. Her gentle laughter made him smile every time.

"I don't think he was all that crazy about her anyway," she offered, rinsing James's mother's old, yellow Pyrex serving bowl around and around under the stream of hot water. "She really wasn't his type."

James wanted to say that he wasn't sure what "type" would appeal to Thomas, but that would've opened up a discussion he wasn't willing to take on. So instead, he crossed over to her, laid his arm around her shoulders, and kissed her neck. She leaned into him. They stood that way for a long second before he squeezed her lightly, then walked into the living room to his recliner. "Maybe we could go visit Tommy together in Boston someday," she'd called after him.

James pretended not to hear her.

He hadn't been to the city in years. Not since he and Anna had traveled with a group of their friends to see the Red Sox in two thousand four, the first year his team finally won a World Series. The bus out of Bangor took them right to the ball field and back home the same day. Not that any of them, Anna and James included, remembered much of the ride home thanks to all the beer they drank. The important thing was the Sox won. It was a great time—a once in a lifetime. He didn't care if he ever went to Boston again; not for anything or anybody.

Anna had gone back to the city once to see Thomas right after he got his job. She rode the bus down. For three whirlwind days Thomas took her shopping, to see his work, and to all the places he liked to go. She'd come back full of stories about their successful son, art, the city, and people.

She'd spent weeks talking about the city. It was foreign to him, the thought that someone could be happy surrounded by crowds and buildings, working inside all day in a stuffy office. He was proud of his boy. He just couldn't relate to it all. Mostly now, he couldn't understand why Thomas hadn't come home when Anna got sick. He'd called every day. But he never came. He still hadn't shown up. The miles between father and son increasingly were becoming far more than geographical.

Their relationship wasn't like some of James's friends whose boys lived in town or worked with them on the same boat or in the same shop. But there wasn't any bad blood or out-of-hand disagreement that had driven a wedge between the two men. Thomas had always been very close to his mother. Why hadn't he come?

James had tried to reach Thomas a few times after Anna was gone. There'd been no answer, and he quit leaving messages after the first few attempts. He knew Sophia talked to her brother at least every couple of weeks. James thought often about asking her about Thomas when she called to check in every Sunday afternoon. But, she was busy, finishing up her graduate degree in Maritime History. They spent their time talking of boats, and the sea, more than anything else. These were safe subjects.

Last week she'd asked about a memorial service for her mother. He'd had nothing to tell her. He simply couldn't get any words out.

"Dad, are you still there?"

"I'm here. Can we not talk about that now?" There was a long silence. He thought for a moment that Sophia had hung up.

"All right, Dad. But we need to arrange something sometime soon. I'm coming home at the end of the month. Can we talk about it then?"

"OK," he managed to say, not meaning it at all.

"I love you. I'll call you next week. Oh and, Dad? Why don't you answer the house phone anymore. I've tried to call you on it at least a dozen times."

"I don't have it anymore."

"You turned off the land line?"

"No, I ripped the fucking thing out of the wall because it never shut up."

He heard Sophia sigh on the other end of the line. "Well, that's helpful, isn't it? What if someone needs to get in touch with you and they don't have your cell number? Not to mention you have voicemail on that line. There are probably a gazillion messages on it by now."

"If someone wants to find me that bad, they can damn well come find me," James growled scratching at his beard.

"Really, Dad. That's pretty unreasonable. Maybe we better talk about that when I come home too."

James grunted, "Probably not. I love you, Bean. Call my *cell* if you need me."

She laughed lightly, an echo of Anna. "OK, Dad. Love you too."

When he hung up it occurred to him he still hadn't asked about Thomas. He would next time. Maybe Thomas would show up soon. Somehow James doubted it.

He crossed back over to the sink, rinsed out his mug, and threw the used tea bag into the trash where he'd tossed the disgusting rotting broccoli a couple hours earlier. At room temperature, the smell was enough to make him gag. He yanked the garbage bag out, tied off the bag, and took it to the can outside. He was glad it was still warm enough to leave the windows open. Maybe it wouldn't take long for the night air to clear the smell from the kitchen.

He set the coffee pot to start at two forty-five am, then went to the bathroom to shower and get ready for bed. He noted that the drip from the cold-water faucet he thought he'd fixed in the spring was back again. Anna had been after him to put in a new one. He'd never gotten around to it. It was past time. Then again, who would know the damn thing still dripped except him? He adjusted the faucets to the spot where he knew the water temperature would be just right and decided everything still worked just fine.

James shed his clothes leaving them in a pile on the floor. He stepped into the steaming cascade of water, The soothing shower ran over his head and down his back. He turned his face to the spray briefly before grabbing the shampoo bottle, squeezed a bit into his hand to wash his hair, then scrubbed some of the the suds into his beard, turning his face directly back into the hot spray to rinse his head and face. He quickly scrubbed his body with Ivory soap and his washcloth from the third shelf on the corner shower stand. As he started to squeeze out the washcloth before hanging it up, he glanced down at the lower shelf of the rack that held Anna's pink scrubbie thing, her shower gels, fancy shampoo, and other mystery bottles. Instead of wringing out the cloth and hanging it where it was supposed to go, he draped the sopping square over the top of all her stuff, turned off the faucet, and stepped out of the shower, grinning. *Now that would give her something to yipe about.*

As he grabbed the towel from the hook by the shower, he caught sight of himself in the full-length mirror on the back of the bathroom door. Water ran in rivulets down his face from his silver-white hair, past bright blue eyes lined with years of working outside. His mustache and beard were close cut, but full and the same color as his hair.

Good thing I have a beard on my face to hide some of the wrinkles. And when the hell did I start looking so old anyway?

His arms and chest were muscular. His stomach was still relatively flat, if he sucked it in. There was that one small scar, right below his rib cage on the right from a few years back—a straight thin line about two inches long where he'd gotten stitched up when he'd lost an argument with the winch and had been thrown into the side of the boat. He straightened his shoulders, turning slightly, further assessing his reflection. He was mostly fit. His back was strong. He was tan everywhere that the sun could hit—which, truthfully, wasn't a whole lot. The parts of his face that weren't covered by his beard were more ruddy than tan because of the almost constant wind on the water. His legs were strong and lean. They still carried him where he needed to go. The mess of hair on his head had been a reddish-blond before it turned the color it was now when he was in his thirties. Anna had always said he had more than enough hair for three people.

He studied himself further. He had more than adequate equipment, and it still worked just fine. At least Anna had never complained.

"You know," he muttered to his own reflection, "You still look pretty good for a half-used up fifty-eight year old."

He wondered for a split-second if he might ever find another woman to share what was left of his life. With a guilty start, he shook the thought away. Where had that come from? He quickly scrubbed his body dry with the towel, hung it back in its spot, pulled on his navy plaid pajama pants that had been hanging on the hook next to the towel, then trudged toward the bedroom.

He stood outside their room, his hand on the doorknob. He couldn't open it. Instead, he turned back to the living room and plopped onto the couch. He shoved one of Anna's decorative throw pillows under his head and pulled the blue and gray crocheted afghan his mother had given them as a wedding gift up to his chest.

James flipped over to his side, punching at the pillow to make it more comfortable under his head. He rolled back over onto his back. He stared out into the darkness. He needed to rest. He needed to stop thinking. Two forty-five came at the same time every morning regardless of when he went to sleep, and he couldn't afford to be sluggish or miss any more days hauling. There were bills to be paid.

Three

The next afternoon when James came in from hauling, the young girl he'd seen the day before was sitting on the edge of the pier watching the boats slip into the harbor. While it was not unusual for local kids to be down at the dock, today she was the only one in sight. He thought he ought to ask around about her family to find out what her story was.

Anna would've frowned and shaken her head. "Inquiring minds think they need to know," she'd say.

She hated gossip. That was the truth. Once James had tried to argue with her saying that he and the other fishermen didn't gossip maliciously, they simply wanted to have all the information. She'd put those soft, gentle hands on her hips and glared at him, chin set, eyes snapping in anger like an electric storm miles out to sea.

"Gossip is gossip, James Edward. Plain and simple. It's a hurtful thing for the good of no one. Not only that, if you need to go behind someone's back to find something out, you probably have no business knowing it."

James had the good sense then just to agree with her. She would know. Then he hugged her and said he was sorry, that he'd never thought of it that way. Not that it changed anything on his end. He just didn't tell Anna what he heard or talked about, if he thought she'd consider it gossip.

The boats tended to arrive in the harbor about the same time at the end of the day, so the dock was busy with work and fishermen's trash talk. The day's haul hadn't been great on James's boat, just enough to pay for fuel and bait with a little left over. Not that he'd ever tell anyone on any day how many pounds of lobster he pulled up from his traps on the ocean floor. He could count on his fellow lobstermen to be just as closed-mouth. Even a good day fishing resulted in a bad haul, lest someone else wanted to put their traps where yours were because you got more than they did. Couldn't that start a war! At least Bustah had come to work today. He was twenty minutes late, but he'd shown up, and he wasn't drunk or strung out on drugs like James suspected some of the others were.

He tossed Bustah the mooring line to tie up the punt and told him to be back at three-fifteen the next morning, thinking that might get him to work on time to put together bait bags before they left out to haul. The young man tied the rope off around the cleat, mocked a salute, and ambled up the ramp to the upper dock calling out to others to wait for him. After trucks pulled away the wharf was quiet, for the time being. James wondered briefly what Bustah's name really was. Everyone seemed to have some nickname these days. Not that it mattered. He couldn't see this one as a keeper. In fact he'd be surprised if he lasted the next couple weeks. Every time James turned around Bustah was either taking a picture of himself, or checking to see if he had a signal on his phone so he could text, or whatever it was he was doing that wasn't fishing. James had to threaten to throw the thing overboard before the kid would put it away. Not only did it tick James off that the guy wasn't taking work seriously, it could be downright dangerous out there if you didn't keep your head up and your brain engaged. Any number of things could go wrong. If you ended up wrapped up in the gear and a moving line hauled you into the water, God only knew if you would get out before you were a goner. Even if you didn't drown right away the water was wicked cold. In a matter of minutes hypothermia would set in. There was no guarantee someone would pull you out quickly enough to stay alive. A forward moving boat takes time to turn around and circle back to wherever it was you went in. That was if you weren't fishing alone and someone actually saw you go overboard .

Few lobstermen wore life preservers. It was a damn pain to do your job with one of those things binding you up. The law mandates all fishing vessels carry survival suits and gear. Training in its proper use is also a requirement, but that does you no good if the gear's not on you.

Over the years James had lost friends and neighbors on the water. A few due to accidents that could have been prevented and others that could not. Some seemed to be taken on the whim of Mother Nature. The sea holds no forgiveness. There's zero room for inattention or just being stupid. James felt a wave of anger wash up over him as he thought about problems that could occur on his boat because of what he considered his sternman's lack of attention and work ethic. He threw the oars into the punt in disgust. They bounced off the seat and slid, ending up in a tangled "X" in a rope coil near the stern.

He kicked at the bow of the punt. As the toe of his boot hit the gunwale the boat wobbled away from him in the water. The mooring line slid off the cleat.

"Dammit all to hell!"

He lunged for the rope. It slithered off into the water just out of his reach.

"Damn kids are so caught up in themselves and their phones they can't even tie a knot right! There's no teaching them anything either! What the hell is happening in the world?"

James gritted his teeth and shook his head as he realized he was talking aloud and none too soft either. He untied the punt moored next to where his had just been, clambered in, rowed to his runaway craft, and retrieved it. As he climbed back out of the little boat he'd borrowed and was tying up both crafts correctly, he felt someone watching him. He looked up to see the girl still sitting on the pier, legs dangling, arms draped over top of the lowest metal rail. Her head was cocked to the side. She was studying him intently, unflinchingly. He looked away, annoyed and uncomfortable in her assessment. She probably thought he was an old lunatic, talking to himself, throwing oars, kicking things, losing boats. He glanced up again, thinking he should smile at her or wave or something to show he wasn't all bad, but she was gone.

Great. He'd probably scared her. Now some belligerent parent would be coming to confront him.

He stomped up the ramp to the upper dock. In the distance he heard the low thrum of boat engines. He turned toward the water—listening. It sounded like the *Allison Rose* and *Max-a-Million*. Both captains were old-timers like himself, and they always had plenty to allow, but he really didn't feel like conversation tonight. He got to the top of the ramp just in time to see the mystery girl on her ratty bike trying to pedal up the impossible hill. He shook his head, amazed again that she even tried.

He wondered once more why she was alone. He figured she had to be about nine or ten years old. She should be somewhere playing or swimming with other kids her age, not hanging out at the dock watching old lobstermen come in off their boats. She'd pedaled as far as she could and was back to pushing the bike along. He took his hat off, scratched his head, then put it back on. He thought that maybe she'd gotten a little farther up the hill tonight before she started walking.

Something about that kid tugged at him. She was different. He continued watching as she disappeared, shoving her bike over the rise of the hill.

Maybe he'd go to breakfast at The Dinette the next time the weather kept the boats in. Any number of the regulars up there had their fingers on all the comings and goings in town. Someone would know something. Besides, it'd been a long while since he'd gone there, and breakfast out was better than anything he'd make for himself.

He glanced one last time at the hill before starting on his own way. Tonight he stayed off the road, ambling instead to the winding gravel path that switched back and forth up the hill toward his dooryard. It was flanked by beach roses, rich in their late summer spiciness. Hung up on a low-lying rose cane at the very edge, a thin line of faded, purple plastic about six inches long fluttered in the air, alone and out of place. He recognized it as a piece of the tassel from the handlebars of the girl's bike.

James gently freed the tattered strand from the thorn that held it. He smoothed it out against his palm, closed his hand over it, and carried it up to the house with him, glad no one was there to see.

Four

The next few days came and went on the tide. The weather was not bad, fishing was good, and his routine kept James mostly away from his thoughts. When you leave for work just before sun-up and come back late in the afternoon, everything else pretty much takes care of itself. There's comfort in the day-to-day rhythm of a hard-working life. Lobstering could never be called an easy job. Most days it isn't what others might think of as fun. But it pays the bills as long as the weather cooperates and a little luck holds out. Mother Nature can turn in an instant and while the sea may seem calm and clear, there's always something unseen under the surface—maybe good—maybe not so good. James knew this as surely as he knew the sun would come up every morning whether he was there to see it rise or not. The sun's continual rising was a fact that had begun to tick him off the past few weeks. He was realizing he'd relied on Anna to do way more than he should have, and he had no idea what might be coming at him each day at home. He no longer was an active participant in pretty much anything in his life, except work. Without Anna to tell him what came next he was bumping around half blind. She'd always scheduled and motored their life along, taking care of most all the details. He'd been perfectly happy to just go along. It worked for them.

He was back sitting on their bench down at the harbor one evening, thinking of this, questioning how and why he'd become so lazy in his life. He wondered if Anna had ever wanted him to do more. He'd been thankful she didn't make him worry about the everyday workings of the household and the kids, but now he was thinking maybe that had been wrong.

The financial end of their world was his job. That part he had without issue. He understood it was an old-fashioned notion that the man would provide, and the wife would take care of the home and children. He also was convinced that women are capable of doing just about everything and usually do a far better job at it than most men. He knew for a fact that many female captains who fished out of the local harbors were more successful in their businesses than their male peers. James also knew that how Anna and he had split the running of their household wasn't anything they'd ever talked about or hashed out. It simply happened that way. It worked. They never seemed to disagree about any of it—even how they raised Tommy and Sophia. They'd tried to teach the kids to be independent and ambitious enough to successfully take on whatever they chose for themselves. They both appeared to be doing fine out there on their own in the world. James would've supported Anna in anything she wanted to change, or do, for the family or herself. And he had. But she'd never mentioned she wanted their roles to be different. It wasn't like he didn't do anything to help at home. With Anna gone now though, he realized that mowing the lawn, taking out the garbage, and picking up here and there didn't make much of a dent in everything needing attention.

Now that he was on his own he was getting by—sort of. Sophia had showed him how to use the computerized washing machine and matching dryer before she left to go back to school. So at least he had clean clothes. He knew enough to make meals for himself, not that he had to just yet. There was still at least a week's worth of food in the freezer. He certainly could keep things clean. He liked order and cleanliness. His boat was always sparkling. With just him knocking around, their small home was easy to keep. It was the other business of life—the living—that had him stuck. Without Anna, it felt like there was no one, and not much of anything to move him about.

When had he stopped making any real choices about his own life? Now he wasn't even sure he wanted to make decisions, and the indecision of that only confused the issue more. Off the water he felt about as useful as a grounded boat—actually more like . . . unnecessary. He was beginning to wonder if that was the way he'd always been.

Well. James grimaced as he stared down at the ground in front of him. *It looks like I've picked up at least one new skill. I'm getting good at feeling sorry for myself.*

He shifted slightly on his seat, lifting his gaze to look past the boats floating idle on the nearly still surface of the harbor. The temperature had shifted in the past hour. It was cooler by quite a bit. The smell of the saltwater seemed thicker, more pungent. The foghorn half a mile away on its tiny island groaned out a warning. An insistent breeze was pushing a thick, grayish white wall of fog across the sea up past the reach. Soon, the fog bank would reach the harbor, then slip up over the hill, covering the town in a blanket of cool mist. Nothing would leave their moorings from now until later tomorrow.

Mid-August into early September you could almost set your watch by the late afternoon fog. Usually, it was gone again before morning, but sometimes it would hang around for days at a time. James's phone had already alerted him that NOAA had issued a dense fog alert until two p.m. the next day. There'd be no going out tomorrow. He'd already changed his plans. It would be a good morning to work on trap repairs, something he hadn't done since early spring. Then maybe he'd come down in the afternoon to give the boat and holding tanks a good scrub.

He rose from the bench thinking he'd like to get home before the fog roiled onto the land. Anna would say that it didn't "come on little cat feet" like that Sandburg poem she'd quoted to him. Instead, it steamed up the streets like a freight train on a tight schedule toward its next stop. She also used to joke that people in the cities paid big money for sea mist facials at salons, but she got one for free every day.

When he grumpily asked her what he got out of the damn fog, she'd pat his hand and smile up at him. "A day off with me," she'd say.

He could never argue with that. She sure had a way of looking at things differently.

Movement near the shore below the rocks caught James's eye. Something was down on the rocky beach just out of sight. Probably a young seal waiting while its mama fished for dinner. Or just maybe it was Anna's errant cat. His bench sat back enough from the rocks that anything on the lower shore wasn't visible unless it had a little height on it. Just as he stood and started to walk toward the rocks to investigate, a head full of wild, long brown hair attached to a young girl clambered up over the rocks toward him.

Well, that certainly isn't a seal, he mused. *A pup, yes, but not one of the seal variety.*

He generally was observant, but today he'd had no idea he wasn't alone. He looked around thinking he'd missed something. Nope—no bike.

The girl spotted him. She stopped short. "Oh," she said with her mouth, only no sound came out. She paused for a second more, then walked directly up to him. She planted both feet and crossed her arms across her chest.

"Hi," she said. She was frowning, her head tilted slightly, studying him with wide, direct hazel eyes. "I didn't know you were here."

"Hello to you," James said smiling. "I didn't know there was anyone down on the beach today either. So, we're even I'd say."

Her gaze didn't waver. She didn't smile back at him. She kept looking at him for a long second, like he was in her way.

"Hmm. Well, I've gotta go," she said, uncrossing her arms, stepping forward.

James moved to the side, allowing her plenty of room to pass. "Have a nice evening."

"Uh, you too." She looked down for a second, then back up at him. "Well, 'bye."

"'Bye,' James returned, but she was already striding past him. Before he could move, she was back, looking at him like he was somewhere he should not be—a trespasser.

"So, you come down here a lot." Not a question—more like she was daring him to disagree with her.

James nodded. "Ayup. I do."

"I do too." She informed him sticking her chin out, glaring at him.

"I see that. I hope there's room for both of us." James was trying not to laugh. He didn't want to seem like he was making fun of the little imp. She was striking out her territory. Far be it for him to impose. She obviously felt this was her very own place. This was something he too felt, and understood, deep within himself.

She stared at him for a moment more. Then she nodded, apparently accepting his offer.

"I'm Natasha," she informed him, narrowing her eyes just slightly—another challenge—although James wasn't sure about what?

"James," he offered and reached out his hand. She hesitated, then shook his hand once forcibly and dropped it. He cleared his throat as he tried again to contain his amusement.

"OK. Well, Mr. James, I'll probably see you around. 'Bye." She started out. He stayed put, watching her leave. She took a few steps then swung around to face him yet again.

"Mr. James, what are you doing, sitting on that bench all the time?"

She waited. James wasn't sure he had an answer, and he had a keen idea that she wouldn't go until he told her something. He also felt she demanded the truth. He briefly wondered why it mattered to him to give it to her.

"Remembering," he offered finally, gazing past her up at his little house on the hill. "Just remembering."

She nodded, apparently satisfied with his answer. Then she scampered off up the hill before he could gather himself up enough to say another word.

Five

Natasha

Mostly, this place stinks. I'd say something worse about it, but Mom would have me tasting Dawn dish soap for a week if I did.

The only good things about it are:

1) The ocean
2) My bike
3) The ocean

My room isn't bad either because it's a cool, kind-of-secret, attic room. You can only get to it by climbing up these steep little stairs that are against the wall by the door to my mom's room on the second floor. Plus, I can see numbers one and three from my *Good Things About Here* list from the window. Mom let me push my bed under the window so I can lie here and look out all night if I want. This is good because I don't sleep a lot. My brain won't shut off long enough to let me.

At night I can hear the waves, and sometimes see the moonshine off the water, but only if the moon is in the right phase and no clouds block its reflection. Just once, right before it started to get light, the water was really still for a few seconds, and I could see the stars reflected in the bay too—like they were floating on top. It felt like the world went upside down and I couldn't tell what was what. Then the water started to ripple again, and the stars were back up in the sky where they live.

I need to add that to my list:

4) The stars here

When I told Mom about the upside-down world, she said that I'd picked the perfect time to look out because the wind that night was still, and the tide was turning just at that moment. She said it's a mermaid's gift to know the sea when it's perfectly still.

I think it would be awesome to be a mermaid. I know mermaids aren't real, but if they were, I think I would be one of them. How cool would it be to live out in the sea all the time? No one would bug me out there.

I was down at the cove this afternoon for a long time watching the water, and the birds, and other stuff. It was breezy and cool, but not like a cold kind of cool. It was the kind that felt like little whispery tickles on your face. Then the fog started to come in, and the wind changed and got pushy. Mostly there's always some kind of breeze kicking up the water. During the day the waves are usually bigger and louder than at night, and the gulls are down there yelling at everything. As far as I can tell, they even yell at each other. Just like people. Mom calls them seagulls, even though I've told her like a million times there is no such thing. There are twenty-eight different kinds of gulls, and not one of them is called a sea gull. So far down at the wharf I have identified three of the twenty-eight of the Family Laridae: Great Black-Backed, Herring, and Ring-Billed. I saw a Herring gull for the first time today. In fact, I saw four of them. According to the internet, the three types I've seen are the only kinds of gulls where we are in Maine, so it's pretty cool that I've identified them all. Still, Mom says she can call them whatever she wants, and they are just seagulls to her. Whatever.

I wonder if Mr. James knows anything about gulls? I introduced myself today, but I've seen him down there a lot. He doesn't act like the other lobstermen. They are all loud and noisy and only go down to the wharf to get on their lobster boats. Then when they come back on their skiffs, they hang around for a few minutes talking and joking with each other. They mostly leave at the same time to go home or down to the pub. That's what my grandfather does when he comes in from fishing. He goes straight to the pub. I know because I heard Mom talking with my grandmother about it. He comes home super late most nights. Sometimes he fights with my grandmother. Well, actually he yells at her a lot. I don't hear her say much. I know to just stay out of his way. He doesn't like me. He doesn't like Mom either. Come to think of it, I wonder if he likes anyone?

Mr. James seems nice. He comes in off the water later than most everyone. Lots of times he goes and sits on this one bench where you can see past the reach, over the ocean, all the way to the horizon. I asked him what he does sitting there all the time. He told me he was "remembering." I get that. I do that a lot down there too.

The only time so far that he hasn't gone to sit on that bench, that I've seen, was the other day when he got mad at his sternman after they came in from fishing. That was pretty funny. He talked to himself and kicked his skiff. The funniest part was the sternman hadn't tied the skiff up right. It went floating off, and Mr. James had to jump into someone else's boat to row after his before it went bobbing right out of the harbor. I was going to laugh out loud. Hah! I had to leave then because I didn't want him to think I was laughing at him. I hate when people laugh at me.

Now I'm lying on my bed watching out my window waiting for the fog to finish coming up over the water, so I can only dream the water is really there. I can hear some kids laughing and talking outside. They're probably walking home from the pool by the golf course. Mom said she would take me up to the pool to swim. She thinks then I'll meet some other kids. I don't want to meet anybody. I only want my old friends back. But I don't want to make Mom more sad by saying that to her, so I just keep quiet.

Mom says we can only go to the pool at night between six and eight because that's when the town kids are allowed to use it. Some *Association* thing of rich summer people own it, and they only let the people in town in after they're done at the end of the day. I told her I thought that was just stupid because what makes them better than us? Besides, by that time at night it's getting chilly, and who wants to swim after supper anyway? She sighed and said money and social status were complicated things. Then she told me the story about how the town kids used to have to climb the fence after hours to swim because back then *The Association* didn't want them to use their pool at all. She said that when the town policeman would walk by, he'd pretend he didn't see the kids in there. Then she told me that she shouldn't have told me that story, and that I was to remember NEVER to break in anywhere that I wasn't allowed to be. That it was WRONG, ILLEGAL, and I COULD BE ARRESTED, and SENT TO JAIL! Did I understand that? I told her I did. I'm not dumb. She didn't say so, but I got that she agreed with me that rich people shutting town people out of the pool is stupid. Not only that, I think it's just plain mean.

Six

James glanced out the window as he was washing up his supper dishes. The fog had thickened enough that he couldn't see past the end of his front yard. Mist stole into the house through the open windows. If he didn't close things up, it wouldn't be long before the whole place would feel cold and slightly soggy. Anna would have turned up the furnace "just to take the chill off," but James left it alone. The raw air felt good tonight.

He shook his head and grinned as his thoughts turned to his earlier encounter with young Natasha. That child had moxie! He remembered their Sophia sometimes being cantankerous. Anna termed Sophia's random bouts of stubborn grumpiness, "attitudinal days." James figured Miss Natasha probably lived that way. She obviously was itching for a fight. James was pretty sure she'd find one without looking too hard if she practiced that spunky attitude at school. He wondered again about who she might belong to. He chuckled thinking of how she'd challenged him about the beach. Her self-introduction was something else. It'd been a long time since anything had made him genuinely smile.

He rinsed out the sink, chasing the last of the dishwater down the drain while mentally planning the next day. Since there would be no fishing due to the weather, he figured it was as good a day as any to go out to breakfast. He hadn't joined his friends for a bite since Anna had been gone. Maybe it was time he started doing a few things again. Besides, with any luck he could do a little gossip gathering. Once again, he heard the echo of Anna's voice in his ear, "Inquiring minds think they need to know . . ."

Ayup. He wanted to know the story and he was going to find out. Why not?

As he was setting up the coffee pot for the morning his phone rang. He looked down at the caller ID—not a number he recognized. Normally he ignored any calls that didn't announce who they were coming from, but for some reason he hit the button to answer.

"Hello?"

"Dad? Where the hell have you been?"

"Thomas, is that you? Where are you calling from? What do you mean where the hell have I been? Where the hell have you been?"

"Don't start with me, Dad. I've only called you almost every damn day since Mom died, and you never return my calls!"

"Now just a minute," James practically bellowed into the phone. "Don't you talk to me that way! You have not called me once!"

"Well then whose voice mail am I leaving message after message on?" Tommy snapped back. "God! Never mind. Forget I bothered you!"

"Listen here . . ." There was an obvious, blank silence on the other end of the line. Thomas had hung up on him! Hung up on his own father! James banged his fist down on the countertop hard enough that the salt and pepper shakers jumped.

That beat all! Damn kid hadn't bothered to call for weeks, and he's the one who gets to be ticked off? Left voice mails. Right. What a crock. Where the hell had he left voice mails? There hadn't been a thing on his cell phone.

"Oh. Shit." James said aloud. "The home phone. I pulled out the stupid thing."

He paced around the kitchen island, turned, and paced back the other way.

He should call him back.

No! The boy had hung up on him. Thomas should be the one to call and apologize. Where was his respect for his father? Where had he been anyway that he couldn't even come home when his mother was dying? And now he calls—just like that yells at his father, and hangs up? Who in God's name did he think he was?

For the second time that evening, he heard Anna in his head. "He's a grown man you know. He told you he called—a lot. You yelled at him and practically called him a liar. It's not like he lives around the corner and can just drop by. He has a job and obligations. Maybe you should try talking with him instead of screaming at him. He is your son, James Edward — the only one you've got. Don't let your stubborn pride get in the way."

James stopped in his tracks. He was gripping the phone so hard his hand hurt. He put it down and placed both palms of his hands on the countertop. The polished granite was solid and cool. His temper come down a couple notches. James hung his head. He'd accused Tommy of not calling and lying about it. He knew that wasn't like his son at all. He was a good kid. He'd always kept in touch with them before.

Fact was, it was Anna that Tommy had pretty much always talked with when he called. James sometimes spoke with him for a quick minute. But he usually got all the news through Anna after her conversations with their son. And who's fault was that?

James lifted his head, reached for his phone, and dialed the last number from the call log.

It rang three times, then went to voicemail. His son's voice came on the line telling James he'd reached the desk of Thomas Edward. James hung up without leaving a message. Of course, Tommy wouldn't answer. That boy could be as stubborn as his mother. James waited a couple seconds, then hit the redial. This time Tommy answered on the second ring.

"Dad, if you're going to yell, I'm not even going to try to talk to you. So, I'm hanging up now."

"Tommy. Wait." Silence. James took a deep breath. "Are you still there?"

"I'm here."

More silence.

"Did you call the home number?"

"Yes, Dad," Thomas' voice was low, angry. "That's where I almost always call. I didn't even have your cell number until today when Sophia gave it to me. I only had Mom's and you know Sophia has that phone now."

"I tore that stinkin' phone out of the wall. It wouldn't stop ringing," James said, rubbing his beard with his free hand. "And here I've been thinking you didn't care enough to call."

"You tore it out of the wall? What . . . ?" James heard Tommy sigh. "Never mind. You do have my numbers. Right, Dad?"

"I think so. Well, not programmed in my cell. The caller ID didn't say who it was. I almost didn't answer it. I'm sure your numbers are written down in the book where your mom kept them. I called and left you messages after your mom first got sick and when she . . ."

James broke off, anger starting to move through him again. He realized he was rhythmically opening and closing his right hand into a fist. He splayed his fingers out to try to relax his hand. He took a deep breath. "You didn't return my calls. I mean, I thought you didn't. I figured you didn't want to talk to me. So I stopped trying."

More silence.

This was going nowhere fast. James knew he'd better turn it around, or there was no way it would end well. He began again.

"I owe you an apology Tommy. I'm sorry. It didn't occur to me that you wouldn't have my cell number. I figured you didn't want to talk. I never even thought about voicemails on the home line. Well, that's not quite true. Your sister did mention something about there probably being messages there the other day, but I still didn't think much about it." He paused to take another breath, calmer now. "Can we please start over? You're at work late. How are things with you?"

What James really wanted to ask now was why Tommy didn't come home when his mother was dying. Why had he been absent after she was gone? But he knew enough to keep that to himself right now. If he started that fight there'd be no talking to Tommy at all.

Timing was everything. He knew at least that much about communicating with his son or anyone else for that matter. He wasn't completely numb.

He heard Tommy clear his throat on the other end of the line.

"It's OK, Dad. I need to apologize too. I could've asked Sophia earlier for your cell number. I just . . . I don't know. This has all been so hard. I can't imagine how awful it is for you. I only know how bad it's been for me. Can we just not yell at each other?"

"Sure." James felt his face get hot. His own son was having to remind him how to act reasonably! "Are you OK?"

When Tommy spoke again his voice sounded more distant and muffled. "I'm all right. I really miss Mom. I thought I would handle it better than I am."

"Me too, Tommy. I miss her too—every second of every day." James tried to swallow the huge lump in his throat. "It's awful good to hear your voice, Son. I'm glad you got my number from your sister." He had a sudden idea. "Hey, you know I text now too. You could always reach me that way. I can text you back."

"You text? Really? When did you join the realm of technology?"

James could practically see the expression on Tommy's face. His mouth was probably half open with one eyebrow cocked in amazement that his father had come out of the dark ages just a little bit. It was the same expression that Anna always wore when she was not sure if she was surprised, or slightly doubtful, about something.

James chuckled, "Well, your mom taught me when she got me this latest phone a while back. Seems my sternman would rather text than get a call. But I still call him a bit, mostly just to tick him off."

Tommy laughed, "Now that sounds like you. But I will definitely text you now that I know you can get them. It makes it easier for me to keep in touch with people too. Especially when I'm at work, which is most of the time."

James cleared his throat. Maybe this was a safe subject. "How's work going?

"Fine. Good. We just opened a new mixed-media solo exhibit in one of the larger galleries. It's this artist's first exhibit here and a huge amount of work, because the pieces are all unique in size and composition. But we pulled it off, and it's been very successful. I had more responsibility for this exhibit than any of the others before. It had me flat out for a long time." Tommy paused. "I'd like to think it was worth all the work. But . . . I just wish Mom could see it. She was really excited about it. The artist's work is bold, geometric, like some of the stuff I used to do, but it also has a lot of textile components to it. It's truly multi-dimensional. Mom was looking forward to coming down to see it in person."

James frowned. The idea that Anna had been planning a trip to Boston was news to him, but he wasn't about to admit that.

"I bet she would've loved it, Tommy. I'll admit I never could understand much about Modern Art, but I do know your mom was thrilled that you followed after her love of the art world. We both are so proud of how hard you worked to get where you are."

Silence answered James.

"Tommy, are you still there? Did I lose you?"

No, Dad. I'm here. Do you know that's the first time I think I ever heard you tell me you were proud of my work? I mean, I always knew you supported my choice of career and all, but Mom was the one who would tell me that. You just caught me off guard . . . It means a lot."

"Really? I've never told you?" James felt his face flush again. That couldn't be true. He must have said something at some point. Or maybe not. He was realizing there was a lot he hadn't done or paid attention to.

"Well," James declared. "I *am* proud of you. You're my son! I may not get what all the art is about. But I know it's important to you, so it's important to me."

"Careful, I think maybe you're getting soft in your old age, Dad." Tommy's tone was playful now. "But, seriously, thank you. You have no idea how much it means to me to hear you say it."

James was still trying to figure out if he really never had told his son that he was proud of him for his success. He briefly wondered if his own father had ever told him he was proud of him. If so, James didn't remember it.

"Dad? Are you doing all right, really? Everything happened so fast. Are you taking care of yourself?"

"Uh, I'm getting along. It's not fun, but I'm getting along."

"Well at least you have Petunia to keep you company."

"Petunia?"

"Mom's cat? She's still around, isn't she?"

"Well . . ."

"Dad, what did you do to the cat?"

"Now, just a minute, Tommy. I didn't do anything! The day I came back after your mom left, the damn furball slipped by me out the door, and I haven't seen it since. I've looked all over the place for it. And, just so you know, I put food out every night, and I keep an eye out for it all the time."

Tommy gave a short laugh that sounded like he was choking. "Geez, the cat skedaddled on you? Wow. Mom would be right ticked off you let her out."

"Tell me about it. I feel awful. I keep thinking she might show up. Petunia, eh? I didn't even remember that was what she named it." He paused. "I have to admit, I kinda miss seeing that cat sleeping in the sun in the kitchen when I get home in the afternoon."

"Well, you could always get another one, or maybe a dog?"

"Naw. I'm OK. I have enough to do just looking out for myself. I'm gone out to fish too much to have a dog. It wouldn't be fair to it unless it came with me. Besides, maybe the cat—Petunia—will show up again."

"I hear that," Tommy agreed. "Being alone is not all that great for animals or humans."

James suddenly remembered he hadn't fed the cat tonight. He shifted the phone to his other ear and moved over to the cupboard.

"You know, Son," he admitted, "I keep forgetting to do little things. Your mom did most everything around here. Now here's something else I hadn't thought about. You and I both live on our own now. I have a pretty good feeling you're better at it than I am."

"Maybe. It's a little different when you live in an apartment building surrounded by other people. You're never really alone. I'd love to have some of that quiet peace you have at home. It is always so noisy down here. You lived alone before you and Mom married, right?"

"Well, not really. I lived in the two-room apartment above the old garage here. I never was by myself much. Plus, your grandmom fed me and did all my laundry too. I was twenty-nine when I met your mom, but still a young fool. I did my share of carousing with friends, and I worked more hours than not. Then your mom spoiled me pretty good these past years. I didn't have much to brag about before she came along. She changed my life in more ways than you can imagine." James took a deep breath. "It all seems a world away now." He stopped. Suddenly it felt like he was talking way too much.

"I bet, Dad." Tommy said quietly. "Maybe someday you could tell me more about your life before you and Mom met. You know, I don't really know anything at all about any of that. One of the things I like most about my job is finding the background stories about the art and artists. But when I'm doing the research, it makes me think how I don't even know my own family history. I mean, Mom told me a little bit about her parents and her dreams of being an artist. I know she didn't finish school. Other than a few other little facts, I don't know much else. Those old photos in the stairwell are the only ones I've ever seen of relatives. I know your mom was around until I was three or four, but I don't remember her at all. Since we didn't have living grandparents or other extended family members, our family story was just the four of us. It would be interesting to know more."

"Not much to tell, Son." What James really thought was that there was a lot he didn't want to relive. Telling it would do just that.

"Maybe not to you, Dad. You were there. But it's like there's a hole in my life, one I didn't realize was there until I became a curator and art historian. I think that family history, and how they lived, play an important role in who we become as individuals. I don't want every single detail, just a few tidbits to chew on."

"Well, next time you're home maybe we can sit down over a beer, and you can ask away." James figured Tommy could ask all he wanted, but there were some things that just didn't need to be shared. Still, he understood what his son was saying. The past shapes our lives, just as surely as the present, whether we realize it or not.

"That would be great, Dad." Tommy cleared his throat. "Uh, I hate to bring this up, but Sophia says that you still haven't made plans about a memorial for Mom. Do you have any idea when you might do that? I need to be able to plan to come home for it. When Mom got sick she made me promise I wouldn't leave to come home to see her, until the exhibit was up and running," James heard a catch in Tommy's voice. "And then she died so fast . . ."

The world fell away from James. He reached for the counter to steady himself. When he felt like he could move, he slowly crossed the room toward the kitchen table, pulled out a chair and sat down.

Dear God. It had never crossed his mind that Anna would've told Tommy to stay away. Of course she would. That was just like her. She probably told Sophia the same thing, but Sophia was at the end of her semester and was coming home for the summer season anyway. He'd been an idiot.

"You there, Dad?"

"I'm here, Son," He closed his eyes and took a deep breath. "I'm so sorry. I had no idea she told you not to come. I didn't know. I thought . . . Never mind what I thought. I just can't think about any service. I don't know . . . I just can't. . . not yet."

"Dad. It's . . ."

James interrupted him, "Besides, with all this COVID crap over the past couple years it's not like anyone is expecting a service anyway."

The last part was a damn weak excuse and James knew it, but he didn't even want to think about some public gathering where he had to feel all that pain, all over again, in front of everybody.

Tommy exhaled forcibly enough that James could swear he felt the air move through the phone. "Dad, I know. I don't want to think about it either. But Sophia is right. We need to face this together and move forward. Mom wouldn't want any of us to be stuck like we are right now. This is important. Please."

There was a pause. When James didn't reply, Tommy softly said, "Maybe we both could come up for a few days and help you get things in order. Soph can drive up from Castine any weekend if she doesn't have anything big coming up with school. She's a little stressed out because this is her last year, and she has a lot of research to complete. So, it's harder for her to take time away, but it needs to happen. This needs to be done for all of us."

Now James felt guilty. He'd been so wrapped up in feeling sorry for himself that he'd basically disregarded that he had two just-grown kids who were grieving and trying to learn to cope without Anna too. It was his job now that she was gone to make sure someone stayed at the helm.

"I'm sorry, Tommy." James grimaced. It sure seemed like he was sorry for a whole lot tonight. "You're both right. I hate it, but we do have things that need to be done. When can you come home?"

After tossing a few dates back and forth, the men came up with two weekends that worked for Tommy to drive up. Tommy would call Sophia to see which was good for her, then he'd pick her up at school on his way through, so they could ride together. James realized he really was excited about his children coming home. He just wished it was for any other reason.

"I'll text you when we figure out exactly which weekend, Dad. I'll see you soon."

"I'm awful glad you called, Tommy. I love you."

"Love you too, Dad. I'll talk to you again in a day or two."

"Text me. Call me anytime," James said with a smile. "You can always leave a voicemail if I don't answer."

Tommy laughed. "Funny. Very funny, Pops. Talk to you soon."

James hung up the phone and stared out the window at the fog. He figured that was the longest conversation he'd ever had with his son. It was different—good. He thought back to his relationship with his own father. They'd never talked much, if at all, about anything but lobstering. His father had been a hard man. He worked hard, and he played hard. When he wasn't working, he was out at the local bar with his pals until all hours. He expected order, meals, and quiet at the house when he was home. James's mom and her mother took care of the house, raised James, and stayed out of the way. He learned at a young age that he was to be seen, not heard. When his father said "jump," James did and hoped it was high enough on the way back down.

James had started to work as his father's sternman when he was thirteen years old. He was quick, did as he was told, and that was that. Thank God he loved the sea and the work. He learned well from his father—some things maybe a little too well.

James had been seventeen when his father killed himself. At least that was how James saw it. His old man left the pub after a night of drinking, took his boat out of the harbor for God knows what reason, and was never heard from again. Two days after his disappearance his boat had been found drifting forty-two miles offshore in international waters, out of fuel, without him. James's father had been an inshore fisherman, same as James was now. They never went more than a few miles offshore to work and certainly not out of local waters.

In James's eyes, his mother was a saint. He was the first and only child after many years of false hope and failed pregnancies. She'd given him all she had. James knew this was his legacy. She quietly taught him how to be a good man—a kind man. Then his Anna had worked to polish him up over the years. Anna had done a fine job with their children too. Now he needed to step up and be there for them. He'd let Anna do way too much on her own over the years. It had been comfortable and easy. The bottom line was he'd copped out. But that could change. It should change. He hoped his children wanted him to be more present than he had been. Maybe they liked things the way they were.

He remembered the pain of losing his own mother. It was nothing like the gut-wrenching, mind-shattering grief he kept getting hit with since the loss of his Anna. Still, it had been a blow. His mom was only sixty-one when she passed away, but she'd been failing for years. Her heart had been like an old clock whose gears wore down, losing a little time each day, the chime on each hour becoming a little less robust, the slowing of its workings familiar in its failing. She died one night at home in her sleep, when her parts were too weak to go on anymore. It wasn't a shock, but still a great loss. He and Anna had gotten through it together. He hadn't been alone in his grief then. He realized he didn't need to be now. He needed to be sure his children weren't either.

He sat for a long time staring outside, sadness holding him there. The fog wasn't helping his mood any. It couldn't be any grayer out there if it tried. You couldn't see a thing.

Except...

"Well, aren't you bold," James muttered, squinting to narrow his gaze, to see more clearly. There was a hint of burnt orange barely visible through the mist, sitting right at the edge of the shed, not fifteen feet from the house, looking straight at James through the window. Damn fox!

"What the hell do you want?" James growled at it through the window. "And don't you think you're going to eat Petunia's food either!"

Seven

James didn't make it out of the house the next morning to join the other fishermen for breakfast. Since he couldn't take the boat out in the fog he hadn't set the alarm, and when he woke he was completely disoriented until he remembered he was sleeping on the couch. The scene out the living room window was as gray and close as the afternoon before. What the hell time was it? He picked up his phone. Holy eight a.m.! Half the day gone and with traps and lines to repair. He knew he'd missed everyone at The Diner. They'd all be on to other things by now.

Still groggy, he headed to the bathroom, splashed cold water on his face, then wandered into the kitchen in search of the coffee pot. The pot was full, but the warmer had shut off hours ago. Good thing for the microwave. James yawned, amazed he hadn't woken up to the smell of the coffee when it automatically brewed at two forty-five. He must've really been out. Fact was, he felt like he could go back to sleep until tomorrow morning.

It took most of the pot of coffee and what was left of *Good Morning America* to get him ready to face the day. Opening the door to the laundry closet to find work clothes, he realized he hadn't transferred what he'd washed the night before into the dryer. He found clean socks, boxers, and a T-shirt in the basket on top of the dryer where his clothes had been living, but no pants or shorts. He'd just been throwing dirty clothes into the washer every day until it was full. He'd run a load, dry it, and toss it in the basket on top of the dryer to dig into when he needed something. Now he either had to wait for the dryer to finish, or go into the bedroom to find clean pants. Shorts didn't take that long to dry, right? Besides, he needed to make some breakfast for himself and clean up the house a bit. He figured the worst that could happen was someone would come by while he was mopping the floor in his boxers. The work outside wasn't going anywhere.

By the time he went out, the mist was pulling apart. The mid-morning sun melted it into wispy, cotton-candy strands that moved away, then dissolved before your eyes.

That's how life is, right there, James thought, watching. *Just like that. Poof.*

"Stop it, you old fool," he said. Great. Now he was actively talking to himself.

He adjusted his baseball cap and strode over to the shed where his tools and supplies for traps were stored. The faded, green wooden rectangle that was a little larger than a credit card and kept the door shut, rotated easily.

James figured he couldn't have been more than five or six years old the summer his father built the shed. He'd watched, fascinated with how boards and nails became a building. His father let him help with small things like bringing the hammer or holding up a board. The little wooden fastener had been one of those tasks—the finishing touch to the shed. It had been there ever since.

The once rectangular piece of wood that swiveled on a single nail through its center really resembled more of an oval now. The corners were worn smooth from being turned again and again. The green paint was more a hint of color within the gray, time-worn wood. The rest of the shed had the same weathered patina. The only thing that had ever been updated was the metal roof James put on after a late January nor'easter, two years before, had torn off most of the old asphalt shingles. The little building was a reminder that there were some things that stood strong against time. It was familiar—comforting.

He swung the door open. It bumped softly into the side of the shed. He wrinkled his nose as a damp, musty odor tinged with old bait, and possibly something dead, seeped out of the open doorway. Probably a mouse or squirrel had decided to call it quits in there.

James took a step forward and stopped short. What a friggin' mess. He hadn't been out here in a long while, but when had this happened? The shed was piled high with everything known to man that had been taken from somewhere else, tossed in with little rhyme or reason. There was no walking room. He couldn't even see his workbench at the far end. James groaned in exasperation. This meant he'd have to pull every damn thing out just to get to his tools. Wonderful.

He shoved his hands into his shorts pockets and glared at the mess. The first thing in the way was Anna's patio furniture that hadn't seen the light of day this year. Being as it was almost September, it seemed silly to set it out on the patio now, but James figured he better at least pull it out of the way to see what to do next.

He reached for a black, wrought-iron chair turned upside down directly in front of him. It was perched on top of another chair with other lawn furniture pieces wedged up against it. When James grabbed two legs to pull it out it refused to move more than a couple inches. He tried to lift it up, then pull. Nothing. He pushed it side to side. It slid a bit, then the back settled down further into the mess holding it captive. James kicked at the bottom chair in disgust. The entire pile screeched as metal slid against metal.

He stood back again eyeing the tangled mess. It looked like one of those weird sculptures that Tommy might have on display at the gallery. It was hard to tell where one thing ended and another began in the ornate, twisted mess. He really ought to take a picture of it and text it to Tommy to tease him a bit. Or should he? James grinned. Why not? Tommy had a pretty good sense of humor. He could show him his old dad did too.

James pulled his phone out and snapped two different shots. Now, how did he get the pictures into a text message? It had been a while since he'd done this. Anna had showed him how so he could send her pictures from out on the water. She'd loved that. Especially sunrise shots.

James stared at the screen willing himself to remember. Oh yeah, there was that arrow thing he had to push. He poked at the arrow, then realized he had to find Tommy's cell number. After a trip back to the house to get the phone and address book on the side table where Anna kept it, he finally had his text ready to go.

"I discovered some modern sculpture in the shed for your next exhibit!"

He put two smiley face things next to his text. He hesitated, then hit *send*. He sure hoped Tommy would think it was funny.

He slid the phone into the side cargo pocket in his shorts and studied the mess in front of him. OK. Fine. Maybe the two chairs had to come out together before he could get them apart. James grabbed the back of the bottom chair at the sides and yanked. They both gave just enough to let him think he had the right idea. He picked up his cap, scratched his head, put his cap back on.

"Come on you sorry son-of-a-snake, you're not getting the better of me. You're coming out of there!" He grasped the edges of the chair again and pulled hard. The tangled mess of metal moved a little more. James yanked harder. He tumbled backward landing on his rear. The chair he had hold of slammed against his chest, while the one that had been on top of it flipped over him onto the grass behind him, nicking his baseball cap off his head as it sailed by. Inside the shed, shrill scraping, screeching, and thumping sounds from all matter of tumbling stuff lasted for at least thirty seconds. It sounded like a junk-yard landslide.

"Holy Mother of God!" James yelled. Then he lay back on the damp grass and laughed until he about cried, still holding onto that damn chair for dear life.

When he finally could stop laughing, he tossed the offending chair to the side and rolled over to get up. His gut hurt, and he was gasping for air. The neighbors were going to think he'd totally lost it. Hopefully no one had been outside to see the show.

James started laughing again. It turned into a bout of coughing, and his eyes started running. A chair had gotten the better of him! In fact, he'd almost lost his damn head over it. It'd been months since he'd laughed like this.

He pulled the worn, navy blue bandana he used as a handkerchief out of his front shorts pocket and wiped his face. Still a little out of breath, hands on hips, he surveyed the disaster area.

What the hell, he decided. It had taken all that work to get the damn things out of there, he might as well set the table and chairs up on the patio. *If* he could get the other two chairs and table out of there. It would give him another place to sit anyway, and the best time of the year to be outside was coming up. Plus the kids would be home in a weekend or two. It would be nice for them. He could even get the barbecue fired up. The grill was somewhere in the shed in that the mountain of crap.

James chuckled. What a sight he must have been. It almost was a shame no one else had been there. He'd have paid money to see it himself.

"Well, if you can't laugh at yourself that's a sad state," he said, grinning as he picked up one of the offending chairs to deliver it to the patio. It was then that he saw the retreating back of a little girl on her banana-seat bike, just beyond his driveway, headed toward downtown. Her ponytail swished back and forth as she worked the pedals. Well, little Miss Natasha would definitely think he was a crazy old man now . . . if she didn't already.

He shrugged and went back to retrieve the other chair. He didn't have time to worry about what little kids thought of him today. He had work to do, and it felt good to be taking on a different chore.

Clearing out the shed to try to get to his workbench was a longer struggle than James anticipated. He untangled the remaining patio furniture and set it up. He also found the cushions for the chairs in the mess, but they'd been claimed as low-income housing by a bunch of mice. Chewed up stuffing, mouse turds, and a couple live rodents scattered as he picked up one of the faded red cushions from the pile on the top of the table.

"Ugh. These things need trashing." He grabbed the entire pile and threw it out of the doorway onto the lawn. Two more mice rolled out of the mess and scampered off.

"That's right, you freeloading varmints. Find somewhere else to live."

James watched the pile for a few seconds to see if anything else was going to appear. He kicked at it once for good measure. Nope. Only little mounds of chewed up fluff and mouse leavings remained.

"Damn rodents. Where did I put those yard bags I bought last fall?" He peered back into the trashed shed as if something might come charging out at him from the mangled pile of junk. "I bet it's been two or three years since I really cleaned this place out. What a friggin' mess. Today's as good as any. But first, I should eat lunch and find those trash bags. No use trying to work on traps today."

Eight

Natasha

Today was hard. Mom works all week at the farm or at the farmers' markets and I have to stay home with my gran all day. That part's not bad, even though I haven't known Gran very long. She's really nice, and she makes yummy pancake breakfasts with real maple syrup. They are my absolute favorite things to eat. She makes them whenever I want, but I try not to tell her that's what I want too much when she asks what we should have for breakfast, because that wouldn't be nice. I'd eat them every day for lunch and dinner too if I could. Breakfast for dinner is the absolute best.

When we were at home in Boston, Mom only made pancakes when my dad left super early for school or was gone on some trip. He didn't like pancakes or French toast or anything like that. He only wanted dark regular toast and coffee every morning. Breakfast for dinner wouldn't have been anything he liked. I guess there were a lot of other things he didn't like. I'm pretty sure I was one of those things. Mom says that's not true, and I should never think that. But I do think about it all the time.

Gran makes me hot cocoa too, even though it's summer. Sometimes she puts a little bit of her instant coffee stuff in it for me and calls it a "mocha." She winks at me and tells me not to tell my mom she's feeding me coffee, but I know that Mom already knows because I caught her smiling and shaking her head the other day when Gran whispered that to me when she brought it to me at the table.

Anyway, Gran doesn't bug me about what I'm doing or thinking or anything. She watches TV during the day sometimes, but mostly she's in the kitchen. Sometimes she'll play Rummy or Sorry with me at the table or let me help her bake stuff. She makes all kinds of things, but I like making cookies best. She made some pies and bread yesterday for a bake sale for some ladies' club thing she does. I love how the kitchen smells when she's cooking, and she smells like cinnamon and spices all the time. It's nice.

If I tell her I'm going out to ride my bike, she doesn't lecture me about being careful and where I can go, or not go, and all that, like Mom did when we first got here. Gran just tells me not to go too far and to ask anyone to bring me to her house if I get lost or need her, and they will. But I won't get lost. I know where things are after I go there just once. It's kind of like I have a map in my head.

I didn't go out on my bike right away today because of the fog. My grandfather couldn't even go out to fish because the fog was in so thick. He was yelling at Gran before I even got out of bed.

It's not like I haven't heard yelling before. A few times my mom and dad got kinda loud at each other when they were arguing about stuff. Old Mr. Cleary down the hall from our apartment yelled a lot around bedtime at night too. But Mr. Cleary didn't yell *at* anyone because he lived by himself and his helper only worked during the day. He didn't even yell in English. Plus, I could only kind of hear him because he was down the hall. And it wasn't ever mean yelling. He was super nice to everyone. Mom said that he was just lonely and getting confused in his old age, and when it was dark out he saw things in the shadows that weren't really there. She said that a lot of times he thought he was back in Ireland and not in Boston. If Mr. Cleary went on for awhile, or got super loud, Mom would go down to his apartment to sit and talk with him to make him feel better.

My grandfather's yelling is not like Mr. Cleary's at all. This morning he was all mad because Gran didn't cook his eggs the way he wanted. He went on and on about how she was too stupid to know what "over easy" was, and she never could cook anything right. Actually, he said a whole lot of swear words too. Then I heard a crashing sound like a plate breaking. But the yelling was the worst. I could hear him all the way up in my room with the door closed like he was standing right beside me, but there's a whole floor between the kitchen and my room. I didn't hear Gran say a word. She usually doesn't say a thing when he starts, she just keeps on doing whatever she's doing and pretends he isn't there. I was glad I hadn't gotten up yet so I wasn't downstairs. I was kinda scared for a minute that he was going to break something else or do more than just yell. Then I heard my mom running down the stairs. She started talking and the yelling stopped. I got out of my bed and opened my door really slowly so I could hear what Mom was saying because I couldn't make out the words, just the sound of her voice low and soft, like when she's super mad. Just when I got the door open so I could hear, the front door slammed. It was really quiet for a few seconds after that. Then I heard Mom tell Gran she wouldn't allow her or anyone else in the house to be hurt anymore by "that man's abusive alcoholic behavior," and if it happened again, we'd be finding somewhere else to live and taking her with us. Gran didn't say a word, but I'm pretty sure she was crying, because Mom told her it was going to be all right, that she knew Gran didn't want to leave her home, and Mom didn't even know where we all could go, but something had to be done. Gran said something about now that my grandfather had whatever it was out of his system, it wouldn't happen again for a long time. Then Mom asked her if she realized that the next time might be worse? Then I heard her coming back up the stairs so I tiptoed back to bed and pretended to be asleep. But that didn't work. She knew I was faking the second she walked in.

She kissed my forehead and sat down on the edge of my bed. She told me she was really sorry about all the yelling. She said she'd been away from home long enough to kind of forget how bad my grandfather could be. Then she said she was going to have to find a better place for us to stay because it wasn't right for me to be around "all that."

I pushed myself up, so I was leaning against the headboard of the bed and said I wished we never had to leave home. I told her I get that we had to pay a lot for rent, and her job wasn't good enough, and we didn't have much money anymore, but that I still wish we could have stayed in Boston.

Her face got all sad, and she looked down at the floor. She told me she knows how I feel, but that she'd tried everything she could to make it work, and we just couldn't stay. Then she said how we are super lucky we had anywhere to go. She said it took a lot of love and courage for Gran to tell her that we could come here.

Then I felt bad. I played with the edge of the blanket so I wouldn't have to look at her. I told her it was OK, and I actually *kind* of like it here. I said maybe things would get better with my grandfather, and I said how I really don't want to move again. She said it was nice of me to be hopeful, but she didn't think my grandfather was going to change anytime soon.

I bit my lip because I didn't want to cry, and I didn't want to make her cry. I could feel how sad and tired she was. Then I suddenly had an idea I thought might make her feel better, so I asked her if she wanted to hear my *Good Things About Here* list so far. She said she shouldn't be surprised I had a list for that, and that she'd love to hear it.

So I told her everything that was on my list. While I told her, I held up my hand and put my fingers up for each good thing so she could keep up. She laughed when I told her the ocean deserved both spots one and three because it's super cool. Then I told her I'd just added Gran's pancakes and mocha, uh *hot chocolate*, for number five. I snuck a peak at her to see if she caught that one, and she was smiling—not with her eyes, but still smiling. Then I told her I added my room for number six, because I really do like it. A lot.

She ruffled my hair like she does and told me she thought it was "a grand list." She said she was glad I'm finding things I like here. She also told me she knows how hard it is to get used to a new place, and she just wished things with my dad had been different.

There was no way I wanted her to start talking to me about my dad again. We'd gone over and over it, and now all it did was make me super sad, mad, and sick at the same time—like someone was stabbing me in my stomach. So I just said I hoped my grandfather would do better. She said again she doubts that's ever going to happen, but that she was going to try to talk to him. She said that no one deserves to be afraid in their own home, that it's time things changed, and that Gran deserves so much better. I get that. But I don't want to move again. I just don't.

I thought she was going to say more, but she just kissed my forehead again and said she had to get to work. She asked what my plans for the day were. I told her I didn't have any except to ride my bike down to the harbor, but she said I couldn't do that until later because it's too dangerous when it's foggy. Then she dropped the big one on me. She announced I was going to have a busy day tomorrow because we're going down to the new school to register me.

I didn't have anything good to say about that. It made me miss my old friends, all two of them, from my old neighborhood. I was sure I wasn't going to like any new school either. Kids are generally mean, and I don't think the same way most of them do, so they like to try to pick on me. Mostly I don't let it get to me, but sometimes it just doesn't seem fair.

As usual, Mom knew what I was thinking. She told me she knew it was going to be strange at first, and she understood how all the new things are hard for me to get used to. She kept saying she was sorry, that the only thing she knew to do was to keep on doing the best she could for us. She promised she was going to make things better, that she loved me more than anything forever and ever, and that she wouldn't let me down. I'm not worried about that part. She's the best mom. I told her I love her forever too. Then I hugged her tight 'cause

I want her to know that I really do get it about why we had to move, and I know it's hard for her too.

I didn't have my pancakes for breakfast today. Gran wasn't there when I got downstairs a few minutes later, so I got myself a bowl of cereal. Mom was making some toast for us when Gran came back. Her face was all puffy and red like she'd been crying. She gave my mom a hug and smiled at me—that fake kind of smile when grown-ups try to act like everything is just fine, and they think you're too stupid to know it's not. I just looked down at my bowl because I didn't know what else to do. Gran told Mom to take it easy going to work and go super slow because the fog was still "thicker than pea soup" out there. Then she started doing the dishes like nothing had happened at all just a little while before.

I told Mom I wasn't really hungry and that I was going to go up to my room. She was getting ready to leave for work anyway, and I didn't want to stay downstairs with Gran. She was different today. It felt weird.

What I really wanted to do was get my bike out and go for a ride down to the wharf, but Mom had already made it clear I couldn't while the fog was in. I don't need to see to know where the road is, but if I even asked to go, everyone would make a big fuss over it not being safe to be out there. Mom doesn't even like me to go out in the yard when it gets this way, which seems like it's about every other afternoon. I sat looking out the window for a while at all the nothing. Then I tried to start reading one of my favorite books I brought from home when we moved. But I really didn't feel like it.

When I told Gran I like to read, she promised that we would go to the library together, and I could get a library card so I could get new books. The only thing is that we have to wait for a day that the library will be open. In Boston, the library was open every day. Balsam Cove is such a small town that the library is only open two days a week and not even for the whole day. I wanted to remind her that she said we could go, but I figured that probably wasn't a good plan today.

When it started getting brighter outside like the sun was trying to shine through the fog, I opened my window to listen. The foghorn was still sounding every couple minutes, but between that I could hear the gulls muttering at each other and the water splashing up on the rocks down at the cove. It smelled like seaweed and bait so I knew the tide was low because when it's in I really can't smell anything except salt. After a while longer I could barely see the water, not clear and bright, but like I was looking through the thin see-through curtains downstairs in Gran's living room.

A couple more minutes after that everything was clear with the sun was shining off the water so bright it made my eyes sting to look straight at it. Off to the right I could see the moorings where the lobster boats are all tied up, facing the same way like they were looking at me, waiting for me to come down and see them. They all move in the same direction with the tide when they are on their lines. Sometimes when the waves are bouncing them around, I think it looks like the boats are all dancing together.

I knew Gran would let me go out then, so I ran downstairs to ask. She said it was fine. I didn't wait for her to say anything else. I was free!

Nine

Natasha

I headed straight for the wharf to see if the tide had brought in anything neat. The shore down there is mostly big rocks, except for a little hidden space between some of the biggest boulders as the shore curves around from the road. There's an actual beach there. Technically the beach sand here isn't sand like when people think of beaches at other places. I know because I looked it up. I love to look up stuff about all kinds of things. I learn tons of cool facts that way. Mom shakes her head and says I'm a research hound, but she helps me all the time and explains things if I don't quite get it.

This is what we learned about beaches. Most ocean beaches in other states are made up of tiny, eroded quartz rock particles that ride down rivers and and streams until they get to the ocean. There the waves roll them over and over for years, making them even tinier and smoother—like silky bits. If the sand is super fine it even might be millions of years old.

Maine sand is different. It's coarser. It's mostly made of crushed mussel shells, other seashells, sea urchins, and eroded granite that the ocean has beat to bits year after year. Here it has a pinkish color to it. The article I read says it looks pink because it's got a lot of potassium feldspar in it, a mineral that comes from igneous rocks like pink granite. Igneous rocks form from molten, volcanic magma as it cools. The shoreline of the peninsula is made of igneous rocks from a volcano that was active like four hundred twenty million years ago across the bay, where Mt. Desert Island is now. Cadillac Mountain—the mountain I can see across the bay—is actually one edge of that collapsed volcano. It's pretty neat to think I live by a once active volcano. Anyway, the potassium feldspar in the pulverized granite bits—I love that word...pul-ver-ized—in the sand makes it look shiny and warm. But let me tell you what. There is nothing warm about the sand, or the water, at my beach.

The bench Mr. James sits on all the time is made of pink granite. The seat is smooth and shiny. It can be polished like that because the granite is made up of quartz, orthoclase or microcline, and mica. The polished mica makes it look like there are bits of gold in it. It's so pretty. All the rocks here are amazing. Down at my beach I've identified pink granite, gray granite, basalt, quartz, and gray limestone so far.

I suppose I should add those to my *Good Things About Here* list:

7) Super interesting rocks

8) My very own beach

OK, so the beach really doesn't *belong* to me. But I never see anyone else down here so I'm claiming it.

My beach isn't very big. It's hidden inside the curve of some huge basalt rocks that have an opening in the front, facing the water. One of the rocks looks just like a whale that stares out at the ocean. I pretend he got beached there a gazillion years ago and turned to stone. I call him Black Whale. That's the common name for the North Atlantic Right Whale. There used to be a lot of them in the Gulf of Maine, but now there aren't many of them left in the entire world, only like three hundred seventy, so they are endangered. The NOAA website Mom and I looked at when we Googled "North Atlantic Right Whales in Maine" says that whale hunting in the late eighteen hundreds almost made them extinct to begin with, and now the whales keep getting caught in fishing lines or hit by big ocean ships. This is killing them off. The article also said that the ocean is noisier than it used to be. This is a problem because it stresses the whales out. The whales don't do well with all the commotion. I get that. Lots of noise stresses me way out too.

Another thing is that the Right Whales that lived in the the Gulf of Maine have left because the ocean's warming up. Even just a few degrees warmer is bad for them and the Gulf of Maine is warmer now than it ever has been. For at least nine hundred years it got colder; then it started slowly warming up. Then suddenly it started getting warmer way faster. In fact, over the past ten years it has warmed up more quickly than ninety-nine percent of any of the other oceans on the planet. The water temperature has been rising an average of point eighty-four degrees Fahrenheit every decade since nineteen eighty-two. That's nearly three times as fast as the rest of the world's oceans. People want to think there's a simple reason for why this is happening, but it's complicated. We found a list that scientists at the Gulf of Maine Research Institute posted online that gives the three main reasons why the water's warmer:

1) Man-Made Global Warming
2) Melting in the Arctic
3) Changing Ocean Circulation

It looks like a simple list of reasons, but there's so much I could read and study about each of the three things that it would take all my free time and the rest of my life. That's why I told you it was complicated.

Anyway, North Atlantic Right Whales like colder water. Now they have to swim farther north to find it. My Black Whale might be the only one left someday anywhere near the Gulf of Maine, if not the whole world, and he's a stone whale. He guards my crescent-moon shaped beach. My beach is just a little bigger than the most massive, full-grown Right Whale could be.

On the other side of my beach, two big round basalt rocks sit together with a much smaller one in between them. I think they look like a rock family—two parents and a kid. They're never completely out of the water like Black Whale is, even at the lowest Neap Tide. It's like they're all swimming together on a beach vacation. Another cool thing about my rock family is that they will be there together for ever and ever, just the same as they are. Sometimes when I think about that it makes me kinda sad.

When the tide is in Black Whale's back is barely above the water, but when the tide goes out, his whole body is there lying on the sand. There are lots of smaller smooth basalt rocks, and sharper gray and pink granite slabs, that make up the curved edge of my beach. They're awesome to look at it and explore. When the sun is shining and the tide is out, the basalt is warm. Then I like to sit on the sand against Black Whale's smooth tail, just soaking in the sunshine.

Today I visited my beach for a while to look for sea glass and other cool stuff. I found a few mussel shells, an old bait bag, some broken pieces of sea shells, and a sea urchin's outer body that was almost perfect. A gull must have had it for breakfast, because when I turned it over to where the urchin's mouth is, there was a big hole that had been pecked out by someone's beak. I swished it around in the water to make sure it was clean. Then I took it up above the tide line where I hide all my treasures I find. There's a bit of granite ledge that hangs over another granite slab there, so it makes a kind of covered shelf that no one can see unless you know right where it is. I discovered it the same day I found my beach. It keeps my stuff safe.

Thinking about the gull eating the urchin for breakfast made me think about lunch. Plus, clouds were starting to move across the sun again, and it looked like it might rain, and I remembered that it was Tuesday, and the library would be open after lunch. If Gran was feeling better maybe she would take me to the library later.

I didn't try to ride my bike up the hill this time. I walked it up while I was thinking about what kind of books I wanted to check out. I couldn't have thought about books and pedaled hard to make it up the hill at the same time. I got to Mr. James's driveway and stopped there to get on my bike. I knew it was his yard because I see him walk up there to his house from the cove almost every day. It's the prettiest little house overlooking the water on Harbor Hill Road. It's white with green trim and green shutters. The paint looks like it's just been done, not chipped and peeling like on Gran's house. The green trim is exactly the same color as the fir trees along each side of the driveway. Those trees aren't super tall. They are perfectly spaced apart and perfectly across from each other. They look like really full Christmas trees to me. I bet they'll be lit up with lights when Christmas comes—at least I think they should be. I should remember to look up what kind of fir they are. I know they're not a pine tree because I know what white pines look like. That's the only kind of pine I've seen here so far. Plus the needles on Mr. James's trees are super short, not long like a pine. I've seen a few different kinds of fir trees around. They could be a type of fir. Maybe I'll make a list of all the kinds of evergreen trees that I find here.

Anyhow, just as I sat down on my bike seat there were some awful metal screeching noises and thumping, bumping sounds coming from Mr. James's yard. Then I heard someone laughing like crazy. I scooted my bike forward just enough so that I could look into his yard to see what in the world? There were a couple chairs that had fallen over beside the shed in the yard, and I could see Mr. James flat on his back outside the open shed door. He obviously wasn't hurt because he was laughing. I mean, he really was laughing, not that fake laugh some people do. For some reason it was so funny to hear him that it made me start to feel like I was going to start laughing too. He stopped and wiped at his eyes. Then he started laughing again as he went to get up. I didn't want him to see me spying on him, so I hurried up to leave, pedaling my bike toward town. It still makes me smile thinking about it. He sure is different; not at all like my grandfather.

Ten

James snagged a spoon out of the dish drainer on his way to the pantry where the jar of peanut butter lived on the middle shelf. When he opened the jar the aroma took him back to boyhood summer afternoons and lunches of a PBJ, chips, cookies, and ice-cold milk prepared by his mom. Back then he'd never dreamed that one day his wife would make their own children the same kinds of summer meals in the very same kitchen. Time had moved on though. Now, it was just him. Everyone else was gone.

He swirled the spoon along the sides and bottom of the nearly empty jar, turned the utensil upside down, and licked every bit of the creamy peanut butter off in one pass. Then he shoved the spoon back in the jar, rattling it around the bottom, fishing around for the last little bit.

Well, that won't do, he thought, surprised to discover that he really was hungry for the first time in a long while. Spoon in hand he tossed the now empty jar into the wastebasket on his way to the fridge. There wasn't a whole lot of what looked to be any kind of quick meal left in there. He opened the freezer. It was about half-full of casserole-type stuff. He closed the freezer and looked back into the fridge. Not a decent piece of bread or anything else needed to make a real sandwich could be found, unless you counted half of a dried-up English Muffin rolled up in a plastic bag and the jar of raspberry preserves in the door. Beside the English Muffin on the second shelf, Anna's supply of yogurt stood in three smart rows, labels facing forward. James would bet they were even arranged by date. She was fanatical about organization and neatness. This was another thing he loved to mess with her about. He grinned remembering how he'd put stuff in the wrong cupboards or turn it around so you couldn't read what it was just to get a rise out of her.

Still smiling, James reached down and turned all the yogurts in the first row around so their labels faced backward one last time. He sighed. It was strange the little bits he missed about her, and about the two of them, that had piled up together over the years to make their world. He retrieved the wastebasket, plopped it down in front of the open refrigerator door, pulled a kitchen chair over, and sat down. For the second time in a few days, he gave a good look at what was left on the shelves. He began tossing things into the trash, starting with the all the expired yogurt.

"Guess I might as well do this while I'm here. Besides, if the kids are coming home, I should make sure there's enough to feed them when they show up. Probably never see yogurt in this house again," he muttered grabbing the last container. "How she could eat this stuff is beyond me."

Ten minutes later all that was spared from the trash was mostly condiments from the shelves in the door: an unopened jar of Dijon mustard, the jar of raspberry preserves, about a third of a jar of horseradish, the butter dish with three-quarters of a stick of butter in it, and a just-opened bottle of ranch dressing. Four brown eggs in their carton and three cans of beer on the top shelf were also spared.

James grabbed one of the beers, cracked it open, and took a long haul on it.

Ayup, definitely time to make a trip to town. Better make a list first.

The local grocery was tiny and carried enough to get by, but when you really needed supplies you had to get yourself off the peninsula and drive the thirty miles into the "Big E" to get them. Ellsworth was also the only place nearby—if you can call twenty-five miles away, nearby—where you could find any fast-food places. James was still hungry, and if he went up to the diner for lunch he'd never get to town.

"Well, why not? Today's as good as any I suppose. To hell with it."

James realized that he was yet again speaking aloud to nothing but air. At least if Petunia cat was still around he could pretend he was talking to her. He sighed again, got up from the chair, nudged the refrigerator door shut, took another slug from the beer, then tossed the mostly full can across the room toward the sink. A splash of beer like an ocean whitecap appeared above rim as the can crashed with a dull thud into the stainless-steel tub.

"Two points! And no mess!" James chuckled, thinking Anna surely would've given him what-for over that move.

He rinsed the can out, then used the faucet's sprayer hose to wash down the sides of the sink. There was something super satisfying about the taste of a good beer on a hot day, but he hated stale beer smell. That was one odor that could take him back in his boyhood memories to places he didn't care to visit.

He dropped the can into the lined and covered bin for redeemables that lived on the mat by the front door. It was just about full. He may as well take them to the redemption center on his way to town. He tied off the bag and tossed it out the door onto the lawn. He did the same to the bag in the now full garbage can. When James opened the drawer to get new bags to put in both receptacles he noted there were just a few left in the box.

Better get more of these too.

He rummaged around trying to find the yard bags he originally came inside to get finally locating them in the pantry on the bottom shelf. There was only a handful left in the box. Since he was going to clean out the shed he was going to need a whole lot more than that. He should pick up something to get rid of the mice too. Writing things down was a definite must. There was no way he was going to remember everything.

He grabbed a pen from the counter and turned toward the pad hanging from a magnetic clip on the side of the fridge. His mother had kept it there. Anna had seen no reason not do to the same. It was so much a part of the appliance that James never took any real notice of it. There already was a shopping list on it in Anna's handwriting:

eggs
15 grain bread
butter
2% milk
peanut butter
napkins
colby jack cheese
angel hair pasta
fresh spinach
salad stuff
cottage cheese
yogurt
plastic wrap
cat food
cat litter
beer for James

He stared at the list. The world stopped. A lingering light scent of vanilla and sugar cookie passed by him. Anna.

In that moment he was certain if he looked over his shoulder she'd be standing there in her bare feet, wearing her favorite baby blue, short-sleeved blouse that she'd chosen at Renys when he took her shopping for her birthday two years ago, honey-tanned legs peeking out from her rolled up jeans. Her head would be barely cocked to one side, wavy, sandy blonde hair wild and tousled from working out in the yard. Those beautiful eyes, the color of the summer sea, would be sparkling as she smiled at him with that funny little look she got on her face whenever he forgot what he was supposed to be doing. He steadied himself, placing the palm of his right hand flat against the list on the door—leaning into it. He couldn't help himself. He turned.

Nothing.

His heart felt like it had been ripped out of his chest, again. *Damn Fool!* What had he expected? She wasn't here. She wasn't coming back. She could not come back.

Screw the damn list! He slammed the pen down on the counter, grabbed his keys, and strode out of the kitchen into the yard. Once he was in his truck he sat with his forehead against the steering wheel until he could breathe normally, and sanity began to return to his brain. Would this ever stop?

James sat for a few more minutes staring out at the yard trying not to think about anything except the fact that he had to go to town to get supplies. After a while he put the key in the ignition. The diesel engine rumbled low as it turned over. Some song that was supposed to be country music filled the cab. James reached over and spun the radio dial down low so he couldn't hear it. "That stuff they play now isn't even country," he growled. "Where's Merle Haggard or Tom Jones when you need 'em?"

He figured that was just one more thing that would never be the same. The world kept going on. Here he was more or less stuck wherever it was he seemed to be, just when he thought things might be easing up a little bit. James thumped the steering wheel with his palm. This was not going to happen today. He had things to do.

He eased the truck into gear and swung around the narrow circle at the backside of the drive to head out to the street. The driveway had been a straight shot from the road when James was a boy. Then one night when his father had roared in drunk from the bar and started his usual carrying on out in the dooryard, one of the summer folks called the locals. When the police cruiser pulled into the drive they'd blocked in his father's old red Ford. He wasn't having any of them, so he jumped back in his truck, threw it in drive, and screamed forward spinning mud up through the grass as he tore around and back out onto the street.

His father spent three days at the county jail for that one—three of the most peaceful days the rest of the family, and the neighborhood, got here and there. When the old man got back, he borrowed a bobcat from a buddy and smoothed over the muddy ruts he'd created in his getaway through the yard. A dump truck full of good-sized rock arrived to cover the mud. That was followed the next afternoon by fine gravel that went over both the old and new portion of the drive just like he'd meant to do the whole thing in the first place. Over James's childhood there had been quite a few *improvements* at the house that had appeared in the same kind of way. James shook his head. At least the driveway was a useful enhancement.

The weather had turned a bit while James had been inside. A smattering of pewter clouds had come up from the southwest chasing away the sun, but it didn't look like it would amount to much. A spit of rain showed up on the windshield. By the time he'd turned off the main road from town onto Route One it was really coming down. He turned the wipers from intermittent to steady and gave his thoughts over to the comforting rumble of the truck and the swish of the rainwater from the tires on the road. After a while he reached over and turned the radio back up for company. A woman was singing something he remembered hearing before. The tune was nice and she at least sounded like she was a country singer. Hopefully the station would play more like that. Some of that newer stuff on the local country radio station just didn't sound right. Not that James didn't like music other than country. Some good rock and roll was fine by him too. He'd even learned to like some jazz over the years, thanks to Anna's influence. But when you want to hear *your* music, that is what you want.

There was a CD player he'd never used in the truck. He should take some of the discs from their collection in the house and put them in there so he could play them. Then again, it wasn't like he ever spent a lot of time in the truck. If it left town once a month that was saying something. He mostly just went back and forth to the wharf or over to the marine supply down the road. Truth was he'd probably never remember to grab the CDs anyway. Ads came on. Then a DJ was yakking at him out of the speakers, then more ads. He punched at the dial to turn it off. What had happened to actually *playing* music without all the yammering? Thinking about that was just another reminder how things were different and would never again be the way he was used to, the way he wanted. He was still chewing on these thoughts when he pulled up into the Walmart parking lot.

Anna wasn't a fan of the huge store, but James only wanted to shop at one place today so he could get back to his chores at home. He could never understand why she had to go to six different stores when you can go to one and get everything. He parked out by the garden center carefully backing the truck into a spot on the far side of the lot. Even though it was a work truck and wasn't as pristine as it used to be, James always worried about some idiot opening their door into it or scraping it with a shopping cart. Years ago, he would've left the keys in the ignition and never worried about anyone bothering with it. Not anymore. He locked the truck and stowed the keys in his pocket. He found a stray cart on his way into the store and grabbed it. Why were people so lazy? How hard was it to return the cart to where it was supposed to go and possibly save somebody's vehicle from a bad scratch?

Once in the store, James headed toward the area where the cleaning supplies were stocked. He went by the automotive section, then books, and was passing by the music when he decided he would try to find something to play in the truck on the way home. There were two rows of vinyl records next to a smaller section of CDs. He remembered hearing a report on the news a while back about how vinyl records were making a comeback. Did they even have a record player at the house anymore? He wondered if his collection of forty-fives and albums from his high school days was still in storage up in the attic.

He'd have to climb up there and look around. He thumbed through the tabs announcing the bands and artists. Many of them were from his glory days. That took him right back. But there wasn't a record player in the truck and he was on a mission to find some good country. He moved on and found the classic country section of CDs. After a few minutes he managed to find one called *Classic Country Gold* that looked promising. Satisfied, he put it in the cart, then steamed on through the aisles, stopping just long enough to toss things in that he thought he remembered he might need, starting with both sizes of garbage bags. He stopped by the pet section to get more cat food. He paused, remembering that Anna's list had cat litter written on it. He should get that too, just in case Petunia showed up. He turned the cart down the next aisle and found the brand he thought she always bought. At least the color of the box was the same as the one in the pantry. He put the box under the basket of the cart and moved on to the grocery side of the store.

By the time he made it to the checkout line, the cart was loaded right to the gills, and he was wondering how in the world he'd managed to fill it up so fast. There was only one cashier open in all of the twenty-some lanes. Most people were using the self-checkout.

James wasn't sure he wanted to try that. He'd probably mess something up and just feel stupid.

When it was his turn, the clerk asked him how many bags he wanted? James stared at him unsure of what he was asking, then remembered you had to bring your own bags into the stores now or buy them at the checkout. He'd forgotten all about the no-disposable plastic bag law. He knew Anna kept bags somewhere, but he had no idea where. He just told the clerk whatever he needed was fine. How could he guess what would fit where for how many bags? Then his purchases were a little harder on the wallet than he'd expected. Oh well. He figured he'd get better at it with a little practice.

Anna had always shopped the sales. She never left home without her list or her bag of bags either. When he did go with her, depending on what stores they went to, he'd wander off to get whatever it was he needed while she shopped for everything else. Then he'd meet up with her and push the cart and load the bags into the truck. He realized he never paid much attention to what she got or where she got it. Considering what he paid today, it seemed she had something with the shopping different places thing—with a list.

The brief storm had passed by the time James left the store. The sun was peeking out from behind layered puffs of light gray and white. Even though the smell of summer rain was still in the air, the pavement in the parking lot was already drying up. He thought it felt a bit less sticky out. Then again, maybe that was wishful thinking.

Back at his truck, he loaded everything into the back seat rummaging through the bags to find the new CD. He tossed it into the front. He returned the shopping cart to the cart rack that was closest to him, grabbing two others on the way that people had left out in the open.

"Lazy buzzards," he remarked to the air. "Nobody gives a crap about anything."

He slid up into the truck, opened the cellophane covering on the cd with the edge of his key, and shoved the wrapping into the bag he kept on the passenger floorboard for garbage. After he started the truck, he slid the new disc into the slot under the radio. Hank Williams's voice filled the cab. James smiled. See, he could figure this out. Anna would be proud of him, and the kids would never believe he had done his own grocery shopping. Maybe he wasn't as helpless as he thought. It felt weird and a little lonely, but if this was how it had to be he could make it work.

His stomach grumbled. He still hadn't gotten anything for lunch. If he'd been hungry before, he was damn near starving now. Considering the amount of food he'd bought he should have eaten before going into the store. Anna had always said that she never liked to shop on an empty stomach because she would be tempted to buy way more than they needed. One more thing to remember before coming to town next time. Eat first.

All right then. He'd just run through a drive-through for some food that was in no way good for him before he headed back home. That'd work just fine.

Eleven

By the time James made it back home—as his grandmother would have observed—his quarter had run out. He smiled thinking of his gram. When James was a young boy, he'd often go grocery shopping with her to the A&P in Ellsworth. She'd always put a quarter into the fiberglass pinto pony that waited on its stand outside the front of the store so he could have a ride. Fact was she'd use that pony ride as a bribe to get him to go to town with her.

The pony would grind back and forth in its slow, jerky rhythm while James pretended he was a cowboy galloping along. When the ride stopped he'd beg to go again, but his grandmother would always say, "His quarter ran out and yours will too, eventually."

It became a time-worn phrase in their family. By the time James's own children were born, the A&P, cowboy pony, and his gram were long gone. He wondered if there were any of those ponies left anywhere.

After three trips into the house most everything was in the kitchen except a few things needing to go down to the boat. The early afternoon rain shower had chased the fog completely out of the bay. An edge of crispness in the air smelled like the sheets Anna used to bring in off the clothesline. It was a comforting scent, somewhere between sunshine and salty sea-mist.

James turned his face toward the gentle puffs of breeze coming in over the bay. He closed his eyes and breathed in deep. He knew the sense of peacefulness on the air wouldn't last. He hoped the weather would remain calm most of the evening even though he already knew there was a small craft advisory for the morning with winds fifteen to twenty knots and gusts up to thirty. He needed to text Bustah the plan for the next day. If the weather report held true, they'd be doing dock work. The remainder of the week looked more promising. Tomorrow would be a good day to make up bait bags for hauling on Thursday.

James had heard there may be some pogies or herring available midweek for bait. It had been near impossible to get them this summer. Herring was restricted and you couldn't always gets pogies, or menhaden, which originally had taken up the slack when herring became scarce. Plus prices had skyrocketed. Lobstermen were often forced to rely on alternatives like pig hide resulting in smaller hauls. Because, for whatever reason, lobster prefer herring or pogies.

The number of lobsters in each trap compared to when James used other baits was the best scientific evidence you could get. The bait issue, along with the facts that shedder lobster prices were down below three dollars a pound off the boat most days and fuel prices were continually rising, made it tough to eke out a living. Peak season would come on in a couple weeks. There was a lot of worry for some folks over whether or not they could continue to afford to fish. Recent bad weather wasn't helping either.

James was hopeful the season should be ramping up soon. Soft shell lobsters, or shedders, are most abundant throughout late summer into early fall. In fact, more than three quarters of what they pulled up into the boat were shedders. These are the lobsters that have just molted, leaving their hard shells so that they can grow new, larger armor. You won't find many hard-shelled lobsters near shore in late summer.

As the water warms near the coastline in the summer months lobsters migrate in, because as they molt, the warmer water promotes new shell growth. When fall temperatures begin cooling the shallow coastal bays, the lobsters move back out to deeper, warmer water. There are lobstermen who fish year-round, following the lobsters migration, going more than thirty miles out to sea during the winter months. However like many of his peers who fished out of Heron

Harbor in Balsam Cove, James was an inshore fisherman. The *Salty Lady* was smaller than many of the newer boats. She was almost as old as he was and only equipped to stay within a couple miles of the shore. This suited James just fine. He'd never had the itch to have a newer, bigger boat or fish waters farther away than he had his entire life.

Of all the lobster landed in the United States, a little over eighty percent come from Maine waters. James figured he contributed his fair share. The latest Marine Resources Report showed Maine lobstermen had hauled in record numbers of lobster the past couple years. While great for the local coastal economy, you could never count on it continuing. This season the price per pound fishermen were paid was almost half what it had been the year before, and prices just kept dropping.

A lot of factors including market variables play into the daily rate co-ops pay per pound. Demand for the tasty crustaceans, including local tourism and exports to the United States and international markets, is number one. Recently, low demand from the overseas market was an issue, not to mention with the sea water temperatures trending upwards, shedders come on earlier. With no one to sell them to prices dive right into the toilet. This happened in two thousand twelve, the year that the selling price for shedders dropped to two dollars a pound right out of the gate. With selling prices that low it didn't make sense to take the boat out of the harbor once you factored in costs for bait and fuel, much less maintenance and other supplies. Many fishermen lost their boats to the bank that summer. They couldn't haul enough to pay the bills. Supply and demand is a finicky mistress at best. It only gets worse when Mother Nature is screwing around with things.

Like most lobstermen in the area, James fished all eight hundred of his allowable traps. That didn't mean he pulled them all up every day. Inshore lobster traps are set up in pairs, triplets, or sometimes quads, on strings of rope. James generally set his in pairs with one buoy attached to each duo. Every lobsterman has their own distinctive colors and patterns on their buoys. James's were bright blue with a four inch black band around the bottom edge of each one, exactly the same as his family had passed down through the generations. One of his grandfather's old wooden buoys was attached to the top of the *Salty Lady's* wheelhouse so that everyone knew which colors belonged to James and his license.

James knew where every one of his traps lay on the ocean floor. He had a routine for which traps to haul, on which days, in which order. As they approach each buoy, the sternman snags the rope attached to it, then feeds the rope into an electric winch—the pot hauler. Once the trap comes up over the side of the boat, the sternman opens it, pulls out anything obviously not a keeper, and tosses it back into the sea. This means not only undersized lobster, but crabs and other creatures that wander into the trap. Sometimes non-marine things find their way in, getting caught as the trap drifts down into the water, or snagged as the winch is pulling the trap up from the sea floor.

They sure found strange stuff in traps sometimes. The most unusual non-sea object that had ever been caught on one of James's traps was a pair of bright pink and lime green thong underwear. There was been plenty of other weird junk that got hauled up in his gear too, mostly litter that seemed to get more plentiful all the time. The bin he kept onboard for garbage had to be emptied almost every day because it filled so quickly with trash they grabbed out of the water.

In James's lifetime, the worst thing he'd heard of being brought up attached to gear was from about ten years back. One of the younger men fishing about twenty-five miles out had his trawl line snag very little of what was left of a man's body. That had stopped the fishing out there just like that. The Coast Guard declared the area off-limits for a time. It turned out an illegal burial at sea had gone awry. Every so often that story would resurface. It always made James slightly sick to his stomach. He was glad it hadn't happened on his boat.

For the most part, what you don't keep is different marine life. After creatures that are obvious non-keepers are sent back to the sea, the lobsters get pulled out one by one. Females whose tails are already notched, indicating they are breeders and illegal to keep, get tossed overboard. Any egg-bearing females needing a notch cut in their tails get one before they also are returned to the water.

Remaining lobster are checked with a measuring caliper along their carapace, to ensure they're keepers. The fines for keeping a lobster that isn't legal size (whether over or under) or egg-bearing or notched females, is not cheap. You ultimately could lose your lobstering license to boot. There are plenty of folks who keep a few they shouldn't. James knew that back in the day his own father had hauled up and kept a few monsters. He knew this as fact because he'd been there to see them. His mother had made some fine stews from them. But James stayed as far on the right side of the laws as he could. Not only did he want to stay out of trouble, but sustainable fishing, and the legacy of working on the sea, meant something to him. Now there was the phone to take pictures if they pulled up a big old bug. Then, at least on James's boat, it went right back to where it came from.

If the lobster is legal, its claws get banded and it's thrown into the appropriate wet tank on the boat—one for shedders, another for hard-shells. The sternman then rebaits the trap, and lets it slide down the rail and off the back of the boat into the water as the captain throttles on toward the next buoy. All this is done in a minute or two for each line as the boats dance around the harbor. Once back in the cove the lobsters get transferred from the boat's tanks into slotted, rectangular crates called cars. The cars are either taken directly to the co-op or a wholesaler or dropped from the side of the boat to sit in the water until sold.

Each grouping of traps needs to sit for a couple days after baiting in order for lobster to find them and crawl in to have a meal. If you pull them too soon there'll be very few keepers because they've not set long enough. If you pull them too late the bait will be gone, and the trap will be empty or at least near empty. Lobsters are not stupid creatures. Since there are escape hatches for smaller marine life to get out of the traps you can bet that lobster often can find their way out too. If you get two or three keepers per trap on any given day that's not half bad.

James thought over whether to buy new mesh bait bags for the months coming up. He knew he had a bunch somewhere in the shed, but God knew when he was going to be able to locate them in that mess. It'd be a good idea to order up more. You never knew when a bait bag would disappear out of a trap or become so bit up it was worthless, no longer able to hold its smelly lobster bait entrée. He took a minute to call Gene, who he'd bought bait bags from as long as he'd been fishing. His old friend didn't answer, so he left a message ordering a thousand.

Now that was done he put away the groceries. After he closed the refrigerator door, he looked at Anna's list again. This time as he read her neat handwriting it didn't beat him up quite as much. Still, he felt deep and empty in his gut, like someone had taken out everything that mattered from underneath his skin, leaving only shredded bits of him dangling into space from his shattered heart.

He reached up with his index finger to trace the curves of the last thing she had written there—*beer for James*. He carefully tore the list off the pad and folded it in half, creasing the fold gently between his index finger and thumb. Then he took his wallet out of his back pocket and placed the small rectangle of paper in the left side of the compartment where he kept pictures of Anna, Tommy, and Sophia, and other items he couldn't be without. He put his wallet back where it lived, then patted his pocket to make sure it was secure.

Early evening turned soft and pinkish gray. The slight, gentle breeze had picked up a bit, but it was nothing like the winds they were calling for in the morning. It was as good a time as any to take the supplies for the boat down.

He eased the truck out of the driveway and turned right to go the two hundred yards down the hill into the parking area at the wharf.

No one else was there. It would only take a couple trips before everything would be settled into his punt for the row out to the *Salty Lady*.

The tide was on the rise. James took his time carrying things down, enjoying the sounds of lapping water sliding in against the shore and rocks by the wharf. The high-water mark was darkly evident on the shoreline rocks and the wharf's pillars. A multitude of barnacles and small sea-plant life clinging to them was suddenly exposed to the elements every time the water retreated. Rocky edges were worn smooth in places by decades of the tide's sway. James watched as a strand of seaweed on one of the outer pilings hung on for dear life every time the tide approached it and left again. It would curl up against the rocks when the water slid in, then get pulled out in a long line as the ocean receded back into itself—a tendril of a strand, barely clinging to the granite its roots called home. He watched it for a few minutes in its graceful two-step with the water until a larger wave rolled in, and the seaweed's root was ripped out of the crevice between the rocks, then pulled away on the roll of the tide.

That's life, isn't it? Time moves in and out, and most times you just move with it. Then one day something happens. You're left uncovered to deal with the raw world around you with no shield of comfort. It wears you down, leaving marks that never go away. Other times you get ripped right away from your mooring to flounder about, drifting on the tide. I guess the question is: how do you find your way to something to hold on to, before you drown?

"Another thing I can't answer," James said aloud. He turned back to his chores, picked up the last two jugs of bleach, and carried them to the punt placing them in the belly of the little boat with everything else. He untied the rope from its cleat, then tossed it into the bow.

As he stepped in the punt it rocked gently away from the dock. The water was calm enough that James didn't bother to sit down to row the hundred feet or so out. He picked up one oar from under the seat and stood in the center pulling the paddle through the water alternately on each side, like a gondolier, steadily moving out to the *Salty Lady* on her mooring.

He put things away, making a quick check to see that everything was still where it should be. For now, that would do. Tomorrow afternoon he'd come out to do some necessary minor cleaning and maintenance.

He climbed down into the punt that he'd secured to the back of the larger vessel and paddled back to the dock. The tide had risen another foot up the pilings by time he came in. Because of this, the sliding ramp from the dock up to the wharf leaned toward the water at less of an angle now.

The swing between high and low tide down in the harbor was anywhere between nine to thirteen feet depending on the moon's cycle. Full or New Moons always brought the highest, or Spring Tide. Right now, they were headed toward the New Moon near the end of the month when the sun, the earth, and the moon would all be perfectly aligned. The tide would be a little higher each day until then. It would back off a bit at Neap Tide, about seven days after the New Moon. The few feet of fluctuation on the Spring Tides each month depended on how close the moon was to the earth.

All this he'd learned from his father years ago, but it was still as fascinating to James as it had been then. The sea and her partnership with the heavens always filled him with wonder. There was mystery, and a little magic, in the vast workings of the universe that made him feel so much a part of it, and yet so insignificant. Out at sea he felt his place in the world much more than when watching from land.

James and his fellow fishermen studied the tides as closely as they did the weather. He figured the high tide tonight at its peak would come in about ten feet higher than its lowest point almost twelve hours before. He knew high tide would be right about eight forty-five p.m. Without looking to check the time on his watch, judging by the water mark and the height of the ocean against the pilings now, he figured the tide would turn in just about two hours.

This had been a game with him ever since he was a kid—seeing if he could predict how much time was left until a high or low tide just by looking at the water marks. He glanced at his watch to see if he was right this time. Yup. He chuckled out loud. Six twenty p.m. Right about dead on. At a rising rate of a little over two feet per hour, high tide should hit right about when he predicted at eight forty-five. He'd just sit and watch a while. It wasn't like he needed to be anywhere.

James wandered over to his bench and sat. He leaned forward gazing out past the reach in his usual pose, hands clasped, elbows on his knees. He believed the most magical thing he could think of was being right there the minute the tide hit its peak and turned, starting the recession to its next low point. There was a palpable stillness, like the cogs of time clicked into place and stood still for that one, silver sliver of a second before life began to move again. In that sliver, it felt like the entire world was pulled in a different direction, and sometimes, you knew that if you could just unglue your feet from the earth, you would go right with it.

"Mr. James?"

In the back of his mind James acknowledged there was a small voice saying his name.

"Mr. James!" The now determined voice suddenly was at his side.

James straightened up, trying to appear like he'd not been caught daydreaming. "Well, hello there, Miss Natasha," he rumbled at her. He cleared his throat.

"Got a frog in there?" she questioned seriously, wide eyes staring at him. Her dark hair was escaping in long tendrils from her loose, cockeyed ponytail, and there was a black smudge of dirt on the tip of her nose. "That's what my mom always asks me if my throat is grumbly."

She put a hand up to her cheek to brush back some hair from her eyes. It immediately flopped back down, and now there was a smudge the same color as the one on her nose on the side of her face too.

James chuckled, more at her grubby earnestness than her question. "No, no. Not a real frog anyway. I just don't talk out loud much these days, and my voice gets rusty I guess."

"Why don't you talk much?"

James shrugged. "Nobody to talk to, I guess. I live by myself. And my cat ran off . . ."

She interrupted him, "Are you remembering today?"

James wrinkled his brow—confused. What was she asking him? Then he recalled his reply to her when she'd questioned what he was doing while sitting on the bench the other day.

"Well, I'm not sure. I just sat down a minute ago."

"I know. I saw you paddling your skiff in from your lobster boat out there." She pointed dramatically toward the wharf, then crossed her arms over her chest.

"Really. I didn't know anyone was down here with me." James smiled at her.

She cocked her head a little to the right, eyes wide and unblinking. She did not smile in return.

This child is some intense! James thought, slightly unnerved by her directness.

"I wasn't. I was at the top of the hill on my bike. And I saw you."

"Oh, I see." He raised an eyebrow. "So you were spying on me."

"I was not! You were down here, and I was up there. I wasn't sneaking around!" Her voice had risen slightly in pitch. She was glaring at him now, and her shoulders were up around her ears in defense.

"Whoa there, Natasha." James put up his hands up in front of him in mock defense. "I was only teasing. I believe you."

She studied his face. He didn't look away as she thought things over. Slowly her shoulders relaxed. Her face softened. "I really wasn't spying. You just weren't paying attention to anything but your boat."

James nodded, "You're absolutely right. I was paying attention to my chores out there." He nodded out toward the harbor, his gaze looking past her, settling on the *Salty Lady* moving restlessly on her mooring.

The child seemed satisfied at his agreement with her. She was already on to the next question.

"Um, if you're going to remember, can I sit and remember with you?"

Something subtly had changed in Natasha's voice. It sounded smaller, like she was scared to ask. James pulled his gaze back from the harbor to the girl. She was staring at the ground, scuffing at the rocky sand with the toe of her dirty blue and white tennis shoe. She peeked up at him when he didn't answer her. He had no idea what to say, so he slid over a little and patted the space beside him.

She hopped onto the bench and wriggled into place. When she was done, she was leaning slightly forward, her hands on either side of her legs, gripping the granite seat as if she would catapult herself off at any second. Her feet didn't quite touch the ground. She didn't look at James. Instead, she stared out over the water swinging her legs back and forth in a slow, steady rhythm. James leaned back, stretched out his legs, crossed his feet, and clasped his hands over his chest. There they sat, watching the sea as it moved in and out—out and in—each time the tide grasping a little higher at the shore before sliding away again.

Twelve

Natasha

I didn't get my library card today. It started to rain again, and Gran didn't want to walk in the rain. I was really bummed, but I understand. I think she was still upset from this morning. She knew I was disappointed, so she promised we would go Saturday, and maybe Mom would come too, if she wasn't working. Then she told me to choose my favorite cookie for us to make a batch together. Chocolate chip, of course. What else?

While she was teaching me how to crack eggs without getting shells into the bowl, she told me about how she didn't drive much anymore, but maybe she ought to start so we could go places when Mom is at work. I just nodded my head at first. But then after I thought about it, I told her I don't know how we'd do that. She doesn't even have a car. Mom drives hers to work, and my grandfather's truck is always wherever he is, which is hardly ever here. Besides, I'd bet he'd never let anyone else drive his truck. Gran sighed and agreed I was right. Then she said, "You're pretty smart, Kiddo."

I already know that, but Mom says I'm not supposed to tell people I know I'm smart, so I just said, "Thank you." Then I had to fish part of an eggshell out of the mixing bowl since I wasn't paying good enough attention because I'd been thinking about how Gran would drive us around in a nonexistent car. Then she handed me the whisk to whip up the eggs. I already knew how to do that. It was the first thing she taught me when we baked a cake together one day.

While I was whisking, she told me that she was really happy Mom and I had moved back to live with her. She said she never thought that would ever happen, and she loves us both so much, and that it's a "dream come true for her" that we're here. Then she was quiet for a minute before she told me she really wanted me to know all that. When I looked over at her she was staring out the window. She said how sorry she is that my grandfather acts the way he does. She looked over at me with her mouth all scrunched up, shook her head, and then said, "He's just who he is, I guess."

It made me feel good that she wants us to stay. But I could feel she was super sad, too. I don't know why, but I felt like I should give her a hug, and I don't really like to hug people. It's smothering. But I went over and hugged her really tight anyway. She knelt and hugged me back. When I wiggled because I felt like I wasn't going to be able to breathe, she let go. Her face was pink, and her eyes were all watery.

I scooted back over to the counter and the mixing bowl. I didn't want to make her cry. I told her I was sorry, and she wanted to know what for? I told her I felt bad I'd made her upset, but she said that I hadn't at all, instead I'd made her really happy because it was the first time I'd ever hugged her. I was totally confused. I made her cry because she was happy? Grownups are so hard to get sometimes.

Gran handed me a wooden spoon and a mixing cup with brown sugar in it. She told me to mix it with the eggs until it was all smooth. Then she added some regular sugar. When it came time to put the soft butter into the sugary mix she took the wooden spoon and scraped the bowl for me. Then she handed the spoon back to me. I started stirring again. She nodded and smiled, so I knew I was doing it right. While she watched me she started talking about my grandfather again. She said he yells sometimes and might say mean and nasty things, but it has nothing to do with me. She said that his problems are no one's fault but his.

I told her how I'd asked Mom if he was sick when we got here, because he shakes all over all the time. I also told her that Mom said he's an alcoholic, and it's poisoning him. She said it's a kind of sickness, but that he did it to himself.

Gran sighed and nodded. She said that was all true. She didn't say anything else for a minute. She just watched me stir the cookie mixture. Then she told me she just wants me to remember that she loves me "very, very much" and that she's so happy we came to live with her.

I just nodded. I didn't figure there was much else to say. Then I tilted the bowl to show her the sticky, yellow mix. She said it was perfect so we put everything else in to finish the dough.

After the first batch of cookies came out of the oven, while we waited for them to cool enough to eat, Gran made us both one of her mochas. We ate cookies and played a game of Sorry while the rest of the cookies baked.

She told me the Sorry game was Mom's when she was little. She said she used to play it with her too and that sometimes they did puzzles. She asked me if I liked puzzles. She said she usually sets one up on the coffee table in the living room to work on over the winter. I told her I didn't know because our apartment was kind of small. We didn't have a coffee table or anywhere to set up a place to do a puzzle. The only table we had was in the kitchen. If we weren't eating on it, it was covered with my dad's books and stuff.

All of a sudden, I got a picture in my head of my dad sitting at the table. That made me think about him, and how he was always leaving for stupid trips. Except the last time he never came back. It wasn't fair. It was like he didn't even care about us at all. He just went away. Poof!

I looked down at the game board. I didn't feel much like playing anymore. So I asked Gran if we could stop. When she asked me if I was OK, I looked up at her and tried to smile so she wouldn't bug me by asking what was wrong. But my smile got stuck halfway, and I couldn't do it. My face got hot. It felt like the walls in the room were getting taller and closer to me. I wanted to go—out of the house, down the street, anywhere but cooped up in there. I stood up and told her I just wanted to go outside, to see if the rain had stopped. She looked at me and opened her mouth like she was going to say something, but then she closed it and nodded. She told me that she thought the sky was brighter, and I could go out on the porch to check. She said she needed to clean up the kitchen anyway, and to let her know if it was nice enough to go for a walk or a bike ride.

I didn't even answer her. I just bolted for the front door.

The rain had stopped. But everything was still wet, so I just sat on the porch step for a long time and looked around from there.

Mom taught me a trick to feeling calmer when I start to feel like the world is too fast or something else makes me feel so feel stressed out that I want to run away from everything. I figured I'd better try it because all I wanted to do was fly down the street as far away as I could, from everything and everyone.

First thing you do is to look for something to focus on. I looked around. I like to try to find something new and different to pay attention to. That was when I saw a big, beautiful cat crossing the street. I mean B. I. G. But not big like as in fat. He was long-haired, with a fluffy tail he held up high like a banner. He took his sweet time getting from one side of the street to the other. He looked kinda like Mrs. Cranston's Siamese cat, from the apartment across the hall in Boston. The silvery fur and darker brown colors on his ears and face were the same as a Siamese. But his face had some white on it too and was rounder than Mrs. Cranston's cat's face. His paws were the neatest thing next to that long fluffy tail. They were all white like he had short socks on. He acted like he never even saw me, but I know that cats have excellent sight, smell, and hearing. I'm sure he knew I was watching him. He just kept strutting along like he was king of the world. Then he slipped into the shadows in the alley where I couldn't see him anymore. This guy was way too pretty and healthy looking to be a stray. Sometimes stray cats hung out at the lobster co-op at the bottom of the hill behind the bank. But he didn't look thin and sad like those. There's no way I'd let him out if he was my cat. Maybe he was lost.

I went to the screen door and hollered inside for Gran. I could see her in the kitchen by the sink drying her hands on a tea towel. She walked to the front door still wiping her hands.. I told her I'd just seen a really pretty cat, and that he was like a Siamese only fluffier with socks on. I told her how he went into the alley between the houses across the street, and that I thought he might be lost.

I was kinda bummed when she told me that he wasn't lost at all, but that he was some summer people's cat that travels with them wherever they go. She said his name is Mojo, and sometimes they let him run around outside. She said I'd probably see him around the next couple weeks while his family is here.

I asked her what kind of cat he is. She draped the tea towel onto her shoulder, put her hands on her hips, wrinkled her nose and tilted her head to one side like she always does when she's trying to remember something. First she said she couldn't quite remember, and she thought that it was a long-haired Siamese something. Then she clapped her hands together. "Got it! He's a long-haired, Snowshoe Siamese."

I said that was cool. I'd never seen one like him before. But I'd been hoping he was a stray or lost, so I could go get him.

She laughed, a short little kind of 'hmph' sound, and smiled down at me. She said he was definitely not lost, that he knows right where he is, and his owner loves him "right to pieces." I think that's a weird way to say how you love something, like you love it so much you'll break it right up. I told Gran that. She said she'd never thought of that, and maybe I have a point. Then she told me we should take a plate of our fresh cookies over later to welcome the cat's owners back, but right then she was going to go watch a little TV. I told her I thought I'd come in too and go read in my room because it was pretty wet out from the rain.

The next thing I knew Mom's voice was calling up to me that dinner was ready. I sat straight up. My book hit the floor. I didn't even remember feeling tired, but I must've fallen asleep. The clock on my bedside table said five fifteen. Wonderful smells were coming up from the kitchen. I didn't know what it was, but whatever it was I knew it would be good. I was starving.

After an awesome lasagna dinner, I helped Mom and Gran with the dishes. Mom washed, I dried, and Gran put them away. While Gran was stacking the plates she told us she was going to take some cookies over to the neighbors. She asked if I wanted to go with her to meet Mojo. Then Mom wanted to know who Mojo was, so I told her all about the pretty cat that I wished was a stray so I could have him. I thought about going with Gran, but then I told her I'd rather stay home if it was all right. I really don't like it when people think I need to meet other people. I'm OK with meeting someone if I want to, but I hate it when I feel like I'm on display. It's like being in a store window where everyone looks you over to decide if they like you or not. Even though I wanted to see Mojo, I just didn't want to have to deal with new people right then.

Gran looked a little disappointed. Mom looked at me like she wanted me to say I'd go with her. I felt like I should at least try telling Gran why I didn't want to. Mom knows, 'cause she knows most everything about how I feel. But Mom also says that sometimes we have to think about what other people want or need. I'll admit that's not one of my strong points. I know Gran just wants to "show me off" as Mom says. But that was the last thing I wanted right then. So I told her that I just didn't want to see any other people today, but that I would like to see Mojo some other time.

Gran looked at me for a second, then she nodded. She said it was fine. She'd forgotten that I wasn't a big people person like her. She said I was more like Mom that way and there would be another time, if I wanted. It felt good when Gran said I was like my mom.

After she left, I asked Mom if I could go ride my bike. She wanted to know where and reminded me it would be dark in a couple hours. I told her I would just ride up past the antique shop to the old playground and down to the harbor. She gave me the same old speech about being careful on the road. She said even though the boats didn't go out today, it didn't mean no one would be driving to and from the wharf, and how some people drive up over the top of the hill awful fast. I told her I promised all that as I headed out the door toward the shed and my bike. She called out after me to be back before dark or if I heard her ring the bell.

There's a replica of an old ship's bell that hangs on the edge of house. Mom showed it to me the first day we moved here. She told me the story of how Gran would ring the bell whenever she wanted Mom to come home if she was outside playing or riding her bike around town. Now Gran and Mom ring it for me to come back when they want me.

My bike was Mom's bike first. She found it in the shed, and we cleaned it up. She had to go to the General Store to get new tubes for the tires and she put oil on the chain, but then it was all mine. I never dreamed I'd have my very own bike, even a hand-me-down one. I only fell off one time before I learned to balance and pedal hard enough to keep it going. Now I can go all over the place and feel the wind against my face. It's the best thing ever.

I was hoping I'd see Mojo the cat while I was riding on that side of town, but he must've been home because there was no sign of him. So, I went to the old playground by the town gym. I love to swing and pump my legs to go as high as I can. But I only stop to swing if no one else is there. To be honest though, I hardly ever see other kids or anyone else there. Once in a while there's a mom with a couple little kids. Sometimes there are boys playing basketball on the ratty old court. You can still see the lines on the cement, but it's cracked, and the green color is dingy and faded almost gray. There's not even a net on the rim. I guess that must not matter to them.

The playground, basketball court, and gym are all that's left of the grammar school where my mom went all the way through eighth grade. Now there's a newer school in the next town over that I'm supposed to go to starting in a couple weeks. I'll have to ride a bus. I'm not a fan of busses at all. They're way too big and smelly and filled with people. Ugh. In Boston Mom walked me the block and a half to school. That's another thing I'm going to miss; school being so close to home that Mom and I could walk there every day.

I was starting to think about Boston and our apartment and my dad again when I turned to go toward Harbor Hill on my bike. I didn't want to think about him. I didn't want to think about how things used to be; about why he left Mom and me just like that. It all just confuses me. It makes my feelings get all jumbled up until I get madder and madder. It's not like I can talk to Mom about it either because I know it just makes her feel a lot like I do. I can see it on her face even when she tries to hide it. I really hate when I think about it. I really do. I started being mad at myself then because I couldn't stop thinking about everything that changed when he left. I pedaled faster trying just to focus on the facts that I was going down to the water and I had things I wanted to do there.

I stopped at the top of the hill like usual. On clear days you can see way out across the ocean. It also looks awesome when there's a fog bank way out that's rolling in toward town. Plus, I love the different colors of the sky and water.

The ocean looks like it changes colors all the time. I know it's mostly because of the sky. The water reflects whatever colors are above it. But I like to think the ocean changes color because of its moods. Tonight, it was grayish, blue-green, kind of like the regular color it is a lot. It's not at all like the dark, navy blue-black stormy color or the bluest of blues on super sunny days when the sapphire water sparkles like it has millions of diamonds floating on top. My very favorite though is the the color of the waves when they crash up onto the huge rocks down at the point in the park loop where Mom and I go sometimes. It's a frothy, frosty, green—almost like the color of the old glass Coke bottle I found in Gran's shed, but not quite. I've never seen any other color like it. I've tried to find a name for it online, but I haven't found one that describes it just right. So, I call it

Schoodic Sea Green, because it's at Schoodic Point. It's my new favorite color of all time. My old favorite used to be Cerulean Blue. Cerulean Blue is on the color spectrum between azure and darker sky blue. I think that Schoodic Sea Green needs to be added to an official color spectrum chart. That way other people could like it too. Then again, maybe adding it isn't a great idea. That might mean people would want to come see the waves and the color, and it would get all crowded here.

I wasn't really thinking about the color of the ocean tonight, though. Tonight, I wanted to check out all the boats on their moorings. I know all the regular fishermen's boats by heart and where their spots are in the cove. I like to make a game of saying each one of the boat names in my head when I look at their spot, even if they aren't tied up at their mooring buoy. I also think one of the the prettiest things I've ever seen, or heard, is when all the boats are in and the water is calm. They bob along with the music of the water, the breeze, and the birds. It could put me right to sleep. It's so soft and soothing.

Since none of the lobstermen went out to fish today, and it was after supper, all the boats should've been there.

I counted them from the top of the hill. Twenty-three. Yup, every one was there. They were all facing the same direction—looking away toward the reach. That meant that the tide was on the way in because boats on their moorings will always point into the current, unless the wind is stronger than the current. Then they point into the wind. There wasn't much of a breeze to push them around tonight, so the tide got to be boss and tell them where to look.

I also noticed only one truck parked down at the wharf. It was Mr. James's pickup. He wasn't near it or on his bench either. Then I counted the skiffs at the dock. There was one space where a boat should've been. So I looked out at the big boats again. That's when I saw Mr. James climbing out of the *Salty Lady* down into his skiff that was tied to her. He untied his skiff, pushed onto the side of *Salty Lady* with one hand to move away from her, and started paddling in.

He didn't sit down on the skiff's board seat. He used one oar, switching sides to paddle. When he got to the dock he slid his boat into the empty space, stepped onto the dock from the front of it, and tied up. Then he went back and doubled-checked the line. That made me giggle, because I remembered the other day when it hadn't been tied up, and he'd had to chase it out into the cove. I guess I'd double-check it too—even triple-check.

Instead of getting into his truck and leaving, he went over to his bench where he sits all the time. I guessed he must've been remembering again. He's always by himself there. I wondered what he was remembering about. Maybe he was a little sad, or maybe he just didn't like a lot of people around him. I can relate to that. But I do still like to be with some people—like my mom and Gran. I used to like being out with my mom and dad, especially when we would go somewhere special, like to the museum or to a movie. I also liked Sundays when we were at home just hanging out. Not that those days happened very much.

There I went again. I felt a little sick to my stomach. Why couldn't I just not think about before? I know that Dad is never going to come back. Mom said so in no uncertain terms when I asked her what if we weren't at our apartment if he came back to us? Mom said he'd stopped answering her calls and texts a little while after he left for his last trip. Then she got a message from him saying he was staying in Sri Lanka and never coming back. That day after she stopped crying, she came in and sat on the edge of my bed and said, "Well, Tashabean, it looks like we're on our own, now. Just you and me."

A couple weeks later we had to leave Boston and move here. I got to bring all my books and toys and clothes, but none of our furniture could fit in Mom's Subaru. It was packed so full of our stuff in laundry baskets, boxes, and trash bags that the only spaces left in the car were the front seats. I didn't even get to finish the last two weeks of school before we packed up and left. I barely had time to tell my teachers and friends goodbye. Mom said she didn't have enough money to pay for rent and feed us too. We would've been homeless except that she'd called Gran. Gran told her to come right home to Maine.

Except this isn't home. It's new, and different, and I miss things from Boston. It's a little lonely.

Suddenly I thought I would go see if Mr. James would let me sit with him. It's not like he's like other people. He sits still and he's alone a lot like me. Maybe if I sat there with him, I wouldn't think about the rotten things I'd been thinking about all day that make me mad. Maybe I'd start remembering good stuff.

Thirteen

Natasha stayed on the bench with James twenty minutes or more without speaking, her skinny, tanned legs swinging like a pendulum as she stared out to sea. James figured that was a long time for a kid her age to go without saying anything. He resisted every urge he had to start asking her questions. She seemed as if she would skitter off like a rabbit if he said the wrong thing. And although he really wanted to know more about her, he was mildly surprised to realize he simply was enjoying her silent company. He was watching two gulls bobbing about on the water near the shore when Natasha popped off the bench, pointing toward the reach.

"Look, look!" She danced around, hopping from one foot to the other in excitement.

James peered out over the water toward the far end of the reach, the area he thought Natasha was trying to show him. Out on the edge of a branch near the top of the tallest spruce, a lone bald eagle sat surveying the harbor.

"Is that an eagle?"

"Ayup. It is." James squinted to get a better look. "From the size of her I'd say she's the mama. There are a pair of eagles that nest in that tree each year. She had two chicks hatch earlier this season. Her nest is a little below where she's perched right now. If you look really closely you can see it tucked in the branches." James leaned forward peering out at the large bird. "I'd say she's thinking about looking for some supper."

"Wow! I saw her all by myself! There weren't eagles where I used to live. I've only seen pictures of them. I knew that's what it is because of its white head!" Natasha was still now, staring at the bird with everything she had.

"You did see her by yourself," James agreed. "I didn't even notice she was out there tonight."

"She's really big."

"Just imagine how big she'd be if she were right here beside you instead of all the way out there." James spread his arms out as far as he could. "When she opens her wings to fly, they are as wide across as this, probably wider."

As if she had heard him, the bird dropped from the branch. She opened her massive wings, flapped them twice, and dipped down and away over the water, disappearing behind the tree line of tall firs on the backside of the reach.

"Oh! She left." Natasha took a step forward as if she would be able to see the eagle again if she were closer to it. "Will she come back?"

James nodded. "She will. It might be a while though. She's probably fishing on the other side of the reach there. There are a couple shallow areas on the backside by the shore where the mackerel like to hang out while the tide is coming in."

"Mackerel? Isn't that a kind of fish? I thought eagles ate salmon. What do they look like? How big are they?"

"Ayup, it is a fish." James laughed. "One thing at a time."

She turned to look back at him, her eyes wide with her questions.

"Let's see . . . .Eagles eat lots of different kinds of fish, not just salmon. They'll pretty much take whatever is available. They eat other sea creatures too, and they hunt small animals like mice and rabbits. They'll even eat other birds and animals that are roadkill, like deer and raccoons. They aren't very picky."

He paused to make sure he remembered her questions. "Mackerel are shiny, blue-green on the top, and silvery-white on their bellies. They're easy to see in the water because they swim in small groups, called a shoal, and they shimmer when they swim. They're a skinny kinda fish; about this big." He held his hands about eight inches apart.

Then he moved them out a little more to show her the fish were not all just one size. "It depends on how old the mackerel are as to how big they are. They're kind of like kids that way. They come in different sizes."

A tiny upturn had appeared at the corners of Natasha's mouth—almost a real smile. "Neat. I wish I could see her catching them. Is she gonna to take them back to her chicks?"

James shook his head. "I don't think so. Her chicks have been fishing on their own for a couple weeks now. I've seen them flying around the bay. Sometimes she'll drop food close by them as they are learning to hunt. But the eaglets are old enough to find their own meals now. She'll just keep an eye on them to be sure they do. Both parents stick close to the young'uns until they're grown up enough to find their own way. Even after they're grown, they'll live and make their own nests near their parents' territory. Next year, that eagle you saw will come back with her mate, spruce up their nest, and lay eggs again. They stay together and raise their families right here, year after year."

The girl stiffened. Any trace of happiness left her face as quickly as a stray summer lightning strike. James thought he must have imagined that a smile was ever there. Her eyes narrowed. She lifted her chin. "Not like people," the girl practically growled low in her throat. "People leave. They just disappear."

She half-turned, staring out at the sea, her arms rigid at her sides now, fists balled up and tight. He could see the muscles in the side of her cheek moving as she clenched her teeth repeatedly.

James felt awful. Something he'd said caused this instantaneous transformation. Anger radiated from the child like a warning beacon. Should he do something? What was he supposed to say?

He cleared his throat and reached to push the brim of his ball cap back on his head a tiny bit. He opened his mouth. Closed it. Opened it again. "I'm . . ."

"Oh, I've gotta go!" Natasha spun back and threw both hands up in the air. "What time is it? I have to be back at the house before dark."

Not waiting for an answer, she dashed over to her bike that was lying down on the side of the parking lot about twenty feet behind the bench.

Her mercurial emotions and dramatic alarm had pulled James to his feet. He was still trying to figure out what he'd said—should say—should do. She turned, right before she got to her bike, and waved a hand at him.

"'Bye Mr. James. See ya later!" And she was off.

He automatically raised his hand to wave back. But she didn't see. She'd already grabbed up her bike and was moving up the hill with it. This time she didn't get on it to try to pedal up the slope. Instead, she jogged beside it, pushing it along. The tattered purple and white handlebar tassels bobbed along in time to her steps. She reached the top of the rise, slung her leg over the seat, pushed down on the pedals, and disappeared from sight.

James realized his hand was still up in the air. He dropped it to his side. He had no idea what had just happened. But he knew enough to understand Natasha was one big ball of angry, all wound up inside a coil of fraying rope. Obviously someone had broken this beautiful child in some way. Who could do such a thing? He may not know the circumstances—yet. But he understood that raw wound. He knew that rage.

He reached down and absently rubbed his palm against his thigh feeling the familiar thin line of the scar just below his right hip. Some scars never went away. He shook his head. That poor child was way too young to have to deal with such pain; whatever, and wherever, it came from.

The thin high-pitched whistling of an eagle in the distance caught James's ear. He turned his face toward the reach to see if the bird was visible either in the air or on her perch. He couldn't see her, but he heard her call again, and then a distant answer from behind the trees—most likely her mate.

There'd been pair of bald eagles that nested each year out on the reach for as long as James could remember. This particular pair had been using the nest for at least the past five years, maybe more. He was so used to them he'd forgotten the excitement that went along with spotting one for the first time. He always looked for them as he motored past their tree on his way out to sea. He appreciated what magnificent birds they were, but he realized that he took it for granted they were there. They were simply a part of his landscape. He scanned the sky once more to see if the bird was soaring up high on a wind draft, although he knew she more likely was perched on a rock on the backside of the reach, snacking on a fish she'd snatched out of the water.

It was quiet. There was no sign of any birds. Even the gulls that had been playing near the shore had flown off. Dusk was starting to slide in on the backside of the tide. All that was left of the breeze was a damp brush of coolness here and there against his cheek.

He took off his cap to brush some imaginary dust off the bill. He wondered if Natasha ever did anything other than ride that beat-up, old bike. Since she seemed so excited about the eagles and learning about what they ate, maybe next time she came down to the wharf James would get the fishing poles out, teach her how to catch mackerel. Then they could leave a couple on the dock to wait to see if the eagles would come to snatch up an easy meal. Sophia had always loved to do that when she was a kid, as James had with his own father once, so many years ago.

A picture of Natasha rigid and upright in her anger, stole into his mind. He felt a spark of malice toward whoever had caused her pain. He knew she wasn't angry like that all the time. The light in her face when she was talking about the eagles told him that. He'd love to coax that big smile out of the girl again. He was going to give it a shot anyway. Maybe teaching her to catch mackerel would be a good start.

James figured mackerel were about the easiest fish in the world to catch. You simply stood on the dock, dropped your diamond jig down into the water, and jiggled it a bit to get the fish's attention. If you had a tree of four or five hooks, it wasn't unusual to haul up a fish on every hook in a single cast. The shiny fishes' favorite meal was smaller tiny fish, and that's how they see the jig. It had been years since James had taken his fishing rod down to the dock. Where was all his fishing tackle anyway? He plopped his cap back on his head and scratched at his beard. He kept one rod on the boat, but the rest were in that damn shed. One more reason to get it cleaned out. Even though the dusk was starting to steal in, there was still a bit of daylight left. Maybe he'd get a start on it.

What the hell. I could dig those fishing poles out. It might be nice to do a little dock fishing tomorrow evening. I can always turn on the lights in the shed. I'm not working until tomorrow afternoon, so I can sleep in if I want.

Softly whistling a random tune, James walked up the path trying to remember the last place he'd seen his tackle box. He wondered if Natasha had ever been fishing or done much else that was fun lately. Somehow, he was pretty sure he knew the answer.

Fourteen

Natasha

I yelled for my mom as soon as I got to the house. I threw my bike down on the grass beside the driveway and ran up the lawn. She was through the door and outside in a hurry asking me what was wrong. She thought I was hurt or something.

I stopped at the edge of the steps just as she was starting down them. I was so breathless from how fast I rode up from the harbor that I couldn't say anything for couple seconds. I shook my head and held up one finger to show her to wait a minute. I leaned over with my hands on my knees trying to catch my breath.

She stepped down and told me to stand up straight and take a deep breath. I did what she said.

"Now exhale." She told me while she held onto my arm with one hand and slowly rubbed my back with the other. Then she told me to do it again.

A couple more times of that, and I wasn't feeling like I was going to pant like a dog anymore.

I told her that I saw a bald eagle! A huge one. And that Mr. James figures it was the female because she was so big, and she was fishing for mackerel fish to feed her chicks that aren't really chicks anymore, and she was so awesome. I was out of breath again, but not as bad as before.

Mom shook her head and threw her hands up in the air. She said the way I came home yelling she thought something bad had happened.

I told her I was fine. I just thought it was so cool I saw an eagle that I wanted to come and tell her right away. I pointed toward the reach to show her where it lived, and she told me she knew right where the nest was. She said there's been a pair of eagles down there for as long as she can remember, but she hadn't thought about them in years. She called them "majestic birds" and she understood why I was so excited. Then she stopped talking for a second, cocked her head to the side, and asked me who Mr. James was.

I was just starting to tell her when my grandfather's truck came roaring around the curve and into the driveway. He got out and slammed the door. Then he walked around the front of the truck and without even slowing down he picked up my bike that was lying in the grass in front of him and threw it as far as he could toward the house. It hit hard and slid on the lawn until one of the handlebars caught on the ground.

Mom put her arm across my shoulders. She backed us up a couple steps away from the path into the yard.

He went right by us and stomped up the steps like we didn't even exist.

Fifteen

What in God's name possessed me to do this tonight?

James was about an hour and a half into the shed. He'd already filled four garbage bags with old junk that had accumulated in the space he'd decided to refer to as "the black hole of broken uselessness." By the time he finally could put his hands on his workbench located on the side wall closest to the door, he was wishing a sinkhole would open up and swallow the whole mess.

For the first hour he'd barely moved as he reached and grabbed whatever he could get at to determine what was trash and what to keep. Everyone so often he'd heave a full bag out onto the lawn, then reach down into the box at his feet to grab another and start again. He'd begun by setting the things he thought should be kept behind him on the floor. It wasn't long before he realized he had to take stuff completely out of the little building to create room to navigate. In truth, he found there was very little that needed keeping.

It turned out there was a whole lot of, "I should put this in the shed in case I need it someday for something," or "I'll throw it in the shed until I get around to fixing it," kind of junk that James was in just the right mood to get rid of. Some of the relics he discovered were parts that he had no idea where they came from or what they might belong to. So far, he'd discovered only a small collection of miscellaneous stuff he considered worthy of keeping. All of that was now sitting right outside the door to be put neatly back in once he had the place cleaned out. He'd started a separate pile for items he thought Tommy or Sophia might want. He was worn slap out, and he'd only gotten through about a third of the mess on the floor.

He'd half-expected to hear, or see, more mice or other critters scurrying about considering the mouse nest he'd disturbed that morning. But so far he'd only found evidence that the rodent squatters had been there. Those stinkin' things sure knew how to chew up stuff and poop everywhere.

At this point, he hadn't even begun to attack the shelves and cabinets that lined the walls. At least he'd made a clear path to his workbench where his tools and materials were neatly organized, just as he'd left them the last time he'd worked in here. He found the string that dangled from the industrial light hanging above his workbench and pulled it. The light hummed, flickered, and caught, casting bluish-white, fluorescent light over the area. He swept a hand across the surface of the bench leaving a marginally cleaner swipe than the rest of the top. He sighed. At least dust was easy to take care of. He was just happy to see one thing still organized the way it should be.

James kept enough tools and trap repair materials on the boat to do quick fixes. He generally repaired or replaced necessary items in the fall when he pulled his traps out of the water, before he brought them up to rest in their neat stacks at the side of the driveway with their rope and buoys placed just so inside each trap. Now he'd at least be able get to his workbench again so he could work on any gear inside.

"OK, where's my tackle box?" James asked the room, scanning the area. In his memory he could see placing the plastic box on a shelf near his workbench. No. He distinctly remembered now that it was under his workbench. It was years since he'd used it. Sophia had still been in high school.

It hadn't been a conscious thing, but one day after putting the fishing poles away, they'd abandoned them. Tommy was already at college and Sophia was growing up, busy with high school, friends, and activities that left her parents on their own to find other things to occupy their time.

Funny how that happens, James mused, holding on to the edge of the workbench with his left hand as he squatted down to look on its shelves. Time keeps on ticking, and before you know it yesterday is years past you.

"Hah! There you are." James grinned as he slid the gray metal box out from the second shelf. It was not too dusty—considering—but there were mouse turds scattered in the indentation where the handle lay folded over.

"Ugh." He wrinkled his nose. "You rodents really are disgusting. I need to do something about getting rid of you."

James reached for the small brush and dustpan hanging on the right side of the pegboard wall behind the workbench. Not wanting to inhale in any of the dusty mess as he disturbed it, James held his breath and gently swiped the top of the tackle box with the brush. The dust and mouse crap fell onto the already filthy floor. He brushed off the workbench top for good measure, then snapped the brush back into the dustpan handle and hung it back up. He wiped his hands on his pants, then reached to unlatch the once shiny, silver-colored latches on each side of the box that were now freckled with spots of rust. They protested slightly as he flipped them up. He pulled the accordion sides of the tackle box outward to open it and scanned the contents. Of course everything was where he'd left it—clean, neat, and ready to go.

His old fishing license was in its plastic sleeve right on top. The plastic was yellowed and brittle in his hand as James picked it up to look at the date—two thousand seventeen. He turned it over. The orange backing of the sleeve was intact, but the edges of the pin at the top used to fasten the holder to his jacket was rusty. Sophia's license, from the same year, lay next to where his had been. He picked hers up and studied them both, thinking how it didn't seem like so long ago, but Sophia would've been a sophomore in high school that year. It was the first year she had to have a fishing license. It was also the year she got her driver's license and her first job besides babysitting.

He remembered the two of them heading down to the wharf many nights in the summer twilight after supper. Sophia was always two steps ahead of him in her excitement to beat him out of getting the first slippery fish out of the water. They had running competitions over who would catch the first—the most—the last—fish of the day.

When she was small and they'd first started playing this game, sometimes he let her win. He'd take his time baiting his hook, waiting for her to get the first bite, or he'd draw in his line at the end of the evening saying he was tired and done, so she would get the last catch. It hadn't been long before Sophia could best him all on her own. Then they'd begun a fierce competition. She'd write about their fishing outings in her "water journals" where she made notes about anything and everything that had to do with the ocean and other bodies of water they visited. Sophia was like her father that way. "Of the sea," Anna had called it.

Anna understood that about James right from the start. She'd nicknamed him Poseidon when they first met. She understood his passion for the ocean and the lobstering life. It made him feel proud to be who he was—important. That woman knew how to puff his ego right up. She said he was deep and mysterious like the ocean he loved. And he believed her.

Anna wanted to be near the water, but not necessarily out on it. She loved to stand with her toes in the surf. She would sit and watch the tide for hours with James, but she didn't share his need to be out there. When James and Sophia would come home soaking wet, loaded up with fish and other treasures that Sophia had found, Anna would shake her head and say that Sophia was obviously his seagoddess daughter. She would tease Sophia, asking her where she hid her mermaid's tail? Sophia played right along with her mother. She started giving Anna gifts that were from or about the ocean. She'd make up wild stories for her mother about where she found the presents. Anna had a whole collection of deep sea and mermaid-themed trinkets that lived in the hutch in the living room. How could it be that those days seemed so far away now?

There was that damn question again. Time. It seemed to James that he was asking himself about time way too often these days. He shook his head.

And here he was. He looked down at the old fishing licenses in his hands. Well, they couldn't use them any more. They were seven years expired. Might as well throw them out. He kept his fishing paperwork in the wheelhouse out on the boat these days, but if he started fishing any lakes or streams again, he'd need to keep a copy of his freshwater license in his wallet, too. James put the old licenses down on the workbench top, closed the tackle box and started to secure it. The latches felt stiffer to close than to open. A little oil would take care of that. He reached for the 3-in-1 Oil that lived on the back left side of the workbench. He put a drop on each side of the hinges, moving them back and forth to loosen them up. He latched the box up, put the oil can back in its spot, and slid the tackle box to the back of the bench top so he could get at it more easily.

He picked the old fishing licenses back up thinking he'd toss them into the garbage bag at his feet. Instead, smiling at the echoes of memories, he reached forward and hooked them by their pins, side by side, on two empty hooks on the pegboard wall behind his work surface.

Now to unearth the fishing poles. He glanced over to look in the corner where he kept them. They were there wrapped up in a mosaic of dusty cobwebs.

That mess requires the broom, or better yet, the shop vac. His stomach growled. *Not tonight though. I found what I was after. The rest of this can wait until tomorrow. Time to clean up and get some food.*

He pulled on the string of the shop light. The familiar clicking movement of the beaded chain sounded as the light turned off. He headed out of the shed. Before he closed the door, he turned to survey his progress.

"Not bad for a first stab at it, eh Petunia?" he remarked to the cat that suddenly appeared out of the shadows. "Petunia?!"

James stood stock still, unsure if the cat was real or a figment of his imagination. She switched her tail at him, softly meowed once and turned, sauntering toward the back door of the house. Once there, she daintily sat beside the empty cat bowl—waiting—most definitely real.

"Well, I'll be damned." James kept his eye on the cat as he closed the shed door slowly and quietly as possible. He meandered up the short path to the house talking to her the whole time in a low, measured voice, hoping she wouldn't run before he got there.

"And where have you been, you stupid furball? I've been looking for you for almost two months, and you've just now decided to show yourself? I was sure you were never coming back, or worse. Now you suddenly decided to saunter your happy ass home. Do you have any idea how crazy upset Anna would be if you'd done that to her?" James continued to watch the cat who was staring at the food bowl. "You've got nothing to say for yourself, huh? You don't look any worse for the wear. Where the hell have you been hiding?"

Petunia didn't take her gaze away from the bowl until James got right up by the door. Then she glanced up at him with her big, round, green cat eyes, meowed again, a little louder this time, and wound herself through his legs. He could hear her soft rumbly purr as she moved in and out around him. Not moving his feet, he reached over and opened the screen door very slowly, about a third of the way, hoping she'd want to go in. She stopped her travel around his legs and waltzed to the other side of the bowl, away from the open door. She sat, staring up at him, the end of her tail twitching back and forth.

"OK. OK. Hang on. I'll get you some." James opened the screen door a little more—just wide enough to slide inside. It hissed closed on its pneumatic hinge and latched with a sharp click. He winced. Why did that sound so loud?

"You stay right there. I'll be back in just a minute with your food," he said.

Dear Lord, please let her still be there when I come back with her dinner.

James opened the cupboard to get the dry cat food. How could he entice Petunia to come in? Maybe . . . He opened the cupboard beside the sink and took down two cereal bowls. He figured he might scare her away if he went out and poured the kibble into the bowl. Maybe he could get her inside if he didn't take her food outside. He could prop the door open just a bit, and slide one dish, with just a few pieces in it, halfway out the door. If he put another full dish of food on the kitchen floor she might come in to get at it. Better yet, it occurred too him that instead of regular cat food, a can of tuna in the second dish might be irresistible to her.

James grinned in self-satisfaction. Now he was thinking. He figured no cat would turn down tuna. This was going to have to be a multi-part operation.

First step: get her a little food to make her want more. He fished around in the bag of cat food until his hand encountered the plastic measuring cup that he kept in the bag. He scooped up some of the star-shaped kibble, making as much noise as he could, rattling the bag so the cat would hear it. Then holding his hand about six inches from the rim of the dish he shook the measuring cup to move the food around and slowly shook it out. It plinked down into the ceramic bowl a few pieces at a time, sliding and settling into a small pile at the bottom. James tossed the scoop back into the bag, rattling it a little more for good measure, before he took the bowl to the door.

"Here Kitty, Kitty," He crooned. "Here Petunia Cat. Here's your supper. Come and get it." He opened the door and leaned down to put the bowl out. There was no sign of Petunia.

James's stomach sank. "Damn cat," he grumbled. What if she didn't come back? This thought made him feel a little queasy. She just had to come back now that he knew she wasn't gone for good. He took a deep breath. "Here Kitty, Kitty. Here Petunia. Suppertime," he sang out.

Hopefully, his neighbors weren't listening. He could hear it now. "That poor old man just keeps feeding a cat that isn't even there. She's been gone for a couple months, and he keeps right on like she's still around," they'd say, frowning, shaking their heads in pity.

James scowled. Screw it. Who cared what anyone might think of him. He was going to get that stupid cat to come in any way he could.

"Here Petunia Kitty. Come on girl, come on in for supper now." He shook the bowl for good measure, then set it down with a clink on the ground, just enough to the side so the door would clear it when it closed. She might come back if she'd heard him set it down. He figured he'd go ahead with his plan and hope for the best.

Holding the door open with his foot, he leaned down and slid the stop on the pneumatic closer so it would stay open just enough for her to slip in if she was so inclined. He stood inside the door peering out into the darkness, searching for a pair of shining cat's eyes. He cocked his head listening, hoping to hear her meow, or to catch any other sound that would indicate she was close by. There was no sign of her.

All right then. On to step two: tuna fish. No self-respecting cat would turn down some good old StarKist! Hopefully there was a can or two in the pantry, and she'd come running when she heard him open it. Anna had remarked once that the electric can opener was the simplest magic trick she'd ever seen, because it could make the cat appear out of nowhere the second it started up.

Here's hoping you're right, Anna Girl. It's worth a shot.

He flipped the light switch beside the pantry and opened the door. The little space was about the size of an old-fashioned phone booth. He scanned the shelves quickly, looking for the short, wide can, banded with paper sporting a blue background and a comic tuna fish on it.

"Ah, there you are. All right then," he murmured, spotting not one, but three of exactly what he was looking for on the back shelf. He ducked one step through the pantry door and grabbed a single can. He backed out of the pantry and walked directly to the electric can opener that was on the counter by the stove, glancing toward the door on his way. The bowl with the kibble in it was just visible on the ground in the dark wedge of night, past the propped open screen door. There still was no sign of Petunia.

He lifted the lever of the can opener, placed the can's lid in place, and pressed the cutting lever down. The machine's blade sank into the top of the can with a metallic pop as the whirring motor began to move the can around. The fishy tuna smell filled the kitchen. James's stomach grumbled, reminding him that he hadn't eaten since early afternoon. He figured that could be easily taken care of. He'd put half the tuna into the bowl to lure Miss Petunia in, and then he'd use the other half to make a tuna salad sandwich for himself. He glanced at the door again checking for any sign of the errant feline. The only movement was a fluttering gray moth, about the size of a dime, that dipped into the kitchen through the opening. It headed straight to the overhead light, where it began to repeatedly bang itself against the bright white glass orb. *Crap!* He hadn't thought of that. It wouldn't be long before every stinkin' bug in town would be headed into his kitchen, especially mosquitoes. Those little whining bloodsuckers were almost as bad as black flies, and he didn't want to become a mosquito smorgasbord. That cat had better show back up soon.

Maybe Petunia hadn't heard the can opener or smelled the fish yet. Hopefully, once he got some into a bowl on the floor, she'd discover it and come in to get it. James removed the can from the machine and pivoted a half-turn to move to the sink. "Holy Shit!" he sputtered as he almost tripped over Petunia who was sitting not two feet from him on the kitchen floor.

"How did you do that? And when?" Her big green eyes were fixated on the can in his hand as if she could will it to drop down to her. "Well, why not? At least you're here, even if I didn't see you sneak in."

Afraid the cat would streak out the door if he moved quickly or took too much time to get the food down to her, James pressed on one edge of the can lid, pushing it down just enough so he could place his thumb under the raised edge. He carefully removed it and set the can down on the floor. Then he slowly backed up, watching Petunia the entire time. She immediately started wolfing down the fish for all she was worth, completely ignoring James. He slid the lid to the can onto the counter. Then as quickly and stealthily as he could, he navigated his way to the door in a circle away from the cat. He was afraid to even look to see if she was still eating, just in case she sensed that he was trying to trick her. He got to the door, knelt, silently released the stop on the door closer, and grabbed the handle of the door to hurry its closing. It clicked resoundingly on its latch. James exhaled, suddenly realizing he'd been holding his breath. Then he shut the inside door too for good measure. Success! He turned to look at Petunia. She still had her head buried in the tuna can like she hadn't eaten in weeks.

James shook his head. "Well, what do you know? I can't believe I actually got you in here on the first try," he told the obviously unconcerned animal. "I pretty much thought that you were going to lead me on one merry chase before I'd convince you to come through that door. And I'd still love to know where the hell you've been hiding out." The only reply he got was his own stomach growling at him again. He really was hungry now.

"That tuna smells like a pretty good supper to me. Mind if I join you?"

He made another trip to the pantry stopping at the fridge to get mayonnaise, bread, and a cold can of Coke. Soon he was leaning on the counter munching on a tuna salad sandwich watching Petunia as she gave herself a good grooming after she'd finished off most of the tuna.

"You really don't look any worse for wear," he said frowning at her. "And even though you wolfed that down, it certainly doesn't look like you missed any meals while you were on whatever adventure you took yourself out on."

Petunia paused from licking her paw long enough to glance up at him, as if to say, "What are you talking about?" Then she went right back to her bath.

James took another bite of his sandwich. "Well, it's obvious you aren't going to tell me a damn thing, but I'll tell you something, cat. You can count on never getting out that door again. Believe it or not, I've missed having you around."

Sixteen

As far as James could see, Petunia spent most of that first night, and the next day, doing nothing much but sleeping on her window seat bed. James brought in the food bowls from outside when he got up in the morning. He washed them, then set food and fresh water up on the mat where Anna had always put it. Petunia got up long enough to eat a few kibbles and make a trip to her freshly cleaned litter box in the bathroom. Then she hopped right back up into her bed, curled up into herself, and went back to sleep.

"OK then. You guard the castle. I've got work to do," he told her as he headed out the door. "Just don't disappear, all right?" He wanted to go over and pat her on the head or something, just to assure himself she really was home. But he thought maybe she wouldn't like that, and he was worried she'd run off and hide somewhere again. Petunia was Anna's cat. She'd always preferred to be by her in the kitchen or to sleep in her lap when she finally sat down in her chair each evening. James could count on one hand the number of times he'd touched the fur-ball for an absent-minded pat on the head or a single pet down her back. That occurred only if she came up next to him while he was sitting in his chair or lying on the couch.

He wanted to make sure she wasn't hurt or broken anywhere. She looked like she was walking just fine. He didn't see any outward signs of injuries. She certainly hadn't lost her appetite or any weight for that matter. It seemed like she should be doing more than just sleeping and eating, but what did he know? At least she was home again. She just could be worn out from whatever, and wherever, she'd been about.

A gust of wind tried to take the screen door out of his hand as he opened it. The weathermen hadn't lied about this morning's forecast. It was blowing up a gale. At least the fog was gone, for now. As he headed toward the shed his phone chirped with a text message. He walked around to the west side of the little building where he was mostly sheltered from the intermittent wind gusts. Wondering who it could be, he slid his phone out of his T-shirt pocket. His sternman wouldn't be texting him this early since he had the morning off, and Sophia usually just called.

"*Morning, Dad. Soph says next weekend works for her. I'll pick her up on the way. Arrive Thursday p.m. Can I bring you anything from Boston?*"

James grinned. Tommy! He typed back, "*Just you two, but a Red Sox win would be nice.*"

"*Lol. Not in my bag of tricks. Let me know if you think of anything. Soph has a class until 3. We should arrive early evening. Love you.*"

"*Love you. See you soon. Be safe.*"

Then he thought to ask, "*Anything special you want here?*"

"*Nope. Will just be glad to be home.*"

"*OK!*" James shot back.

James was grinning so wide his face hurt. This texting thing was going to be good. It already felt like he could talk to Tommy more and maybe without them butting heads so much. James just hoped they'd be all right when Tommy finally came home. Anna often had been a needed buffer between the two, especially as Tommy had gotten older. She'd always tried to help James understand his son. They were just so different.

James couldn't wait to see both kids. Next weekend couldn't get here fast enough. He decided he'd only haul Monday through Wednesday, weather permitting. He wasn't going to go out while the kids were home, unless Sophia wanted to take a pleasure ride out of the harbor. Maybe they'd all go out on Saturday afternoon for a run around the back edge of the reach to watch the sunset. That would be nice. It was something they hadn't done in years. Fact was, James couldn't recall the last time both kids had been out on the boat with him for any reason. Hopefully, Tommy would want to go.

Thinking of fishing and boats, he needed to remember to save a few lobsters from next week's haul for dinner one night—crab claws too if he pulled up any. One thing there was no arguing about. They all loved their seafood.

What else would he need to get for a nice homecoming dinner? He remembered, thanks to Anna, that both kids were big into fresh, organic stuff. Wasn't there still a farmer's market Thursdays across from the post office? He could run down there to get some fresh veggies in the morning before they arrived. Then he could slide over to The Dinette for a cup of coffee and a bite. Now there was a plan.

James left the shelter of the shed wall. His step was light and quick as he hurried to his truck. He was surprised to realize that he was looking forward to the rest of the day. It had been a long time since that had been the case.

Not only that. The cat came back!

Seventeen

Work kept James busy for the rest of the week and into the next. He and Petunia settled into their new routine together. He'd leave her breakfast when he went out in the morning, and she'd be there on her window seat when he came in off the boat. After they both ate supper, he'd make a cup of tea and go to watch TV. In a few minutes she'd saunter in and stare up at him. He'd pat his lap, she'd hop up, then turn around a couple times before she settled in and started purring. If James started to get up for any reason, Petunia would protest with a soft mew, but she'd move to the arm of the chair until he left. As soon as he was up, she'd settle down in the middle of the seat, curling herself up into the leftover warmth. James found he was talking to the cat like Anna used to. She was a good listener. He'd come to realize he was glad to have the company, as well as something to take care of every day, besides just himself.

He'd seen Natasha down by the wharf a couple times when he was coming in from fishing. But she'd been gone by the time he and Bustah finally made it to land after they were done with the end of day chores on the boat. Yesterday, Bustah needed the day off, so James had gone out alone. Since he was by himself, it took a good while longer to haul all the traps he had on his schedule, and he came in later than anyone else. As he steered the *Salty Lady* past the edge of the reach toward her mooring, he noticed Natasha picking her way through the rocks above the tiny stretch of beach on the eastern side of the cove. She looked up as if she recognized the sound of the boat, then began to wave wildly at him. He waved back, then sounded the boat horn twice for good measure. She clapped her hands together and waved at him again. When he came in on his punt about half an hour later, she met him down at the dock as he tied up.

"Hi. You're late today." Her tone was matter of fact, but James felt like it was almost accusing.

"I am." He smiled at her. "That's because my sternman couldn't go out with me. It takes me a while longer to finish my work if I'm alone."

"Oh." She looked down into the punt. "You didn't bring any lobsters in."

"Nope. The co-op is closed for the day, so I'll come down tomorrow and take them over. They're sitting in their cars over the side of the boat, waiting on me."

James leaned over to check that the punt was securely tied up to its cleat on the dock.

"Oh." She said again. "I know what those are. They're plastic crates with holes all in them. My grandfather has a pile of old wooden ones out in the backyard, too."

"Ayup," James said straightening up. "In the old days they were wooden, but now we all use plastic cars."

"That's interesting," Natasha said. "Well, now that you're in, I've got to get back for supper. See you later, Mr. James."

She turned and started up the gangway.

"You waited for me to come in today?"

Natasha turned back around. She nodded. "You were late. I wanted to be sure you came back." Then she scampered up the gangway leaving James staring after her.

"'Bye, Mr. James." She called back over her shoulder. She waved and was off, leaving him behind wondering what in the world had just happened.

Eighteen

While James was still shaking his head over the idea that Natasha had waited down at the cove for him to come in just to be sure he was safe, it occurred to him that she'd mentioned a grandfather. A clue. As he was walking home, thinking about the fishermen in town who might have a granddaughter Natasha's age, his phone rang. James fished it out of his pants pocket. It was Tommy.

"Hi, Dad. How's it going?"

"Good, good." James realized with some surprise that it really had been going pretty well.

"How about you? You're still coming home, right?"

"I'm fine and you bet. That's why I was calling. Don't forget that Soph and I will be there tomorrow night.

"As if I could," James was smiling. "I'm thrilled you're coming home. What time do you think you'll be here?"

"Oh, I'd say a little after five," Tommy answered. "I'm going to work half the day. I should be at Castine to pick Soph up after her last class for the week, about half past three. By the way, we both were able to get a little bit of time off at the beginning of next week, so we're going to stay until next Wednesday night. Is that all right?"

"Is that all right? Hell, Son, I wish you'd both just come back home to stay. That's great! I can't wait for you to get here." This was true. James felt a bit like a kid waiting for Christmas. He was going to get to see both his children. It had been way too long.

"Great," Tommy said. "I better run. I need to pack and take care of a few errands yet this evening. Love you, Dad. See you tomorrow."

"Love you too, Tommy. Take it easy on the drive. Be safe."

Tommy chuckled, "You got it. 'Bye, Dad."

"'Bye."

James put the phone back in his pocket. There was still a lot he should get done before the kids arrived tomorrow evening. He wanted to clear his schedule so they could spend the whole week together. He could still give Bustah plenty to do so that he could make his paycheck while they weren't hauling. He'd contact him first, then clean up the house. It could use a go-round with the dust cloth and vacuum. He needed to open the kids' rooms upstairs—air them out. He should make sure the bathroom was sparkling and had fresh towels. Finally, he'd go to the store to get some real food for meals for the next couple days. After the kids arrived, they could figure out what else they wanted for the rest of their time at home. First things first though, he needed to feed Petunia and get some supper himself.

Nineteen

As James was running the vacuum over the living room carpet the next morning, he formed a mental list of tasks. Breakfast first, then the farmer's market, or maybe the market and then breakfast. Yup, that worked better. He wanted to get there before all the best stuff was gone.

The truck needed cleaning out after he took the catch from yesterday over to the co-op. This thought reminded him how Natasha was unexpectedly waiting for him at the dock the day before. Then there was the little tidbit she'd dropped about her grandfather having old wooden lobster cars in his backyard. But she didn't ever seem to be waiting for her grandfather while down at the dock. Who was this kid?

James was pleased he could take the time today to run over to The Dinette for breakfast. He was tired of eating the same old stuff every morning. Breakfast out was always nice, and it'd be good to catch up with anyone there to hear about the latest happenings in town. He had been out of the loop lately. He might even find out some information on Miss Natasha and her family.

"The kids are coming home today," he told Petunia after he put the vacuum back in the broom closet. She was eyeing him from the top of the sofa where she'd fled when he first turned on the noisy machine. "I'm going out to breakfast and to buy groceries. You're in charge."

At the door, he bent over to grab his shoes from the mat where they sat neatly next to Anna's old slippers. Seeing them there, the now familiar sadness stole over him. She would never be there to see their children again. She wouldn't make their favorite meals anymore or celebrate their adult milestones. She wouldn't spoil grandchildren someday. The two of them wouldn't grow old together like they'd planned. Grief didn't punch him in the gut like it had a few weeks earlier, but it was there; hollow, yet solid at the same time.

I can do this. The kids are coming home. She'd would want me to be there for them—with them.

A picture of her, hands on hips as she told him to take care of whatever it was that needed doing, appeared in his memory. He smiled sadly and swallowed the lump in his throat.

"Don't you worry, Anna Girl. I can do this," he said aloud. "You just wait and see."

He stepped out of his slippers, slid into his shoes, then placed his slippers neatly on the mat beside hers.

As he closed the door on his way out, he grabbed at his cap to keep it on his head. The wind was at it again. He strode out across the yard, and just as he got to the truck, a gust kicked up that felt like it might take his feet right out from under him. Good Lord, it seemed like there were a lot more blustery days this season than any before. No one with half a mind would be out hauling. Some fellow fishermen would surely be at the restaurant for breakfast. He climbed in, turned the key, and the truck rumbled to life.

Anna, would ever believe that he was shopping at the farmer's market. She'd be telling him to watch for the lightning strike, or for the ice to appear, since hell was going to freeze over any time now.

James swung the truck into a space in front of The Dinette. He tugged on the brim of his cap to secure it on his head before getting out to cross the street to walk the short distance to the market.

Half a dozen or so vendors were set up in a neat row. Vans and trucks were parked behind white or navy tent gazebos that were puffing and complaining at the wind that threatened to lift them from their moorings. There were a few empty spaces between vendors, evidence that less tenacious folks had given up or not shown up at all. Those that had braved the wind were doing their best to keep their goods from tipping over or flying about, weighting lighter products down with whatever was at hand. A couple vendors hadn't even bothered to set up their tables, selling directly out of the backs of their open vehicles.

You could almost always count on at least a slight breeze off the cove, so most were normally prepared for that. Today's wind was stiffer than usual, and although it was not cold, the sharp gusts had a chilly edge to them.

Here on the peninsula, the weather isn't just something to make conversation about. It is king to the queen that is the sea and so rules the peninsula's and much of the state's livelihood. How folks react to this mercurial master is an unspoken indicator of what they're made of and how they stand up to the world. James sometimes thought, especially on a day like today, that it was simply an indication of how stupidly stubborn people could be.

He slowed his stride as he got to the first awning attached to the back of an old VW bus painted like a colorful, tie-dyed shirt James had worn in his youth. He paused long enough to check out what was on the portable racks and tables. A woman who looked to be about his age, dressed in an orange slicker with a vivid yellow tote bag hanging from one arm, was chatting over a collection of brightly colored yarns and knit hats with a younger, pony-tailed woman sporting well-loved blue jeans and a sweatshirt that matched the vehicle behind her. There was no food there, so James just smiled at them both as he moved on to the next stall. Here, a single table held neat rows of different breads and rolls. This would be good. He hadn't thought there might be baked goods. He hadn't had any homemade bread for a long time. James picked up a loaf marked whole wheat, raised it to his nose, and inhaled deeply. *Nothing better than the smell of fresh-baked bread.* He was considering a package of huge cinnamon rolls when a lanky, young man emerged from the back of the white van parked sideways behind the stand. He looked to be about Tommy's age, with a full ginger-colored beard that could use a good trim. A wild mass of curly hair, the same color as his beard, whipped around his face and into his eyes. James couldn't help but think there was no way a comb would ever get through that mess.

"Hey there! Can I answer any questions for you? I was about to give up and head back home for the day. This wind is killing me!"

James grinned at him. "Aw, it's not that bad. At least it's fairly warm and not raining—for the moment."

"I guess," the kid laughed. "Still, I'm done in. It's been a slow morning so far."

"I'll take these," James said holding up his choices.

"Sure. Do you need a bag?"

"I guess I do. I didn't think about bringing one."

Pushing his hair back out of his eyes yet again, the young man shrugged. "Some do, some don't. We keep a small supply of 'em handy just in case."

He motioned toward a short stack of wrinkled, brown paper bags at the edge of the table held captive by a smooth rock not quite the size of a grapefruit. He lifted the rock slightly, slid out the top bag, took the breads from James, and placed them in it.

"That will be eighteen fifty."

James reached into his back pocket for his wallet. That seemed like a lot for one loaf of bread and six cinnamon rolls, but what did he know? They were homemade after all, and the wonderful aroma of the fresh bread mixed with the sea air was almost good enough to pay for all by itself.

"Here you go." He handed over a twenty-dollar bill. "Keep the change," he added as the kid started rummaging in his pocket. "I don't need it rattling around."

And maybe you might could save for a haircut, he thought. Immediately, in his mind's eye, he saw Anna glaring at him. Feeling guilty, he smiled at the youngster.

"Thanks, Man. Hey, have a great day."

"You too."

James moved on to the next vendor. There were plenty of vegetables in crates on a table and some buckets with leafy, green tops poking out of them. A forest green and white banner hanging from the edge of the table broadcast the name of a local organic farm the next village over. He knew the Dawson family that owned the place. They were always looking for help during the growing season. They also offered internships for college kids who were studying sustainable living and organic farming. Tommy had worked for the farm one summer when he was in high school, but James figured it was more because he'd been enamored with one of the Dawson's daughters than he was in learning anything about farming. At any rate, his interest in both had only lasted the one summer.

As he approached, a fresh-face woman who looked to be in her mid-twenties stood up from behind the table where she'd been sitting on two, black plastic milk crates stacked upside down. She was tall and lithe. Her ankle-length blue cotton dress, the color of old blue jeans, flowed about her in waves with the wind. A darker blue sweater lay across her shoulders, its arms tied loosely across her chest. Her dark chestnut hair was pulled to the front over one shoulder, secured with a small black ribbon just above where her sweater was tied. She held a book in one hand, her index finger stuck in between the pages to hold her place.

"Good morning." Her voice, soft and low, was almost carried off in a wind gust.

"Good morning to you," James smiled over at her. She was about as tall as he was. Her deep brown eyes were accented by prominent cheekbones that were flushed from the wind's buffeting, but there wasn't a hint of make-up to mar her honey-toned skin. Although she returned James's smile, it didn't reach up to her eyes, and suddenly the wind felt like it had a little more of a nip to it that hadn't been there the moment before.

"Are you looking for anything in particular?" she asked, meeting his gaze directly.

"Well, this is the first time I've come down, so I thought I'd see what there is and go from there."

She tilted her head slightly and nodded. "It's getting late in the season for greens now, but we still have some, and the corn is just coming in." She motioned with her free hand to his right, where colorful hues of the red and deep green peeked out of wooden crates. "If you want cucumbers, tomatoes, or peppers, there's plenty. Oh, and I do have a few of the first beets and parsnips left today; wax beans too. Everything else went quickly first thing this morning."

James nodded. He looked over the offerings. The sweet corn looked amazing and would be great with the lobster dinner. Fresh salad would be nice too. He realized he didn't even know what kinds of vegetables Tommy and Sophia might like. Anna had served anything and everything. The kids would never have dreamed of complaining, or if they had he'd never heard it. He wondered what their favorite meals were. He'd never thought about that, either. He'd just have to wing it. He ended up choosing corn, wax beans, two tomatoes, some long-leafed lettuce of some sort, a cucumber and a red bell pepper—a good start.

The girl set her book to the side. "Do you need a bag? I don't think you want me to put all this in with your fresh bread. It probably wouldn't be good for it."

"Yes, please. I keep forgetting I'm supposed to take my own shopping bags everywhere." He thought she frowned slightly as if he had committed some kind of social faux pas.

"Yeah, most folks bring a re-useable bag when they shop. I'm out of any extra paper ones. I might have a little box in the truck. Let me see . . ." She half-turned to start walking back to the truck behind the stand. "Oh wait!" She spun back around. "I've got just the thing." She grabbed a tote bag from beside the milk crates, peered into it, and began rummaging around in its depths for whatever it was she considered 'just the thing.' "Got it!" She held up a little red package about the size of her fist that looked like a tiny pillow.

James stared at it. He was thoroughly confused.

She started to laugh, a low melodic sound, but quickly looked down and hid it with a small cough as she dropped the large tote on the ground. She was grinning when she looked back up at him. He couldn't tell if it was because she was pleased with her find or amused at his confusion.

She pulled open a small drawstring at the top of the little red bundle and turned it inside out, so its contents were now outside of it. "Voila!" She grabbed a piece of the fabric by the drawstring and gave the thing a sharp shake as if she were cracking a whip. As it unfurled, James could see she had hold of a handle, and the pillow had become a tote about the size of a brown paper grocery bag. It was made of the same kind of fabric as a windbreaker jacket. She pushed her free hand down into the bag to flesh out the shape of it, then held it up triumphantly. "Magic, instant produce bag." She held it out for his review.

"Well, I'll be damned." James shook his head. "I couldn't figure out what you had there for a minute."

She grinned at him again and this time her eyes crinkled at the edges. For a second, from somewhere deep in his memory, he swore he saw a spark of a younger, mischievous child he'd known.

"That's a neat trick," he remarked. "I never saw one of those before."

"Yeah, it's kinda cool. I haven't ever had the chance to use it for anything. I almost forgot I carried it around."

She carefully started packing up the vegetables he'd chosen. The greens of the lettuce that peeked up over the top of the bright red bag reminded James of Christmas colors. Christmas memories always reminded him of Anna's plays at the church that the town kids put on. He looked back up at the young lady's face. He knew this girl!

"Justine Connor! Is that you? And all grown up. I haven't seen you since Tommy left for college."

She smiled, a real smile this time that made her hazel eyes sparkle and her face light up from within. James was startled by the transformation. The girl was pretty, no doubt, but when she smiled like that, she was absolutely stunning. He thought if there ever was a mermaid that came to live on shore, she'd look just like her.

"It's me, Mr. Edward! I knew who you were right away, but I wasn't sure you would recognize me, or want to recognize me..." Although her mouth was still turned up at the edges, the light dimmed as the smile faded from her eyes. She reached across the table to hand him the now full, red nylon bag.

"Please just call me James. And, Sweetie, why would I not want to recognize you? It's wonderful to see you again. How long have you been home? Are you back for good?"

She looked up and nodded, peering past him instead of meeting his eyes. "Yes. I mean, I think so. Oh, I don't even know . . ." James saw her eyes were brimming with unshed tears and her voice had whispered away. She waved her hand as if to dismiss something—someone. She sighed.

Suddenly uncomfortable, James glanced away.. Great! Now he'd made her upset. What should he say? Probably nothing because it appeared he'd stuck his foot in it already. He opened his mouth, then closed it again.

"Look at me. What a mess. Sorry." She gave him a little half-smile as she met his concerned gaze. "I'm fine. Really. I think I'm just a little overwhelmed today."

James cleared his throat. "I'm sorry if I was too personal. I was so surprised to see you, and so pleased I recognized you, that I just spouted off questions."

"Oh, no. You're fine. I'm so happy to see a familiar, friendly face. I've been back about three weeks now. And yes," she added firmly. "I hope I'm back to stay."

Justine tucked a few wispy stray hairs behind her ear. She looked steadily at him. "I wanted to tell you how sorry I am about Mrs. Edward. She was one of the most wonderful people I've ever known."

"Thank you." James looked down, internally bracing himself for the familiar pain of acknowledging Anna's loss. But this time there was just a hard, quick, pinch near his heart. Then it was gone. He took a deep breath and looked back up at Justine. "She is definitely missed."

"Mom said that you are waiting to have a service later?"

James nodded, surprised at himself for agreeing. "Yes. Tommy and Sophia are coming up this weekend. I guess we'll figure things out then." He held the red bag aloft and grinned. "Hence, my first trip ever down here. They like fresh veggies."

Justine smiled, but it was guarded again. James wished he could somehow make her light up like she had before.

"I know they'd both be so happy to see you. I hope you'll come over while they're home."

She shook her head. "I'd love to, but I'm not so sure that's a good idea."

"I think you're wrong. But I understand. Still, do you mind if I tell the kids that I ran into you, and you're back?"

Justine ducked her head. "I don't mind at all. It would be great to find a time we can get together. I really would like that. I've missed them both." She paused. "Life sure hasn't turned out the way I thought."

"It has a way of surprising us, that's for sure."

"Oh, listen to me!" She put the palms of her hands up to her cheeks that now were flushed bright red. "Here I am starting to moan and complain about life being unfair, and you've just lost Mrs. Edward. I'm so sorry!"

James hardly heard what she said. He suddenly saw a much younger girl in Justine's flushed face and too bright eyes. He shook his head in sudden realization.

"You're Natasha's mother!"

Justine lowered her hands. "You've met Natasha? When?" She wrinkled her nose, like she was trying to figure something out. Before James could answer, Justine clapped her hands together, "Oh, of course! She told me last night that she met a Mr. James. I didn't know who she meant. All I finally got out of her was that you were a lobsterman with your own boat, and she met you down at the wharf." James opened his mouth as she took a breath, but he didn't get to answer her. "You must have introduced yourself by your first name. I never thought of that. I told her that she was to stay away from you, because, well, I had no idea. I mean I've been trying to figure out who an older lobsterman from town was that was a Mr. James. I thought I knew all the fishermen down there, and she was perfectly safe running around like us kids used to, but . . . Oh, I'm sorry." She'd put her hand over her mouth. Her face was an even deeper red now.

James chuckled and shook his head. "No need to be sorry. Your thoughts were perfectly understandable, and smart. You can't be too careful. But, you know, I really didn't have any choice but to tell her my name. She pretty much insisted. I had no idea she was yours. I've been trying to figure out who she belongs to ever since I first saw her."

"Oh no! What did she do?" Justine stood stock still, waiting.

"Nothing at all bad, I promise." James grinned at her and held up the bag of goodies. "Tell you what. I'm going to put this in the truck. Why don't you let me buy you a late breakfast, and I'll tell you all about how I met your little girl. She's really something, you know."

Justine tilted her head to one side. "I'd like that. I don't think many more people are going to come by with this wind howling around the way it is. I'll text Deb to let her know I'm giving up for the day. She'll be fine with it. But," Justine paused and looked down. "Is it OK if we go to The Coffee Stop and not The Dinette? I haven't been in The Dinette since I left after. . . Well, I'm just not ready to go in there."

Twenty

Natasha

The wind is weird today. It's acting like it doesn't like anyone and is in a super rotten mood. It's blowing kinda steady, then all of a sudden it puffs up and rattles the window in my room all mad-like. That's kinda how I feel today.

I came right back up here after breakfast. I wanted to go to work with Mom for the whole day, but she said today wasn't good because she has to be at the farmer's market thing downtown again, and I really wouldn't have anything to do there but sit and wait for her. She said if the wind slowed down, I could ride my bike over to see her or maybe walk down with Gran. But I'm not allowed to go down to the wharf again until she figures out who Mr. James is because she says she doesn't know him, and that means he's a stranger, and I'm not supposed to be talking to strangers. I told her over and over again that he's really nice, and he's not a stranger, but she said there was no discussion. Period. Not only that, the old wind isn't giving up anytime soon. It'd just push me all over the place 'cause I'm a lightweight. Gran is quiet and seems kind of sad today, too. I don't want to bother her. So here I am, just staring out the window, remembering.

At least we've hardly seen my grandfather here lately. After he threw my bike into the yard I was so mad. I wanted to yell at him and ask him why he was so mean. But Mom had me hugged sideways to her, and I knew I wasn't supposed to say a thing, or I'd get in trouble with her. It's not like it mattered anyway. He acted like we were invisible.

He didn't have any reason to do that. My bike wasn't in his way or anything. He had to go out onto the yard to pick it up and throw it. I was sure it was going to be broken to bits, but when I ran over to pick it up it wasn't hurt. Just the tassels on the one handlebar were all muddy from where they'd slid along the ground. Mom said she'd help me clean it up later, but right then we should put it away for the night. Then we could go for a walk together and take a look at the pool to see if I'd like to think about going swimming there some evening. "Out of sight, out of mind," she'd said.

I asked her what that meant. She said that if we weren't there, then it would give my grandfather time to cool off, and he'd most likely be gone again when we got back.

Then we didn't talk at all for a while. We just walked. I figured she was thinking about my grandfather and how he was and what she'd said that morning about how we might have to find somewhere else to stay. I didn't mind she was quiet. There's a lot to see, and it all looks different when you're walking instead of riding a bike. Plus, I was still mad at the way my grandfather had thrown my bike like it was a piece of junk in his way. I know I should've put it away instead of laying it down in the yard. But jeez, what he did to it was just plain mean.

We walked up the hill, past the General Store, the bank, and the arts center building where I always turn around when I'm riding my bike that way, because that's as far as I'm allowed to go if I'm by myself. Then we turned down the street beside the art center. The sign at the corner said "Sandy Ln." After we went down a little hill and backup again, there was a small cove with a sandy beach.

I told Mom how I thought it was really pretty. She said she knew I would like it. Then she told me all about how she used to hang out with her friends there after they went swimming at the pool. She pointed down the road the ran along the edge of the cove to show me where the pool was, up a little hill and around a curve. The road is the only thing between the rocks by the water on the left side and the emerald-green golf course grass on the right. She said she was too worn out to want to walk all the way up there tonight, but maybe next time we could.

There's a wooden bench on the little hill where the cove first comes into view as you go up the road. A wide set of granite steps goes down to the beach in front of it. I was so excited when I saw them that I hopped up and down, all-around Mom. I told her how neat I thought it was and how beautiful the beach looked. I asked if we could go down the stairs to the beach and maybe even swim there sometime?

She laughed and agreed it was neat. She says the beach is the biggest sandy beach in town. But we can't swim there. It's too dangerous because there are a lot of sharp rocks in the water. She said we are allowed to walk on the beach though, but since it was starting to get dark, we'd have to do that some other time. Then she said we could sit on the bench and watch the water for a little bit before we walked back to Gran's.

While we were sitting there, she pointed out the little sailboats moored on the outer right side of the cove. They bobbed on the water just before where the land disappears, and you only can see ocean forever. She said the boats were a kind of sailboat that aren't even made any more. The people that own them are members of *The Association's* yacht club, and they race them every Thursday and Sunday afternoon during the summer. She said the old yacht club building is on the shore there too, but I couldn't see it because there are a ton of trees in front of it. She talked about how she'd been a server in the dining room there for two summers when she was in high school, and how there's a big deck outside the dining room, that hangs out above the cliff overlooking the ocean. She and her friends would go there late at night after work to just sit and talk. She said they hung out there even more during the seasons when the yacht club was closed. I guess sometimes big fancy yachts that belong to the summer people, or their friends, come into the deep water in Sand Cove to stay for a few days. I'd like to see that, especially at night when they're all lit up.

She also told me about the big resort hotel that had once been on the hill and how there'd been a salt-water swimming pool right by the outer edge of the cove before you get to the yacht club. She said that when the tide came in, it would fill the pool. Then they closed big gates to keep the water in while people swam. I guess at low tide you can still see where the old gates were. I asked her if she saw the whole pool when you she was growing up, but she said it was gone way before she was born. There was a fire like 80 years ago that destroyed the hotel and everything around it. It never got rebuilt.

Then she told me how there are some big, beautiful homes up on the avenue behind the golf course that were built years and years ago. Balsam Cove was a resort town then. People came from cities to spend whole summers. She said that only a few summer people still come for the season. Now mostly, folks only visit for a week or two. So those big houses are empty almost all the time. I can't believe that no one lives in them and I told her so. She said that Gran told her a few of them have been sold to people who want to live in them year-round. But the cottages are so old they need a lot of work to make them warm enough for winter. I guess some of them don't have any way to heat them, except for old fireplaces. I like fireplaces, but I don't think one could heat a big house very well. I think it's just crazy that there are houses people only visit and don't really live in.

Mom said she thinks the same thing, that it's sad for the houses to just sit empty when so many people need places to live. I know that's true because I keep hearing her and Gran talk about how there aren't many houses for families to buy around here. No only that, apartments to rent, like the one we had in Boston, don't exist here.

We both were quiet after that. We just sat looking out over the water. It was just getting dark. Mom pointed up to a single star that had just popped out in the sky.

"Star light, star bright," she started.

"First star I see tonight," I said.

"I wish I may. I wish I might. Have this wish I wish tonight." We both said together.

She put her arm around my shoulder and hugged me to her. I was staring at that star—wishing with all my heart. I wondered if she wished for the same thing. But she can't tell me, and I can't tell mine either, because then the wishes will never come true.

Twenty One

The Coffee Stop was the only eatery open year-round, besides The Dinette, within ten miles. Unlike The Dinette that was available all day every day for three meals, the tiny cafe on the edge of town was open five days a week for breakfast and lunch, closing promptly at two p.m. every afternoon. Tucked back in off the road, it had a cozier atmosphere. Few tourists noticed it, or stopped, as they zipped by on their way to town.

James opened the door and stepped back so Justine could enter before him. As he expected, everyone stopped talking. Each and every eye in the place turned to see who was arriving. James ducked his head in greeting toward the regular crowd sitting at the front table they always claimed as their own. He put his hand gently on Justine's upper back, steering her toward an open table farthest from the others.

"Pay no attention to the vultures on their perches," he said softly, trying to keep a straight face.

"Oh, I remember how it is. I've got this." After they walked by, she turned, smiled brightly, and wiggled her fingers at the table of fishermen. Instantly, they became extremely interested in their coffee and plates.

It took all James had not to bust out laughing.

"You are enjoying this way too much," Justine remarked, arching an eyebrow at him as he held the old ladder-back chair out for her to slide into.

James plopped down in the seat across from her, grinning from ear to ear. "I guess I am. You don't seem to mind, though."

She shook her head. James could tell she was having a hard time not giving in to laughter herself. "Let 'em talk. It'll keep the old boys busy for the rest of the day."

"The rest of the day? Lady, this will keep them going for weeks. Imagine, James Edward and Justine Connor out to brunch together!"

Justine couldn't help it this time. She started to giggle, bringing a hand up to cover her mouth as she tried to contain herself. It was no use. Her shoulders were shaking. Soft laughter bubbled up over her hand.

"Hey, it's not that funny." James tried to appear wounded, but her laughter was contagious. He couldn't contain his amusement, and the more he thought about it, the harder he laughed. Pretty soon he was just about rolling on the floor. Now no one in the place was even trying to pretend to be interested in anything but the two of them. Half of the group they'd just walked past had their mouths open wide enough to catch flies.

Justine was wiping her eyes with the back of her hand, gasping for air. But every time she thought there wasn't any more to laugh about, she'd look at James and start all over again.

"Oh, Oh, this is awful!" She grabbed the edge of the table with both hands and took a deep breath. "I'm sorry. I'm not laughing about . . ." She put both palms up to her cheeks as she dissolved into giggles. "Oh," she gasped, "I'm not even sure what I'm laughing about!"

James waved a hand at her, while he held onto his aching side with the other. "Who cares? I haven't had a really good laugh in ages. Holy moly!"

"Well, I don't know what the big joke is, but you two certainly brought some life into the place today." The waitress who had wandered over plunked down two glasses of ice water, then reached into the pocket of her server's apron for straws. She slid them onto the middle of the shiny, mottled-gray, Formica tabletop. "It's been a long while since you've come around here, James. And I don't believe I recognize you, Deah." She looked at Justine.

James knew this was nothing but bull since Sherry had been a waitress at one place or another around town long before James and Anna had gotten married. She'd never forgotten anyone who'd crossed her path, and she knew most everything about them to boot. James thought that Sherry had to be going on seventy now, but she still worked a few days a week serving breakfast and lunch to the ever-hungry locals, and summer folks when they wandered in.

"Oh, Sherry," Justine smiled up at her. "You know perfectly well who I am. Quit fishing for details just because you haven't seen me since I last sat at one of your tables with three other high school girls ordering a large French Fry to share and Cokes with maraschino cherry juice poured into them."

"Well, if it isn't Justine Connor all grown up." Sherry smiled and winked at her. "What brings you back to town?"

"Good try, Sherry. Got anything else? I'm sure that everyone who knows I'm back has some theory of why. I'd love to hear them all."

Sherry waved a hand in front of herself like she was batting at an insect. "That's true. Everybody's an expert. Except me, of course." She sighed, "I should put out a shingle and charge by the hour. I hear it all in this place."

James smacked the table lightly with the palm of his hand. He was still a little short of breath from laughing so hard. "And you love every second of it. Just like the rest of us old gossips."

"As we say, 'true story, real life,'" Sherry shot back at him. "But you know, I only want the details so I can set people straight. I wanna make sure no one is spreading hurtful rumors. That kind of talk just ain't right."

Justine reached out and patted Sherry's arm. "I'm not worried about what they're saying or are going to say. Trust me. I'm just fine. You can go back over there and tell them anything you want. I couldn't care any less."

"Well, I tried." Sherry shook her head. She pointed to the folded menu card standing between the salt and pepper shakers by the wall at the far edge of the table. "Do you two comedians know what you want? Or are you going to keep providing the floor show?"

"Now Sherry, don't be that way." James said.

"Oh, I'm good. I can tell them all that I've been sworn to secrecy. Then they'll just have to keep guessing." She winked again at Justine. "I do hear that you have a young'un in tow and a right cunnin' girl at that."

Justine smiled. "I do. Thank you for asking."

Sherry turned to James. "This girl is good. There'll be no cracking her."

She beamed at Justine. "You're gonna be fine. I hope you stay home this time. We could use some girls with backbone around here. This new generation are just a bunch of privileged whiny brats." She shook her head again. "Now how about it. You eating or not? I've got work to do."

"Can you give us a few minutes? If you don't mind. I haven't even had time to pick up the menu to see what's on it." Justine replied.

"The same as when you were here last time, Deah. That menu hasn't changed since I started slopping food on tables in this town when I was fifteen, and I doubt it will change before I'm in the ground. But I'll be back in a few minutes with a cherry Coke for you and coffee for Mr. Chuckles. You know I still make my cherry Cokes just like I used to, but I don't think I've had an order for one in a while. I hope the cherries are still good."

As she walked away, Justine leaned over the table toward James. "Did I order a cherry Coke? I think I missed something."

"Just go with it, Kiddo. She's gonna get you one anyway, and unless you hate them now you might as well not fight it. I don't know why she bothers to ask any of us what we want when we come in here. We pretty much get the same thing every time." James paused, "I do hope you are going to eat more than French fries today, though?"

"What's good?" Justine asked. "I try to eat healthy now, and I remember the burgers here could give you an instant heart attack. We used to call them gunk burgers."

"They haven't changed. I think they train every cook that comes through the door to open cans the same way, because no matter how many of them come and go, the food is still the same. Anna used to say some of it was just this side of awful. But they can do up some things really nice, like their fried Haddock lunch. Breakfasts are fairly good too. But I guess it's hard to screw up toast, bacon, and eggs." James paused. "It's not the food though . . ."

"It's that this place is ours," Justine finished for him. "That's it in a clam shell. True story, real life."

James smiled, his eyes distant. "I do remember you were one smart cookie. You stood out from the others, even when you were a youngster. Seems like that hasn't changed a bit."

Justine looked down at the table. "Oh, I don't know. I've made some pretty stupid choices in my life. Some turned out to be major mistakes. I'm not sure that coming back here wasn't one of them."

"I can't speak of your life. But I've been around a good while. I'd like to say that coming home is always a good plan. But I think it's more what you do with life once you finally get where you're headed. After all this time, your compass must have pointed you in this direction again for a reason."

Justine started to say something, then stopped. James held up his hands as Justine started to speak again. "I don't need to know. The reasons are your own. I'm just happy to see you all in one piece. Not to mention that snappy little sidekick you brought!" He was surprised to realize he really meant what he said about not needing to know—and after all that thinking that he had to figure out all about Natasha and her story.

"She is quite a sidekick," Justine agreed. She paused as Sherry reappeared through the swinging gate behind the counter with a coffee pot in one hand and a tall glass full of ice and cherry Coke in the other.

"Here you go, Youngster." Sherry set down the glass directly in front of Justine. "I found a brand-new jar of maraschino cherries to open. I even put three cherries in it, just for you."

"Thank you, Sherry." Justine smiled up at her. "How in the world did you remember what I like after all these years?"

Sherry poured coffee into James's mug and set the pot on the edge of the table. "I wouldn't be much of a waitress if I didn't remember what my customers like, now would I? I'm thinking that daughter of yours probably likes them too, and I bet she never had a real cherry Coke." She sniffed. "Those sodas in the can just aren't the same. Now do you want breakfast or lunch?" She looked at James. "I'm assuming lunch for you. You're pretty late for breakfast even if the weather is bad enough to keep you in from hauling. So, you'll want the Haddock burger."

James grinned up at her. "I guess I must."

"Don't be a smart ass. It's not like you ever get anything else for lunch here. You haven't graced us with your presence for months, but I can still remember what you eat. Yes, I know," she said without taking a breath, "Extra tarter, and fries, not chips."

James shook his head. "Not quite. I think I want coleslaw. No fries." He pointed at Justine's drink. "And I'll have one of those cherry Coke things too."

"Really." She studied James for a second trying to see if he was serious. She shrugged. "Ok, it's your lunch."

Sherry looked down at Justine. "What about you then?"

"Oh, I haven't even looked. But I think I'd like an early lunch too. I had a bit of breakfast first thing this morning. Do you have any salads?"

"There's a Cobb Salad and a Tuna Salad, same as always."

"I'll try the Cobb Salad. That sounds good."

Sherry nodded. "You'll want some bread with that. Ranch dressing? It seems like you young'uns live on that stuff."

"Umm, do you have any other dressings?"

Sherry cocked her head. "Sure. Italian and Thousand Island. That's it."

"Italian, please."

"Ok. I'll be back." Sherry got halfway to the counter before she realized she'd left the coffee pot on the table. She swung back around, picked it up without a word, and sauntered into the kitchen.

Justine leaned over the table toward James. "I think I've been caught in a time warp. How many people can say that home is exactly the way they left it?"

"I'm not sure that's a good thing. I would've hoped that at least some things would've changed for you, and your mom, over the years."

Justine scrunched up her mouth, her expression guarded. "I know it's no secret how things were at our house. I'm afraid they mostly are still the same on that front. But my father does spend most of his time away. By the time he gets back from the pub, or wherever it is he goes at night, he's usually too sauced to do anything but fall into bed and pass out. I tried for years to get Mom to come and stay with me. But she wouldn't have any of it. Considering how things worked out, in some twisted sense, I'm glad she didn't leave."

Justine picked up a straw from the table. She began to pull the paper wrapping away from the top. "I don't have much to say, though. In a lot of ways I did the very same thing Mom has done—stayed where I wasn't wanted, thinking it would change."

She slid the paper down the straw and plunked it into her drink. She took a long sip and closed her eyes. "Ah, that is perfect. I'd forgotten how much I loved these things."

"Justine, he's not hitting her again, is he? He's not trying to hurt you or Natasha?" James leaned forward his hands flat on the table. His face suddenly felt hot, and he could feel a dull throb in his temples.

She looked up at him, startled. "No. No! I didn't mean things hadn't changed that way. After all that happened, he hasn't moved to touch Mom, or anyone else, that I know of. It's all words and yelling. He's still as miserable as he ever was, and he makes sure everyone around him knows it. All those years of drinking have made him into nothing but a mean old drunk." She gazed into the distance and lightly shook her head. "I'm working hard to save enough money so I can rent a little place for Natasha and me. But it's so hard to find anything in town or even close by. Right now we have the whole upstairs to ourselves. I'm in my old room and she's in the attic bedroom. We hardly ever see my father since he's usually gone before we're up and in long after we're in bed. Mostly he doesn't even acknowledge we're there anyway, so it's OK."

"I'm not sure how, 'OK' that really is, but I'll have to trust your judgment."

James relaxed and leaned back in his chair. The 'that' Justine referred to was the catalyst for a chain of events that had changed more than a few lives. It had also involved the man who once had been James's friend—Justine's father, Homer.

James and Homer Connor had been buddies all through school, bound together by losing their fathers when they were young. The thing was, that right after high school graduation, Homer had taken up after his father and began a life of hard partying. Homer's new crowd and their lifestyle wasn't anything James wanted any part of. Still, even though they hardly spent any time together as time went on, James and Homer had remained fairly friendly right up until Anna arrived in town. When she didn't pay Homer any mind at all despite all his best efforts, and started seeing James, that was then end of any friendship between the two men,

The rift between the two widened and became unbridgeable once Homer decided that James had stolen Anna from him. Not a month after James and Anna married, Homer married Cora, a close friend of Anna's.

Truth be told, Anna hadn't entertained any thought of dating either one of them. But she'd turned both men's heads the very first day she showed up in town. They'd chased her relentlessly until James wore her down enough to agree to go out with him "just one time." Well, that one time had turned into two. Before long James was begging her to marry him. Homer never got over the fact that Anna had never looked sideways at him. It also didn't help that Homer imagined he needed to be in competition with James over just about everything. He'd always been that way. Plus, he was a right sore loser.

Anna's friend Cora had fallen hard for Homer right from the start. But for Homer, Cora was the consolation prize, and he treated her that way, and worse.

Less than three weeks after Anna and James's wedding, Cora came running into their kitchen to show off a plain gold wedding band to Anna. Cora and Homer had just come from the courthouse in Ellsworth. She'd convinced him they should get married too.

Anna tried to be happy for her friend, but she confided in James that she was sure Homer wasn't in love with Cora. She was afraid it was going to be a rough road ahead. At first, after Homer and Cora married, the two ladies had tried to mend the relationship between the men. The couples did a few things together, but it wasn't comfortable, so they soon drifted apart. Cora was enamored of her husband and unfailingly loyal. It wasn't long before Homer made it clear to Cora that she was to stay away from her friend Anna. So, she did—at least in public.

Cora and Homer's one and only child, Justine, arrived three months after Anna had Tommy. The kids grew up not one block from each other, but her father expressly forbid Justine to be friends with anyone in the Edward family. Still, it was a small town and the kids hung out at school, went to the same church with their mothers, and were all tight with the group of town kids that did most everything together. Justine could be found every so often over at the Edward's home. Homer Connor had become a notorious drunk; an obnoxious blowhard with few fans and no followers. There wasn't a soul around who was going to tell him they'd seen Justine consorting with the enemy.

A little over a year after Tommy and Justine graduated and left for college, Anna came home from church one Sunday and related that Cora had told her Justine was home for a visit. She'd breezed in the evening before, announced to her mom that she was in love with a boy she'd met in one of their classes at school, and now she was pregnant. They had everything all planned out. She was dropping out of school at the end of the semester. Her boss at her part-time job at Bloomingdale's in the mall at Chestnut Hill was thrilled to hire her on full-time and with benefits to boot. After the baby was born, Justine would take six weeks maternity leave. Then the little one would go to a daycare center right down the street from the mall while Justine was at work. By the time Justine came home to share her news, she'd already moved out of the dorm on campus, into the boyfriend's apartment. It was a done deal.

Anna said Cora had been blind-sided. She'd asked her daughter why she hadn't brought the boy home with her to meet them, and wouldn't they be getting married? Justine told her that he was working and studying for exams, so he couldn't get away to come with her this time. As far as getting married, they hadn't really talked about it. Besides, she told Cora, plenty of couples lived together without being married.

Anna said Cora was in still in shock and not sure what to think. It certainly wasn't how she had imagined her lovely daughter's future. But here it was.

As usual, Homer hadn't been home when Justine arrived. Cora told her she'd give Homer the news. She thought it might be just a bit easier on them all if she was the one he heard it from. As Cora expected, when she finally got the courage up to talk to Homer a couple days later, he went off the deep end. He blamed Cora for the whole situation. He began publicly accusing her of all kinds of shortcomings and nastiness, most of which Homer was guilty of himself. He declared down at the pub, in front of God and everyone, that he was going to kick Cora's "whore-of-a-daughter" out, and she was never to step foot in his home again.

Friday evening, two days after Homer's speech at the pub, there was hell to pay. That awful night was as fresh in James's mind as if it had just happened.

There hadn't been an empty table at the Friday, all-you-can-eat fish fry at The Dinette. In between huge bites of fried haddock, an already half-drunk Homer was loudly, and tirelessly, verbally tearing apart the two women in his life. Obviously mortified, Cora helplessly tried to excuse herself from the table.

Homer yanked her back down onto the bench next to him. "You worthless bitch, you'll go when and where I say you can go. And when I do say you can go, you'll be gone for good, and you can take that stupid whore of a daughter with you."

Everyone was watching. There was nowhere else to look. No one knew what to do at first, including James. It was no secret Homer had absolutely no respect for his wife, but he'd always been just a blowhard—at least as far as anyone knew. Besides, you stayed out of your neighbor's business, right?

When Homer saw that Cora was crying, he gained steam, sneering at her. "You're nothing but some weak excuse for a woman. You know that? If you had any backbone, your worthless daughter wouldn't be knocked up with some bastard kid."

There were audible gasps from some of the tables.

Anna started up out of her seat. James was already out of his. He shook his head and put a gentle hand on her arm. He closed the space between the tables in two strides.

"That's more than enough, Homer. Why don't you clear out and sober up."

Three other men had come over right behind James. They stood there letting James take the lead, waiting to see how things were going to play out.

Cora tried to rise from the bench again. Homer shoved her with both hands. James tried to catch her as she came tumbling out of the booth, but she ended up on the floor in a heap.

"Why don't you take the bitch, you son-of-a-whore!" Homer roared. "You stole her friend from me to begin with. You can have her too!"

James was lifting Cora to her feet as Homer shot up out of the booth. He took a drunken swing at James hitting nothing but air. Then he kicked hard at Cora, catching her on the shin.

"Oh!" Cora was all out sobbing now. She crumpled back toward the floor. James scooped her up, handed her over to Nat Baker, turned around, fist cocked, and laid Homer out with one shot to his jaw. Then he dragged him up off the floor by the front of his shirt bringing his own face three inches from the red-faced, lolli-headed drunk.

"If you ever, and I mean ever, think of hitting Cora, or any other woman again you sorry son-of-a-bitch, I will cheerfully kill you with my own hands." He threw Homer to the floor. Homer's head hit the edge of the booth with a dull thud. He didn't try to get up. "And God help you if you do anything to hurt young Justine." James growled at Homer, fists curled at his sides, thinking how he'd like to keep beating the life right out of the coward.

"Call the Sheriff," he instructed the open-mouthed waitress behind the counter. "Maybe they'll make sure he doesn't show up at home for a few days. I'll wait outside for them." He turned to go out to the parking lot. There wasn't a sound from anyone in the place.

Nat had taken Cora over to Anna who had promptly herded her out the door to their truck. James sent them up to their house while he stayed behind to wait for the cops. He remembered pacing up and down in front of the building for what seemed like an hour, fists jammed in his pockets, thinking that if he'd ever wanted to take up smoking, it would be the perfect time to do so.

Right after James talked to the law and started for home, Homer was on his way to the jail in Ellsworth. James figured he'd be in there until at least Monday morning when a judge saw him. The sheriff told James the state would file domestic abuse charges, and drunken disorderly conduct, then it would go from there. James was free to go because he'd only defended himself and Cora.

At home, Anna was sitting with her friend at the table, teapot in front of them, but neither had touched the tea in their cups. Cora's upper arms were already bruising. Anna had propped Cora's leg up on a chair with an ice pack laid gently on the angry, purple, baseball-sized lump from Homer's boot.

Anna wanted to take her to the hospital to be sure she wasn't badly hurt, but Cora was having none of that. She just wanted to go home. James didn't say a word. He figured Anna had said enough. Cora was right on the edge. She couldn't even look either of them square in the face. They helped her climb back into the truck and drove the quarter-of-a-mile between their two homes in silence.

By the time they got to the Connor's residence Justine and some of her girlfriends had returned from wherever they'd been for the afternoon. A group of about half a dozen kids was in the driveway. Young Sam Dean stood in front of them, gesturing wildly as he told the story. Justine was sitting on the porch stoop, her head in her hands.

James vaguely remembered Sam had been at The Dinette with his parents, but that didn't mean the story would be even close to what really happened. There'd be all kinds of dramatic embellishments to the tale. That boy had no sense. James could see all the girls were clearly upset. Why in the world would anyone go over to the Connor's place so you could tell Justine, in front of all her friends, all about how her mother and father had been publicly shamed?

He asked Cora and Anna to stay put while he dealt with the youngsters. He gave young Sam a good talking to about minding himself, then sent everyone on their way assuring them he'd be keeping an eye out for the ladies. Then he and Anna helped Cora out of the truck to the front porch steps. Justine hugged her mom and Anna herded both of them into the house. A moment later she reappeared to send

James home, saying she was going to stay awhile just to make sure they would be all right.

When Anna came back home after dark a couple hours later, James was already in bed. He wasn't sleeping. Anna slid into bed without a word and turned to him. He kissed her and held her tight, knowing better than to ask any questions. She was lost in her own thoughts. She'd talk to him when she was ready. He drifted off to sleep, one arm around her, her head on his chest, thinking how lucky they were to have each other.

Justine left town before her father finished serving those few days in the county lockup. She hadn't been back, until now. After the incident, Anna checked in on Cora every few days when Homer wasn't around. As the years passed, Cora kept even more to herself. She was rarely seen out and about, except at church. She never had much to say.

About a week after Homer came back, James left out to haul one morning only to discover that over half of his traps had been cut from their buoys. That was one hell of a loss. The authorities were notified. There was no doubt in anyone's mind who had done the dirty work, but there was no way to prove it.

James entertained the idea of beating Homer to a fine pulp, but Anna had convinced him otherwise pretty quickly. He knew she was right. He might feel better for a minute or two, but he didn't need assault charges against him. Besides, Cora would end up being the one who suffered from it all. He hated backing down, but what else could he do? After the incident, there wasn't a lobsterman in town that would give the time of day to Homer. They simply ignored him.

Homer became more of the miserable drunk he was, but at least he appeared to leave Cora alone. There wasn't a sternman worth a damn who would work for him. Most of the crew he ended up with weren't from town, were about as trustworthy as frayed rope, and no one you'd ever want to meet in a dark alley.

There was always plenty of talk about how in the world Homer got by. It seemed he spent most of what he made down at the pub or at the casino in Bangor. There were rumblings of Homer getting involved with a burglary ring and maybe even drugs. God only knew and James didn't care. He made it his business to steer clear of the fool like everyone else. He'd given very little thought to Homer Connor for the past ten years. Which was probably one reason why he didn't put two-and-two together when he first saw Natasha.

"Mr. Edward? James? Are you ok?" James mentally shook himself as he realized Justine was talking to him.

"I'm fine. I was just remembering a long time ago." James shook his head. "It seems I do that a lot these days. In fact, your Natasha has been remembering with me."

Justine was staring across the table at him, obviously confused. "I'm not sure I understand," she said.

"Well, I promised I'd tell you how I met your little girl. So, I guess I owe you the story." He paused and smiled at Justine thinking how much Natasha really did resemble her mother. "I first saw her down on the beach by the wharf, and I wondered where in the world she'd flown in from . . ."

Half an hour later they were almost finished with lunch, and James had related most of how he'd come to know Natasha. He left out how she heard him cuss out his sternman, as well as the debacle of losing the punt that wasn't tied up right, but he told her most of it. When he related how Natasha had asked if she could "remember" with him on the bench, Justine smiled.

"That's just like Tasha. I hope she didn't seem disrespectful. She really does mean what she asks you. She's very curious. Intense, too."

"She's just fine," James reassured her. "I'm hoping that you're all right now with letting her spend some time with me. I'm not sure how you feel about that, considering." James paused. "I was thinking I'd like to teach her how to fish for mackerel. I bet she'd like that. Her excitement over the eagles gave me the idea. I can just imagine how she'd love to watch them snag the fish off the dock if we leave some there."

Justine picked at what was left of her salad with her fork. "I think that would be nice," she said after a few seconds, "I definitely will tell her right away that I know who you are now, so she can have her bike riding privileges to the wharf back and be able to talk with you. I can't believe I thought you were some stranger that I had to worry about." She smiled over at James. "Sorry about that."

He chuckled. "Well, it just shows you're a good mom to worry. I could say I'm stranger than most, but I don't think it's in any bad way."

Justine set her fork down. "Another thing, truth is I really don't care what my father thinks. It's not like he'll notice anyway. He's perpetually sauced. Do you think maybe I could come along sometime too? I used to love fishing from the wharf. God, that was so many years ago. It seems a lifetime away."

James grinned, "I'd love it if you did! You know Sophia and I used to fish together all the time until she got so busy with school and all. She's getting ready to graduate from Maine Maritime with her Master's degree," James added.

"I heard that," Justine nodded. "Good for her. She's doing it right."

James studied her face for a moment, "You know, Kiddo. Just because your life is on a different path doesn't mean you're doing something wrong."

Justine shook her head. She cleared her throat. "I sure don't feel that way right now."

"Give yourself some time. You'll see. I know I don't know your circumstances, but I still see one smart young woman in front of me. I'm betting you'll figure it out soon enough."

"I appreciate that, Mr. Edward."

"James. Justine. Just call me James."

She smiled at him and ducked her head. "OK. James. I'll try to remember. But Tasha still has to call you Mr. James, all right? I want her to address her elders with some respect."

"I like that fine. It sounds kinda nice and it's refreshing to find a young'un with some manners these days. She introduced herself to me as Natasha, but does she prefer Tasha?"

Justine wrinkled her nose. "You'll have to ask her, I guess. If she told you, 'Natasha' then I'm guessing that's her preference." She laughed. "You know, I just call her whatever nickname or pet name I come up with at the time. She's never complained, but I've never thought to ask what she might like to be called."

"I imagine she'd let anyone know if they called her something she didn't like. But I think she'll just be Natasha to me until she tells me otherwise."

Justine looked earnestly at him. "I'm so glad she found you. She could use a positive male influence in her life that cares about her and what she thinks. The past few months haven't been easy. I hope that when school starts she'll find some friends. You know it's hard to be the new kid in town, especially one as small as ours."

"It's a pretty tight bunch here for sure," James agreed. "When Anna came here she made friends with your mom right off the bat, but it took a while after we were married, a couple years, before she felt at home and other folks were more friendly. Of course, we kept to ourselves quite a bit, for the first while anyway. I guess it was after Tommy was born that she really got out and about, and folks got to know her. Then it seemed like she'd always been here . . ." He looked down at the table and then back up. "Listen to me! Going on. Sorry about that, I seem to get a little lost sometimes."

Justine put her hand over his and squeezed it lightly before letting go. "It's fine. I know just what you mean. Sometimes I get stuck for a minute back in the past, too. At least your memories with Mrs. Edward are good. She was such a wonderful person. I don't think I've ever heard anything but nice stories about her."

"She was something else—my Anna. Don't I miss her. She'd be so happy to see you and your girl. She always had a soft spot for you, with your mom being her first friend here, and you being born right after Tommy." James grinned. "Natasha's sass would tickle her for sure."

"She definitely has sass," Justine remarked dryly. "Too much, most of the time." She looked down at her phone on the table. "Speaking of time, I better get the truck back to the farm and head to the house. I need to take Tasha down to the school to get her registered so she's all set when it starts. I was hoping to have the time to do that today, after market and all." She smiled at James then with that smile that lit up her face. "This was so nice. Thank you for asking me."

"I've enjoyed every minute of it. We'll do it again sometime. I can't tell you how happy I am to have run into you. I hope you'll come by the house when Tommy and Sophia are home. Bring Natasha too. Please. Besides, I want to show Natasha the fishing gear, and see if she's interested in trying her hand at mackerel fishing."

Justine chuckled, "You'll never get rid of her then."

"Fine by me. It's been kinda lonely at the house. It's just me and the cat. Wouldn't hurt my feelings a bit to have a youngster hanging about."

Twenty Two

Natasha

Mom came home a little early this afternoon. She said we had time to go down to the school to get me all set up. I didn't want to go, but she said I should. She said it would be mostly empty since only the office staff was there. She thought we might get to see where my classroom would be, but I wouldn't get to meet my teacher yet. I knew she was trying to make sure I understood that we could look around without a lot of people around, so I could figure out about the school building before I went the first day. But I didn't want to go at all anyway, so who cares?

She also told me when we were done we could go into the park and drive the loop to look at the waves. Then we could stop for an ice cream cone. Even though I didn't want to go down to the stupid school, and I knew she was just bribing me, I was kinda glad to be able to go for a ride. I'd been cooped up in the house all day. I also knew if I started arguing with her, it wouldn't do me any good. Plus, the wind should have the waves whipping up high against the rocks, and I'd be stupid to turn down ice cream. The ice cream stand close by was a nice thing about here, but there had been ice cream near our apartment in Boston, so that didn't make my *Good Things About Here* list.

I did add "bald eagles" to my list after I saw them with Mr. James. That's number nine. Then, after Mom walked with me to Sand Cove, I added "long walks by the ocean with Mom" for number ten.

When I ride my bike, I have to concentrate on where I'm going. Everything goes by pretty fast. I get to see more details when I go for a walk. Not only that, it's great walking with my mom because she tells me details about the stuff we walk by and about the people in town. I love to hear her talk about growing up here. When she tells me stories and things she remembers, her voice sounds different and her face looks happier, not like the sad and tired one she wears almost all the time since Dad left, and we moved.

That was what had made me grumpy before Mom got home. I was thinking about leaving Boston, and wondering why my dad never came back, and the fact that he made us move here because he left, and all the other things that changed; like Mom being gone more now, and having to live with a grandfather that hates all of us, even Gran. It's not fair. None of it.

On our drive to the school Mom told me she'd seen Mr. James at the farmer's market and even had lunch with him. She had asked me again who Mr. James was at bedtime the day my bike got thrown into the yard after we came back from seeing Sand Cove. She was trying to figure out who he was by how I described him, but she kept getting stuck on his name. She kept saying she didn't know any old fisherman with that name. I was tired by then, and having a hard time concentrating, so I guess I wasn't helping with enough details. I could tell she was worried about who he was. Sure enough she told me I couldn't talk to him anymore. And I got a big lecture on talking to strangers. No matter what I said she didn't believe me that Mr. James wasn't like a stranger. On top of that, now I wasn't even allowed to go anywhere near the cove, or the wharf, until she figured out who he was. That stunk in about six different ways, mostly because of my beach and the fact I really like Mr. James. He's nice and not fake, like a lot of grownups act when they talk to kids like me.

Now my worry doesn't matter though, because Mom figured out who he is. It turns out that she's known him all along. Not only that, his kids went to school with Mom. They were good friends. She even knows all about Mr. James's boat and his pretty house. She said Mr. James's last name is Edward, but it's perfectly fine to call him Mr. James just like he introduced himself to me. I told her he said he was all alone except for his cat. That's when she told me his wife suddenly got sick and died a few weeks before we moved here. Mom said she was one of the nicest ladies she ever knew, and how much Mr. James loved her, and how hard it must be for Mr. James to have lost her. I get that.

Then I started wondering why people say they "lost" someone when they die. I mean, they're dead right? Saying they lost them seems like they might be able to find them again, like if they lost car keys or phone. I didn't get to ask Mom about it though, because we were turning into the school parking lot by then.

I'm just glad it's still OK for me to talk with Mr. James. Mom said he really likes me spending time with him. That made me feel good. I know he only has his cat at home now. I've never had a pet, so I don't know what kind of company they might be. I think it could be super lonely. I may not like crowds of noisy people, but I still like some people, and I know what it feels like to miss someone.

Twenty Three

"Dad. We're home."

James was already out of his chair and halfway to the door by the time he heard Sophia calling out to him from the driveway. He'd been waiting for over an hour for the sound of Tommy's car. He opened the screen and stepped out just in time for Sophia to fly up the flagstone walk, her arms open wide to hug him. He held her close, lifting her up just off her feet. When she was younger and smaller, he would have twirled her around before setting her back down. But she was all grown up now. When he put her back down on the ground and let go, she stepped back and wiped at her face with the back of her hand. Tears pooled in eyes the same sky-blue color as his own. He gathered his little girl back up to him. She laid her head on his shoulder.

"Hey now. What's wrong with my girl?"

"I'm just so glad you're here, Dad."

"Me too, Bean. Me too. I've missed you something fierce."

James looked over Sophia's shoulder searching for Tommy. He was straightening up after pulling things from the back seat of his blue Ford, the same car he had bought the summer before he graduated from college. He had a black, carry-on suitcase in one hand and Sophia's navy-blue duffle bag over his shoulder. He turned toward the house, shoving the back door of the car closed with his foot before starting up the path.

At the sound of the car door slamming shut, Sophia released her father and turned around. They watched Tommy's progress up the path. James kept an arm around Sophia's shoulder, not wanting to let go just yet.

"Hey, Pops. We made it."

"So, I see."

"I figured you'd be out to haul, but that wind." Tommy said as he came toward them.

"Ayup, not today. I'd already planned to take it off anyway, to get ready for you two."

"I bet that made Mack happy. He never likes to cut a day hauling."

"True. But Mack hasn't been with me for months now. When your mom got sick, and after, I didn't go out for a long time. He has a family to feed. He's fishing with another old timer out of Beals. I'd love to have him back, but it's not right for me to ask or to take him from someone else. I do miss him. That's a fact."

"I'd have asked him," Sophia said as they went up the walkway. "He'd be loyal to you and come back."

"Maybe so, but that's not the way to do it. At least, it's not the way I operate. I told him he needed to do what he had to for his family. He lives about halfway between here and there, so his commute isn't any different." James paused. "I will admit that this new kid I've got can't hold a candle to Mack work-wise. Got no damn sense of humor either. Watch the cat," he said holding the screen door open for them to go through, "I think she's hiding in the living room. She hasn't tried to go out since she came back, but I'm not wanting to lose her again."

Tommy dropped the bags on the floor of the kitchen. "So, I'm betting you mess with the new guy every chance you get," Tommy said raising an eyebrow.

"God, Son. Don't look at me like that. If that's not your mother right there. She'd be telling me to be nice and get along."

"Oh, I'm not saying you should do anything different," Tommy chuckled. "I'm right though, aren't I? I know you, Dad. You can't help yourself. And I'll admit, I'd pay good money to watch the show."

James shook his head, "Truth is, I don't know him well enough to give him any good ribbing. I doubt this one's gonna stick, but at least he shows up sober and on time, mostly."

"Huh," Tommy grunted. "Well, I'll just take these bags upstairs. Be right back. Soph, you need anything out of yours before I take it up?"

"Nope, thanks."

Sophia turned to James as Tommy started up the narrow, steep stairway to their old bedrooms. "I'm starving. What are we going to do about supper?"

James shrugged. "Up to you kids. I bought a whole bunch of stuff earlier. I figured we'd do lobster Saturday night. Do you want to grill something, or do you want to go out? Doesn't matter to me either way."

Tommy came down the stairs ducking his head so he wouldn't hit the low beam above the bottom step. "I vote for going out tonight," he offered. "It's been a long drive. Head of the Harbor is still open, right? They don't close for the season until late October if I remember right, and we can walk there. I know it's geared more for the tourists, but it does have a great view. I'd love a bowl of good fish chowder."

"Sounds fine to me," James said. "I haven't been there since we celebrated Sophia's graduation from high school. I still hear good things about their food." He checked his watch. "They should be open for supper by now, it's after five."

"I'm in. Let's go." Sophia was already out the door and halfway down the walk.

"She's in a hurry," James remarked as he and Tommy followed.

"I think it has more to do with not wanting to be in the house than being hungry," Tommy said. "I had a hard time walking through the door myself knowing Mom wouldn't be there. I still expect to see her standing in the kitchen cooking up something for us. Soph and I talked a lot on the way up about Mom not being home. Even though Soph was back at the house right after Mom died, it's still hitting her hard. I imagine it will for a long while."

James slowed his pace. "I should've thought of that, Tommy. I've been so busy worrying about how I feel . . . I'm sorry."

"Stop apologizing, Dad. There's nothing to be sorry for. It's something we need to work out for ourselves. It'll take a little time, that's all."

"It's still taking me time," James admitted. "I guess we'll get there someday."

"I imagine we will. I've been talking with a grief counselor. A friend at work recommended it to me. I had—no, I'm still having—such a hard time dealing with not being here for Mom, you, and Sophia when Mom got sick."

James didn't answer for a moment. "I wondered why you didn't come home," he said, his voice low and measured. "You know, I didn't know she asked you not to."

Tommy shook his head. "Dad. She *ordered* me not to. I thought I was being a good son, being respectful, for obeying her. I should never have agreed to stay in Boston until the show opened. Plus, I should've known that she wouldn't tell you. She tried to shield us all, starting with not saying anything when she started feeling sick; then later not wanting us to interrupt our lives to be with her. I really wanted to believe she was going to get better, or at least hang on, until I got home. I know that she thought she was protecting us. But in the end, it wasn't that way at all." He cleared his throat. "I suppose as individuals, we all keep things pretty close, don't we? I'd like to try to talk more, as a family, about what's important. Seeing the counselor is helping. I've learned a lot about myself these past couple months." Tommy stopped to look out over the sea. He took a deep breath. "Sophia, hold on, will ya?" He called out. "It's too nice a night to be running by the cove without stopping for the view."

His sister turned to make her way back to them. James draped an arm over her shoulder. She turned slightly and pointed to the right, up over the edge of the cove. "Look, you can see the top of the big maple right before our driveway from here."

James squinted as if it would make him see better. "Sure can. You know, way back, before that maple and the other trees on the street weren't so tall, you could see my father's truck in the drive, or the roof of the bait shed if his truck wasn't there. That old house up there has been home to me my whole life, just like it is for the two of you. I remember coming back from being out, turning the corner here, and looking up to see if my father's truck was there so I'd know who was home. Now you can't even tell there's a house behind that tree." He hugged Sophia's shoulder lightly. "Things are always changing."

"Isn't that the truth," Tommy agreed. "What a pretty night. Let's go watch the water from the restaurant. It's early enough that we might snag a front table by the window."

Twenty Four

"Are you going out to haul tomorrow?" Sophia looked up at her father. She was sitting on the upper wharf, her legs dangling over the edge. They'd decided to walk down the path from the house after supper to enjoy the cooling evening. The lobster boats on their moorings dipped and swayed gently on the mostly calm water. Tonight there were two sailboats on moorings out past the working boats. The furled sails rigging clinked softly against their masts in time with the tide; a muted lullaby announcing the oncoming night. The eagles had been calling out to each other from the reach earlier, but there was no sign of them now.

"Nope. I've taken the time off while you're here. Work can wait. I just set new bait in about half the traps yesterday. They need to sit a while anyway."

"Oh. I was hoping to go out with you," Sophia allowed.

James smiled. "Well, why don't we take the *Lady* for a run-about and head over Bar Harbor way—scoot around the islands a bit as we go. I was thinking Saturday, but we can do tomorrow instead."

"Oh, I'd love that!" She looked up at her brother standing beside her. "Tommy will you come too?"

"Why not? It's been a long time since I've been out on the boat. It'll be fun."

"You sure, Son? I thought you didn't like the water much."

Tommy laughed. "No, Dad. That's not it. I love the sea and I like boating. I just don't like *working* on the water. When I was a kid it felt like you were hell-bent on making me a lobsterman. I respect your work, but it's not anything I ever wanted any part of."

"Well, I guess you're right about that. I thought I tried not to pressure you, but I did always figure you'd take the business up, like I did after my father. Your mom worked hard to get me to see I needed to let you find your own path. I had a rough time with that," James admitted. He gazed out at the boats. "You know, your mom was right. She usually was. Some do well generation-after-generation, but I've seen a few boys here take on with their father just because it was expected. Not much good comes of it. You have to have a passion for this way of life. Your mom always said the water has to be in you, or working it'll just make you miserable."

He turned to look at both of his children. "I know you understand what I'm trying to say, Bean."

Sophia nodded.

James scratched at his chin through his beard. "I'm thinking it's probably the same way with your art, Tommy. If it's in you, it's part of who you are as much as anything else that makes you. I think when you're lucky enough to know what makes you feel whole, and you're able to follow whatever that passion is that makes work not feel like work, then it's about the best thing there is. The only thing that makes it even better is when you have someone special to share it with. Someone who knows and understands you—who loves you for who you are—loves all of you." James swallowed hard. "Your mom, she was that for me. . .for all of us." He cleared his throat. "You know, I've had more time alone than I ever wanted, to think about a whole lot, over the past couple months. I need you both to know that all I really want is for you kids to have good lives; to be happy in whatever you choose. And I'm not at all disappointed you didn't take up fishing, Tommy. You're both doing so well. I'm more proud of you both than I could ever find words to tell."

"Thanks, Dad," Tommy said quietly. "That means more than you know. And I'd love to take a ride out tomorrow."

Sophia got to her feet. She hugged her father. "I love you, Dad. Tomorrow will be great. I just wish Mom was here." She looked down.

James saw a tear fall onto to the surface of the weather-smoothed wharf.

"Me too, Bean." James cleared his throat again, not trusting himself to say more.

"We'll always miss her," Tommy said quietly. "But she'd be so happy we're going out together. You know, thinking about it, Mom wasn't much for the boat. Was she, Dad? I remember her saying she'd rather be on the shore."

"That's true." James gazed out toward the *Salty Lady*. "Do you remember how your mom would come out on the punt with me and sit on a chair on deck while I cleaned and did my chores? She'd bring a book and sometimes a sketch pad while she kept me company. But she really feared the open water. It was fine as long as the boat was on her mooring, but that was about all she could do."

"Yeah, she always was super worried when we were out on the water. I got lectured for half-an-hour every night before I went out to haul with you." Sophia sniffed and wiped her nose on her sweatshirt sleeve. "I used to hate it, but now I'd give anything to hear one of those lectures again in the kitchen, while she made our lunches for the next day." She turned to James. "Say, Dad, do you have stuff at the house to take for lunches?"

"Probably more than we need," James said. "I went on a bit of a shopping spree earlier today. I even went over to the farmer's market and picked up some fresh veggies and home-baked bread for you."

"No way. You at the farmer's market?"

"Yup. And guess what? I ran into one of your old school friends, Justine Connor. I took her out to lunch. She's moved back to town with her daughter."

"Really?" Tommy said. "I knew we were both down in Boston, but I haven't seen or heard from her since she left town. Did she ever marry that guy?"

"I have no idea," James said. "But she's back and she's brought her youngster. There wasn't any mention of any husband. I got the distinct impression the two girls are on their own. I tried not to pry. It seems she's having a rough time of it right now, and I figured she doesn't need anyone poking around asking questions. Before I ran into Justine, I had actually met her daughter, Natasha, down here at the wharf. She's something, that kid. Kinda reminds me of you sometimes, Sophia. She's spunky as all get out."

"Our Sophia? Spunky? Come on. No way. More like a complete pain." Tommy grinned and gave his sister a slight poke in the ribs with his elbow.

"Ouch. You big jerk! You'll pay for that!"

"Gotta catch me first, Brat." Tommy took off at a lope toward the path to the house, Sophia hot on his heels.

James followed them in the failing light, grinning from ear to ear at their antics.

"Well, Anna Girl, our kids are home," he said, stopping to watch them run into the house. The screen door slammed. The light blinked on in the kitchen. He could hear the muted sounds of his children laughing and teasing each other. "And guess what? We're all going out for the day tomorrow. But I figure you already know that." He smiled, shook his head, then continued up the path. "In fact, I'm willing to bet you had this planned all along."

Twenty Five

"Cup of tea, Dad?" Tommy had the kettle going on the stove by the time James made it up the hill and into the kitchen.

"Sure, thanks, Son." James went to the pantry and opened the door.

"I've already got everything," Tommy said.

"Oh, I'm just getting Petunia's food. She's going to be wanting supper now." He closed the pantry door. On cue, James heard the soft thump of cat feet hitting the floor in the living room. Petunia sashayed into the kitchen a few seconds later. She wound herself in and out of James's feet as he poured the kibble into the bowl and opened the can of tuna to squeeze the juice onto the top.

"Geez, she's got you trained."

"Well, I'm just glad she came back. For a long time, I was sure I'd lost her for good. I had no idea where she was—still don't. But I kept putting food outside for her. One night she just showed up. We have a deal now. I keep her fed with her favorites, and she doesn't try to leave. At least, she hasn't yet." Petunia was waiting by the mat. James took the dish over, put it down, and patted her head as she dug in. "Isn't that right, Girl? We have a deal. We keep each other company now."

"More like she's sees the big 'S' on your forehead for 'Sucker.'"

"Hey now." James clutched at his chest, acting like he was wounded. "You're probably right," he admitted with a chuckle. "But that's fine by me. I've gotten pretty attached to her. She's what kinda kept me going for a good while. I had to get out of bed to look for her when she was missing. Then I had to keep putting food out in case she showed up. Now it's my job to make sure she gets what she needs every day. Funny, I hadn't thought of it before, but taking care of something else besides me, and having to go to work, were about the only things making me move some days."

"I get that," Tommy nodded. "If I hadn't been in the middle of setting up the new exhibition at work, and so busy I couldn't think, I know it would've been a lot worse for me. As it was I crashed pretty hard after opening night. That's when I knew I needed some help, or it was gonna be bad."

James studied his son's face. He took a breath. "Umm, do you want to talk about it, Son?"

Tommy shook his head. "No, Dad, but thanks for asking. I'm doing better, working through things. You know I was lucky a friend of mine saw how rough I was. He suggested someone I could go talk to."

"You mean your new counselor?" James asked. "And it helps?"

"Yes. And it does," Tommy reached over and slid the mugs closer together on the countertop. "I had a hard time even thinking about talking to a stranger about what was going on in my head. I guess I'm a bit like you that way. I hate talking to anyone about what I'm thinking or feeling. But it has really helped." He glanced over at Petunia who was still eating her supper. "I still feel guilty about not being here. I think I always will. Somehow I thought Mom would get better—that it wasn't that bad. I'd convinced myself that since she told me to stay in Boston at work that I was being a good son by respecting her wishes. I know she was worried about me leaving the middle of the project, since it was my first big assignment, but I should have been here. I should have come home no matter what she said. Family is what's important. Work will wait. I know that now." He took a deep breath and grimaced. "Truth is, I knew that then, too. It was just easier to immerse myself in work and convince myself that she would somehow get better." He rubbed his forehead with one hand. "Well, how's that for not wanting to talk about it?"

James closed the space between them in three strides. He hesitated for a split second and then reached out and pulled his son to him, hugging him hard. He stepped back, keeping his hands on Tommy's shoulders. "Look at me, Son."

Tommy's gaze met his father's.

"You did what your mom asked. You were respecting what she wanted. You know, she never told me she asked you to stay in Boston. I'll admit I couldn't figure out why you never came. But I could have called you myself and told you to come home. I should have called you. I was so caught up in my own grieving and suffering that I let you and Sophia try to navigate all by yourselves. I'm the one who should have been at the helm when your mom got sick. I feel like I failed all of you, especially your mom." James dropped his hands to his sides. His guts felt like they were unraveling, again. "She never said a word about not feeling well, and I was too wrapped up in other things to notice. What if . . . "

Tommy broke in. "Dad, listen to yourself. You can't blame yourself for any of it either. We need to pull together now, find a way to go on—as a family."

James smiled sadly at Tommy. "I know you're right about that. You know you sound a lot like her. She was so proud of you kids. She was thrilled with Sophia's decision to continue right on through to get her master's degree, and she couldn't have been happier about your education and career. I really think your mom was able to recover some of her lost dreams through your art and your work in Boston."

Tommy suddenly looked confused. "What do you mean, 'her lost dreams' . . .?"

Just then there was a startled shriek from down the hall.

"Dad. Help!" Sophia yelled.

James was already headed out of the kitchen toward the bathroom with Tommy barely a step behind him.

Sophia stood in the doorway wrapped up in a towel, a strange look on her face. She was holding onto a water faucet handle. They could hear water spraying against the wall of the bathroom while a puddle was growing behind her on the floor.

"Um, I broke the cold water in the shower. It just came off in my hand when I turned it on." The cold pool of water reached her bare feet. "Oh! Damn!" She started, and danced out into the hallway on her tiptoes. "And it's spraying everywhere!"

James chuckled, more at the look on Sophia's face than anything else. "Oh that," he said. "Well, it was ready to go. Let me get in there and shut the water off to the shower." He splashed into the wet room. "Tommy, grab me the Phillips head screwdriver from your mom's little toolbox. You know, the one she keeps in the hallway closet floor. I've got to unscrew this panel to get to the pipes."

"Got it."

In the couple minutes it took for James to get to the water supply and shutoff valve, the entire bathroom floor was flooded. The water was now trickling in a stream down the hallway. James tossed a bath towel to Tommy. "Here. Put that at the end of the stream so it doesn't go any further. The bathroom and hallway floor needed a good mopping anyway." He cocked his head to one side. "Boy, you sure can tell the old floors in this place aren't level."

Tommy rolled the towel up to catch the running water just as it reached the edge of the bedroom door.

Sophia had disappeared upstairs. Now she reappeared dressed in sweats and a sweatshirt.

"I was really looking forward to a hot shower." She shook her head. "I'll get the mop."

"I guess we'll be using the old tub until I can get to town." James observed. "The water is still on to it. You know," he added, "Your mom would be scolding me right now, telling me how she was right, yet again. She never let me update that ancient tub. It's been in here since the house was built. She said nothing newer could hold a candle to a good soak in that cast iron claw-foot. Not only that, she'd been after me for a while to put new fixtures in the shower."

"Well, she *was* right," Sophia said handing him the mop and bucket. "Tommy, grab me the laundry basket. Let's get these soggy bathmats into the wash machine."

"I would," Tommy said from the doorway of the laundry closet, "But the basket is full of clothes, and the washer is packed too."

"Oh, damn." James said. "Just dump that basket onto the couch. Then we can put the rugs in the basket to wash in a bit." He set the mop bucket down. "I'll start the washer now with that load that's in it."

"Don't you want me to just take the clean clothes into your room?" Tommy asked.

"Naw, it's OK. I'll take care of that later. Let's just get this mess cleaned up quick as we can, so your sister can get her bath."

Twenty Six

"Are you two slackers ready?" Sophia burst into the kitchen from outside. "I've already been down to the boat. She's loaded and ready to go. I made lunch for us and everything. Come on, it's a gorgeous morning, and you two are wasting it flapping your gums."

"Hmmph. Now she's the one sounding like Mom," Tommy remarked to James. He looked at his sister. "All right. All right. We're coming. We were just having our coffee."

"Well, bring it with you for God's sake. I'm ready to go."

"I've got to get a bite to eat, Soph. I can't be out there on an empty stomach," James said, taking another sip of his coffee. "There are some bagels and cream cheese in the fridge. Why don't we grab them to take with us?"

Sophia had the refrigerator open before James even finished his thought.

"I guess you are in a hurry," he said.

"Well, it's beautiful out there. Everyone left out to haul hours ago. I got up and started getting ready the minute I heard the first engine start up this morning. This is the first thing I've had to look forward to in months. I want to go before something happens, and we don't do it. I'm going back down to the boat." She headed out the kitchen door with their breakfast.

"I get it," Tommy agreed. "I'm right behind you. Ready, Dad?"

"Sure." James took the last slug out of his coffee mug, set it in the sink, and followed his children. Before he shut the interior door he turned to the cat, sitting beside her food bowl, grooming herself. "Guard the fort, Petunia. We'll be back this afternoon."

Tommy was waiting for him at the end of the walk. Sophia was way ahead of them on the path toward the harbor.

"Bean," James called after her, "I'm thinking since you've already done all the hard work anyway, I'll just let you take over today. If you've got the *Salty Lady* ready to go, you can captain her. I'll just come along for the ride. Sound good?"

Sophia stopped. She turned around beaming from ear to ear. "Really, Dad? I'd love to. Thanks."

"Sure you remember how to drive that thing?" Tommy asked winking at his dad.

His sister glared at him. "Shut up, Goober, or I'll dump you overboard first chance I get."

James laughed out loud. "You know she probably would."

"Maybe," Tommy agreed as they caught up to her. "But I'd give her hell first."

James rolled his eyes. "Damn, it's good to have you both home."

Sophia grinned. "Love you too, Dad. Now come on. You guys are sooo slow."

Twenty Seven

"Tommy, would you please take this up with you and tie her off?" James held up the coil of rope that was attached to the bow of the punt. "I think we'll tow her along today, just in case we want to take a side trip to one of the islands."

"Got it," Tommy said taking the rope from James.

Sophia was already up in the wheelhouse flipping switches and checking instruments; preparing to fire over the *Salty Lady's* engine. Tommy could hear her humming some tune between bouts of talking to herself, reciting some technical checklist from memory. Although he knew his sister was an adult now, her voice still sounded like when she was small, chanting jump rope rhymes outside on the driveway with her friends, as he sat at the kitchen table drawing in his sketchbook, keeping Mom company while she was cooking up some treat for them all.

"Time," he thought, "It keeps on, but somehow it circles back to you in sounds and sights, so that it never really goes anywhere." He shook his head to bring himself back to the present, climbed the four rungs up, secured the rope, then turned back to see if his father needed a hand up. He didn't. James was already stepping off the ladder onto the stern of the boat.

"Dad, I really want to talk more about what you mentioned about Mom a few minutes ago at the house."

"What's that?" James turned toward the wheelhouse, but he stopped to look back at Tommy.

"You know, what you said about Mom and 'lost dreams.'"

James looked up at the sky, studying clouds that weren't there. "Someday," he said after a few seconds. He looked back at Tommy. "Today, let's get this old girl out on the bay and enjoy a little running about. Days like this don't come along often enough. Today I just want to concentrate on having some fun with my kids. OK?"

James didn't wait for an answer as he moved up to the bow of the boat. "Do you have everything ready to fire her up, Bean?"

Tommy followed a few steps behind. He knew enough not to push. "Someday" was as good as a promise from his Dad, and it was the best he was going to get, at the moment. He stopped on the port side, a few feet from the wheelhouse, looking out over the water. A slight movement on the sparkling surface of the water caught his eye. About three feet away from the boat, a sleek brown head popped up out of the water like a buoy that had been dragged under and suddenly let go. A harbor seal held a slim, silvery fish firmly in its mouth. Long whiskers arched downward toward the water from the edges of a black, button-like nose. Two dark brown orbs stared up at him.

"Got yourself a mackerel breakfast, have you?" Tommy asked quietly, trying to hold the seal's gaze. He swore he saw a twinkle in its eyes before it ducked back down under the surface with its prize. Tommy watched for a moment to see if he could tell where it swam, but the surface was quiet and still, like nothing had ever been there.

"Did you say something, Tommy?"

"No, Soph. Well, actually, yes. I was just talking to a seal who is catching mackerel for breakfast."

James chuckled. "Plenty of them out here. He and any fish will be moving away from us in a second. Sophia's done all her checks and she's ready to start the engine."

Tommy wished they could just sit for a few more minutes, so he could watch for the seal. He wanted to see it again. He should've taken his phone out and snapped a picture. Why do you always think of that when it's too late? No. It was all right. It had been something just to look at the little bugger and have him look back right into him. That feeling was better than any picture would ever be able to show.

The boat's engine coughed, sputtered, and grumbled to its low thrum of life. Sophia laughed aloud. Tommy smiled at the joyful sound and the promise it held. He gazed back at the shore, at the wharf, the co-op, the neat rows of houses on the hill, and the church steeple just visible beyond the houses. It was a different perspective to see your hometown from out on the water.

James checked to be sure they were free from the mooring. He gave a thumbs-up to his daughter at the helm and moved over to stand beside her. Sophia opened the throttle slightly. As the *Salty Lady* started to slide out toward the open water, she turned and grinned up at her dad. He returned her smile and patted her on the back. She returned her attention to the water in front of them, moving the wheel slightly to the left maneuvering between a smattering of buoys marking lobster traps just outside the mouth of the harbor.

"That's it. Take her nice and easy," James said. "No need to be in any hurry today."

Twenty Eight

Natasha

This morning when I woke up it was one of those sparkly mornings where the ocean reflects the sky's bluest of sapphire blues, and diamonds shimmer all over the top of the water. Mom said when she was little, she pretended on days like this that the stars had fallen from the night sky to rest and float on the sea where they'd soak up the sunlight so they could shine bright again at night.

That sounded kind of funny. I asked her if she meant recharging, like rechargeable batteries. She laughed and said she'd never thought of it that way. She told me she'd imagined the stars just floated down from the sky before everyone woke up, so they'd be there on the ocean to sparkle and soak up the sun all day. I like that idea. Stars just floating down, kind of like snowflakes, would be soft and so pretty.

At first when she told me what she'd imagined, I thought about shooting stars falling into the ocean, but that would make a whole lot of splashing and commotion. Mom and I both know that there's really no such thing as a shooting star anyway. What we call shooting stars are really rocks or particles that come in contact with Earth's atmosphere as it orbits around the sun. Then there are meteor showers. Those are different than single shooting stars. I know because a meteorologist I saw on TV was talking about the best time to see the Perseid meteor shower. He said that the Perseids are bits of rock and ice that the comet Swift-Tuttle throws off from its tail. The Swift-Tuttle comet is the largest natural object in space that comes anywhere near us. The fact that the meteorologist said the comet is gigantic, and comes close, made me worry for a minute that it could hit Earth. But mom said that "close" still means light years away, and the comet could never hit us in a million bazillion years. She even Googled it to prove it to me, but I already believed her anyway. 'Cause, well, she's my mom and she'd never lie to me.

But it is neat to know that the comet hasn't passed close by us since nineteen ninety-two and it won't again until twenty-one twenty-six, because it takes one hundred thirty-three years for it to go around in its orbit. Then it will be fourteen point two million miles from Earth, so there really is no way it could hit us. The cool thing is that every time it comes by it leaves pieces of rock and ice behind. Some of the pieces are just as small as the smallest grain of sand. They're called space dust. When Earth passes really close to any single bit of a floating thing, that's what astronomers call "debris," it enters the earth's atmosphere, bursts into flame, and burns up. That's what everyone calls a falling star. When Earth passes through a whole cloud of the stuff, it burns up one right after the other, and we get a meteor shower.

I asked Mom why this one meteor shower is named the Perseids if it comes from the Swift-Tuttle comet. So, we looked that up too. The article we found said that a meteor shower is named after the constellation of stars that it seems to come from. They call that point "the radiant." The radiant for the Perseids is the constellation Perseus. This confused me because we just read that meteors don't come directly from stars or constellations. But I get that sometimes the way things get names, or get explained, don't make perfect sense. Mom said that science changes all the time as we get to know more and more. I wonder if the Perseid meteor shower got named before scientists knew about comets speeding through space leaving dust for the earth to run into. Mom told me I could look up more about it later on my tablet if I wanted.

She also said we could go out and look for the meteor shower. We tried twice, but we didn't see anything. It was cloudy one night.

The other time the moon was way too bright. Mom said we might have seen something on the clear night with a telescope even with the moon trying to outshine everything. But we don't have a telescope, so oh well. Earth passes through the Perseids debris every year in late summertime, so maybe next year I'll be able to see it. If we're still here.

I didn't have time to think about that any more this morning because I wanted to eat breakfast and get down to my beach. It was a perfect day to find treasures.

Mom was already at work. She gets up early to get to the farm on most days. When I asked Gran if I could go out, she told me to be careful and be back for lunch when I hear the fire station whistle blow in town. The old whistle blows one time at noon. Boy is it loud! I can hear it anywhere in town. I can even hear it like it's right beside me when I'm down at my beach. I guess it's good it's so loud though, because sometimes I get so busy riding around and seeing stuff that I forget that I need to go back to Gran's for lunch.

Today when I got down to the harbor there were only a couple boats left on their moorings in the cove. Mr. James's boat was just moving out past the tip of the reach. That was weird. He was awful late going out today. Usually, all the boats would be out fishing long before then. His skiff was tied up to the stern too, just bobbing along behind. That was different. I wondered if something had broken, so he hadn't left early like usual. Nothing looked like it was wrong though. I could see his sternman on the back of the boat, and I could hear the *Salty Lady's* engine humming right along while she was moving out to sea. I reminded myself to ask him about it next time I saw him.

When we first got here, I would wake up every time the boat engines started up out in the harbor before morning. Now I'm so used to it, I just sleep right through it. Mom says she'd really missed the early sounds of the fishermen going out, especially the rumble of the boats starting. She says the lobster boats' engines are the heartbeat of the working harbor, and each one sounds just a little bit different. I agree. It's like each one has its own voice. Mom says that after a while, if I pay close attention, I'll be able tell which boat belongs to which lobsterman just by the sound of its engine.

I can't do that yet. But I can always tell Mr. James's boat when I see it. It looks older than than a lot of the other ones. It's smaller, not as wide and flashy as some of the others. It sits different in the water too—lower. Plus, it's painted bright white with a sky-blue stripe all the way around it on the hull just below the deck rail. Then there's a smaller black stripe right underneath the blue one. The buoy on top of the wheelhouse is exactly the same colors as the stripes around his boat. It's mostly the blue with a thick black stripe all the way around the bottom part of the buoy head. His buoy colors make me think of the sky during the day and then at night. The only thing missing is some stars in the black night stripe, but they don't paint buoys with stuff like that except if someone makes an artsy one for the tourists to buy.

I was just getting off my bike to go walk down over the rocks when a bunch of people showed up in a van with a trailer full of different colored kayaks. They got out and started making a big fuss over getting ready to go out paddling, putting on their lifejackets, and jabbering at each other. It was like a circus of color and noisy voices, kind of like how the gulls sound when they are super excited about something out in the water or food someone dropped in the parking lot.

All the commotion made me feel anxious, and I didn't want anyone to watch me because they might see where my beach was. So, I decided to go ride my bike around town for a while. Then I could come back down later when it was all quiet again. I figured I'd try to get farther up Harbor Hill pedaling this time. The first time I tried to ride up the hill, I couldn't even push the pedals around twice before I had to stop. If I could get past the telephone pole by the only driveway on the way up the hill, I would beat my best run so far. I circled around the parking area a couple times to warm up and then started pedaling as hard as I could to get a running start. I wasn't even halfway to the top before I had to stand up on the pedals to keep moving them around at all. Then I couldn't push on them anymore, and I felt like I'd start going backward if I didn't get off.

After I put one foot on the ground, I had to stand there for a couple minutes just holding on to the handlebars until I caught my breath. My legs felt like rubber and were burning from pedaling so hard, but I made it past the telephone pole. It was only by a few feet. But I did it! I'm going to get all the way up that old hill someday. Just watch me.

Twenty Nine

"That's funny," James remarked as they walked up to the house later that evening.

"What?" Sophia asked.

"Bustah was supposed to go over to Gene's to pick up new bait bags, then to Austin's Marine for the order I called in. I didn't want him to not have any income while I was taking time off. There's plenty of boat chores that can be taken care of before we go out again next Wednesday. So I gave him some stuff to keep him busy. I left a check for him to take to Gene. It looks like he never came and got it." He stopped by the shed door and pulled out a white envelope that was stuck halfway in the door, right above the old latch. He opened it up. "Still here," he observed. He walked around to the back of the shed. "I told him just to leave everything here, and I'd get it ready so he could come back on Monday to get a few more things done. But . . ."

"Do you think he might have dropped off everything and someone took it?" Tommy asked.

"Stolen? Naw." James lifted his ball cap and swatted at a fly buzzing around by the corner of the shed. "Not that it couldn't happen," he added. "But, it looks like he didn't show up at all. Something must've come up. Could be he just decided to take the day off." James put his hat back on. He shook his head and frowned. "I wish he would've let me know, though. Gene was expecting him to get those bait bags, and I promised to pay for them today. I better run over there later."

"Dinner first," Tommy said holding up the five-gallon bucket full of lobsters he'd toted up from the boat. "I'll get the pot out so we can steam these bad boys up."

"Sounds like a plan," James agreed. "You both go on in. I'm gonna make a couple phone calls."

Tommy and Sophia were well into dinner preparation when James finally made it into the kitchen. Petunia was sitting by Sophia's feet as she shucked ears of sweet corn.

"Listen, you," Sophia was saying to Petunia. "You aren't getting any of this corn. Maybe you can have a bite of lobster later. Not that you need it. You're obviously not lacking in the grocery department, Miss Fatty."

"Hey, there's no need to insult my cat," James protested. "She's just well-loved that's all." Petunia was purring loudly while winding herself around James's legs.

Sophia laughed. "Look at her. I never would've thought you'd be a cat person, but she obviously has you wrapped around all four of her paws."

"I guess she does," James knelt to pet the cat running his hand all the way from the tip of her head to the end of her tail. She bumped her head against his hand for more. He gave her one more pat and stood up.

"Anything I can do to help?"

"I think we've got it. You have everything we need for an old-fashioned lobster dinner," Tommy replied as he picked up the ears of corn Sophia had laid on the edge of the sink. He placed them on the countertop by the stove where two large pots were warming. Steam was curling up over the largest one. He reached down into the five-gallon bucket on the floor to his right and grabbed a lobster. He carefully placed it in the steaming pot, adding two more before placing the lid on.

"All righty then. Twelve minutes and round one will be steamed and ready for consumption," Tommy announced. "Soph, if you'll make the salad, I'll cut the bread. The corn should be able go in anytime now. The water's just about boiling."

James's stomach growled.

"You get your calls made? Everything OK, Dad?" Tommy asked.

"Yes. Well, not entirely. But I'll make it work. Gene said just to come by in the morning for those bait bags. I'll run over to the marine supply then too. They'll be open until noon. But damn if I'm not down a sternman again." James frowned and shook his head. "He didn't even have the decency to give me any notice. Seems he's taken on as third man on a boat out of Milbridge that fishes year-round. I tried to call him twice. He didn't answer, so I sent a text. He finally responded telling me he wouldn't be back."

"Huh. That's a great way to get done. Just don't show up. No communication. No notice. No nothing." Sophia dropped an arload of greens and veggies onto the counter. Then she scooped up the corn husks from the sink. As she turned to put them in the trash, she almost tripped over Petunia. "Good Lord, Cat! Dad, feed this fat thing before I end up stepping all over her. She obviously thinks she's starving."

"Come on, Petunia," James said on his way to get the cat food. His stomach growled again. "You're certainly not starving, but you do like to eat. Just like me."

"So now you've got to look for a new sternman," Tommy observed.

"I don't know. Maybe."

"What do you mean, 'you don't know?'" Sophia stopped cutting a tomato in mid-slice and looked at her father. "You have to have help," she said. Her voice was a pitch or two higher than normal. "You can't go out hauling by yourself."

"I certainly can." James raised an eyebrow at her. 'There's no need to get all excited. It's a little slower going, but I can still do it. I'm not that old, young lady."

Sophia took a breath and exhaled. "That's not what I mean and you know it, Dad. I know you can. But you'd be the first to say that it's not a good idea for anyone to be out there all alone. It makes for super long, hard days no matter what. It's not safe. And here the season's just ramping up, too."

"One more reason why it'll be hard to find someone. There's a small pot to choose from this time of year, especially now the bigger boats are hiring on their third man. That leaves me with only the lowest fruit to pick from—if there's any at all." James shook his head. "Nope, I think I'm just going to go it alone for the rest of the season. I can do it for three months. Besides, it's not like I have to hurry home at night. I can do it."

"Hmph. You're the one who always says to 'work smarter, not harder.' I think it's a bad idea." Sophia went back to her tomato.

Listening to the exchange, Tommy had decided to stay quiet, busying himself with cooking. He knew better than to get in the way of any discussion that involved his father and working on the water, much less just questioning his judgment; even if Tommy agreed with his sister. Sophia always could get away with telling their dad what she thought. It was just the way it was. Plus, she knew all about what it was to be a lobsterman. She'd worked out on the boat since she was a kid, first as a third man, and then as sternman. She'd been eight years old the first time she convinced James to take her out with him to work. By the time she was ten she was out with him every chance she got and itching to be a captain. At sixteen she'd made it happen. After that, the sea, fishing, and the lobster trade were her world. She'd chosen a course of study at school so that she could ultimately work to make a difference sustaining the history, traditions, and future of the lobster industry that was at risk more and more each year.

"Four more minutes," Tommy announced.

"Great, I'm starving," James said. "Let's eat."

"Oh crap. I almost forgot the butter." Tommy opened the fridge door to grab it.

"Here, give it to me. I can at least do that," James said. "I know how to work the microwave really well."

Tommy knew that Sophia would have plenty more to say later about their father's idea to fish alone. But thank goodness, at least for now, it appeared the discussion was closed.

Thirty

"Dad," Sophia began. They were all sitting in the living room together after dinner. Sophia was curled up on the couch with her legs tucked to the side. Tommy was lounging on the other end, his stockinged feet extended in front of him, resting on the coffee table that doubled as a footstool. James was leaned back in his chair with his feet up. The TV was on to the Red Sox game, but the sound was low enough that they could easily talk to each other.

"Uh, oh," Tommy thought. "Here we go again over the sternman issue."

James must've thought the same thing because he frowned slightly. "Go ahead, Sophia. Out with it."

"Why are you sleeping on the couch and not in your room?"

James started. This was not the conversation he'd been expecting, nor one that he was prepared for. "What makes you think I'm sleeping on the couch?"

"Come on, Dad. I got up way before you guys this morning, and you were out cold in your pajamas. Besides that, your bedroom door is closed all the time. It hardly ever was closed when Mom was alive. And I haven't seen you go in there at all."

"Well," James cleared his throat. "I . . . I guess. . . ." He looked over Sophia's head at the wall behind the couch. He cleared his throat again and took a deep breath. "I just can't seem to make myself go in there since she's not here. I just can't do it." He stopped and looked helplessly at Tommy. "I just can't."

"It's OK, Dad. Really." Tommy said. "We don't need to talk about it. It's really none of our business." He looked over at his sister. "Right?" He asked her pointedly.

Sophia looked down and picked at an imaginary something on her leggings. "I'm sorry, Dad. I just wondered that's all."

Tommy saw a tear drop into her lap. "Oh, Soph. I'm sorry. I didn't mean to make you cry."

She sniffed. "It's fine. Really."

James left his chair to go to his daughter. He held out his hand. "Come here, Bean."

She wiped at her eyes with her sleeve and stood up. James wrapped her up in his arms. She was actively sobbing now.

Tommy had gone to find tissues. When he brought them James looked up into his son's eyes. They were full of unshed tears.

A flash of anger shot through James. His throat tightened. He felt the threat of tears in the back of his own eyes. It shouldn't be this way. It just wasn't fair—none of it was fair.

He squeezed Sophia, then stepped aside, keeping her in a loose one-armed embrace. He reached out toward Tommy at his other side and grasped his shoulder. "I miss her so much too," he said looking from one to the other. "But, it's going to be all right. I promise. It has to be."

Tommy held the tissue box out to Sophia. "I really am sorry, Soph. I didn't mean to sound so harsh."

"No, you're right." She shook her head and took a tissue, wiping her face, then grabbing another from the box to blow her nose. "What Dad does isn't any of my business. I know I can hardly stand to be in the house without Mom here. I can't imagine how it must be living here all the time. It was insensitive and stupid of me to ask what I did, Dad. I'm sorry."

James sighed again. "There's nothing to be sorry for. You didn't do anything wrong. I'm just stuck, I guess. I know at some point, we need to talk about all this and plan a memorial service." He took a breath. "I suppose tonight's as good a time as any to start."

Sophia sniffed again and wiped at her nose with the balled-up tissues she was holding. James hugged her to his side. He kissed the top of her head, then he released her. He looked directly at his daughter. "Bean, here's the thing. I'm not going to share the details of why I can't seem to go into my bedroom. Hell, I don't even want to think about it. This is all I can tell you. That room was your mom's and mine together, and I never, ever, wanted it to be just mine. I don't even know how to be me without us." He looked away, over the top of his daughter's head, and closed his eyes. He swallowed. "She was my whole life, and now . . ."

Sophia nodded. "I understand, Dad." Her voice was muted and small. "I really am sorry. I didn't mean to pry or anything." She shrugged. "I'm just trying to figure it all out I guess."

"I know. There's a lot to talk about. I've just been muddling through myself, and I know that's not right. It's damn hard to go on some days." James turned toward the kitchen. "I'm gonna get a cup of tea. Do either of you want anything?"

"Do you mind if I grab one your beers out of the fridge?" Tommy asked following his father.

"Go right ahead. That sounds like an even better idea. I'll join you. Bean? Do you want anything?"

"No, thanks. I'm good. Wait, on second thought, I'll have a beer too."

James stopped. "Well, why not? You're certainly legal. But I didn't know you like beer."

"I like white wine better, but a nice cold beer would be fine. Can I have it in a glass, please?"

When James handed Sophia her drink, he was shaking his head.

"What? I don't live in a closet. I do have a social life you know."

"It's not that at all," James said. "I just can't get over that I have two grown children, and I'm sitting in my living room having a beer with them. I must be getting old."

"Hardly," Tommy said. "You're what, fifty-eight now? That's not old at all."

"Sure doesn't feel like that some days." James took a swallow from his bottle. "Oh well, life goes on, doesn't it? Even when we're not paying attention."

"Especially when we're not paying attention." Tommy raised his beer in a salute toward his dad. "And then we have to deal with the fallout."

"So," Sophia said, "Where do we start?"

Thirty One

Natasha

Today was a library day! Finally. Mom, Gran, and I walked over. We went to Sand Cove first, then stopped at the library on the way back, because it wasn't open yet the first time we went by. On our way, Mom told me how the library used to be a chapel with just a little library space inside. We read about its history on a fancy plaque thing in the parking lot in front of it. To go inside, you have to go through the parking lot and around to the back of the building. You can't even see the door from the road. I didn't tell Mom I'd already read the plaque at least a dozen times because I stop to sit on the steps when the library's closed. Plus, she knows extra stuff about the library that isn't on the sign.

Once you get around to the back, there are trees and a little garden off to the side of three gray, granite steps that go up to the door. There's a small porch at the top of the steps, with square stone pillars on each side. It's a perfect place to sit and think. The heavy, old, wooden door makes a really cool sound when you open it—creaky—like how an author describes a groaning, ancient door in a book about a haunted house. Inside, the library is super small compared to other ones I've been in. I said that to the librarian who was sitting at the desk right when you go in the door. But it turns out she's not a librarian. She's a friend of Gran's from church who works as a volunteer library lady. What I said got me in trouble with Mom. She said I was being rude. I wasn't really. I was just telling the truth. But

I had to say sorry anyway. Then I told the lady that there's still plenty of books, and it smells just like a library should, so it was all good. She just smiled at me kind of weird, and asked if I was there to get a library card.

Well, yeah, that's why we came here. Plus, to check out books, I thought. But all I said out loud was "Yes, thank you," because I could tell Mom was already grumpy at me. That kind of made me grumpy at her, but I got over it pretty quick because the library lady said I could choose three books at a time to check out. And I could even come in myself without my mom or my gran when I wanted to return books and get more. She told us if there was ever a book that we wanted that wasn't there, as long as we weren't in a big hurry, they could get it on loan from any other library in the whole state. Whoever had the book in their library would send it here for us to borrow. So it's almost like the library is expandable to as big as we need. I imagined the walls of the library magically opening up and out, getting bigger until you couldn't see the tops or the ends of the stacks and stacks of books. That would be way cool if it really happened that way, but kind of overwhelming too. So, I guess it's good that it doesn't.

Anyway, in our tiny library, there's also a media center to look stuff up on a big desktop computer. But, best of all, besides the books, is that in the front, up two steps, where the chapel altar used to be, there's a cool reading room with comfy chairs, a little electric fireplace, and even a hot chocolate maker. There are stained glass windows all around it. The sun shining through them made patches of colors on the wall in different shapes that reminded me of a kaleidoscope I got to look through once. I could just stare at the cool shapes and colors all day, especially if they change when the sun moves across them. When I got home, I put "Cool Library Reading Room" on my *Good Things About Here* list.

I picked out three books: a field guide about the different kinds of sea life in the Eastern Atlantic Ocean, another one about trees in the northeast, and a novel from the young adult section that had a cool cover with a girl looking at the stars. I can't remember the title of that one right now. Sometimes I like to choose stories just because of what the cover looks like, without reading the synopsis thing on the back. Then it could be surprising when I read it, because I have an idea in my head what it might be about just because of the cover. But it might not be about anything I thought. Sometimes I get close though. Mostly, ones I choose that way are pretty good stories. If it's not, I just stop reading it and turn it in for a new one. Now that I can sit in a reading room when I'm at the library, I'll be able to start reading anything I want before I actually check it out. So I can see if I like it first. That's awesome.

The library lady looked over my head at my mom like I was nuts when I put the books I chose up on the desk. Mom told her that I'm a very advanced reader for my age, and I know what I'm allowed to read, so I could pick out any book I wanted, anytime. Just because I'm only almost ten and scrawny, people think I'm a baby and can't read anything except little kid books. Sometimes they treat me like I'm a dumb little kid. I'm used to it, but it still makes me mad. I'm not a baby. And I'm not stupid.

I'd gotten back into a great mood while I was looking at all the books and choosing. But the way the library lady looked at my mom made me all grumpy again, even though she smiled at me and told me she was glad to meet me and to come anytime. Gran didn't choose any books. She said she was just along for the walk. When Mom put her choices on the checkout desk, she told Gran and me we could go ahead outside to wait for her. I knew that Mom wanted to stay inside by herself, so she could tell the library lady to make sure anyone else that works there knows I'm allowed to come in and check out what I want. She did the same thing when we went to the school to register me, only I was there when she was telling them. It wouldn't have been any big deal for me to hear her tell the public library lady, but it's nice that she didn't want me to feel embarrassed.

School kind of gets it because they know there are other kids like me. Mom says sometimes it's hard for people to understand when others are different. I kinda get that. Still, no one needs to treat me like I'm some weirdo. Maybe they're the weird ones. Nobody ever thinks of it that way, though. It's always me.

On our way back to the house, Gran and Mom were talking about something the church was going to do with the library at some fall fair in September. It sounded boring to me, so I opened the book about sea life that was on the top of the stack I was carrying and tried to start reading. You know, it's hard to walk and read at the same time. I finally gave up because I kept tripping over bumps in the sidewalk and losing my place on the page.

We were about to turn down the street to Gran's house when I saw Mr. James coming up Main Street in his truck. His window was down and his arm was hanging out the side. He smiled and waved at us, but he didn't stop to talk. He must've been in a hurry to get home. That was OK with me because I didn't have time to talk with anyone. I wanted to get back to the house so I could start reading.

Thirty Two

James left a note for the kids on the counter in the kitchen the next morning.

Headed to Austin Marine, then to Gene's. If you want me to pick up anything while I'm out, text me. Back shortly. Love, Dad.

The night before turned out to be long, but good in the end. It had been awkward at first, all of them trying to think about somehow moving on without Anna, much less the idea of publicly saying goodbye.

"I think we're going about this all wrong," Tommy said. "My counselor told me that everyone mourns differently, in different ways. There's no playbook you're supposed to follow, or any rule that we should get over losing Mom after a certain time, because that's not ever going to happen."

"I'd say that's true." James rubbed the front of his forehead where a dull ache was threatening to become something more. "I know I'm never going to 'get over' it, as you say. I can't tell you how pissed off I get thinking anyone expects that would happen. It's like I'm supposed to just pick up and go on like every other day before she left. For me, her being gone is nothing like when others have died over the years. Not even close. Sometimes when I think of my mom and my grandmom, it physically saddens me that they're gone, but it feels more nostalgic than painful. Losing your mom, and way too soon, and so sudden . . ." James rubbed his forehead again. He closed his eyes. His gut felt hollowed out and his heart was physically sore.

"Are you all right, Dad?" Sophia started to rise to go to her father. He waved a hand at her.

"I'm fine. It just . . . hits me sometimes."

Sophia nodded, but she stayed perched on the edge of the couch, studying her father's face.

He smiled at her. "I'm fine, Bean. Really. It just hits hard sometimes. You know." James exhaled. He put the footrest down on his recliner and leaned forward. Forearms resting on his knees, he clasped his hands together. "Look, I know people think we should have some kind of service. But truth is, I don't know as I could even get through one. It seems . . . I don't know. So public and final."

Sophia looked down at the floor.

"Is that wrong of me?" James asked, concerned she was unhappy with his admission.

Sophia shook her head. She looked up at her father. Once again her eyes were too bright.

James's face prickled as frustration washed over him. "Oh, damn. I didn't mean to make you cry again. I shouldn't have said anything."

"No. No, Dad. It's fine. Really," Sophia protested, wiping a single tear from her cheek. "I totally get what you're saying. Really. It's just . . . hearing it out loud. You know, the 'public and final' part."

Tommy cleared his throat. "I really don't think we need to be concerned about what anyone else wants in the way of any service, or anything else," Tommy said. "I'm not saying they don't matter. I get Mom was a pillar here. She had so many friends who loved her, too. It's just that I think the most important thing is to figure out what we need ourselves, first individually, and then as a family, to heal and move forward. My counselor is always reminding me that grief is personal. No one else's expectations of what we should, or shouldn't, do is as important as honoring what we *need* to do as we process our personal loss. We all have different ways we cope. We need to respect that about each other."

"But, what about what Mom would want?" Sophia asked. "I think whatever her wishes were are important, too." She looked at her father. "Did she ever say what she'd like done when she died?"

James shook his head, "No, we never really talked about it. And we didn't ever get around to having wills written up. The only thing I know is that she didn't ever want to be buried in a box in the ground. The only reason I know that is because after a graveside service for a friend a few years back, she told me no one better ever put her dead body in a box that would just take up space for no good reason. She made me promise that wouldn't happen. She wanted to be cremated. She said we started as dust, and that's where she wanted to end."

James reached over to the end table beside his chair and picked up the beer bottle resting on the coaster there. He took a long drink.

"Speaking of that, where are Mom's ashes?" Tommy asked.

"Ummm," James looked down at the bottle he was holding. He studied the label. "I haven't gone to get them."

"What? Dad!" Sophia sputtered. "You didn't go get them? What if they've given her to someone else? Or worse, thrown her away?"

James looked up, eyes wide. "Jesus! I never thought of that. I just couldn't face that I should go pick up her ashes."

The horrified look on James's face was so out of character for his father that Tommy didn't know whether to feel bad for his father or to laugh at the absurdity of the conversation. "Oh stop. They're not going to do anything with them except store them. We can't be the first folks who took a long while to pick up loved one's ashes. But I do think we better go get them, sooner rather than later. I hate to think of her sitting on a dusty shelf in Bangor. I'm surprised they haven't called to remind you."

"The home phone," Sophia said, shaking her head, grinning. "I bet they only have the home phone number."

"And Dad ripped that out of the wall." Tommy took a sip of his beer in an effort to hide the laughter bubbling up out of him. He sputtered and coughed, almost choking.

Sophia giggled. "You all right there, Bro?"

"OK, So I'm an ass," James said. "Thanks for the reminder. Seriously, though, I just couldn't face going to get pick them up." He sighed. "I guess it was another way for me to pretend she isn't really gone."

They were all silent for a moment.

Tommy was the first to speak. "So first things first, we need to pick up Mom's ashes right away. I can call the crematorium tomorrow to see if we need an appointment. We can go over there together. Is that all right with you, Dad? There's no need for you to go alone."

James nodded. "I'd like that. Thanks. I still feel like a damn fool, though."

"Oh, Dad. It's fine. I just never thought you wouldn't have picked up her ashes. I figured you'd have it all taken care of. That was a childish assumption on my part." Sophia took a sip from her glass. She set it back down on the braided wool coaster on the coffee table, then leaned back on the couch, tucking her legs up under her. Petunia wandered in from the hallway, hopped up next to her, turned around twice and snuggled in. Sophia absently stroked the cat's back. "Now that we figured that part out, what about a service?"

"I don't think your mom would want any big to-do." James said. "She preferred to just *do* and not talk about it or be talked about. I think she'd tell us she never wanted to be on display."

"I'd agree with that," Tommy said. "But funerals aren't for the dead, they're for the people left behind. Mom would tell us to figure out what we want and make it happen. So, if we start there, maybe we can come up with something that works for all of us." He was turning the bottle he held around and around in his hands. "What do you think? You know, since COVID folks have been putting off or not even having services. I still say we don't need to worry about anyone else. It wouldn't seem too strange if we chose not to do anything publicly."

James was silent—thinking. He already knew what he wanted. Well, he knew what he didn't want. He also realized he needed to consider what his children needed. The trick was figuring out how to compromise. If Anna had been here, she'd have reminded him that compromising wasn't anything he'd ever been very good at.

"You don't think we should do anything." Sophia spoke up, while James was still wondering how to say something without making it feel like he was putting his foot down. She also sounded like she was about to get wound up.

"No, not necessarily," he said cautiously. "But I don't want to do something where I have to get all trussed up and go where everybody is crying and feeling sorry for us, hanging all over me telling me how awful it was that she got sick and died so fast, and how wonderful she was, and how much they miss her, and how awful it must be for me." He took a breath. "I know all that already. And I don't want her, and her cancer and death, being hashed out repeatedly by every person in town. I feel bad enough as it is. I don't need any help. On top of all that, I think she'd hate that. I know she'd hate it. She never was a person that liked to be in the spotlight. Not to mention, after all the hoopla, it's supposed to be over. Everyone goes on about their business just like that. Boom. Final. Done."

James glanced over at his daughter. She didn't look happy. But at least she it didn't seem like she was about to yell at him or jump off the couch and run off like she used to when she was a kid and things didn't go exactly the way she thought they should.

"Well, I think we have to do *something*," Sophia said, her voice just slightly louder than normal. "It doesn't seem right to just go on like she wasn't ever here."

"That's not what I'm saying at all," James protested.

Sophia reached up and ran a hand through her hair, catching a handful, holding it scrunched up on top of her head. "I know, Dad. I'm sorry. That came out wrong. I didn't mean it like that. I get what you're saying." She let go of her hair. She reached for her glass. "Really, I do. I also agree with Tommy that it kind of doesn't matter what people in town want. We just need to remember they'll have plenty to say if we don't at least have a memorial service, and most of it would be made-up gossipy bullshit, because that's how it is around here."

"I'm sure there's plenty of that already," James interjected. "They can yap all they want. Nothing can make me feel much worse than I do already." He fell silent again as a ragged gnawing at the hole in his gut took over.

"Well, I care," Sophia said firmly. "You know that kind of talk would hurt Mom a whole lot more than having folks come together to say goodbye and say nice things about her. I understand that you don't want a full-blown funeral and I can deal with that. But there has to be some kind of something to celebrate Mom's life." She looked over at her brother. "Tommy? What do you think? You haven't said anything about what you want."

Tommy shrugged. "I'm on the fence to be honest. On one hand I'm like Dad and don't want to feel like we're on display as we're navigating through losing Mom. But on the other, I do think that it's good for everyone to have a way to come together to celebrate her and say goodbye." He paused and leaned forward staring at the floor, then looked back up at them. "Maybe I'm not as ambivalent as I thought. There must be something we can do without the big formal service—something more casual where it's more like neighbors coming to visit to remember her. That way maybe you'd feel less on display, Dad. She was a huge part of the community whether she wanted to be singled out for that or not. I, for one, would love to hear what others remember about Mom. Sophia and I only know her as Mom. But she was a whole other person to so many in town—a much respected, well-loved person. I'd like to hear what her friends and neighbors remember of her."

James sighed. The bottom line was that he didn't want to hear all about Anna from anyone else. He wanted to be left alone with his memories. If everyone was in one place talking about her, he was afraid he'd fall apart and never recover. Or worse, they might call him out for not realizing something was wrong and not getting his wife the care she needed before it was too late.

It was this last thought that jolted James. He needed to do better. Here he was trying to hide. Anna would have been riding him up one side and down the other for wallowing in self-pity. "Get over your bad self," she'd have said.

James knew he needed to respect how his kids, and some others, felt too. It was past time. Anna had been an important part of many lives and that mattered. If people had things to say to him, about how he had or hadn't acted, that was something he'd just have to suck up and deal with. This wasn't all about him.

"I'm sorry. I'm being selfish. You both make good points. Let's figure out how to do this. But, please, no stuffy funeral or morose church memorial service. Whatever we come up with should be as informal and cheerful as we can make it. Your mom was all about keeping things simple and staying positive, no matter what. She'd want folks to remember her with smiles and good thoughts."

It suddenly occurred to James that Anna probably would like to know if people had nice things to say about her. "You know what? I say that your mom hated to be talked about or highlighted for things she did, but I don't think that's all true. She hated malicious gossip and big to-dos where folks bragged about all they accomplished. But I bet she would love to know that her friends admired her efforts and cared about her. As humble as she was, she still loved to know when she'd made a difference somewhere. I remember she always lit up when someone would thank her for doing even the simplest little thing for them. And she did a lot." James smiled. His distant eyes crinkled at the corners in genuine amusement. "Too much sometimes."

Tommy laughed. "Sounds like there's a story in there, Dad."

James chuckled. "Oh, I've got a few."

"You gonna share?" Sophia asked, teasingly.

James shook his head. "Not now. Maybe someday."

"Aww, come on, Dad. No fair."

"Oh, hell. Why not. You're both old enough to appreciate this. There was this one time . . ."

The rest of the evening passed with the three of them trading stories and memories. There were a few tears here and there, but mostly there were smiles and even some genuine laughter.

They never did get around to deciding what they should do about a memorial service before they headed to bed. But James felt like the weight of that decision had lightened since he'd been able to share some memories with the kids without the bottom dropping out from under him.

Thirty Three

James's friend Gene was sitting on his front deck in his faded white rocking chair when James pulled into his dooryard. He raised a hand in a casual wave as James climbed out of the truck and strode toward the older fisherman who'd been a part of his life since his first memories.

"Well, look what the cat drug in," Gene said. "You're looking none the worse for wear, I suppose."

James hopped up the three steps to the deck and stretched out his hand, giving Gene's a quick shake.

"You're looking fine too, Gene-O. What's news?"

"Eh, not much. Same old tune you know. It's mostly quiet around here. Just me and old George here." He nodded at the dog lying to the right of his chair; a scruffy golden retriever mix that looked about as old as his master. "We do fine most days. Don't we?" He reached down to pat his dog's head. He turned back to James. "Been a long while since you've come around, Boy. Not since your Anna got sick." Gene stood up. "Have a sit while I get more coffee." He snatched his mug off the table beside his chair. "I'll bring you a cup too. Then you can tell me all about what's going on down at the wharf."

James sat on the deck at the top of the steps and leaned against the railing. He looked around the tidy yard. Gene hadn't hauled for at least five years, but there were still about a dozen traps stacked neatly against the boat garage. He now worked repairing traps for folks and tying bait bags for orders like the one James had placed with him. He'd told James once that he missed being out on the water, but he'd gotten too old and slow to do the physical end of it all. James understood that all too well. Gene still worked hard. It was just different work. James only hoped he'd be as spry and sharp as Gene by the time he was his age.

The old timer pushed the wooden screen door open with one shoulder and stepped through it holding a steaming mug in each hand.

"Here ya go," he said, handing one down to James. "Camp coffee—black, boiling hot, and strong enough to stand a spoon up in."

"Finest kind," James replied. "Thanks."

"So, tell me what you hear at the wharf. I don't get down there much. It takes more energy than I care to use most days. You'd think I lived a whole town away instead of just the other side of the hill. Just lazy I guess," he mused.

James laughed. "I think 'lazy' is not a word that applies to you, my friend."

Gene shrugged. "It could. I don't move around as much as I did. Anyway, you back fishing full-time? I heard you were having some sternman issues a couple days back."

James chuckled. "You know more about what's happening down at the wharf than any of the rest of us. You see way more of folks than I do." James took a cautious sip of the steaming brew. "Ah. Good stuff." He raised the mug in salute. "You could tell *me* all about all the goings on. Especially the past couple months."

"Well, I have heard talk that you don't have much to say to anyone these days. I saw Malcolm Scott last week. He said you leave out early and come in late most days, and you don't give the time of day to most anyone." Gene paused and rocked back in his chair. "But I get that. I didn't want to have anything to do with anyone for a long while after my Gracie died."

James took another sip of coffee, hiding the brush of emotion that threatened. The brew was still too hot to take a good slug of it. He nodded. "It's true. I've been keeping mostly to myself. And, yes, I've lost my new sternman," he added. "Figures you'd know about that before I did. I'll tell you what. These darn kids don't seem to have any loyalty, and they're just after the quickest buck. He took on with Roger Jones as third man."

"Ayup, that's what I heard. Jones just took delivery of that brand-new Young Brother's forty-six he ordered last year. Now he's gotta pay for it. He's hot to haul every second he can. Price per pound don't come up though, he'll be in a world of hurt. He won't do much without good help either." Gene shook his head. "You're better off without that Bustah kid. Seems like he's one to go whichever way the wind moves him. Didn't he come up here from down south somewhere?"

"Mass," James said. "He's not much of a loss, to be honest. He showed up most days. That was about the best of it. Wasn't much he could do right."

"Now what? Not like there's any good sternmen available out there this time of the season."

James toyed with the mug perched on his knee. "Guess I'll be fishing on my own. Try to make it through to the end of the season without any loss. The price of bait and fuel is hitting me hard," he admitted.

"It's getting everyone, and there's no good reason for it. Damn politics and wars," Gene growled. "No one can make a decent living these days what with the government always sticking their nose in somehow. If it's not the manipulation of supply and prices, it's crazy regulations they want in place. Back in the day it was simpler. Our grandfathers knew what to do to keep things right—sustainable. They knew enough to set up reasonable regs to keep the bays healthy and thriving. Now big business has their say in everything. Mark my words, they're in it to drive us right out of the water so they can use the sea for their own interests. Big money. If you follow the trail, it all comes down to corporate greed in the end."

"Sure seems that way," James agreed. "It's like everyone else wants to use the Gulf for their own projects or agenda. Most of them have nothing that will benefit any of the local working folks, towns, or even our state. Just look back a few years ago at that proposed commercial fish farm at the old sardine plant. What a circus. It was all backed from foreign interests. Any real scientific studies show its byproducts would've kill most anything within fifty miles of it. Their own country kicked them out, so they came here.

"And don't get me started on what I think of wind turbines out there. The fact that anyone would think that's a good idea is beyond me. It seems to me the folks wanting to do these projects all cry about how we need to preserve the environment and all, but they only look at any aspect of it that suits them for profits and leave the rest of it out. You hear all about how these 'green energy solutions' are supposed to make things so much better for the planet. I'm all for that. Really I am. But I want to know, what about any collateral damage? You don't hear about that.

"My Sophia is studying all about this kind of stuff. She told me how those wind turbine blades up on the mountains are killing off eagles and osprey all the time. They also emit sounds that are harmful to other animals. But that end of things is buried away from public knowledge. Now they want to put those monstrosities in the bay. What about how that will affect not just our fishing grounds, but all the other sea creatures?" James paused just long enough to take a breath. "Anyone worth his salt knows everything out there depends on something else to survive and thrive. Fishermen with half a brain know that and respect that. We have the privilege of having a part in that too, as long as we do it right. The fact that we're hauling up record numbers of bugs is good evidence our sustainable fishing laws here in Maine work. Plus we change our regs and gear all the time to comply with good environmental practices. But there's those wingnuts who say we're killing off other marine life, like whales. And if you think that doesn't have everything to do with big business."

James was on a roll. He took another deep breath and kept on going. "Sometimes, I think big industries think up more crap just to drive us out, so they can run rampant out there. They think lobsterman don't care about the whole picture. They think we're just a bunch of backward numbnuts who can't do anything except bait a trap and bring it up; that all we care about is the money we make." James scowled. "Yeah, Buddy, there's sure a whole lot of money in what we do. No one takes into account all the costs we face, and that we only haul four or five months out of the year, if we're lucky. I'd like to see all that money they think I'm bankrolling. They'll find a way to spin what they want to do so it looks like they care about the the planet and all that, but they'll leave out any research or data that shows the downside and harm of their projects. They just do whatever to find a way to line their deep pockets even more. Seems like we're always having to defend our bay and our way of making a living from outside threats." James stopped. He took a long slug of coffee. He stared down into the mug. "Geez, sorry about that. I guess I got a little wound up. It's just that not much of it holds any logic in my mind. No common sense."

Gene chuckled. "Ayup. You get no argument from me. I sure hope that fish farm thing is dead for good now. It looks like the town acted just in time to get that moratorium for projects like that in place. Now they just have to make sure it sticks down the road. Seems like a lot of times we get a good head of steam up front, then it slows down when the initial threat is past. That's when the big money moves in again. And bam! All that work for nothing."

"Yup. I guess all we can do is keep on keeping on."

"I hope more young people like your Sophia come through. Old guys like me don't have what it takes to fight without young blood to carry on. Funny," Gene mused. "Seems like just yesterday us old geezers were saying how your generation would have to come forward and fight for fishing and our way of life. 'Young James and his friends will need to step up', we'd say. But now you're not getting any younger either."

James chuckled. "I'll give you that. Lately I feel a whole lot older than I used to. I'm not sure that many of the youngsters out there these days have the motivation, or understand what needs to be done. Hell, I don't think I even know what to do."

They fell silent, each with his own thoughts.

"How're you really holding up, James." Gene said after a minute. "I know it's not been easy on you."

James shrugged. He looked down at the dark pool of coffee in his mug. "I'm gaining. I think. It's a struggle. I can't seem to get out of my own way a lot of days."

Gene's chair creaked as he shifted. "Ayup. Not that it helps at all, but it was like that for me too, when Gracie passed. I mean, we were getting older, but I never figured she'd go before me. Then one morning—poof. I was all alone with just old George here." He reached down to pet his dog. "That stroke took her from me in the middle of the night. I didn't even get to say goodbye. It still hurts me just about every day."

"Does it get any less, Gene? The real pain? The kind that knocks you flat?"

Gene tipped is head to the side, then nodded once. "It does. Slowly. It's been over two years now though. I'll miss her the rest of my life. I never imagined I'd be here without her. We were married fifty-seven years. Fifty-seven. You know we got hitched when we were just kids —both of us eighteen. Then we never had children. Gracie and I always wanted a big family. Lord knows we tried. But we ended up just the two of us. Now I'm going to be seventy-seven next month, and she's been gone a while. I keep wondering if I'm gonna be stuck here alone forever." He gazed out over the grass. "I don't think I want to be here much longer. Ya know?"

James nodded. "I get it. I prayed every night for weeks after Anna left that God would take me too. But I still woke up every damn morning."

"It's good that you at least have your kids. I heard they're back in town."

James smiled. "I am lucky for that. They'll be home for the week. It's sure nice having them around. You know, with them both living away, I got so damn caught up in myself and losing Anna that I left them hanging out there in the wind for a good while. I just wish I'd done better for them right off."

Gene grunted. "Sometimes we can only do what we need to survive. You seem on track now. No use beating yourself up about it. You going to have a memorial service?"

"That seems to be the question of the hour," James said ruefully. "The kids and I decided last night we're going to do something. We're just not sure what or when. I guess we'll get that all worked out in the next couple days."

"Well, when you do, let me know. I'd like to pay my respects. My Gracie loved your Anna. She always felt bad that Anna didn't have her own parents. Gracie'd tell her she'd always hoped she'd have a daughter just like her. Anna was sweet as can be to us old folks. She stopped by about every week to spend an hour or two just to visit. She treated us like family. You know she and her friends up at the church took care to see that George and I wouldn't starve when Gracie passed. Later on, she came with Cora to help me box up and clean out all Gracie's things so they could be donated. I could never have done any of that on my own. She was one of the good ones, for sure."

"She was one of a kind," James agreed. He realized that while it hurt to acknowledge to someone else that Anna was gone, it didn't hurt as badly as he'd thought it would to hear Gene talk about her. In fact, he felt proud to know that his wife had meant that much to his friend and his wife.

The two men sat together a while more enjoying their coffee, catching up. After James drained his cup, he nodded toward the box on the porch marked, "James E." "I see those must be mine. I hate to run, but I best grab them and be getting on with my other chores. I wanna get back to spend the day with the kids." He fished the folded check made out to Gene out of his shirt pocket and reached over to hand it to him. Then he set his empty coffee cup down on the table beside his friend. George got up, padded around the front of Gene's chair and sniffed to see if there was anything in the mug that he wanted. The dog sat and laid his head on Gene's lap, looking dejected.

James chuckled at the dog. 'Sorry there, George. Nothing for you in there. Thanks for the coffee and the conversation, Gene-O. It's been awful good to see you."

"It's been nice. I'm glad your sternman didn't show. It meant I got to bend your ear a little. Now that you're getting out and about again, stop by. Coffee's always on, and I haven't had a decent game of chess with anyone for months. You still remember how to play, don'tcha?"

James laughed. "Oh, I think I can still remember how to beat you."

Gene raised an eyebrow. "Don't forget who taught you, youngster. A little respect."

"Yes, sir." James gave a mock salute before he bent over to pick up the box of bait bags. He hoisted it onto his shoulder and headed toward his truck. "Don't work too hard, Gene. I'll be back, and we'll have that game."

"I'm holding you to it." Gene called after him. "Stay safe out there."

James lifted the box over the tailgate into the bed of the truck. "I'll do it," James promised. "See ya soon."

Thirty Four

"Hey, Dad. Need some help?" Sophia came out into the dooryard as James exited the truck.

"Mornin,' Bean. There's not much to put away, but I'd love the company. I'll just get the bait bags into the shed. Then I'm going to take everything else down to the boat." James lowered the tailgate. He pulled the box out of the back. Sophia was two steps ahead of him, opening the the shed door.

James slid by her. "Thanks. What's your brother up to?"

"He went for a walk about half an hour ago. He said it's been a long time since he just wandered around town. Plus, he wanted to go down to the arts center to see what they might be exhibiting down there."

"Ah. Well, it's a nice morning for a walk for sure." James set the box on the recently cleaned off bottom shelf of the storage rack where he kept trap maintenance supplies. Then he closed up the shed and headed toward the truck. Sophia fell into step beside him.

"You know," James said. "It's too bad you both weren't here for the arts festival at the end of last month. Town was hopping while it was going on. I remember Tommy used to do something with that when he lived at home."

"Yeah, I think he did some work down there a few times. I thought it was just classes you could take to learn art stuff."

"Well, I don't know for sure, but there seemed to be a lot going on: concerts in the park, pop-up exhibit things, and the old schoolhouse where they hold their art classes was jam-packed every day for two weeks. You couldn't even find a place to park. The harbor master had to close off the road at the top of the hill because folks were trying to come down to the wharf to park. Anyone coming in off the boats in the afternoon couldn't get to their trucks to get home 'cause they were all hemmed in."

"Sounds like a circus. I bet you loved that."

"Yeah, you know I'm not a fan of the crowds for sure. And then there was the boat races and lobster festival. Lots of people in town." James shrugged. "The boat races are just one day. But the arts thing is two whole weeks with lots of coming and going. I steer clear of town those days. I take stuff down to the boat after everyone's gone for the day, and I walk down to go haul. When I come in I swing the boat over and unload at the co-op dock like everyone else. It's just easier."

James opened the truck door. Sophia went around to the passenger side and climbed in. She slammed the door.

"Whoa, kiddo. Take it easy with that door. This old girl likes a gentle touch. You don't need to be so rough."

"Oops. Sorry, Dad. I'm used to Mom's old beater. The driver's side door sticks sometimes. I usually have to slam it to get it to shut all the way."

"Hmmm. I better take a look at it the next time you drive it home. Sounds like it needs a little adjusting. Is she running OK?"

He put the truck in drive and pulled out onto the road.

"Oh yeah. Same as always. It's not like I drive much at school anyway. I can walk almost everywhere from our apartment. I haven't even put enough miles on her to get the oil changed lately."

"Do that every three months regardless. You know that."

"Yeah, I bet it's about time. I'll have to look at the sticker to see. I've just been way busy with trying to get my thesis project up and running. I have so much research. Now I need to wade through everything I have and find a narrow enough focus to present my position."

"Better you than me." James shook his head. "I never was the school-loving type. I'm glad you kids take after your mom that way. Education is important. I just never thought to go further than high school. Back then it didn't make sense anyway. I knew from the start

I'd fish my whole life. I remember telling my math teacher that I didn't need to know algebra because as long as I could do the figuring for bait, fuel, supplies, and how that stacked up against selling bugs, that was all I needed for math skills. Course it's not that simple at all, but you get my point."

Sophia laughed. "You must've been a teacher's nightmare, Dad."

James grinned. "I guess I could've been, some days."

He pulled into his usual parking spot. They both hopped out.

"Who owns that fancy rig?" Sophia pointed toward a long, sleek, black and chrome speedboat perched on a trailer, hitched to what looked like a spanking new, matching Ford Super Duty. All you saw was high gloss black and chrome.

"Bobby Mac's pup," James frowned.

"Riley? Really?"

"Yup. And don't get me started." James kicked at a stone in the parking lot, obviously disgusted. "More money in those shiny pieces of crap than in three, good old working boats."

"Is he still working sternman for his dad?"

"Supposedly."

"Supposedly? What's that mean?"

"Nothing," James grunted.

"Doesn't sound like 'nothing' to me."

"Some things are better left alone, Bean. None of our business. Let's get this stuff out on the boat. I've got a little tinkering to do on a few things before I take her out to haul again."

"Dad, about that."

"I know what you're going to say," James interrupted her. "But I don't know that I have any choice except to go it alone for the rest of the season. There just isn't any good help out there. And it's not like I can afford to pull my traps out early. I know some guys are talking of doing just that if costs continue to rise, but I don't have a bankroll to support not working for the next eight months. Without having to pay a sternman, I might can save a little. As long as I bring in even a slight profit, I'm going to haul. If I start just breaking even, I'll have no choice except to bring it all in."

Sophia held up her hands in surrender. "OK, OK. I get it. I do. I'm just worried about you hauling alone." She cleared her throat and looked down. "I don't want to lose both my parents in one year, all right?"

"Oh, Bean." James cringed. He'd gone and made her cry—again. "Please don't worry. I'm not going anywhere. I've gone out plenty, just myself. I won't be stupid about it. I'll be fine. I promise."

Sophia looked up at him, her blue eyes flashing in anger. She wasn't crying. In that instant, he saw fire like there had been in Anna's eyes the few times she'd been truly mad at him—hurt and accusing. It jolted James to his core.

"You can't make promises like that. You can't." She was almost growling. "So, don't even."

Then she turned on her heel and began marching up the hill. James watched her go, unable to move, not knowing what to do. She was nearly to the rise of the hill when a young girl went flying past her on a bike. Sophia didn't even seem to notice.

Thirty Five

Just before she got to James standing at the back of his truck, Natasha slammed her heels back on her bike pedals. The tires slid sideways. For a moment James thought that she was going to topple over, but Natasha placed one sparkly, tennis-shoed foot on the ground stopping the movement, keeping the other on the opposite pedal. She had a small denim backpack strapped to her back. She casually leaned over her handlebars and stared up at James.

"Hi," she said.

"Hi yourself," James replied absently. He glanced back to Harbor Road. Sophia was no longer in sight.

"Are you sick, Mr. James?"

Startled, James looked down at the youngster. "No, no. What makes you think that?"

"Your face is all red and you kinda look like you're gonna be sick." Natasha sat up straighter on her bike and grasped the handlebars like she was getting ready to ride off, or at the very least move quickly out of the way.

"Oh. No. I'm not sick," James said. "I'm just a little upset that's all."

Natasha eyed him suspiciously. "You sure? You still don't look like you feel so good. Like you might throw up or something."

"No. Really." James tried to smile down at her, but he only managed a brief grimace. He glanced at the crest of the hill again. The road was empty. He looked back down at Natasha who obviously was thinking he was not being truthful.

"Are you waiting for someone?"

James picked up his ball cap off his head. He brushed an imaginary speck off the bill. "No. Actually my daughter just left and walked up the road."

"Oh. Was that the lady I went by?" Natasha asked.

James nodded and put his cap back on.

"My mom said you had grown-up kids that were coming to visit you." She wrinkled up her nose and pursed her lips to one side, obviously thinking. "Aren't you happy they're here? You don't look happy."

"No. I'm thrilled they're here. It's just that . . .well, I just upset Sophia. That's my daughter," James offered. He was gazing over Natasha's head at the road as if he could will Sophia back into view. "We had a bit of an argument, and she got mad at me and left."

"Will she come back?"

"Oh, yes. She'll be back. She's likely just going for a walk. She'll be at the house when I get there."

"Are you sure?"

Natasha's voice sounded insistent, almost frantic to James. He looked down to see her stepping off her bike. She set it gently on the ground. She looked up at him her face serious, eyes searching. She truly was concerned.

"I'm sure," James said firmly. "She used to run off to be by herself all the time when she was a kid and got mad at her mother and me for something. She just needs some time, and a little space, to get over being upset. That's all. She'll be back, or at least she'll be home when I get there."

Natasha didn't say anything. She stood there eyeing him, her hands balled up into fists at her sides. "Not everyone comes back," she said flatly. "You don't know for sure she'll be there."

James could see she personally was angry and hurt. She looked like the first day he'd seen her, all coiled up, ready to fight. For the second time in less than ten minutes he didn't know what to do or say.

Natasha's gaze didn't waver. Either she was waiting for him to respond, or she was trying to decide if she should say anything else. Just as James opened his mouth again to tell her that everything would be fine, that she didn't need to worry about Sophia coming home, Natasha began to speak. Her voice was so soft at first that James had to turn his head slightly to hear her.

"I know all about this kind of thing because my father got mad at me, and he left, and he never came back. He said he was going to visit his parents in Sri Lanka. That's in a whole different country, you know," she added helpfully. "He told us that he had to go to take care of his father who got COVID. I didn't want him to go because . . .well, because I didn't want him to leave. We never got to go with him when he went away places. Sometimes he was gone for weeks and my mom was always so sad when he left for his trips." She paused barely long enough to take a breath. "I was always sad too, but not like my mom. She always got really, really quiet, and she cried a lot. But then he'd come back after a while, and she'd be happy again. Anyway, Mom and I got home from school that day, and his suitcases were in the kitchen. He was all ready to leave. My mom looked surprised like she didn't even know he was planning any trip. I got mad when he said he was leaving right away. I yelled at him and told him that it wasn't fair that he left and didn't ever take us with him like other families that went to visit people or go on vacation. I mean sometimes he went with us to do stuff in Boston, but we never went on trips with him, and he was gone a lot to other places. Mom said it was because of his working on his doctorate or doing research, or seeing his family that lived in Sri Lanka, and that it was too hard and too expensive to take us. Plus, I had to be in school. But I thought we should get to go with him at least sometimes, you know?"

James didn't have any idea what he should say. But that didn't matter because Natasha kept barreling on, not waiting for any answer. "Usually, he told Mom about his trips a while before he was leaving. But this time he was already packed. We didn't even know anything about it. When I got mad at him and yelled, he just looked at me, and then at my mom. He didn't say anything. Not anything! He picked up his suitcases, and he just left."

Natasha looked down at the ground. Her fists were still tight at her sides and her cheek moved like she was clenching and unclenching her teeth over and over. "Mom told me that night that the COVID thing was an emergency, and since people could die from it he wanted to get to his father as soon as possible. She said it was a long trip so he was in a hurry." She paused again, still staring at the ground. James thought her balled up fists were turning a lighter color than the rest of her arms from being clenched so tightly. He didn't know what to say—if he should say anything. He stood stock still, waiting.

She looked up at him, her eyes narrowed, angry. "He never came back. He left us and . . . Never. Came. Back. He called my mom and told her that he was staying in Sri Lanka for the rest of his life, and that he wasn't going to pay the bills in Boston anymore, and he didn't want us to come there. Ever."

"Oh." It was all James could manage. He still had no idea how else to respond, but Natasha kept on like he hadn't even spoken at all.

"Mom says none of it has anything to do with me getting mad and yelling at him. She says it has to do with a whole lot of things that I'm too young to understand. She says she knows now that he was never going to marry her, or stay in Boston after he finished college and got to be a doctor, but . . ." Natasha shook her head. "I know a lot more than she thinks I do. I know that she didn't plan on having any babies before she got married and that she dropped out of college when she had me—*because* she had me. Even though she says she wouldn't change any of it, I think she's just trying to make me feel better."

She took a deep breath. "But it's not better. It won't ever be better. I know my dad wasn't like a lot of other dads. We didn't always do much stuff together like my friends' dads, and he wasn't home a lot. But, I thought he loved us. Then he just left. At first he called and texted Mom. But he's never talked to me ever again. One day Mom tried to call his phone, but it didn't work anymore. She couldn't get hold of him any way she tried. It was like he just disappeared off the planet. Then Mom's job wasn't enough to pay for the bills anymore, and we had to leave most everything in Boston and come here to live in Gran's house so we wouldn't be homeless.

Gran is nice and all, but my grandfather is mean even if he mostly acts like we don't exist. He doesn't want us here. And now Mom works really hard at a farm instead of an office. She's tired and sad almost all the time. And I don't have any dad anymore—at all."

Natasha had finished her story. She unclenched her fists, rubbed the palms of her hands on her legs a couple times, then folded her arms over her stomach grasping an elbow in each hand, her already diminutive frame folding into itself. Then she dropped her arms and took a hesitant step toward James. She stopped, straightened her back, squared her shoulders, and moved until she stood directly in front of him.

"Mr. James." She looked up at his face. Her searching gaze cut right into him. She reached out hesitantly and touched his arm. "You have to go find her," she said earnestly. "You have to talk to her and make everything all right. I know that her mom just died. Now she doesn't have her, not like I still have my mom to take care of me. What if your daughter doesn't come back? Then she won't have you. And you won't have her either. That's too awful to even think about. I know because I worry about stuff like that all the time. I mean all the time. You have to go find her and make whatever it is right again." She dropped her hand from his arm. She took a deep breath and closed her eyes briefly. When she opened them, deep brown pools drilled into his own. "Please."

Thirty Six

Natasha

When we got back from the library, I was going to go up to my room to read, but then Mom and Gran decided they were going to do some deep cleaning thing in Mom's room. They were talking loud and laughing. There was all this thumping and bumping and scraping of furniture moving around. I couldn't even concentrate. Once the vacuuming started, forget it.

It was nice out anyway, so I thought I'd go outside on the porch to read. When I went down the little stairs from my room into Mom's room, she was dragging things out of the closet that goes along the whole side of the short wall. Mom said a lot of the old houses have closets like that along the knee wall. That seems like a funny thing to call a wall, but Mom told me it's named that because it's so short it barely comes above your knees. I told her it should be called a "hit your head wall" because whenever you get close to it you end up hitting your head on the ceiling where it slopes down to the top of the short wall. She laughed and said she could agree with that. I was glad to hear her laugh. It makes me feel happy.

She kept pulling things out, adding it all to a big pile of clothes, cardboard boxes, purses, and other stuff. She kept saying she couldn't believe all the crap that was in there. Gran said that she hadn't been in that closet since Mom left home.

There was a little blue jean backpack thing on the top of the pile. I asked Mom if I could have it. She said I could. She told me she used it when she was in high school. I told her I thought it would be great to put books in. That gave me the idea that I could wear the backpack with stuff in it while I ride my bike. So I asked if I could take my bike and go read by the water. I'd started reading *A Field Guide to North Atlantic Wildlife*. I thought maybe I would see some of the animals in the book down there. She thought about it for a minute and then said that was fine as long as I was smart and safe. She also reminded me to be super careful with the book, so it didn't get dirty, or worse, wet. I don't know why she told me that. She already knew I'd never let anything bad happen to a book. I know how to treat them right.

My new backpack is big enough to hold a couple books, but still small enough that it fits on my back. I slid the book into it. There was still plenty of space for other stuff. So, I had another idea. I went back up to my room and got my little drawing pad that's about as big as a paperback and my small box of colored pencils. I figured if I saw something down at my beach that was in the field guide I could draw my own picture of it and then write facts about it from the book on my illustration. There was still room for something else too, like lunch. I told Mom that and she agreed. So she went downstairs with me and made me a PBJ. Then she told me to grab some fruit snacks from the shelf in the pantry and a juice box. I asked if I could take some of the cookies Gran and I made yesterday too. Then I had a whole picnic lunch to go with me. Perfect.

Mom laughed at me again, but in the nicest way, because I was so excited about my book and a picnic. She hugged me tight and said it was good to see me going on an adventure. Then of course I had to hear the same old lecture I get every time she's home before I go out on my bike: be careful, remember to respect the water, don't get in anyone's way, yada, yada, yada. I promised. Then I got out of there fast before I had to hear it all again.

I pulled my bike out of the shed and headed straight for Harbor Hill Road. I was pedaling as fast as I could to get down there. I passed a lady who was walking up, but I didn't have time to wave at her or anything.

I love to go down the hill fast because it feels like I'm flying. At least I think that's how flying must feel. I have to be careful and slam my brakes on just right to stop when I get near the bottom though, because the road ends in the circular parking lot, and most of the time the lobstermens' trucks are parked in all the spaces that face the water. It wouldn't be good if I ended up hitting one of them, or worse, if one of them was backing out and hit me. I try to stop before I get to the first parking space, but sometimes I slide a little bit if I'm going super fast.

Today, Mr. James was standing behind his truck at the space where he usually parks. His parking spot is the one that is very first on the right side, next to the wharf. Mom says that the fishermen all have their own spots where they always park, and some of their dads and granddads parked for years and years in the same place. I asked if they're assigned, like how they assign lockers at school. She told me no, that it's just what they do. It's habit. I think they're like the eagles that way, they come back to the same spot all the time. I even park my bike the same place when I go down to my beach. I hide it off to the left behind the first couple big rocks that aren't right at the edge of the parking lot. I know it'll be safe there until I come back to get it. No one can see it unless they're right at it. Even if I climb up on the back of Black Whale and look back at where I hide it, I can barely see it between the rocks. So, I can check on it, too. Mom says no one would want it except me anyway because it's so old and beat up. But I love it, and I don't want it to disappear.

I didn't end up parking my bike, or going to my beach, or reading, or eating my lunch there, because I stopped in front of Mr. James to say "Hi" to him and that changed everything. He didn't look so good. When I asked him if he was OK, he said he'd had a disagreement with his daughter, that she was mad and had run off. I didn't even know what their argument was about, but all of a sudden I felt really upset and super anxious at the same time. Then I ended up telling Mr. James all about my dad leaving and why we came here and other stuff about Mom and Dad. I couldn't help it. It all just spilled right out.

Then I went and told him he had to go find his daughter right then and there, that he couldn't let her leave. I told him that I knew her mom had just died. I felt so worried that she wouldn't have any parents. Then she'd feel like I do a lot of the time, only worse because she wouldn't have anyone at all like I still have my mom. Then Mr. James would feel even more sad than he does because his daughter might be mad enough to never come back.

He didn't say a word to me after I said all that stuff. He just looked at me for a couple seconds, cleared his throat, got into his truck, and drove away.

Now I'm afraid Mr. James hates me and will never want to talk to me again because I had to open up my big, stupid mouth. And that's just awful because I really like him. I think he's about the nicest grownup I've ever met—next to my mom and maybe Gran. Even worse is that now I'm going to be in the most terrible trouble ever with my mom, because I told someone I only got to know a little while ago all kinds of personal stuff that I'm not supposed to talk about to anyone. But the very worst is that I disrespected a grownup by telling him what he should do—someone who is old enough to be my grandfather—a super nice old grandfather who knows way more than any dumb kid like me. I ruin everything.

Thirty Seven

James looked down at Natasha's earnest face. She had a point—a good one. Her anguish was palpable, raw, and beyond her years. She was right. He needed to go after Sophia.

He turned on his heel, got into the truck, and headed up the road to find his daughter.

At the very least he needed to apologize and make things right. But that wasn't all. He also needed to stop dismissing Sophia's arguments and concerns, and really listen to what she had to say. Her fears about him fishing alone, being out on the sea for long hours by himself, were real and practical. But he realized they were just the surface of other deep-seated fears she was dealing with. He saw now that he'd just been pushing her away when she tried to discuss options with him. He'd been treating her like she was still a little girl that didn't know what for— that he was the father who knew best, and what he decided was law.

For all his thinking that he should be there for his children more, and his trying to do the right thing, he was still acting like they were young kids. Both Thomas and Sophia were smart, able adults. He had to stop thinking of them as just his children. He should sit down and talk to Sophia, really listen to what she had to say, see if she had any ideas about how to approach the rest of the season. She knew the industry, most likely better than he in some ways, what with all her studying and research. She knew his boat, his fishing territory, and the ins and outs of every aspect of the business itself. He knew deep down that she was only trying to make sure he was working smart and staying safe.

James heard Anna's voice in a distant echo. "Stay safe, Love."

He shook his head. "I'm trying. But I'm still making a damn mess of things down here, Anna Girl," he muttered as he turned into the driveway. "Now I'm taking advice from a baby sea urchin. The worst thing is that she's right."

Tommy and Sophia were both sitting outside at the patio table. As he predicted, Sophia hadn't gone far. Her temper was a lot like her mother's. She'd lightning and thunder, but then the storm would pass quickly, and all would be fine. This time though, James wanted to talk about why they'd disagreed.

He'd hated it most times when Anna made him sit down and talk over things anytime they'd argued. He'd always wanted to just be done with it and go on. She said that if you didn't work out what the real problems were that started any issue in the first place, then they'd just fester and be worse the next time. There were a few instances over the years that they'd spent long hours working through things before going to bed. He had to admit she'd been right. There wasn't anything they hadn't worked through, even if it did take most of the day and night. As much as he hated it sometimes, she'd been big on communication.

Communication. Holy Hannah! He put the truck in park and smacked the steering wheel with his palm as he realized he'd left Natasha standing down at the wharf without even so much as a goodbye.

You're batting a thousand today, dumb ass. One more thing you'll have to go apologize for; later though.

James got out and walked straight over to the patio. "Mind if I join you?"

"Help yourself," Sophia said. "We were just thinking about some lunch."

James pulled out one of the wrought iron chairs. The harsh screech across the patio stones made him wince. He sat down. "Well, before that I need to talk to you."

Sophia glanced at her father. She didn't say anything. It was clear she was still simmering.

Tommy stood up. "I'll head in and see what I can rustle up for food. Any requests?"

"I'm not picky," Sophia said. "Thanks."

"Me either," James agreed. "Thank you, Son."

Tommy left them. James cleared his throat. "Bean, look at me, please."

Sophia looked over at him. She didn't look overly angry, but he could tell she still was frustrated.

"I'm sorry. I really am. I didn't mean to dismiss you and what you have to say like I have."

She raised both eyebrows at him. She still didn't say a word.

"God, sometimes you are so like your mom." He paused, trying to think of how to better say what he meant. "OK. So maybe what I said before is not all true. Maybe I did mean to shut you off like I did, but I didn't even think about it like that." James groaned and pushed his cap back as he rubbed his forehead with one hand. "Hell, I can't even say what I mean." Now he was feeling frustrated. "What I mean is that I didn't stop to think that you are not a kid anymore, and you might have some good suggestions that I haven't come up with on my own. I was just trying to take care of things myself and take care of us too. Does that make any sense?"

Sophia didn't blink. Then she leaned back, staring at the sky. She took a deep breath, exhaled, then looked over at her father. "I'm still mad at you, but I guess I can understand that. Dad, do you know how that makes me feel when you swat me away like some pesky bug?"

"I didn't mean to make you feel like that. I didn't," James insisted. "I didn't ever think of it that way. I'm just so used to making all the decisions about my business, the boat, myself. Your mom never got involved in any of it."

"That's because she wasn't a fisherman, or better, a fisherwoman. I am. And, have you even thought that it might be in my plans to be part of 'your business' as you say? This business has been in our family for five generations, right?"

James nodded and opened his mouth to speak. Sophia put her hand up.

"I'm not done, please." She leaned forward and put her hands on the table. "This is my business too. Unless you're planning on telling me I can't take it over when you're ready, because I'm a girl, or not good enough, or some stupid bullshit like that?"

"Whoa. Just a minute," James sputtered. He could feel his face flushing as his anger rose. "When did I ever say anything like that? You never told me you were interested in taking over someday. I thought you were going to get some fancy job where you worked at the upper levels of the industry, not out on the boat."

"Did you ever even ask me? Yes, I want to be working at a level that can help the industry as a whole, but I also want to fish and keep the family legacy alive." She sat back, eyes narrowed, waiting.

"I guess I never did ask," James admitted. "But all you ever talk about is what you're learning from all your research and all the book stuff."

"That's only part of it, Dad. That's some of my point. If we don't have real working lobstermen and women in the upper stratosphere of the industry, we're all going to be run right over by big interest groups. Or worse, we'll kill ourselves off by not leveraging all we can to keep the fisheries sustainable. I'm talking *all* the fisheries in the Gulf of Maine, not just lobstering." She leaned back again. "And here's the rest of it. I need to be out there. I love being a captain and a lobsterwoman more than anything. It's who I am. You should know this better than anyone else. I am your daughter, after all."

James smiled tenderly at his girl. "Ayup, you are." He paused to choose his words carefully. "I'm so sorry, Bean. I'm just having a rough time remembering that you're grown up now. I need to start listening to you instead of trying to tell you what I think all the time."

Sophia looked down at the table, then back up at James. "I'm sorry I lost my temper too, Dad. It seems like I'm pretty emotional these days. I could have tried to talk to you more reasonably. At least I'm not bawling my brains out *all* the time like I was when Mom first died."

"You don't need to apologize, Bean. It's all me. Let's just start over, OK? I assume you have some ideas about my sternman issue and what should be done about it?"

Sophia nodded and stood up. "I do, but first I think we should go rescue Tommy from the kitchen so he knows it's safe to be with both of us in the same room. Besides these chairs are darn uncomfortable without the cushions. Where are they? We looked in the shed, but didn't find them."

James grinned. "Well, that's a story I can tell you both about over lunch. I also have a couple other things I'd like to bounce off you and Tommy." He rose out the of the chair to walk to the house.

"Who's the little kid?" Sophia asked pointing to the end of the driveway. James could see Natasha's back. She was slowly pedaling away from them down the road toward town.

"That's Natasha, Justine Connor's little girl. They're living with Cora and Homer right now. She's something, that little one."

"Hmph," Sophia grunted. "I bet that's a picnic, living with old man Connor. But then, you get what you ask for. I hope her kid is smarter than she is."

"Just what's that supposed to mean?" James asked as they were walking toward the house.

"She was stupid enough to go and get knocked up right out of high school. Then she quit college and threw her future away for some idiot guy who obviously didn't care one way or the other for her in the end. She had a full scholarship to Boston College, and she just gave it up. There were other options. She chose to go with some fairytale idea of true love, having babies, and all that crap like it was the fifties. Now she's ended up back here with nothing to show for any of it." She frowned. "Except she's got a kid in tow, and she's brought her back here to live with her parents to go through the same exact crap she did as a kid. She hated her life at home. Now she's bringing up her kid in it. She needs to get it together—stand on her own two feet."

By now they were at the door to the kitchen. James reached for the handle. "That's awful harsh, Sophia. We don't have any idea about all the circumstances around Justine ending back up here or what her plans are. Even if we did, it's not on us to judge her for what she has, or hasn't done, or what she's going to do. That's her business."

Sophia tossed her head, flipping her long hair over her shoulder. "Well, I for one think that she gets what she deserves. Why would she even come back here?"

"Because she had nowhere else to go." Tommy turned around from making sandwiches at the counter. He had a tomato in his hand. "Dad's right. We don't know anything about her circumstances. But I can tell you this." He looked directly at his sister. "Justine is not any kind of stupid, and she's certainly not any 'shrinking violet' as Mom used to call it. She's got backbone; more than most of us have."

"You're just saying that because you had a thing for her in school." Sophia proclaimed.

"No, I'm not. It may be true I had a crush on her, but she never had any interest in me other than as a friend. You know as well as I do that she's damn smart. Hell, she was near the top of our class. She never would've gotten that scholarship to BC if she wasn't super bright."

"She may be book smart, but she's proven she has no common sense at all," Sophia protested.

Tommy shook his hand that held the tomato at his sister. "Listen, you can't say anything about her 'common sense.' You know what she had to put up with as a kid at home. Her father is a verbally, emotionally, abusive alcoholic. Justine's mom did her best to shelter her from old man Connor and get her the hell out of here," Tommy took a breath and shook his head, "Even if Mrs. Connor wouldn't, or couldn't, leave herself. None of us has a clue what it's like to be in an environment like that. Justine's a newly single parent and has become basically homeless. I'm pretty sure she came back as a last resort. At least that's how it seems."

Tommy looked at his father. James nodded, "That's true. Justine indicated that when we were at lunch the other day. I didn't pry for anything else. Now she's working her tail off while trying to find a place for the two of them to move into."

"Not one of us in this house knows anything at all about what they are going through over there." Tommy repeated. He turned back to the countertop and began slicing the tomato.

"Well, I do know that she was stupid enough to get knocked up and throw away her education. She had other choices!" Sophia insisted. "She at least should have known enough to prevent getting pregnant, even if she was dumb enough to think she was in love. She threw everything away. Now she'll never do anything worthwhile with her life since she has a kid. She couldn't even find a place on her own. She just ran back here."

James stared at his daughter. This was a side of her he'd not seen before, and he didn't like it.

Tommy turned back around, glaring at his sister. "Do you think that about Mom? That she didn't do anything worthwhile with her life because she had kids?"

"No, of course not!" Sophia's face flushed and she looked down. "But Mom chose to get married and then had kids. That's the way it was back then. You went to school, found someone, fell in love, got married and raised the family."

"You do know Mom left school when she married Dad, right?"

"Well yeah, but that was relatively common in those days. Besides, she was at college in New York. What was she supposed to do? Dad was established here, lobstering. It's not like he could move all that to New York City while Mom finished school. A lot of women started school back then. They quit when they fell in love and got married. After that they started their families. Many of them only went to college with the idea that that was where they would meet their future husband. It's completely different now. Besides, Mom never would have gotten herself in the circumstance Justine got herself into."

"You're being completely unreasonable," Tommy retorted.

"Now, hold on," James interrupted, firmly. He held up a hand. "Just stop. Both of you."

"But," Sophia tried to argue.

"Stop. I think there are a few things you both need to see. Lunch can wait. Come with me. I'll need help getting some things from the attic."

Thirty Eight

James led them upstairs. He stopped at the top of the tiny landing where you would either turn right to go into Tommy's room or left to go into Sophia's. Both of them stood on steps below the landing. James unlatched a framed wooden panel that was flush to the ceiling, exposing a hatch to the tiny attic above them. He pulled down on a strap on the front edge of a second hinged plywood cover. Ladder-like stairs unfolded until the bottom of them sat on the floor. He locked the hinges in the middle of it, then pushed against the center edges with both hands to make sure it was secure.

"As I remember, there's not a whole lot up here. We may as well pull it all out and go through it. There was something else I was thinking about the other day that I need to find up here, as well as what I'm after right now."

James climbed up the first couple steps. He looked back over his shoulder. "If you two stay down here, I'll hand things down to you. He went up the steep stairs until his waist was at the same height as the attic floor. He peered into the room.

"Sophia, would you please run down into the kitchen and grab the flashlight that's in the junk drawer by the stove? The light from this filthy old window isn't enough for me to see much by. I can't even tell where the string to the light is, not to mention, the bulb might be blown. It's been years since I've been up here."

"OK. Be right back."

"Dad, what are you after?" Tommy asked standing at the base of the attic ladder looking up.

"You'll see," James said his voice muffled. He was trying to make out what all was up in the dusky space. "Just let me get this stuff out of here where we can actually go through it."

"You sure you don't want me to go and hand things down to you instead of you crawling around up there?"

"Naw, I've got it. From what I can tell, I was right. There's not all that much up here—just a couple boxes and a big steamer trunk. That'll be the hardest to maneuver down."

Sophia was back with the light. She handed it to Tommy.

"Soph found your light. Here." Tommy held it up toward James in the opening. It was made of steel, about ten inches long. Originally painted red, silvery steel shown through the paint in the middle where hands had held it throughout the years. "This thing's heavy enough to be a weapon. How old is it anyway?"

"It was my dad's, if that tells you anything about its age," James replied as he leaned down and took the handoff from Tommy. "And you're right. It could be a weapon. These old steel flashlights were made to be a form of protection, too. Let's just hope its batteries are good."

He switched the flashlight on and moved the beam around the ceiling of the roughly eight-foot by eight-foot space until he located the cotton string hanging from the bare light bulb fixture near the middle of the room. He climbed the rest of the way into the attic and pulled the string. The light bulb flickered once, then glowed steady. "Well good. The light works. That helps. Now I can see a little better," he called out toward the hole he'd just come through. Tommy's head poked up in the opening.

"What's up there?" Sophia asked. "Let me see, Tommy. I've never even looked up in there."

"Well, there's the trunk and three cardboard boxes that I can see from here. And I think an old dress form," Tommy answered.

"Ayup, that was your grandmother's. She called her 'Matilda the Model.'" James went over to the first box near the far edge of the tiny room. "I'm going to get everything else first, then the trunk since it's back in the corner. If you go down to the bottom of the attic steps, Tommy, I'll slide stuff down to you. Then if you wouldn't mind, you and Sophia can ferry it right into the living room."

"Got it," Tommy said. "Ready when you are."

It only took a couple of minutes to get the few boxes over to the hatch and out of the attic. The trunk took a little longer, with more finagling, because it had to be slid, just so, in order to make it through the small opening before Tommy could guide it down the stairs. Within fifteen minutes, everything except the dress form was down in the living room.

"I'm just going to leave Miss Matilda up there," James said as he climbed down backwards from the attic. "I have no idea what to do with it anyway."

"Does anyone even use those things anymore?" Tommy asked. He helped his dad fold up the access stairs and lock the hatch in place. "I think tailoring your own clothes is kind of a lost art."

"Hmmm, maybe," James answered absently. He followed his son and daughter into the living room.

"What's in the boxes, Dad?" Sophia asked. "I knew there was an attic space, But I didn't know there was anything up there."

James raised an eyebrow at her. "I seriously doubt that. I can't imagine any kid that wouldn't be nosy enough to go up there and look around. I know I did."

Sophia laughed. "Oh, I'm not saying I didn't try a couple times. But I couldn't get the stair thing to pull down. I asked Mom what was up there and she said it was a dusty old room with storage and nothing I'd want to see. I guess that was good enough for me." She wiped a hand across the old trunk. "You know this thing isn't very dusty for being up there for years."

"I went up there a couple times," Tommy said. "Mom sent me to get the box of stuff for the church Christmas pageant. This one right here." He pointed to the larger box, marked 'Christmas Costumes - Church.' "I bet your Harold costume is still in there, Soph."

"Harold costume?" James asked.

"Yeah. You must remember, Dad. Sophia was about five or six and we were getting ready for the kids' play at the church. Mom was telling everyone what part of the Christmas story they would be. She told your bossy daughter here that she was going to be an angel. Soph got all huffy and said that the only way she'd be an angel was if she could be Harold. Mom couldn't figure out what she meant and was trying to reason with her. Sophia stomped her little foot and said, "You know, hark Harold the angel sings. I want to be Harold!" Everybody busted out laughing. After that, Mom told her she could certainly be Harold if she wanted."

James shook his head. "Damned if I don't remember. But I can see how it would've been, plain as day." He smiled at his daughter. "You always have known what you wanted. I do remember you were a cute little angel."

"Yeah, right," Tommy said drily. "I bet that costume is in that box. Mom even wrote, 'Harold the Angel' on the inside hem of it."

"It probably is," James agreed kneeling down in front of the trunk. "But right now, it's what I'm sure is still in here in this old trunk that I think you both need to see."

Thirty Nine

"Great. It's locked," James said. "It's an old skeleton key. I have no idea where it might be."

"I think I know where it is," Sophia said. Both men looked at her.

"Really?" James asked.

"Yeah, Mom kept old keys and other weird little bits of things in a mayonnaise jar in the pantry."

"She did?" James shook his head. "Well, then. Go get it, and let's see."

Sophia hadn't waited for her father to tell her to find the jar. She was already on her way. It took all of thirty seconds for her to reappear with it in hand. It was about three-quarters full of a jumble of small things. Sophia poured the contents out onto the coffee table. In among a couple glass marbles, a piece of pink granite shaped like a heart, some spare screws and old rubber bands, four antique skeleton keys held together with a black, bread twist-tie tumbled out.

"Let's hope one of these fits this lock because I'd really hate to pry it open and break it," James said. "This trunk was my grandfather's from when he was in the Navy during World War Two. I can't believe how good it still looks after all these years."

Sophia handed him the keys. She perched herself on the edge of the coffee table.

"I bet one does," she said. "What's in there anyway?"

"Give me a minute," James said. "You'll see."

Tommy kneeled on the floor next to his father. "Try the biggest one first," he suggested. "It looks like it's hardy enough to just fit the size of the keyhole."

James slid the key into the lock and turned. It clicked into place and easily unlocked the top. "That's funny," he said. "I don't think this trunk's been opened in over twenty-five years, but the lock turns like it was oiled yesterday."

He gently lowered the unlocked center latch, then reached to each side of the front, outer edges of the trunk, lifted the side latches and folded them down out of the way. He paused before opening the lid. He looked at both of his children.

"Now mind you, your mother had her reasons for not wanting anyone to see what's in here. I've respected her wishes all these years. But now," he looked directly at Sophia, "Hearing you talk the way you did a while ago," he shook his head. "Well, I just think if your mom had heard what you were saying she'd be the one opening it."

He lifted the lid. They all leaned over, peering inside. There was a tray with a package of sorts, wrapped in white tissue paper. James gently lifted it out and handed it to Sophia. "I think that you'll find the christening outfit in there that my mother made me. You and Tommy both wore it at your baptisms too. Just put it on the table for right now. We can look at it later. Here's the blanket that my mom knit that we brought both of you home from the hospital in," he said picking up the next tissue wrapped bundle. He handed that to Sophia, too.

Petunia wandered in and stood on her hind legs to investigate the trunk. She hopped up onto the tray.

"Oh no you don't." James scooped the cat up gently under her belly and placed her back on the floor. "You don't need to be shuffling around in there." Petunia swished her tail and waltzed toward the kitchen. "I swear, she always wants to get in any little space she can find, cat-sized or not."

He picked up a large manila envelope that had been beneath the tissue wrapped packages he'd already handed to Sophia. "Here it is," he said. He got up and went to sit on the middle cushion of the couch. "Both of you come on over here by me." He patted the cushions beside him. Once his children were settled on the couch, he turned the envelope over and unwound the string that held it closed. He reached in and slid out a handful of papers. Then he placed the envelope on his lap, laying the contents on top of it. "I'm going to show you something that I promised I would keep secret. I want you to promise me that you'll keep it in confidence too."

He looked to each of them for their agreement. "I mean it. I don't want this to go further than here. I made a solemn promise to your mom. I've always respected that vow. But I know that if she could, she'd be right here with me today to tell you all this. She would say it was necessary and the right time, and that's why I'm a going to share it with you."

"I understand, Dad," Tommy said. "I promise."

"I do too," Sophia agreed.

James took a deep breath. *I really do think you'd want me to do this, my Anna. I sure hope you'll forgive me if not.*

He picked up the papers he'd laid on top of the envelope. He looked at the top one and slid it to the back of the stack. He did the same with the second and third papers on the pile. Then he looked at the next document. He bent the top toward him to see the one beneath it. These were what he was looking for. He laid the pile back down on his lap so they all could see the paper on top. "Here. This is what I want to show you."

Both Tommy and Sophia leaned in to look at it.

"It's a birth certificate, "Sophia said. She looked up at her dad.

"That's right. Now take a good look at it," James said.

Tommy was already silently reading through the form. He glanced up at his father's face. "This certificate is for a son born almost exactly a year before me." He looked confused. "But you and Mom got married in September of that year. You'd only been married for about two months when he was born."

"That's right," James said. "Your mom was pregnant when we got married."

"Wait," Sophia said, "Tommy's birthday is actually a year earlier than he thinks?"

Both men stared at her.

"Are you nuts? No. It's not. Don't be numb," Tommy said. "Geez, Soph. Read the details. The baby's name was John Christian Edward, not Thomas James Edward, and his birthdate is fourteen months before me; not exactly a year before."

"Just a minute." Sophia held out a hand. "Can I please see it? It hurts my head to try to read sideways."

James handed her the certificate.

"We had an older brother? How? I mean, why weren't we supposed to know? What happened to him?"

Tommy picked up the next piece of paper from the pile in James's lap.

"Here's a death certificate dated the same day as the birth." He looked at James for a moment. "He was stillborn, wasn't he?" He asked quietly.

"Yes," James nodded. He was surprised to feel a soft wave of sadness cross through him. He cleared his throat. "He came way early. The doctors said there was no way he could've survived. You mom was just over five months along with him." He took the death certificate from Tommy's hand, looking it over. "She didn't even really look pregnant yet," he added. "Your grandmother and I were the only ones who knew."

"Mom was pregnant when you got married," Sophia murmured. She laid the paper down in her lap. She turned her head, looking out the window.

"But the baby wasn't yours, Dad. Was it?" Tommy searched his father's face.

"What?" Sophia choked out.

"No," James said shaking his head. "The baby wasn't mine. But that didn't matter one bit to me. I thought of him as my own as soon as I found out she was pregnant. I loved her beyond all else. To me that meant every bit of her, no matter what."

He looked over at his daughter. She was staring at him, obviously stunned.

"She was just a few weeks along when I met her," James began. "Of course, I didn't know it then. She'd met a guy at college, and they'd become a couple—of sorts. They were intimate, but weren't serious about each other. She ended up getting pregnant after a drunken party one night when their birth control method failed. Once she realized she was expecting and told him, he broke off the relationship and all but disappeared. That was that—for him. Your mom was left on her own trying to figure out what to do."

"What about her family? Weren't her parents still alive then? Didn't she tell them? How did she end up here? I don't understand why she never told us about him." Sophia obviously was thoroughly confused. She seemed a bit hurt too.

James held up a hand. "Just wait. I'm going to tell you the whole story," he said. "Now I don't want any interruptions or questions until I'm done. Then I'll answer anything you want to ask. Agreed?"

Forty

"Well? Are you both willing to let me get through the story without interruptions?"

"I can respect that, Dad. Go ahead," Tommy agreed.

"But," Sophia started.

"No buts, Bean. I mean it. I only want you to listen. Then you can ask or say whatever you want when I'm done."

Sophia studied her father's face for a moment. She sighed. "All right. I just can't believe this. But if that's what you want."

"That's what I want," James stated. He placed the pile of papers on the coffee table in front of him. He stood up and walked to the window that overlooked the side yard and Anna's now neglected flower garden.

It was wild with just-blooming, oriental lilies. A chorus of jumbled color combinations—yellows, pinks, whites, oranges, reds, even some dark purple, poked up straight and tall through tangles of green weeds, clover, and the ever-present thistle that also was in full bloom. The fluffy, brilliant fuchsia thistle heads swayed above the bell-shaped lilies like adorning crowns. Anna had loved the thistle out in a meadow, but continually fussed about it in her garden. No matter how much she pulled it out of her tended space, there was always more of the prickly plant poking its head up the next time she went out to weed. She never would have let it flower and go to seed like it was now.

Tommy and Sophia were silent, waiting.

"I hope you both know that the decisions your mom and I made were always with the best intentions," he began. "We never wanted to hide things from you. I'm sure that your mom would have told you both all about this herself someday; maybe if, or when, you married and had children."

James turned back around and crossed over to his chair. He sat down and rested his arms on the sides of the recliner. "Tommy, you asked me about your mom's dreams and wanted to know more about our lives before we met. I guess this will give you a little of that history too. So here goes." He cleared his throat.

"You both already know that your mom and I met when she came up here to Maine on vacation after her first year of college. Well," James smiled, his eyes distant. "She was the prettiest thing I'd ever laid eyes on. I think I fell for her the first second I saw her. She was standing on the wharf, watching when we came in from hauling that day. It looked like she was just taking it all in. You know, like she didn't really see any one thing. She looked like part of a living painting. She had on white pedal pushers and a navy-blue blouse, and her hair was floating back from her face with the breeze." He shook his head. "I can still see that picture in my head clear as if it was today. Anyway, she was a sight. I wasn't the only one who noticed her either. Pretty much every single, hot-blooded boy in town thought they wanted to get to know that girl. But by the time we were up on the dock, she'd disappeared. I almost thought I'd dreamed up what I saw. But that night there was a contra-dance, right up at what's now the arts center, and she was there with Cora Young —now Cora Connor—and Cora's cousin Pam, who lived down Portland way. Your mom and Pam were classmates in art school in New York City. Word was that they'd come up here to stay and work for the summer with Cora at The Dinette where she waitressed."

"Mom was a waitress once?" Sophia busted in. "Oops, sorry," she said when James raised an eyebrow at her.

He went on. "Well let me tell you, everyone wanted to partner with Anna at that dance, but she didn't even go out on the floor once. Cora and Pam introduced everyone to her. Boy, didn't we all crowd her when we first got there. It's a wonder she didn't run screaming from the building with all that attention. We all knew Pam already. You'll both remember her. She's been one of your mom's closer friends all these years. Pam's mom was a Young before she married and left. Pam and her brother Tim have come up here most every summer since they were kids. She's been back and forth quite a bit this season. She and her husband bought her grandparents' old place and have started to remodel it." James paused for a second. "Where was I? Oh, yeah. Well, we all knew Pam; had for years. She was engaged to some guy from New York City that summer. She had a big old diamond on her hand that I swear flashed bright enough it could rival the head light out at the island. She was clearly off-limits for anyone to date, but she still hung out and danced with the crowd. Your mom just watched everything from the sidelines, smiling and tapping her foot. Cora told us that your mom had a boyfriend in the city too, and the rest of us could just forget about her. But there was no ring on her hand, and I was bound and determined to get that girl. I just knew she was the one for me. Unfortunately, so did Homer Connor, but that part comes in a little later."

James took a breath and grinned. "Once I found out she was working at The Dinette, I made it my business to be there whenever I wasn't out to haul, for whatever meal Anna was waitressing, no matter what shift she was on. I about went broke buying food in there every day. I asked her out every time I saw her, and whenever I wasn't working, I would be 'just passing by' at the end of her shift to walk her home. The first few weeks she was here she turned me down for a date more times than I can count, but she did let me walk with her. We got to know each other pretty well on those walks. I was head-over-heels for her from the start. It became a private joke between us, my asking her out every day, but one day when I asked her to go to Ellsworth to the movies with me, she said she would. You could've blown me over like a feather. I had to stop and ask her to tell me she would again before I could believe it." He rubbed his beard absently for a couple seconds as the memories flooded back. "After that night we spent every second together that we could," he went on. "Because she was an artist I showed her all the most scenic points around the peninsula, took her out to see the lighthouse on the old Navy base, down to the rocks at the point to watch the waves, and anywhere else I could think of to make her fall in love with this place, and me. I'd decided I was going to marry that girl no matter what. I didn't care if she had some city boyfriend waiting for her back in New York or not. I had this idea that she could stay here and be an artist, that this was way better than any city.

"I told her a few days after our first real date that I loved her, and I hoped she felt the same for me. She didn't say a word. She just looked at me with those big mermaid eyes, all sad-like. I felt like I'd been sucker-punched because I thought she didn't feel anything for me like I did for her. She started to say something, but I stopped her because I didn't want to hear it. There didn't seem to be anything else to talk about, so I took her back to the Young's place.

"That night I figured I'd be a heartbroken bachelor the rest of my life. I couldn't even begin to think there'd ever be anyone else after falling in love with her."

He looked earnestly at both his children. "I hope that someday you both have someone you feel that way about. That you find love like I did, like I had, with your mom. And that they feel the same for you. I don't think there's anything that makes you more complete than finding that person that you can share every bit of your life with; every little bit, good or not."

James shook his head. "Anyway," he continued. "I didn't go to The Dinette the next day after my failed declaration, and I didn't go to walk her home. I just wallowed in self-pity." James grimaced. "And plenty of whiskey, too. Let me tell you, I think that was the worst time I ever tied one on. Cured me of wanting to drink booze much ever again." He cleared his throat. "Speaking of drinks, I need something. My throat's a little rough. Let me go get some water."

"I've got it," Sophia popped up off the couch. "You just keep talking."

"Thank you, Sweetie. I'll wait." James leaned his head back and closed his eyes.

Tommy was itching to ask his father some things, but he knew better than to say a word. Sophia was back in no time with a glass of water and two cans of soda.

"Here, Dad." James opened his eyes and took the glass from her. "Thank you, Bean."

She handed her brother one of the soda cans.

"Thanks," Tommy said.

"Sure." She sat back down and popped the top of the can she'd kept for herself. James took a long drink from the glass of water. He kept the glass in hand, resting it on his knee.

"So, to get on with it. After about three days of drunken misery and avoiding Anna, Cora shows up down at the dock with her cousin Pam one afternoon as I'm coming in off the boat. They tell me I have to go see Anna because she's a miserable mess and wants to talk with me, but she won't come see me herself. Remember, we didn't have cell phones, or texting, or any of that. You either called the land line where that person lived, or you went to see them in person. Or maybe you wrote a real letter. Usually, since it's such a small town, we'd just go over to each other's places if we had something to say. Well, I wasn't keen on seeing her, regardless. I'd already had my heart broken. I wasn't about to go through that humiliation again. Cora and Pam kept insisting that they knew Anna had feelings for me, but that she had this boyfriend in New York. They thought that was standing in the way of our being together. They figured they'd already convinced her that he should just be forgotten about, and now if I just went to see her she'd tell me how she really felt about me—about us." James shook his head ruefully. "I was a stubborn, proud cuss, back then."

Tommy almost choked trying not to laugh. He finally gave up. "Back then? OK, Dad."

James chuckled. "I'll give you that one, Son. I'll own it. Let me rephrase it. You both know I'm a stubborn, proud cuss, and I was then too. Better?"

Tommy grinned back at James. Sophia giggled.

"Well," James went on. "I told those two I wasn't ever going to talk to Anna again. She'd let me know without saying anything at all that she wasn't interested in being with me. I told them the only way I'd ever see her again was if I went to ask her to marry me, and that would be a cold day in hell. Then I left without another word and marched my happy ass up to continue drinking with the boys. Trouble was, by the time I got to the pub, I was thinking that I might really have a chance with Anna, and what if I didn't go talk with her? I'd never know. It didn't take me too long before I decided I was going to go see if she'd see me. And by God, if I did that, I was going to be good on what I'd told Cora and Pam. I was going to ask Anna to marry me." James stopped and took a deep breath. "And so that's what I did."

Sophia was holding her breath trying not to say anything. She couldn't stand it. "And then she said, 'yes'. Right?"

Tommy poked at his sister's leg. "Be quiet," he ordered.

James chuckled. "Not at first. It was almost dark by time I got to the Young's place. I banged on the door. Cora answered and went to get Anna. When your mom came to the door, I told her I that I had something to say. She came outside and we walked out into the yard. Cora and Pam were standing right inside the screen door, just waiting to see what was going to happen, I guess. I turned to face her, got down on my knee right there in the wet grass. I told her I loved her more than life, that I wanted to be with her forever, and would she please marry me? The way she looked down at me I could see that she really did care, maybe even really loved me like I did her. In that moment I was sure she was going to say 'yes' and that would be that. But then she shook her head no and started crying."

James turned the water glass resting on his leg around and around. "I remember I was so confused. And I felt like a damn fool—again. I could see that she felt the same about me as I did about her, but here she was crying, refusing my proposal. Then I felt terrible that she was so upset. So I stood up and held on to her and let her cry. I just let her cry it all out. When she was done, I told her that I would respect her answer, but I felt she at least owed me some explanation since it was plain as day she cared for me. Cora and Pam had long since disappeared back into the house; I guess after Anna had said no to me. At least we didn't have an audience anymore. I asked her if she wanted me to leave, but she said she wanted to go for a walk down to the cove, where we could have privacy. We didn't say anything on that walk. I just held her hand and waited."

He stopped turning the glass, picked it up, and took a long drink. He sat it down on the end table next to his chair, stretched his legs out in front of him, and leaned his head back. He stared at the ceiling. "I think that was one of the hardest things I've ever gone through, waiting for her to tell me why she wouldn't have me. When we got down to the cove, we went over and sat down on what we call 'our bench.' You know, the one right there to the right not far from the base of the path up to our house."

"Everyone knows that's your and Mom's bench," Tommy remarked. "The whole town."

"Shhh." Sophia glared at her brother.

"I guess that's true after all these years," James agreed. He lowered his gaze from the ceiling to look at his children. "Well, we sat down on our bench. She still wasn't talking. I was afraid if I said anything, she'd never give me any explanation at all. So I waited, just watching the water with her as the tide came in and the stars came out. I remember that the water was so calm that night. You could just barely hear the lapping of the tide against the wharf. The sky was clear as a bell. The stars popped out one by one, and you didn't even have to look up to see them because they were reflected in the water. I remember thinking that if you didn't know the stars were in the sky, you might have trouble figuring out if the water was reflecting the sky or the other way around. It was that clear and still . . . Well, after a few minutes, she finally started talking. The first thing she said was that she loved me too, but that she couldn't marry me even though she really wanted to. She said that after she told me what she had to say, I would never even want to admit I knew her. You can just imagine how much more that addled me. I promised her that would never happen, that I was sure nothing could change how I felt. She wouldn't even look at me. She'd tucked her hands under herself and sat looking at the ground for the longest time. I was starting to get frustrated, thinking that I should just get up and leave, because she was never going to tell me anything.

"Finally, she looked over at me. She said, 'I'm pregnant. I don't have a boyfriend back in New York like everyone thinks. At least not anymore and I was never in love with him anyway. I'm single, and I'm three months pregnant. And I'm going to keep the baby.'" James paused. "I still remember her exact words because it truly was the very last thing I'd ever expected to hear her say. She could've told me anything else; like that she was more in love with the boyfriend in New York, or that she wouldn't leave school, or even that she'd robbed a bank. The fact that she might be pregnant wasn't even on my radar of any reason she would give me for not wanting to marry me. I was trying to wrap my head around what she'd said, but she was still talking. She told me she loved me." There was a catch in James's voice. He cleared his throat and took a breath. "She told me that she loved me. She said that she'd never loved anyone else, but that I didn't want to marry her—that I deserved better."

Sophia and Tommy were silent, waiting for James to go on. Since they had found out about Anna's pregnancy before James started telling his story, her admission hadn't surprised them, but they both were thinking of how James and Anna must have felt that night.

Sophia was the first to say anything. "Wow," she whispered. "I can't even imagine."

James nodded. "I was so shocked that I couldn't even think what to say, or really what to think for that matter. Then your mom stood up and said, 'Now you know.' She also told me she'd decided that she was going to leave early to go back to the city. She said she couldn't stay any longer, trying to pretend everything was just fine. She told me that she was going to find a job and a place to live, to do what was right for her baby. I grabbed her hand when she turned around to walk away and I said, 'Not without me, you're not.' I'd realized while she was telling me she was going to leave that it didn't matter to me. I loved her, all of her, and that included any child whether it was mine or not. I just knew we were meant to be together."

"Did she finally say yes then?" Sophia asked.

"Not right away," James admitted. "But, after a few more tears and a lot of convincing I wore her down enough to get her to agree she didn't want to be without me as much as I couldn't see my life without her." He grinned. "By about midnight we'd started making plans for a small wedding."

Tommy leaned forward. "Dad, did you really mean what you said about you going to New York with her?"

"At that point, I would have," James replied. "I was young and head-over-heels. I'd have followed her anywhere. In the end, she really didn't have anything to go back to there since she was quitting school. Plus, she'd fallen in love with Maine just like I knew she would. She said she couldn't imagine tearing me away from here because I was as much a part of it as the sea is. Even then, she knew me better than I knew myself." His voice caught again. He swallowed. His chest felt tight and sore. He absently rubbed at it, trying to ease the ache.

Sophia cleared her throat, pretending to be interested in the soda can she was holding.

James shifted in his chair. "She was really worried about what folks in town would have to say once they figured out she was already expecting when we got married. I told her if that was the only thing they could find to talk about we were lucky. I'll admit that didn't help to make her feel any better. But in the end she agreed with me that it really didn't matter what anyone said, so long as we didn't let it get to us. She did make me promise that we would talk to your grandmother right away. She wanted to tell her everything. Even though they'd only met a couple weeks before, they'd hit it right off. She wanted to be honest with her. Your mom had so much respect for your gram. Over the years, she came to love her as if she was her own mother."

"What about Mom's parents?" Tommy asked. "Where were they?"

"They were at their home in Philadelphia. They were a huge part of the Philadelphia social scene. Her father was a high-powered corporate attorney, and her mother was a socialite who came from old money. Your mom went to private schools as a child. Then her parents sent her off to New York for art school. They hadn't been happy when she decided to come to Maine for the summer. The expectation was that she would go back to Philly to attend all the fancy parties and other social stuff. They told her if she decided to come up here for her summer vacation she'd be on her own. They basically forbade her to come. When she told them she was an adult and old enough to decide where she wanted to vacation, they cut her off. She was more than ready to break away though. She sold a couple paintings before the semester was over. That funded her trip up here. Then she took the job with Pam and Cora at the diner. That was the first, and last, paying job your mom ever had." James chuckled. "She wasn't that great a waitress either. She could forget your order between the table and kitchen and have to come back to ask again."

"I couldn't believe it when you said Mom waited tables," Sophia said. "I didn't know she ever worked. Besides taking care of us and home, I mean."

"That was no small task. I think that's more 'work' than most people who have some jobs ever do," James said.

"I know that," Sophia retorted. "I didn't mean it like she should have had another job. She worked her tail off twenty-four-seven for all of us. I just thought you never wanted her to work outside the house. She was so involved with us and did so much volunteer stuff I don't think she could have found the time."

"I never said a thing about working or not to her." James looked startled at the mere idea. "She could've done whatever she wanted. I never would have told her what she should do, or tried to stop her either." He gestured, hands out in front of him palms up. "Can either of you imagine me telling your mom what to do with her time?"

"Yeah. No," Tommy said firmly. "There would've been a mushroom cloud over the house if *anyone* did that; much less you."

"I'd say," James agreed. "She was in charge of our home and family right from the start. I have no complaints. Never did." James sighed.

Except that I was so comfortable I let you do too much, Anna Girl, and I didn't pay attention to what was really important. If only I'd seen you were sick—that something wasn't right. If . . .

"Dad? Dad?"

James realized Sophia was trying to ask him a question. He focused his eyes on his daughter. "Sorry. I got lost for a minute. What, Bean?"

"What happened next? Did mom call her parents? I know they didn't come to the wedding, because there are no pictures of them from then." She paused, thinking. "In fact, the only pictures I ever saw were of just the two of them and from before you got married. Mom told me that they were dead. But . . ."

"That's right. You were just a baby when they both died in a train accident while they were on vacation in Germany. I'll tell you what I know about that later, but let me get through this first." James leaned forward, both feet on the ground, his elbows resting on his thighs. He clasped his hands together. "Your mom told me that her parents would never give their blessing for her to marry a lobsterman. They had it in their heads that she was going to get her college degree and then come back to Philadelphia where she'd marry some young lawyer or doctor that ran in the same circles they did. She said that she was sure they already had a few candidates picked out, but that when she left for college she left with the intention of never going back to that life, not ever. She also said that if she told her parents she'd allowed herself to get pregnant they'd disown her completely, and she'd never hear from them again." James frowned and shook his head slightly. "I couldn't believe that would really be true. Later, after we had a family of our own, I couldn't imagine in a million years doing something to you kids like what they did to your mom—to slam the door and pretend your child never existed. Unbelievable. Anyway, I still thought we should at least call them to let them know we wanted to get married. I thought that while they may not approve completely of her choice of a husband, I was a good person. I had a decent income. I even owned my own business. I convinced her that we should call them, but I agreed that we would just tell them we wanted to get married. We'd leave the part about her expecting a baby out of it, for a little while anyway. I foolishly thought that because we were in love, everyone would be happy we found each other."

"You're an old romantic at heart, Dad. Mom was too. There's no fault in that," Tommy said. "I believe we need more of that old fashioned, 'love can conquer all,' ideal in the world."

"Well, that wasn't at all how your mom's parents saw it. When I finally convinced Anna that she should call them, it was awful. Once she got them on the phone she didn't even get the word, 'hello' out of her mouth before her father started lecturing. The first thing he said was that if she had come to her senses, he'd get a plane ticket for her that night to fly to Philadelphia, that she was never to pull a stunt like she had again—meaning going against their wishes, taking off somewhere they didn't want her to go. Then he said that for the remainder of her schooling she would be getting only a small allowance for expenses. Anything she thought she wanted to get, or do, above that would have to be personally approved by him until she graduated, returned to Philadelphia, and 'settled down.'"

"What was that supposed to mean?" Sophia asked.

"I bet it meant when she married whoever they deemed an appropriate keeper for her," Tommy answered.

James nodded. "That's what we figured too. Now mind you, she hadn't even been able to say a word yet. When he finally stopped his tirade your mom was right worked up. Those eyes of hers were flashing and her chin was set, and I just knew the rest of the conversation was going to be bad. She didn't let him start in again. She told him she was an adult, that it was time he listened to her. She was having a wonderful summer in Maine. She had a job. She'd fallen in love, and she was getting married. She wouldn't be going back to New York to school and would never move back to Philadelphia. She was staying right where she was. There wasn't a thing he could do about it and by the way, she was having a baby, too!"

"Oh boy," Tommy remarked. "I bet that was just the beginning."

"Ayup. Then the yelling started on the other end. Both her parents were on the line, and her mother started screaming at your mom. And I do mean screaming. That woman said some of the most hateful things I've ever heard come out of anyone's mouth. I still can't believe a mother would say what she did to her daughter—her only child. I could hear every word like the woman was standing right next to me, and I wasn't even the one holding the phone. I wanted to grab that receiver and give those awful people some of what they were dishing out, but your mom had a death grip on it. Besides, I knew that this was her fight. I had to let her handle it. She was so angry her face was the palest I've ever seen, before or since. She was shaking all over. Her mother yelled that she'd never see them, or anything from them, ever again. But she didn't stop there. She screeched that your mom was dead to them, and she wished she'd never had her. That was the moment your mom took the phone away from her ear, quietly hung it up, and walked out of the house."

Sophia and Tommy were both staring at James.

"Oh my God!" Sophia gasped. "I can't even. Poor Mom!"

Forty One

"Wow. Just wow." Tommy looked at his dad. "So, that was the end of her family to her wasn't it? We know Mom was an only child. She told us her parents had no siblings either, and that all her grandparents died when she was a young girl. She had no one. No one except you."

James nodded, "That's right. Me and my mom, my grandmother, and then you two. She made me promise after that awful call that I would never bring up her parents ever again, not a single word."

"You never even met them, did you?" Sophia asked.

"Nope. Never spoke to them either. God knows, I wouldn't have been able to be trusted if I had." James absently cracked his knuckles. "I did what your mom asked. She would say something about them every so often, mostly when you kids asked questions. I just left it to her to handle as she saw fit. Your mom poured every ounce of everything she had into this family—into our community, too. She was the most kind, giving, and forgiving person I've ever met; probably ever will meet. That was just who she was, inside and out. I think that she never wanted to be anything like her parents, so much so that she worked hard to be the complete opposite in every way." James's voice trailed off. He closed his eyes for a second. When he opened them, he looked toward the window, out at the sky. "She wasn't perfect. I'm not saying that. Her temper was fiery enough to burn a dragon's ass. But she always tried to put others first, especially the three of us. She loved with every single bit of her whole heart. There will never, ever be anyone like her. Never."

They all were silent.

Sophia broke the stillness. "We should all try to be more like her." She put a hand to her forehead and closed her eyes. "I feel awful. Mom would be so ashamed of me for what I said earlier about Justine. She always taught us not to judge other people because we never knew what they might be going though. Not to mention, it's none of my business." She sighed and opened her eyes to look at her father.

"I understand why you wanted to tell us about this now. But I don't get why it was such a big secret. What happened? I mean with the baby. I know all about your wedding because Mom loved to tell us the story of how you got married down at the cove, and how Gram and Great-Gram cooked up a huge reception, and just about everyone in town came to the party. But what happened after that?"

"Well," James began again. "There was talk because we got married just three weeks after we got engaged. Of course, I wanted to marry right away anyway, and your gram was all about protecting your mom and her reputation the minute we told her the whole story. She'd already fallen in love with your mom, too. She told me that she knew the day I introduced the two of them that Anna was the one for me. I think she knew we loved each other before either of us did." He rubbed his cheek. "My mom was like that. She knew about things way before anyone else." James paused.

"Dad? Then what?" Sophia prodded.

"Oh, right. Sorry. There were rumors that your mom was a runaway. And there was one that she was an orphan and another that she was some rich kid who had been disinherited. And of course, there was talk that she and I had been sleeping together from the first. And that she was pregnant, so we had to get married. There was all kinds of speculation. But we just kept 'smiling and waving' as your mom would say."

Tommy laughed. "That was one of her favorite sayings. I have to admit I use it all the time. In fact, I say it so much at work that a couple of my co-workers just do the beauty-queen wave now when we come up against an issue we need to plow through."

James laughed. "I can see your mom doing that wave thing to remind me to just keep on moving along. She didn't have to say a word."

"Come on. I want to hear the story," Sophia complained. "No more interruptions, Tommy."

"All right, all right. Sorry." Tommy held his hands up in mock surrender. "I do too, Soph. It was just so clear in my head just now, Mom saying that. Go ahead, Dad."

"It's fine. There's not much else to tell. It's good to know that you both carry things that your mom taught you through your own lives. She would laugh to know that about you and your buddies at work, Tommy."

"But what happened then?" Sophia insisted.

"I'm getting there. Like I said, we just ignored all the rumors as we started our married life. I'd been living in the old studio apartment above the garage for a couple years. It wasn't much. You know, just three rooms. But it was fine for two newlyweds. Your mom didn't have many belongings to add other than what she'd brought up here for the summer. When Pam went back down to the city, she packed up what little your mom had left there and sent it on up. As far as anything from her childhood, there was no getting any of that. Your mom didn't seem to want any bit of it anyway. Of course, your gram knew Anna was expecting, but we never told another soul. Not even Cora or Pam suspected. As far as I know they never found out. We figured once the baby came we'd just say he was early, and let folks think exactly what they'd been saying about us sleeping together right from the start. It was the nineties, after all. It wasn't like that was any big deal. Some folks around here changed partners like they changed their socks." James frowned slightly. "Still do as a matter of fact." He backhanded the air like he was swatting at a pesky bug. "Anyway, we knew the talk would pass. It wouldn't matter after a bit. No one ever had to suspect that she'd come up here already pregnant."

"Wasn't she showing at all?" Sophia asked.

James shook his head. "Not really. She was a tiny thing, but she was really fit. Your gram told us that since this was the first baby she wouldn't really start to look pregnant until the last three months. That was true. You couldn't tell a thing when we got married. Plus, a lot of the time, she wore these loose little sundresses that just fell from her shoulders. They hid a whole lot. She'd just started to fill out a bit, and maybe look like she might be expecting, a couple weeks before we lost him."

James looked down. He clasped hands again and pressed his thumbs against each other. "I'll never forget that night. It was one of the scariest times of my life. Your mom hadn't felt great during the day. She'd never had any kind of morning sickness to speak of or anything like that, but every once in a while she'd feel tired and a little off. She'd felt like that all day, except she was a whole lot more tired than usual. She'd gone to bed early. I'd stayed in the house here with your gram and great gram to have supper and talk a while. When I went up to our apartment later that evening it was dark, and the lights weren't on. I didn't turn on any right away because I didn't want to wake her. But then I heard her crying in the bathroom. I went over to the door. She wouldn't tell me what was wrong, and she wouldn't let me in. She asked me to go get my mom. So, I did. I flipped on the light as I was headed back out. That's when I looked over at our bed and saw there was blood on the sheet on her side. I knew right away what was happening. I about fell down those stairs to get your gram. We got her in to the emergency room in town as fast as we could. She was having a contraction every few minutes by the time they saw her. They did an ultrasound. They couldn't find the baby's heartbeat. The doctor said that the only thing they could do was to let the baby come."

James closed his eyes and rubbed his forehead. "She was in so much pain, and it seemed to me like there was so much blood. The doctor said I couldn't go with her in case they needed to do surgery. Then they took her away. It seemed like forever before it was all over. The whole time I was terrified I was going to lose her." He swallowed and exhaled. "The baby was already gone by time he was born. They didn't have any answer for why it happened. He was so tiny, and perfect." James held his hand out, palm up. "He could've fit right here in the palm of my hand. It was one of the hardest nights of our lives. We'd just started thinking about what we needed to do to get ready for a baby to come. We didn't even know whether it was a boy or girl yet. The ultrasound appointment to see if they could tell was supposed to be that next week. Then suddenly everything changed."

"Oh, Dad. How awful. I still can't believe it," Sophia had risen and was standing at the window, staring out toward the shore across her mother's garden. "I never would've thought something like that would have happened to Mom and you. Any of it."

"And no one ever knew? In this town?" Tommy pressed.

James shook his head. "Nope. Oh, don't get me wrong. There was plenty of talk and nasty rumors. But your mom didn't even stay in the hospital for twenty-four hours afterwards. They sent her home after they made sure she wasn't having any complications. It was surprising that we didn't see anyone we knew the whole time since we'd gone to the nearest hospital, in Ellsworth. Everything happened on Saturday night. Sunday we didn't haul, so no one missed us back here. When we came back home late that next day, no one was any the wiser. We just said she was under the weather for the next few days if anyone asked where she was. She had to have some procedure a few days later to make sure everything was all right, but that wasn't a hospital stay either. Since her regular doctor was in Bangor, no one ever knew a thing."

"Is he buried in a cemetery somewhere?" Tommy asked.

"No. Remember what I told you about how your mom feels about buried pine boxes. Plus, then everyone would've known about her being pregnant. He was cremated. The two of us scattered his little ashes down at the shore one night."

James rose from his chair. "Well, now you know," he said. "I hope you can understand the reasons why your mom wanted all of it to be kept secret."

There was silence.

Sophia sighed. "I won't lie. I feel a little hurt that she never told us."

"Come on, Soph," Tommy protested. "Can you imagine telling us kids about that. It opens up all kinds of questions about Mom's life before she and Dad got married. I don't think she'd have wanted to rehash those memories. Plus if she told us when we were younger, even if we'd wanted to, I bet we wouldn't have kept it a secret."

"Let me finish, already." Sophia scowled at her brother. "I was going to say that as I heard the whole story, I kept wondering how she could be such a positive, giving person after all she went through. I can't even imagine. You too, Dad. It's like her life before she met you was the total opposite of anything I would've thought."

James nodded. "She hated her childhood and her life in Philadelphia. She never wanted to talk about it much. She said she'd lived in a made-up world where money and social standing were all that mattered. She'd been sent to the best schools to learn all about how to become some high-powered, bigwig's wife. She said the main pastime of her mother's social circles was to talk about anyone and everyone in the worst way possible in order to make themselves appear superior. So that will give you a little understanding about why your mom hated rumors and anyone talking about other people's business."

James headed into the kitchen, toward the back door. He stopped and turned around just before he went out. "If you have any more questions, I'll try to answer them in a bit." He looked at his watch. "We missed lunchtime entirely, but why don't you both grab a bite of what Tommy started making earlier. I'll make a sandwich when I get back. Later, I'll show you what else is in that trunk."

"I'm not sure I'm up for any more shocking revelations today, Dad." Tommy remarked.

"Don't worry, Son. It's nothing crazy, just some of your mom's artwork from before we got married. I think you both would like to see what a good artist she was. Please wait for me though. I won't be too long. Right now, I've got something I need to take care of."

Forty Two

Natasha

Mr. James was just here. I was up in my room when Mom came upstairs to get me. Well, actually, I was totally hiding out in my room, because I didn't want to tell my mom what had happened at the wharf. You know, me telling Mr. James stuff I should keep to myself, and how I'd acted like a know-it-all telling him what he should do. Mom and Gran were downstairs cleaning when I got back. I just told them that I decided to come back here to read because it was too noisy down at the cove. Mom looked at me funny, but she just ruffled up my hair—which I absolutely hate by the way—and I went up to my room.

I didn't read though. What a waste of a library day.

I couldn't even eat my picnic lunch, because I still felt really bad. Let me tell you that's a big deal, because I'm hungry most of the time, and I really like to eat. Mom says it's because I burn so much energy running all over the place. She says she wishes she could eat like I do. But I wasn't hungry because I was so worried. I knew that if Mom found out about my big mouth she was going to be mad at me. Then I would get a good, long talking to at the very least. I might even be grounded for life. Then I wouldn't be allowed to see or talk to Mr. James ever again. That part made me sad. I really do think he's not like any other grownup I've met before. He doesn't ever seem to be in a hurry when he's not at work out on the boat. He doesn't act like he has to be in a rush to get somewhere or do something else. He likes to sit and watch the water and the birds, like me. The best thing is that he listens. I mean he really listens to me when I talk. He makes me feel like what I say or think is important. My mom does that part too, most of the time. But it's different with her. I'm her kid, you know? So, she has to.

When Mom came upstairs calling for me, she didn't sound mad or anything. Then she told me Mr. James was here to see me about something. That's when I started to feel like I was going to throw up. When I went down my little stairs into her room, she gave me that funny look again and asked me if I felt OK. I said, yeah, I was fine, that I was just a little tired. That was a complete lie. I was *totally* not fine. Plus, I was so worried, there was no way I could be tired. She told me that it was a real surprise for Mr. James to come over because he hadn't come to the house in years. Then she asked me if I knew why he might want to talk with me. She said she'd asked him if everything was all right and he'd said he hoped so, but that was up to me. By then we were almost into the living room and Mr. James was standing there. So thank goodness, I didn't have to answer her. He was holding his baseball cap in his hand. I'd never really seen him without his hat on before. He looked kinda different without it. I know that sometimes old guys wear hats to cover up bald spots on top of their head, but Mr. James's silvery hair is thick all over and messy curly, like the front of mine gets around my face when some of it comes out of my ponytail.

Gran smiled at me as we came into the room. She said that they were just talking about how much Mr. Edward liked to see me riding my bike down at the wharf, like my mom used to.

"Oh," I said. I couldn't think of anything else I should say.

Then Mr. James told Gran that he was just "James" and that we were on a "first-name basis." He smiled down at me and told me thank you for coming down to talk to him. He didn't look mad or upset at all, but I couldn't really tell for sure, because sometimes people smile and pretend to look one way when they really feel the total opposite of what their face shows. I didn't know if I was supposed to say anything or not, and my stomach was feeling queasy, so I just kept looking at him. He cleared his throat and sat down on the edge of the chair that was right behind him He looked straight at me all serious-like. Then he said he was sorry that he had been rude to me earlier!

I felt my face get all hot. This wasn't what I'd expected at all. Even though I wasn't sure what I'd expected, it wasn't this. I felt like I might cry and that was totally weird. But I just told him it was OK.

He shook his head and looked down at his hat, turning it over and over. Then he said he appreciated I said that, but that it wasn't OK at all.

Oh, boy, I thought. Here it comes. I'm gonna be in so much trouble.

But then he said that he wanted me to know that I was absolutely right about what I told him that morning. He said it meant a lot to him that I took the time to talk with him and that he'd needed to hear my advice.

I still didn't know what to say, so I just said, "you're welcome" to him.

I looked over at Mom and Gran. They were just standing there looking as confused as I felt.

Mom asked if we would share what we talked about. I thought for sure that I would have to tell then. I just knew I was going to get it. But Mr. James answered her before I could say a word. He said that we were talking about how hard it is for people to talk with each other sometimes and how things can get mixed up because of it.

Then he stood up and told Mom that he and his daughter had a little argument at the wharf this morning and when I rode down on my bike I gave him some good advice about making sure that I didn't let a "small misunderstanding become a big deal."

Mom raised one eyebrow at me like she does when she wonders if she's not getting the full story.

But Mr. James told her that I was just fine and respectful. He said I have a way of putting things that make anyone, "even a stubborn cuss like him" think. Then he said that I was right to say what I did, and that he really meant it. He said he went to find Sophia, and they talked, and everything is just fine now. Then he said he was really sorry he left without saying good-bye. He said he "forgot his manners" because all he could think about was going to find his daughter to talk with her right then.

I told him it was all OK. I know what it's like to be so focused on doing something that you forget about other things.

He thanked me for accepting his apology and then he told me that I was a "very smart, special young lady." He said he really likes our conversations and he hopes we get to talk a lot more. That made me happy, because I really like talking with him too.

That was when I first thought he might not say anything else about exactly what I'd said to him earlier. Maybe I wouldn't get grounded after all. Then he said that he'd been wondering, if Mom thought it would be all right, would I like to go mackerel fishing at the wharf tomorrow? He told Mom it would be nice if she would come too, and that we could have lunch at his house first. He also invited Gran, but she said even though she'd love to, they both knew that wasn't a good idea. Mr. James turned his hat around and around in his hands and acted like he was going to say something else to Gran. He didn't though. He just smiled at her with this sad kind of smile.

I wanted to know why it wasn't a good idea for Gran to go with us. But I was barely avoiding disaster already because I didn't know how to shut up, and Mom would be all over me about getting involved in grown-up conversations if I did ask about what Gran said. Sometimes I just can't help myself.

Luckily before my big, stupid mouth opened up, Mr. James said he hadn't heard from me if I thought it would be fun to go fishing. Boy, did I! And I told him so. Then I felt so excited about the idea that I could barely stand still. I wanted to dance all around the room. But I didn't, even though I thought I might burst right out of my skin trying to stay calm.

Mom said since tomorrow was Sunday and she didn't have to work, that we'd love to go over for lunch and spend the afternoon. Mr. James seemed happy about that. He smiled super big. He said he had to get back home, but he'd see us tomorrow. On his way out, he told Mom not to worry about needing any fishing stuff because he had all of it. Then he told me I should ask Mom all about mackerel and how to catch them because she used to fish for them at the wharf with her friends when she was my age. He put his hat on, said he'd expect a "full report" on what I learned, then he winked at me. That's when I knew for sure that everything was good with us and he wasn't going to tell anyone what I'd said before.

Mom had other ideas. As soon as Mr. James was gone, she turned around to me with that look that meant I was in for a grilling. Before she could say anything though, Gran put her hand on Mom's arm and shook her head a little. She said that if Mr. James said everything was fine and just between us, then it was. She said of all the people she knows he's the one she'd trust the most to do the right thing. She also said I had the best person to talk to and be friends with in the whole town.

Mom looked at Gran's face for a few seconds. Then she sighed and said, "OK."

I beat feet right out of there let me tell you. I knew better than to wait around for Mom to change her mind and start asking questions. 'Cause no matter what, I can't ever not tell her what she asks me, or worse, lie to her—not that I wouldn't like to sometimes. For some reason if she looks right at me, I just can't. I've tried. Believe me. But the second she looks me straight in the eye I start giggling. Then I can't say anything except the truth. It's like her eyes can see right into my brain to make my mouth open and spill it all out.

I've been thinking about what Gran said about Mr. James being my friend. Is he really? I never thought of it that way. He's awful old to be friends with a kid my age. I guess he could be. It seems weird to think of him that way, but I don't really know what else I could call him.

I'll have to think more about that. Right now, it really doesn't matter. The bottom line is, I didn't get in any trouble at all. Not only that, I get to learn how to catch mackerel tomorrow!

Forty Three

"That didn't take long," Sophia remarked as James came striding back into the kitchen a few minutes later.

"Nope. I had to go see my young friend, Natasha, for a minute. I owed her something. Where's your brother?"

"He's out wandering around in the yard. He said he needed a little fresh air." She shook her head. "It's kind of hard to process what you told us—this side of Mom we never knew, you know?"

James crossed the room to his daughter. He pulled her close resting his chin on the top of her head for a second before he took a step back. He put both hands on her shoulders and looked down into her eyes. "I know this is all shocking and seems out of character for your mom. This was one of the reasons she wanted it kept secret. She didn't want it to tarnish what you thought of her. She didn't ever want you kids to lose any respect for her."

"I can get that. But I've been thinking about it. Knowing about her past only makes me respect her more. I mean, I always felt like she could conquer anything, but I can't imagine how strong she had to be to go through all she did. I just wish she'd trusted us enough to tell us about her parents, and our baby brother and all."

"It wasn't a matter of trust, Bean. It was protection—of you kids, of me, of our lives together, of herself. She truly wanted to forget the part of her life, pretty much *all* of her life before she moved here. Those memories never brought anything but pain. She didn't want to hurt us, or our lives, by sharing them. Whether right or not, in the end her intentions were simply to protect us all."

Sophia was silent. James dropped his hands. He could see she was busy turning things over in her mind.

"I think I'll make myself a sandwich now," he said. "I just realized that I'm half-starved."

"Oh. Here." Sophia opened the refrigerator and took out a plate covered with a napkin. "Tommy made you one already. I had to put it in the fridge because your fat cat thought she might like some ham for herself. There are chips on the counter too, if you want them," she added.

"Thanks. Would you mind handing me a soda?"

Sophia reached back into the fridge. She handed a can to James. "Dad?"

"Hmm?" James mumbled since he'd just taken a bite of the sandwich.

"Do you think one reason Mom was so involved in the community was so no one would ever have a reason to think she had any past to haunt her? That she was like, perfect? I mean, she was so into the church stuff and all."

James swallowed. He took a long drink from the can of soda. "No." He paused. "At least I don't think that had anything to do with it. You know better than to think your mom wanted to appear to be 'perfect' as you say. She forever was reminding all of us that no one is flawless or even close to it. Also how we need to remember we always have room to grow," he added. "Her faithfulness to the church was the one thing I think she continued from her past. Churchgoing was just lip service and a big part of the social circle of her parents. Your mom said she never saw it that way. She really was a faithful believer. She'd loved going to church as a child. She found peace there and a higher purpose. She told me that once when I asked her. Mostly, I think that your mom just wanted to do the opposite of what she'd been exposed to growing up. She wanted to be as far away as possible from people who throw money at things and pretend to be noble and helpful, when in truth they aren't that way at all. All her parents and their circle did was viciously criticize and look down on anything that wasn't up to their false standards. She always said that any time talking about what you had done, or were going to do, was time wasted. You should 'walk the walk and let the talking alone.'"

"Yeah, I remember her telling us many times to just keep quiet and 'walk the walk' and that 'talking doesn't hold up to doing.' What you say makes sense, Dad." Sophia went over to the sink. She turned the water on to rinse the dish in her hands. "It's just a lot to think about, you know?"

"It is," James agreed. "Still, I thought it was necessary for you both to know. Especially with what you said about Justine and young Natasha. The way you acted, your comments, gave me quite a shock. It was harsh, and nothing I would ever have thought to hear from you," he admonished. "We don't know much of anything about their situation except through gossip. Plus, it isn't any of our business. Regardless of circumstances, Justine is still Justine. She was your friend since you were tots and all through school. I have a feeling she could use some of that friendship right about now."

"I don't know what I was thinking," Sophia said, hanging her head. "Actually, that's not true. I know exactly what I was thinking. I've seen more than one girl drop out of the academy since I've been there; giving up on her dreams because she was stupid enough to chase after some guy, then get pregnant to try to trap them. All they were thinking was that they'd have this fairy-tale life they dreamed up because they were 'in love.' I lumped Justine into that bunch and ran with it. I was assuming, judging, and wrong. Mom would've ridden up one side of me and down the other if she'd heard me."

"I thought that too," James sadly smiled at his daughter. "That's why I decided it was time to tell you about your mom's past. Like I've said, I think she would've wanted you to know, now."

Sophia nodded. "She would have. I'm sure of it. And I'll have to make it a point to go see Justine while I'm home. Just to say, 'Hi.'"

"You can do that right here tomorrow if you want," James said between bites of ham sandwich.

The screen door opened. Tommy stepped into the kitchen.

James continued, "I invited them to lunch and to go mackerel fishing down at the wharf. Natasha loves the eagles so much I thought we might could catch a few fish and see if they'll give us a show when we leave a snack for them."

"Invited who?" Tommy asked.

"Justine and her daughter, Natasha," Sophia offered.

"Cool. That sounds like a nice time. I'll be glad to see Justine and catch up. It's been a minute."

"Good, I was hoping you'd both be open to the idea. I can't wait for you to meet Natasha either. She's a pretty neat kiddo."

Tommy went to the kitchen sink. He stood there looking out the window.

"You doing all right, Son?" James asked. "I know I threw you both a curveball without warning."

Tommy turned around to look at his dad. "I'm good."

James looked hard at his son, not sure if he should believe him or not.

Tommy smiled. "Really, Dad. I'm fine. I'll admit at first I was kind of put out. I wondered why Mom and you never wanted us to know that we had an older brother. But I think I can understand how she would've wanted to put her past behind her to start over in a brand-new life. The more I thought about the circumstances of that pregnancy and all, I realized she never wanted us to think that we were anything except her 'everything' like she always told us. Her words make more sense to me now than ever. She put her past behind her to create her world here—with you, then with me and Sophia, too. That was her choice. I can respect that. Then I started thinking about how you must have felt through all of this, Dad. I just can't get over the fact that you accepted a child from a relationship Mom had before she met you. You accepted him as your own, like it was no big deal. You make it sound so simple. But I can't believe that it was."

James took a sip off soda. He shook his head. "Oh, it wasn't simple. I had some real back and forth with it at first, believe me. But in the end it came down to some basic truths. I loved your mom, everything about her. She told me that she'd never been in love with anyone but me, that her previous boyfriend had never been a serious consideration. Her getting pregnant was not purposeful in any way. She wasn't keeping the baby because she loved the father, she was keeping the child because she believed that it didn't ask to come into this world, and it was part of her. She couldn't anymore end the pregnancy, or give up the baby, as she could cut off her right arm. The moment I fell in love with Anna, she became part of me, I think some of the best part of me. So, the baby was part of that too. I truly thought of him as my own, as ours, after that. When we lost him, we both grieved for a long time about all that could have been. It was a hard time. For a little while, we were scared that we wouldn't be able to have any other children because we didn't know why your mom miscarried. But the doctors told us there was no indication there was anything wrong with her ability to have babies. Then it wasn't long before we were expecting you, Tommy. You both need to know that your mom loved her life. She loved all of us more than anything. She showed us that everyday. Her past was her own, and she asked me to leave it there. So, I did. Until now." He put the last bite of his sandwich in his mouth, chewed slowly, and swallowed. "Well, I don't suppose you might want to peek at what else might be in that old trunk, or have you had enough excitement for today?"

Forty Four

"Oh, come on, Dad." Sophia rolled her eyes. "You already said that there's no other bombshells in there, just some of Mom's old artwork."

"I, for one, would really like to look at them," Tommy said. "I saw Mom sketch things once in while, but she never showed me any finished pieces or any of her work from when she was in school. I wonder why?"

"I can answer that," James said. "I always told her she should show you kids; that she should be proud of her pictures. But she said she never wanted to influence your own art in any way, Tommy. She said you saw the world with a different artist's eye and she wanted you to develop that without feeling you should be painting or drawing things like she did."

"Well, I can tell you that it never would have influenced me in any way," Sophia remarked dryly. "I haven't got an artistic bone in my body. Tommy got all those. Still, I want to see too. It's something about Mom that we never knew much about, you know?"

"Well then, let's take a look." James led the way back into the living room. "I haven't seen them since Pam sent your mom's things and we packed them away. I don't think there's many pictures in there. I remember her keeping just a few favorites; a dozen or so."

"I can safely say there's a few more than a dozen in there," Sophia offered.

"Really?" Tommy stopped. "Geez, Soph. Dad asked us to wait. What'd you do? Open it up the minute we both went outside?"

Sophia grinned. "Pretty much. I'll fess up. Even though Dad told us to wait, I took just a little peek under the tray."

"You're an incorrigible child," James chuckled, shaking his head. "I see you still aren't very good at following instructions, are you?"

"Guilty, as charged." Sophia held up both hands in surrender. "I just couldn't help myself. I didn't actually look at any of it. So, I didn't really disobey you, Dad. But it's not any 'dozen or so' pieces. It's filled right to the top under that tray with a stack of stuff that looks like it could be drawings. It's covered with some tissue paper."

"That's strange." James lifted the tray out of the trunk. "Huh. You're right. It's jam-packed. I would've sworn that the main compartment of this thing wasn't even a third full. Either I remembered wrong, or she added a lot more to it over the years." He handed the tray to Tommy. "Put this over there on the floor, please."

Tommy placed the tray on the other side of the room out of the way. He went to stand by James who was lifting off the tissue paper that lay over the first drawing. He revealed a scene they all recognized at once. It was a rendering of the head of the harbor on a foggy morning, from the end of the main road where you had to turn one way or another onto Main Street, or you'd end up in the harbor. There was a single sailboat moored in the cove about two hundred feet from the pebbled shore. The ghost-like apparition of the boat bathed in a sliding mist, sails slack and tied to its mast, almost seemed to bob slightly on the gently moving surface of a near-calm sea. It looked as if Anna had framed her perspective from the exact spot where the three of them had stopped to admire the view before going to dinner on Tommy and Sophia's first night back home.

"That's absolutely stunning!" Sophia exclaimed looking over her father's shoulder. "It looks so real. I can almost feel the mist. And there's just a hint of the sun beginning to seep through the fog in spots, like it's filtered through lace. You can just tell it was going to be a beautiful day."

"Dad, can I see that?" Tommy asked holding out his hand.

"Sure, Son." James lightly grasped the over-sized, semi-stiff, sketch paper by its edges and carefully transferred it to Tommy.

"It's all done in colored pencils," Tommy observed, carefully taking the drawing James offered. "This isn't like any of her rough sketches I ever saw. I mean, I never saw her develop any of those into polished pieces. Soph is right. This is stunning." He sat on the edge of the couch and perched the lower edge of the drawing on his lap, holding gently to the top edges. He studied it intently.

James tipped his hat back and rubbed his forehead. "I knew she could paint and draw like this. I saw some of her finished work from school. But I know I've never seen this one. I'm sure of it. All the paintings and drawings your mom put away in here years ago were scenes from New York—buildings, people, a few of Central Park. She used to sketch stuff from all around here at home. But you're right, Tommy. The things she drew weren't what I would think of as finished. I don't remember her using colors either. She kept her supplies in a portfolio thingy in our closet with her pencils and a couple different sized sketch pads in it. She used to pull one out once in a while and sketch in it. But I never saw her working on the one you're holding or anything else like it."

He reached into the trunk to move away another layer of tissue exposing a watercolor painting of the town church, all decked out in Christmas garlands, the ground around it covered in a fine layer of snow. "Here's another one." He picked it up and sat back on the couch a little farther, holding it at gently by its edges at an angle, resting it against his lap. He gazed at it for a few moments, then shook his head. "She was so talented. This is amazing. It seems more alive than just a picture. Like you could step right into the painting, and you'd be there for real." He sighed. "I never understood why she didn't want to keep on with her artwork. I tried to convince her she should, but she said she just wanted to 'scribble' a little now and then." He set the painting down in his lap. "Fact is, she'd get right irritated with me whenever I tried to talk to her about it. She said that she didn't tell me what I should want to do with my time, and I should let her alone to make her own decisions about what she wanted, or didn't want, to do." He shrugged. "So, I did. I just wanted her to be happy."

"She was, Dad. You know that. And it looks like she kept on anyway. Plus, she took care to store them so they wouldn't get damaged," Tommy observed. "I guess she had her reasons for not sharing her work with anyone."

"Well, this explains how little dust was on the trunk's lid." Sophia had moved around to stand beside her brother so she could look at the drawing of the cove that he still held. "I wonder how often she put things in there."

Tommy turned the drawing in his hands around so he could look at its back, careful not to touch anywhere but the very edges of it. "This is dated here on the back—April second of this year." He looked closely at his mother's neat handwriting. "She named this one too. 'Safe Haven.'" He turned it back over in the same manner. "It's also signed with her name and just the year here on the front at the bottom right. "See?" He tilted it slightly toward his sister.

"Uh huh. What about the one you've got, Dad? Is it dated?"

James started to flip the paper over.

"Be careful with that," Tommy warned. "Try just to handle the very edges. We don't know if any of them are fixed with anything to keep them from smudging or getting damaged."

"Oh. I never thought of that," James said. "Like this?" He barely pinched the top corners of the painting.

"That will work," Tommy said. "Before we take out any others, I'm going to wash my hands and grab a pair of gloves from my kit in the car. I keep supplies in there in case I need them when I'm looking at fragile or unframed artwork."

James peered at the upper right corner on the back of the drawing. "There is a date here. January six, twenty twenty-two. But it doesn't have any name on it like on the one you have, Tommy."

James turned it back over taking in all the details Anna had captured of the church and its surroundings. One side of the double wooden door at the top of the steps was barely open, as if someone had just slipped through and was closing it behind them.

"Hopefully she dated them all. It would be nice to know when they were created." Tommy stood up making sure to keep the drawing he still held away from his body. "As we get them out we should put them somewhere safe with the tissue between them like she had them in the trunk." He looked around the room for an empty, flat surface that they could use.

"What about the top of the buffet in the kitchen? Sophia asked. "I can take off the silver chest and the other things that are on there."

"That'd be perfect," Tommy agreed. "I'll just put this one back into the trunk for now, while you get it ready." He placed the drawing on top of the row of tissue that was covering the next piece. "I'm going to run out and grab my kit so we don't get any dirt or oil from our hands on any of them while we're checking them out."

He glanced at James. "Do you want me to put that one back in here for right now too, Dad?"

"No," James said softly. He was thinking of all the times he didn't go to church with Anna when she asked. Now it seemed such a little thing that he could have done for her; a small sacrifice for something that would have made her so happy. He was sure there were other things he hadn't done over the years that were important to her. Things that wouldn't have taken him any time at all. Things he would've realized if he'd just paid more attention. Holding Anna's painting he could feel her energy and her love for her life. His heart physically hurt with the longing to hear her voice, to see her, to hold her just once more. If only he could go back in time. "No," he repeated. "I want to look at this one for a just a while more."

Forty Five

It was well after suppertime when James lifted the last piece of Anna's unframed artwork from the bottom of the steamer trunk. Tommy had suggested that they make a list that included a brief catalogue-type description of each of Anna's works. He also said they should note things like the medium she'd used and any dates and titles. Sophia volunteered for this task. On a notepad she grabbed from her room, she meticulously wrote down any details her brother relayed about piece after piece. It turned out to be less of a list and more a descriptive narrative as they uncovered renderings and interpretations of the peninsula, their town, their neighbors, friends, even themselves. As they'd neared the bottom of the trunk, they finally came across Anna's oldest works from art school. James had been right about what he remembered of them. There were five paintings and six drawings of images from Anna's days in New York City.

"This last one of the pond in Central Park makes a grand total of forty-seven pieces." Sophia set down the notepad on her lap, placed the pen she'd been using on top of it, and folded her hand over them both. "Forty-seven. Wow."

James was exhausted. Tommy had given him a pair of white cotton gloves to wear so he could lift out each piece without damaging it. They'd developed a kind of routine along the way. James removed the tissue covering and handed that to Sophia. Then he'd carefully take the picture out of the trunk, holding it so they all could look it over. This part took a few minutes because each was a fresh surprise. There were so many details to discover, and point out to each other, as they found themselves continually amazed by Anna's expressions and talent. After they'd initially looked at a piece, James handed it off to Tommy. He would study it looking for identifying dates, titles, or other marks Anna might have made. Then he'd tell them what kind of pencils, paints, or other tools she'd used to create it. After that, they all offered ideas of how to describe the work while Sophia wrote it all down.

The original plan had been that they would place the pictures flat on the buffet top in the kitchen protected by the same tissue paper that had covered each work originally, thus basically reversing the order of how they were stored in the trunk. That idea became convoluted almost immediately, because before they began the process James propped up the watercolor of the church on top of the oak bookcase by his chair.

"I just want to leave that one there for right now."

"Sure," Tommy said. "You can do whatever you want. We don't have to stack them all back up. I just want to make sure we don't hurt any of them."

The next drawing, of the Mark Island Light, was laid out on the buffet. But after that, less found their way onto the pile in the kitchen as more were carefully propped up around the room on different surfaces. It wasn't long before there wasn't anywhere to squeeze another in. They'd even stood four up in James's chair—one on each arm and two in the seat.

Tommy took the last scene that depicted Anna's views of New York into the kitchen to join the others on the top of the buffet. They hadn't placed any of those works in their makeshift gallery in the living room.

Sophia looked down at her notebook. "According to the dates on the backs of the pictures, she didn't draw or paint after she left school, until after she had Tommy. She finished at least couple a year after that, except for all of two thousand one and the first few months of two thousand two."

"That was about the time her parents were killed in the train wreck," James mused.

"That certainly could have influenced her creativity. It must have been a hard time for her," Tommy remarked from the kitchen doorway.

"Oh, it was," James agreed. "She told me the worst thing about her parents' dying was that it ended any thought that things could be reconciled. She said that even though she knew deep down they would never have come around, she was most sad for the end of the hope that they might change their minds, maybe want to meet me and you kids someday. Any chance of that was gone—just like that."

"How sad," Sophia remarked. "You know, I always wished for grandparents like a lot of my friends had. But, knowing what I know now about Mom's parents, I'd say they're the ones who missed out. They must have been bitter, lonely people."

"You're right, Bean. They are the ones who missed out," James said. "In so many ways."

Tommy, still standing in the doorway, scanned the paintings around the room. "Mom was so talented. This is wonderful. I never would've guessed in a million years." He took a faltering breath. "I wish I would've known."

"Me too," Sophia said. "It makes me think about how things would've been for us as we all got older. You know? Maybe she might have told us about her life when she was a kid. Maybe she would have shared her artwork. Maybe since we're grown now and wouldn't need so much of her time, she'd have done more painting. . . and not in secret. Maybe she would've told us about our older brother. Now we can't ever ask her about him or anything else. Now we only get to wonder and guess." She looked down at her hands still clasped over the notepad. "It just makes me miss her so much more," she whispered.

James didn't know what to say, not that he could have gotten any words out anyway. His throat was so tight he was having trouble breathing. He understood their pain. He felt it. He knew there was nothing he could say that would make it any better. Nothing to do. Worst of all, nothing that could bring Anna back to them.

Tommy walked over to stand in front of a watercolor that clearly depicted his sister and himself playing in a wooden sandbox next to a trellis dripping with climbing apricot roses. While that sandbox wasn't in their yard anymore, the trellis still rested against the chimney of their home where it continued to support Anna's favorite antique rose bush. "At least we have our memories. And now we have these."

Sophia rose from her seat. She set the notebook on the end table and went to stand beside her brother. "I remember that old sand box. Dad finally took it apart not too long ago. Maybe when I left for college. But that trellis is still there. I haven't looked, but I bet Mom's old rose bush is blooming like crazy right about now. The detail in this is unbelievable. I don't ever remember seeing a photo of us like this. How did she paint it so perfectly?"

Tommy shook his head. "She had a gift for sure. She put in a whole lot of hard work, too. You can tell how much she truly cared about all her subjects. She had an amazing way of using color and light. You can't help but get drawn into each one." He put his arm around his sister's waist and gave her a slight hug. "But, then again, we're pretty biased too."

"Not completely," Sophia said. "You'd have to be numb not to see how talented she was."

"True." Tommy moved away to look at a colored pencil rendering of the cove and wharf busy with all kinds of activity as fishermen came in from the haul. It wasn't like the usual, idyllic lobster boat harbor scenes that seem iconic to Maine. It was more. Beautiful yes, as far as the scenery and boats went, but it contained depth that brought it alive. Tommy swore he could physically feel the vibrant hum of the lives, and community, of the lobstermen finishing their long day's work.

"She really nailed this one," he remarked. "Even though I can't see individual features on faces, I can pick out some of our neighbors here just by their stance or by their boats. And there you are, Dad. You're the last boat coming into the cove past the reach. Your signal buoy is clear as day on the top of the wheelhouse. I can even make out the silhouette of you at the wheel."

"First one out, last one in—all the time." Sophia laughed. She walked across the room and gently picked up a colorful drawing overlooking a garden. "Mom sure knew how to make you take notice. I swear I can almost smell the flowers in this one."

"You said it." Tommy tipped his head. "She knew how to translate what was important to her onto the paper, not only what she saw, but what she felt. She did a remarkable job of depicting more than scenes. She captured life."

"Art imitates life. Life imitates art," Sophia remarked.

"That's the classic philosophical debate about art for sure," Tommy said. "But that's not exactly how I see it. In a way, that's too simplistic an argument. Mom's work proves that. I think that art is all about individual perception, not just 'imitation.' I don't mean just the different forms of fine gallery art that I deal with in my job, but all artistic endeavors in any form: music, writing, theater, cinema, architecture—any way that an artist creates a work to express concepts or emotions about life. The artist translates their perceptions into a form to be shared and appreciated in an attempt to communicate what they view—how they see it and how they feel—an intimate interpretation of their vision. Most importantly, they aspire to evoke the same emotions and attachments related to their individual perception of each subject, which ultimately is linked to how they relate to our world. This validates their art and themselves."

"Perception is reality," Sophia mused.

"Yes. Exactly," Tommy agreed. "If the artist is successful in creating that perceptive link with their audience, and it can be just an audience of one, then they've effectively created a kind of bond with that person. Of course, the hope is that many see the work and share an appreciation of it. It's a way to open up communication with others. It's an avenue to find or create shared interpretations of life. It could even be a way to take us away from our human existence and limitations by creating visions or imaginings of what life might be on some different plane of existence, in a different realm or time."

"It sounds pretty complicated, not to mention awful personal to me," James said. "Your mom was always trying to explain to me how art works, especially modern art, because I couldn't ever seem to get it. I still don't," he admitted.

"And that's fine, Dad. You don't have to 'get it.' You don't even have to like it. You just need to appreciate that there are people out there who see and communicate imagination, concepts, and feelings in diverse ways. I like to think of it as a kind of artistic empathy. If an artist can open up enough to effectively relate their experience with their subject and their inner vision so that others are able to empathize with it, or better yet to really be drawn into it, then communication is opened between the viewers, readers, or listeners. Hopefully this leads us to understand that while each of us may view things differently, we can openly acknowledge and learn to accept that. In turn, if we find common elements or shared views, we might better understand and appreciate each other and our entire existence."

Tommy turned back around to look at the painting of his sister and himself building a castle in the sandbox. "Of course for us, that higher connection is easy to find in Mom's work, because we lived in her world, and we shared her love."

"True. But I like the idea of an 'artistic empathy,'" Sophia said. "Thinking about art in general, I don't need to like the art, but I can try to see what the artist sees and feels by putting any prejudice of my own perceptions aside." She looked down at the vibrant, multi-hued rendition of the flower bed behind their house overlooking the bright azure sea in the late afternoon. "But I don't need to always think about art so deeply, right?" She gently picked up the drawing again, turned around and held it in front of her for them to see. "I simply love this one just because Mom made it. And it's home. And it's all her. Look, you can even make out your mooring down in the cove, Dad. She must have drawn it one afternoon while you were out to haul."

James smiled. "It is beautiful." He felt a tug at his heart. "And you're right, that is 'all her.'"

"I've got it!" Tommy exclaimed. "I think I've got it!"

Sophia started, bumping her elbow against the edge of the bookcase just behind her. "Ouch! Geez, Tommy. Got what?" She leaned the drawing back up on the top of the bookcase and rubbed her elbow.

She and James both turned to look at Tommy. He was grinning from ear to ear. "A way to honor Mom. I know just what to do. We could rent out the gallery at the arts center, and we can create a show of Mom's work. Then we can have a public reception where everyone can come and see her interpretations of her life." He gestured around the room. "Just about everything and everybody in town is all here. And they're beautifully rendered. We also can put a book in the front of the gallery where people can write things if they want. You know, remembrances, condolences, messages, whatever. After the initial reception we can leave the exhibit up for a couple of weeks so people can visit whenever they want."

Sophia clapped her hands together. "It's a great idea!" She tilted her head. "But aren't there already exhibits in there?"

"The last official showing for the center ends the tenth of September. That's only a couple weeks away. Then they don't have any other art exhibits scheduled until spring. I ran into the new director this morning," Tommy explained. "He told me all about the plans for the space for the next couple years. The main room is available for rental for anyone who wants to use it for private parties, or whatever, as long as there is no exhibit. You know, that's the great room where they have all the tracks to hang art. They also put tables and pedestals in there for sculptures and such. There's a fiber arts show going on in there right now, but it'll be cleared out soon. I remember him saying there isn't anything else booked in the main room until the holidays."

He turned to his father. "What do you think, Dad?"

James looked slowly around the room taking in Anna's work.

Tommy broke the silence, clearing his throat. "You don't have to decide right now. And if you don't like the idea, it's fine, really."

James looked over at Tommy. He smiled at him, his bright blue eyes crinkling up at the corners. "No, Son. Your idea is perfect. How do we make it happen?"

Forty Six

Natasha

I've been awake since just before four this morning. The sky was still dark and I could see the stars when I first opened my eyes. Just a few minutes after I woke up they started fading away as the sky began to lighten. Sunrise is still early right now, but not as early as in June when the sun came up over the edge of the ocean before five. I usually wake up about the same time the sun rises because my window faces due east so it shines right in at me.

Today though, I woke up early when I heard my grandfather start his truck to leave out to haul. Most of the time I don't even hear him in the mornings, but I didn't sleep all that great last night. I was so excited to go fishing today that I had a really hard time turning off my brain. Once I finally fell asleep I dreamed all night about swimming underwater in the ocean with schools of long, silvery fish darting and swirling around and around me. By the time I woke up I was feeling good and guilty about even thinking about trying to catch the flashy fish that had been swimming with me in my underwater dreams. They were so pretty. Their big eyes kept looking at me like they were telling me they just wanted to be left alone, and why did I want to catch them anyway? It's a good thing they didn't talk in my dreams. That would have made me feel super terrible. I already feel bad enough.

I mean, I really like to eat fish. I've never had mackerel before, but I bet I will like it. Mom says it's got a stronger fishy flavor than whitefish like halibut or haddock. Those are two kinds of fish I really like. Halibut cooked with butter and lemon just about melts in your mouth and Gran fries up fillets of haddock for us almost every Friday. She makes this batter stuff that she dips it in before she fries it. It's super delicious—crunchy on the outside and soft and flaky inside. Mom says Gran cooks mackerel totally different than the halibut or haddock. She said sometimes mackerel gets mixed in with cornmeal and seasonings into patties, then gets fried in a skillet, the same way as the crab cakes Gran's made us a few times since we got here.

We eat a lot of different kinds of fish and other seafood, but why wouldn't we? It's all right here, right out our front door. We eat a lot of other things too like hamburgers and chicken and mac and cheese and spaghetti. But my grandfather brings lobster and crab claws in from his boat all the time. At least a couple times a week I go down to the corner store or the co-op with Gran. She chooses what fish to cook depending on what's just come in fresh from the boats. I asked her about getting fresh shrimp from here. It's one of my favorite seafoods. But Gran told me they are hard to get and super expensive since the Gulf of Maine was closed to shrimping for a few years because there weren't as many shrimp out there. The rule-making people decided that shrimp can be caught again, because not catching them for a while means there are more of them now. It doesn't make a lot of sense to me that just shrimping too much is why there aren't as many in the gulf, especially if there's always been rules about how many pounds can be netted. There has to be something else. I wonder if Maine shrimp like colder water, like the Right Whales? Has their habitat changed so that new shrimp aren't hatching? I'll have to look that up. I might ask Mr. James too because I know he knows a lot about the ocean and everything in it.

Anyway, I really like shrimp because Mom used to make it for us at home for a special treat. Sometimes she'd put them in a pasta with crab meat, butter, and a creamy sauce. But a lot of times she'd just steam them and put them in the fridge for us to eat cold later. My dad didn't really like shrimp or even lobster the way Mom makes them. He said they didn't have enough taste to him. He liked seafood, but he liked it best when it was spicy and in a curry. When we all lived together we ate a lot of different curried stuff and rice. Mom said those were the foods he liked best because he grew up eating them in Sri Lanka. I like most all food except if it's super spicy hot. Who wants to eat something that could burn your mouth up? You can't even taste it then. Usually Mom made us shrimp when my dad was off on one of his trips. I like them cold the best, because if Mom cooked them that way, I knew that we were going to have a movie night; just the two of us. She'd mix up a dipping sauce with ketchup and horseradish and put it in a bowl. All the shrimp went into another bowl. Once we chose a movie to watch, we'd make a picnic on the floor with chips and soda and the shrimp. Then we'd watch the movie while we peeled, dunked, and ate every last one of those tasty buggers.

Even though I like to eat seafood, I haven't ever caught any of it myself. Mom and I watched a couple YouTube videos before we went to bed last night that showed people fishing for mackerel from a boat. Mom says we won't go out on a boat. We'll just stand on the pier and drop our lines for the mackerel as they come in on the tide. It looked pretty easy. Then I saw that there were other videos that showed the mackerel swimming around. So, we watched some of them too.

In the underwater videos there looked like there were hundreds, maybe even thousands, of fish in big schools. When the sun shone through the water, they darted and swirled all together. It reminded me of a laser light show, all in silver. Mom said that sometimes when the mackerel come in toward the shore on the tide, they'll jump up out of the water as they are swimming. She said when the sun catches the fish in the air, they reflect the same silver bursts of light, and she feels like they're showing off for the world. She also told me when you touch the fish, the silvery color from their scales is sticky, and rubs off on your hands. But she said it just looks white and not silver then. It has to be on the fish to be all flashy.

Then she explained all about the gear you use to catch mackerel. It's simple. You just need a fishing pole with a mackerel jig hook thing. You don't even have to bait the hook. You just drop the shiny jig down in the water, and they bite it! Once you catch some you put them into a five-gallon bucket full of sea water to keep them alive until you're ready to clean them for cooking. She says you want to keep the fish alive as long as you can, then clean and cook them right away, because the fresher they are the better they taste.

Of course, you have to kill them before you clean them. I had to go and ask her how that all is done. That's what got me—the killing and cleaning parts. It's way different to have someone else cook me fish they got from the store than to have to think about catching the fish myself and killing them so I can eat them. What if I was a fish and someone wanted to catch me? I can tell you I'd be terrified. I mean fish don't have the same kinds of brains as humans, but I'm pretty sure they can think about *some* things. I know they have instincts that make them react certain ways. Like they may not get scared the same way I do about stuff, but they can feel something that's kind of like fear. I know this fact and also that they feel some kind of pain. I Googled it on my tablet after Mom and I looked at the videos of the mackerel schools swimming. It said that fish don't hurt like we do, but they still feel sensations like pain because they have neurons called nociceptors in their brains to tell them when something doesn't feel right.

No matter what kind of pain it is they feel, I bet they don't like biting into a big hook that goes through their lips, getting yanked out of the water, and being clubbed on their head with a rock to die.

So now, I'm thinking that fishing might not be much fun after all.

Forty Seven

"I need to run down to the corner to grab a few things. Anything either of you want?" James rinsed the coffee carafe out and set it into the dish drainer to dry.

"Are you walking or driving?" Tommy asked.

"I figured I'd walk," James answered. "It seems a shame to waste the chance for a stroll on such a nice morning. I just want to grab some meats and cheese from the deli at the market for our lunch."

"I'll come along if you don't mind the company." Tommy got up from the couch and ambled into the kitchen, empty coffee mug in hand. "Is the General Store still open Sundays?"

"Only in the summer months when the tourists are around. So yes, he should be open today."

"Good. Hopefully, he still carries some art supplies. I want to grab a couple things to work on preserving Mom's pictures."

"Sure. We can stop there first or on the way home if you want—either way. What about you, Bean? Wanna come along?"

"No thanks. I'm good," Sophia replied. "I think I'll grab a shower and just chill. What time are Justine and her daughter coming over for lunch?"

"About noon," James replied crossing the room to stand in the doorway where he could see Sophia and hear her more clearly. She was curled up on the couch with Petunia napping in her lap.

"Cool." Sophia stroked the cat's head lightly. "That gives Petunia and me a couple hours to be lazy."

James smiled at her. "You do whatever you want. Be lazy all day if it makes you happy. You should take advantage of having a little mini vacation from school for the next couple days."

Sophia leaned her head against the back cushion of the sofa and closed her eyes. "Thanks, Dad. I might even take a nap. For some reason, I feel wiped out today. Take your time. I'll probably be right here in the same spot when you get back."

"You don't feel sick or anything, do you?" James asked anxiously.

Sophia opened her eyes. She smiled at her father. "I promise I'm not sick, Dad. Just tired. Yesterday was kind of rough. You know?"

James nodded. "It was."

"But it was good, too."

James walked toward his daughter. He leaned over and kissed the top of her head. "I think it was. Is there anything special we can get at the store for you?"

"Nope. But thanks."

"OK, then. We'll be back. Love you." James joined Tommy in the kitchen.

"Love you, too. Have a nice walk," Sophia called after them as they left.

They strolled out and down the driveway. Tommy fell into step with his father. They turned left toward town, walking along the edge of the pavement in companionable silence. The mid-morning sun promised the day would be typical for mid-to-late August; warm, perhaps even hot by Downeast Maine standards, but not overly humid. As they came to the corner where the sidewalk began a breeze kicked up, swirling dust and bits of fresh mown grass in front of them.

"I love that smell," Tommy remarked.

James sniffed the air. "What smell?"

"Fresh mown grass mixed with beach roses and a dash of salt air," Tommy said. "Summer at home. You don't smell anything like that in Boston."

"Ah. I guess you wouldn't. I don't even notice. I guess it's one of those things I take for granted."

"You're just used to it. I was too, before I left home. It's funny the things that I miss about not living here. It's mostly stuff you never think about when you're a kid growing up."

"I suppose." James thought for a moment. "I wouldn't know. I've lived here my entire life, hardly ever leave the area, much less the state. I don't know if that's a good or bad thing, but there it is."

Tommy chuckled. "It's all a matter of how you look at it, I think. If you're happy with your life then that's what matters."

"I can agree with that." James motioned toward the blue and white storefront on the corner to his left. "Do you want to go to the General Store first or stop on the way home?"

"Let's go in now." Tommy looked at his watch. "Is he open yet? It's only nine thirteen."

"Dunno," James turned the corner. "But we'll find out. I'd think so. I can't imagine he'd open any later. The day's half gone already."

Just then the door opened. The sound of jingling tin bells hitting the door glass sounded briefly. A man who looked to be about halfway between Tommy and James's ages stepped through the door, then held it open for them. He was clean cut, neatly dressed in a white golf shirt, pressed khaki dress pants, and light tan deck shoes that looked like they'd just been taken off the shelf.

"Mornin'," he greeted them.

"Mornin'," James and Tommy replied in unison.

"Thank you," James said as the took the door in hand and stepped through the opening into the store.

"Have a nice day." The man put on a pair of dark glasses and headed down the sidewalk toward the bank.

"Do you know who that is, Dad?"

"No idea. Never seen him before. He's sure spiffed up. But you know how it is in summer. All kinds of different folks from all over."

"Feds." A male voice floated over to them from behind the counter beside them. "They've been crawling around town the past few days. Mornin' James. Hi there, Tommy."

"Hey, Ron. How've you been?" James asked. He moved to stand in front of the glass-topped, honey colored oak counter. Tommy followed.

"I'm good. It's nice to see you both. It's been a while. You back for good, Tommy?"

"Oh no. Just a couple days. Feds?" Tommy asked.

"Yup. Haven't you seen those black SUV's driving around?" Ron went on, not waiting for, or expecting, any answer. "Hot onto something, I'd say. They try to fit in, look like tourists, but they all wear exactly the same outfit and drive the same fancy, modified cars." He pursed his lips and shook his head. "They think we don't know they're from the government. They act like everyone up here is a bunch of backwards yokels who don't know this from that."

"What're they after?" Tommy queried. "They aren't part of the Coast Guard or anything are they?"

"Nope," James answered. "If I had to guess, I'd say it doesn't have anything to do with fishing."

Ron leaned over the counter and lowered his voice. "I'd say you've got that right, James. I hear they're looking for drugs." He paused dramatically. "But I think they're way off base up here. Everyone knows the real problem is down the southern coast. No one here would be involved in that kind of stuff."

James didn't respond to the shopkeeper's observations. "Tommy here is looking for some art supplies," he said. "Do you still carry stuff like that?"

"Of course." Ron gestured toward the rear of the shop. "Right there in back, Tommy. You'll find most of what I've got on the wall next to the sewing supplies. But I have that special order in the back room. Is that what you're after?"

James raised an eyebrow. "Special order?"

Tommy looked confused. "I didn't order anything."

"Not you. Your mom," Ron said coming around the side of the counter. "It's some papers and paints Anna had me get before . . ." He trailed off. He looked down at the floor then back up at James. "I'm sorry. I just assumed you'd come to get them. They're paid for already," he offered. "Do you want them?"

Tommy cleared his throat. "I guess. I mean, sure. But then I have some other things I'm looking for."

"Well, you go look and see what I've got back there. I'll go grab her package." Ron started walking toward the back. "If I don't have what you need on the shelf, I can order anything you want from my suppliers. That's what your mom had me do. She'd just tell me exactly what she wanted, brand, and all that, I'd call them up and they'd send it. She kept me busy the past few years finding certain colors of paints and stuff. You know, she could've gone right on-line like everyone else seems to do these days. I know that my prices aren't always as cheap as other places. But she told me she liked being able to talk to a real person about what she wanted, and she wanted to make sure she kept her money here at home. She always pre-paid too. That sure was nice."

He scooted off, disappearing into the back of the store.

James turned to look at Tommy. "Well, I guess now we know where she bought her supplies."

Tommy nodded. "I'm curious about what she got." He started toward the back of the store where Ron said the art supplies could be found. "Myself, I'm looking for acid free backing paper to replace the tissue paper mom used. I need some pencil fixative too."

James stopped. "Hey, does that fixative stuff come in a can?"

"It does," Tommy said.

"I think I know where a can of it is." James said. "It's in our bedroom closet by your mom's portfolio thing that her sketch pads are in."

"Oh good. That means she may have already fixed them. But I think I'll see if he has some anyway, just in case I need it. I really would like to see what's in that portfolio, too."

"I guess we need to think about getting in there anyway," James admitted. "It's probably time to go through your mom's things. Not today, though."

"Whatever works for you, Dad. I'm not pushing."

"Here you go." Ron appeared around the corner holding a box a little over a foot square and 4 inches deep. James reached out to take it from him. It wasn't heavy but was obviously full. He held it close to his chest with both arms—this little part of Anna's life.

"Did you find what you need, Tommy?" Ron asked.

"I just started looking," Tommy replied. "You've got more here than you used to carry. In fact, you've got a little bit of a lot of stuff."

"Yeah, I keep the lists of whatever the arts center requires for any classes they offer, plus a smattering of other things for any tourists wanting supplies. I even keep some clay, and supplies for potters out back in the storeroom, because I don't have enough room out here." Ron looked around his little store. Every spot available displayed an amazing variety of items. There wasn't any space to be had on the neat, well-ordered shelves. Where shelves didn't span the entire height of building, hooks suspended from the ceiling dangled a myriad of treasures: baskets, wind chimes, stuffed toys, and more. "I should expand, but there's no way unless I went up. Since we live up there, I don't think the wife would like that very much."

James barked out a short laugh. "I'd say not."

Ron turned his attention back to Tommy. "What is it you said you need?"

"I didn't, yet." Tommy scanned the crammed shelves in front of him. "I'm looking for some pencil or charcoal drawing fixative and some eleven by seventeen, or larger, acid-free archival paper. Ah, here's some fixative." He plucked the aerosol can off the shelf and looked it over. "This will do. In fact, it's the same kind I'd buy down in Boston. It's a great price too, Ron. I know I usually pay more for it than this."

"I try. But I only can keep the prices down when I can buy in bulk. I can only buy in bulk when I sell enough of it. That's the brand the art center lists on their supply list for drawing classes, so it moves in and out of here quickly. Your archival paper, not so much. I do have a couple pads of it, but it's not cheap." He pulled out a package of fifty sheets from the bottom shelf where it was tucked under a graduated stack of sketch pads.

"Here you go."

"Thanks. This will do just fine."

"What're you working on," Ron asked casually. He put his hands in his pants pockets and rocked back and forth on his heels. "Something for The Institute?"

"Just some standard drawing preservation," Tommy said. 'I've always got something going on. You know."

"Sure," Ron nodded. "You looking for anything else?"

"Nope, not today. Thanks. This'll do."

Ron led the way back toward the register. He rang up Tommy's purchases on the sleek, squat, ivory machine that sat on the counter next to the original cash register that had been in the store from the beginning. James could remember coming in with his gram when she shopped, and how Mr. Evans, the shop owner back then, had pushed the manual buttons down on that register to ring up every single item. The sharp ca-ching of the bell when the cash drawer opened still echoed in James's mind even though he hadn't actually heard that sound in over thirty years—certainly not since Mr. Evans had sold out. When Ron took over, he'd updated the equipment in the store right from the start. As the years went by he added more modern technology. But he'd left the old register bolted right to the wooden counter where it'd always been. It was somehow comforting to James to see it there.

"You got that, Son?" James asked as Tommy reached for his wallet.

Tommy grinned at James. "Sure, Dad. No need for you to buy my work supplies. Thanks anyway."

James nodded. "I'll be right outside." His arms were full with Anna's box, so he pushed the shop door open with a shoulder and stepped onto the sidewalk. The string of bells on the door tinkled and swung, hitting the glass lightly as he went out. Tommy was only two steps behind, pushing through the door to join him as it began to close.

They walked on together, back to the corner.

"Shouldn't we take this stuff home before we go get your lunchmeat and stuff? Tommy suggested.

"Good idea." James chuckled. "You're pretty good, you know?"

"What?" Tommy asked, his tone innocent.

"Oh, come on. Ron was dying to know what your project was, but you managed to lead him on a completely errant path."

"I learned from the best. Besides, can I help it that he figured I was working on something for my job? Old Man Nosey doesn't need to know what I'm doing. The whole town would hear what our plans are by noon, and we don't even have them in place yet."

James laughed out loud. "Old Man Nosey, huh? That's a good one."

"That's what the kids in town always called him. He pumps everyone for any information he can get so he can broadcast it all over. He's gotten more subtle about it over the years. Still, I'm not telling him a damn thing. He'll just make up what he wants anyway —stinkin' president of the Downeast Busybodies Association."

James chuckled again. "Oh, I'm not saying you shouldn't just let him think what he wants. He's harmless, but he does dig for information like a squirrel after a fat acorn. I'm just saying you handled it like a pro. It couldn't have been smoother, especially what you said when I asked if you needed me to pick up the tab for what you got. Which by the way . . ." James slowed his pace, stopped, and took a breath. Tommy stopped too. He looked over at his father.

"I'll be paying for everything," James continued. "I'll give you what you just spent as soon as we get to the house. You need to keep your money. Anything and everything you need, or want, to put together this gathering and art show for your mom, is on me. No arguments. Got it?"

"Yes, Sir." Tommy said clicking his heels together. "So ordered."

"Come on, Son. I didn't mean it like that." James frowned. "Really."

"I know, Dad. I'm just horsing around. Lighten up a little. We're all in this together you know."

"Yeah. I know. I just wish . . ." James clutched the box he carried a little tighter to his heart as he began walking toward home again.

Tommy followed half a step behind. "Me too, Dad. Me too."

Forty Eight

"Is that you guys? Sophia's voice floated down the hall and into the kitchen. "That didn't take long."

"It's us. We didn't make it to the market yet," James responded. He walked into the living room and set the box he was holding on the floor in front of the bookshelf. He looked around. "I guess we should find somewhere to put this stuff from the attic before our company comes. But I still have to get food for lunch."

"Let's leave the pictures where they are," Tommy suggested. We could just put the trunk and the boxes back up in the attic again."

"Naw, I was thinking that we'd take the box of costumes to the church. They can do whatever they want with them. The other box is just some old keepsakes from my mom and grandmom that you kids might like to see. We can go through it later and put the stuff from it into the trunk." James looked around the room again. "But where to put it after that?"

"You know," Tommy offered. "The trunk is in pristine shape and nice to look at. There's room at the top of the stairs for it to sit up against the knee wall. You know, straight ahead, before you turn into either bedroom."

"Now there's a thought. Let's move it up there now. I think the other box of keepsakes will fit right inside, as is. Grab an end, will you?"

James took hold of the thick leather handle on one side of the trunk. Tommy slid his hand through the other. It was fairly light since nothing was in it except the small sheaf of papers that James had returned to the upper tray of the trunk the night before.

As they turned into the hallway by the stairs, James stopped and put his end of the trunk down. Tommy immediately followed suit. James moved to stand in front of the open doorway to his bedroom. He glared into the room.

"What the hell do you think you're doing?" His deep voice was loud and accusing.

Sophia appeared in the doorway in her robe and slippers holding a hanger with a muted coral colored sundress on it. Looking past his sister, Tommy saw that the basket from the top of the dryer that held James's clean clothes, now sat on the cedar chest at the foot of their parent's bed. "I had to wash my clothes, and I don't have anything suitable to wear today. I thought I'd grab one of Mom's sundresses . . ."

James didn't wait for her to finish. "What made you think that you had any right to go into our room without asking? And why is my laundry in here? Put it back!"

Tommy could see a muscle in his father's cheek twitching rhythmically. A flush of scarlet appeared at the base of his neck and washed up into his face. His fists were clenched at his sides.

"But . . ." Sophia eyes were wide in alarm and confusion.

"Put it back. Now!" James growled. He strode into the room past his stunned daughter, grabbed the basket of clothes from the chest, and turned on his heel. Tommy stepped out of the way without a word as his father came barreling back through the door. James stomped to the laundry closet, slammed the basket on top of the dryer, took off his hat, threw it into it, and practically ran out of the house.

Tommy turned to look at his sister. She was standing in the exact spot she'd been in the whole time, still holding up the sundress. Tears were streaming down her face.

"I didn't mean to make him mad," she gulped out between sobs. "Mom always let me borrow her clothes when I came home, and since I was doing wash, I just thought I'd clean up a little and put his clothes away." She looked up at her brother in confusion. "I was only trying to help. I didn't mean to do anything wrong. Honest," she choked out.

Tommy went into the room and gently took the dress from Sophia's grasp. He laid it on the bed. Then he hugged his little sister. "It's OK," he said as she cried into his shoulder. "It's OK. You didn't do anything wrong."

"Dad's so mad at me. Why is he so mad?"

"Oh, Sis. It's hard to say. I just don't think Dad's ready to face this room and what Mom left behind. That's probably most of it. For him, you opened the door to more than just the bedroom." Tommy stepped back. Then he gently steered her from the room, closing the door behind them.

Sophia was hiccuping now from crying so hard. She wiped at her face with the sleeve of her robe.

"Why don't you go wash your face," Tommy suggested. "I'll make you some tea, and we'll wait for Dad to come back. Then maybe you can explain about Mom letting you borrow her clothes when you needed, and how you thought you were helping. I'm betting he'll cool down in a few minutes. He'll feel terrible about how he reacted even before he gets back here."

"Do you honestly think so?" Sophia wiped at her face again with her sleeve.

"Yup. I do. It'll work out fine. You'll see."

"Mom used to say exactly the same thing to me when something was wrong." Sophia sniffed. "I sure hope you're both right."

Tommy looked down at his sister's feet. "I do think you might want to put Mom's slippers back by the door before Dad realizes you're wearing them. I've seen him straighten them up a couple times when he's come inside. It seems important to him that they're still there on the mat."

Sophia stepped out of the slippers on her feet. She handed them to Tommy. "I guess Dad and I," she took a shaky breath, "And you too. We're all trying to stay close to Mom in different ways, aren't we?"

Forty Nine

Natasha

You know, I have a new hypothesis. Grownups may be bigger and more practical and know a little bit more because they've been around longer, but deep inside I think they're still just like kids. Grownup is a weird word to explain getting bigger and older anyway. Maybe it just really means that you grow in inches. You know. grown up, instead of grownup. Maybe spelling the words altogether in one, like it's supposed to mean a lot more than just getting taller—kinda like trees do—is not the way it really is. I mean, who thought to call it that way anyway? I can tell you it wasn't any kid. I think most kids have better things to do than worry about what to call themselves so they look all important and official—like they morphed into something entirely different just because they get bigger and older in years. Besides, I don't think that's any great prize either.

I've been turning this over in my mind while I'm getting ready to go to Mr. James's for lunch. I'm pretty sure I'm on to something. Plus, there were a couple things that happened this morning that showed me I could be right.

First, at breakfast Mom was super quiet. She usually only acts that way when something isn't going well, or she's worried. So, I asked her if everything was all right? She told me she was fine, and she was just was a little tired because she hadn't slept very well. I asked her why, because I wondered if she'd had swirling fish dreams like me. But she said she'd been thinking about going to lunch at Mr. James's house and seeing her friends for the first time in years. I asked her if she was excited. She said she kind of was, but she was a little nervous too, because it had been so long since they'd been together. She told me she wasn't sure if they'd be glad to see her or not. I thought that was a little strange since they'd been good friends. Both Mr. James and Mom had told me that part. But I didn't ask her why. I just told her I was a little nervous too, because it was new people and all. She gets that because I'm usually anxious about meeting anyone new because they always seem to expect me to be a certain way. I honestly have no idea what that way is, so it always feels like I'm on trial or something.

Mom smiled that weird little smile she does when she's going to say I should just be myself, and everything would be fine. And wasn't I right? The next words out of her mouth were, "Well, I'm sure it will be fine." Then she told me to "just be myself." She said she was sure we'd have a nice afternoon, and we were going to go fishing too. And wouldn't that be fun?

Why do people say stuff like that anyway? It's like telling a river that if it just relaxes and remembers it's just water, it won't matter when it hits the edge of the cliff, and crashes down two hundred fifty feet in a raging waterfall.

I've noticed a lot of adults try to be all brave and pretend stuff doesn't bother them. I guess maybe sometimes it's because they're setting an example and don't want kids to feel more scared or nervous about things. But most times I wonder if it's just all an act because they think they're not supposed to feel stuff like that when they get grown up. Mom isn't really like that. Most of the time she doesn't tell me when she's worried or feels bad or something, but I can tell by how she looks and acts. And if I ask her, she doesn't lie to me. Even if she won't tell me what the problem is because she thinks it's none of my business, she'll still be honest that she's worried or upset. It made me feel better to know that she was anxious about going over to Mr. James's and meeting everybody, too. At least then I didn't feel like I wasn't just being a stupid kid who was scared about nothing.

I decided not to tell her about my fish dreams. Instead, I asked her if I had time to ride my bike around town and down to the wharf. She said I had at least a couple hours, and she'd ring the bell on the porch if I wasn't back by time we should leave. I didn't want to tell her, but I wanted to see if there were any mackerel around. Maybe they wouldn't be coming in today if the tide wasn't quite right. Then I wouldn't have to worry about whether we'd be catching any.

I took my time. It was like the perfect summer morning. Because it was Sunday, there really wasn't anyone around yet, so I parked my bike in my hiding spot and went down to my beach to talk to Black Whale first. He's a really good listener and I know that he can't ever spill the beans to anyone about my secrets since he's made of stone. I've told him most everything since I first discovered him there. I think people might think I'm nuts to talk to a rock, but oh well. Some people talk to themselves or their pets. One of our old neighbors in Boston did that. He used to tell his little dog about all kinds of stuff. I know because I heard them whenever he took it out for a walk. But I don't have a pet to talk to and sometimes I just need to talk about things that happen and say stuff I'm feeling out loud, so it gets out of my head. A stone whale is good for that.

He was warm and dry where he rests on the sand because the tide was almost all the way out. I checked out the two small tidal pools by his head. They are so cool—a whole miniature world in a clear-as-a-bell puddle. There were a few baby mussels and a tiny crab in one. The other one just had lichens and rocks, but it was still neat. Since the tide was on its way out, that meant it would be absolutely perfect timing for fishing in the afternoon when it started to roll back in. I should have known it would be since Mr. James had picked when we'd go. Because the tide was out, I knew I wouldn't see any fish this morning. They'd be out swimming around in deep water.

I sat in the curve of Black Whale's tail on the damp sand and just watched the sun on the ocean for a few minutes. It was so warm and cozy there that I started feeling tired. I didn't want to fall asleep, so I got up and went down by the water to look for some sea glass or other cool stuff the tide might have left. I found a few broken pieces of different kinds of shells, including a piece of a sea urchin armor, but they weren't worth putting in my hidey spot, so I left them there for the tide to take back. Then I decided to go over to the wharf. I figured even if there wasn't any fish, I could at least look at the seaweed and mussels that would be exposed on the pilings. I didn't get all the way over there though, because when I climbed up over the big rocks that guard my beach, I saw Mr. James sitting on his bench, so I decided to go see him first.

It was after we talked for a while that I really started thinking about my hypothesis about grownups, and feelings, and what being grown up means.

As I walked closer to Mr. James, I could tell that he wasn't in a very good mood. He wasn't leaning back like he does when he's just relaxing. He didn't have his hat on either. That was weird. He was sitting up pretty straight, kind of leaned forward, and he was holding on to the seat of the bench with his hands, one on each side next to his knees. It looked like he was ready to push right off of it and run. I know just how that feeling looks, because I feel that way a lot when things aren't good.

He didn't even notice me. I was going to leave him alone. I even turned around to get my bike to leave to go back to the house, so I wouldn't bother him. But then I changed my mind and decided I better go see if he was all right. I thought that even if he wanted to be by himself, I should at least check on him. Because another thing I know from personal experience is that sometimes it's nice to know someone cares about you, even if you think you don't want them to right then.

Fifty

"Are you all right, Mr. James?"

Startled, James turned toward Natasha's voice. She was standing about three feet away from the back corner of the bench.

"You sure do have a way of sneaking up on me, young lady. You've got to be the quietest child I've ever known."

"Sorry," Natasha took a hesitant step forward, stopped, and cocked her head to one side, studying James's face. "Are you all right?" She repeated. "Are you remembering again?"

James sighed. "I'll be fine. I was just thinking." He patted the bench beside him. "Come on over. Have a seat if you like."

Natasha slid onto the bench beside him. "What were you thinking about?"

"Life. I was just thinking about life."

"Oh," Natasha wrinkled her nose. "There's a lot to think about in life."

"True," James agreed, turning his attention across the sea toward the horizon.

Natasha stood up. "Well, I just wanted to be sure you were OK."

James looked over at her. "I appreciate that. You don't have to run off if you'd like to stay a while. I don't mind the company at all. By the way, what made you think something was wrong with me?"

Natasha shrugged and pushed stray strands of her dark hair away from her forehead. "The way you were sitting. You looked all tensed up. And you don't have your hat on like usual." She plopped back down pushing herself to the back of the bench, so her feet dangled off the ground.

"You're very observant. I was not fine when I first came down here. I was pretty upset. But I'm feeling better now."

"That's good. Do you want to talk about it?" She asked casually.

James was touched and amused, but he kept his face poker straight. "Not really, but thank you."

"Sure. I understand. My mom always asks me if I want to talk about it when I'm upset or mad, but usually I don't want to, either. I just want to sort it out on my own, you know?"

"I do," James said. "Thank you for understanding."

"You're welcome."

James leaned back against the bench and stretched his legs out. His thoughts turned back to where they'd been before Natasha had appeared.

He didn't want to tell anyone about how he felt about Sophia opening his and Anna's room, going through the closet, moving things around. He knew on one level that his feelings might seem unreasonable, even ridiculous. But where was the respect? It was his bedroom. It was his decision if he wanted to keep it closed and undisturbed for as long as he wanted. Maybe forever. He knew he'd have to talk to Sophia reasonably when he went back home, explain it somehow even if it didn't make any sense to her. Still, there had to be boundaries. What was she thinking? He'd never just waltz into her room and start rifling through things.

"I hope everything is all right with your daughter," Natasha said softly as if she were reading his mind.

"What's that?" James asked.

"I mean, you looked like you might be mad when I first saw you. I wondered if she was mad with you again."

So much for not talking about it. James sighed. He didn't want to upset another girl today. "No. We're not arguing. This time it's me that's angry with something that she did."

"Oh. That's not good."

"No. You're right. It's not good. Something happened and it wasn't what I wanted or expected. Then I acted badly."

"You did?" Natasha peered at him, her head cocked to one side, her eyebrows knit together.

"Ayup. I threw a nasty, grownup temper tantrum by yelling and stomping off. So, now I'm mad at myself, too."

"Hmmm."

Natasha's noncommittal response only made James feel worse. He knew his reaction to Sophia's intrusion into his room was irrational and petty. But he still felt she didn't belong in there to begin with. For some reason, he felt like he needed to defend himself.

"I know I should have handled it better, but I was surprised and hurt and . . ." James frowned.

I know how that is," Natasha interjected, her expression serious and intent. "Sometimes I get so mad I can't help it and I act like that. Mostly I cry instead of yell, though." She paused. "Plus, I run off when I'm super upset. I guess I kind of think I can run away from whatever the problem is."

"Well, you're not alone there. I ran down here. But now I'm thinking I'm the issue, and it's awful hard to run away from yourself. I didn't control my temper, and I know better."

Natasha was quiet for a moment. She leaned forward looking out across the water. "Does the way you feel about stuff change just because you're grown up?" She asked. "I mean, I know that grownups are supposed to act certain ways because they're adults, and know better, and all that. But maybe just because you're a grownup doesn't mean you don't have the same feelings you had about things when you're a kid. I didn't ever think about it before or ask anyone. But how would feelings just get less or turned off? It doesn't seem to me like they would. Does how you feel about things go away or get less when you get older, Mr. James?"

James thought for a moment. Natasha waited, watching him. "Well, no," he finally responded. "How feelings work doesn't get less.

In fact, sometimes it's the opposite. There's a lot more to care about when you grow up. The problem is that there are right and wrong ways to handle issues. It's hard sometimes not to let emotions take over. There are times you do have to pretend you don't feel the way you do about something, or at least be able to control how you react to how you feel. It's not acceptable to throw a fit, no matter how old you are."

Natasha nodded. "I get that temper tantrums aren't cool. I understand people might learn how to think and deal differently with things as they get older. Plus you learn more about stuff, right? But I wonder why it matters that everyone thinks there are certain ways people are supposed to feel and act. What if it's all just some stupid made up idea to have to pretend we don't like something, or that we don't feel something? How do you get rid of the real feelings? What happens when you squish them all down inside instead of letting them out? How come we're supposed to tell our brains that we don't care just because we grow up?"

"It's a bit more complicated than that."

"Is it. Really?" Natasha frowned. "It seems like sometimes grownups try to make stuff too confusing to deal with. I think you can't help but feel how you feel. It seems to me it might really hurt you to keep all the feelings inside and not let them out." She shrugged. "But what do I know? I'm just a kid."

James smiled at her. "Don't sell yourself short, Natasha. You've given me some interesting things to think about. And not just from this discussion. I don't think anyone who knows you could ever accuse you of being 'just a kid.' You're one of the most unique people I've ever met."

"Is that a good thing?" Natasha asked, her eyes narrowed, guarded. "Sometimes when someone says something like that to me, they don't mean it in a good way."

"It's very good," James assured her with a smile. "You're a breath of fresh air for this grumpy old guy."

Natasha grinned, apparently satisfied. She leaned back against the bench and closed her eyes.

James followed suit, listening to the harbor's song: the outgoing tide rhythmically lapping against the rocks and the wharf pilings, the occasional bump of a punt against the dock or its neighboring boat, the tops of the fir trees whispering lyrics to the breeze high above the crystal water while gulls patrolling for a snack cried out intermittently.

"Would it be OK if I talk more?" Natasha asked. "I'd like to tell you something else."

"Absolutely," James said opening his eyes. "What's up?"

"Umm, I just wanted to say thank you for not telling my mom about what I said yesterday about my dad and how I told you what you should do. I've got a big mouth sometimes. It gets me in trouble." She drew in a deep breath. "A lot."

"You're welcome, but I would never tell someone what a friend tells me in confidence."

"You mean, like a secret?"

"Yes, or when someone tells me something that isn't a secret, but isn't anyone else's business, and I know they told me because they trust me not to say anything. Sometimes people just need to talk to someone they trust."

Natasha's face was solemn. She nodded in understanding. "That's good. A lot of people like to blab to other people about everything. I think it's because they think it makes them look important or something."

James chuckled. "It's interesting you say that. My son, Tommy, and I were just discussing the same issue a little bit ago." He looked over at the youngster. "Natasha, I promise I will always listen to you, and I will keep what you tell me in greatest confidence; just between us. But . . .," James paused. "Please look at me."

Natasha looked at James, her hazel eyes direct, questioning.

"Listen very carefully to what I'm going to say," James took a breath and went on. "I want you to know that you can talk with me about anything—anything at all. I enjoy our chats, and I'm truly interested in what you have to say and what you think about things. The only time I will tell anyone else, most likely your mom, about what we talk about, is if you ever tell me something that is a danger to you, or someone, or something else. If anything that you tell me could cause harm to you in any way, I have to let your mom or someone else who can help know. But, if that happens, I will always tell you first that I need to share what you've said. I care about you. That means I have a responsibility to your well-being. Do you understand what I'm saying?"

Natasha nodded, "I think so. That makes sense. You want to be sure I don't get into trouble and that I'm safe; like my mom does. I would do the same thing for you too. It's important."

It hit James that Natasha really meant what she said about doing the same for him. Suddenly there was a lump in his throat. He swallowed.

Natasha pulled her knees up to her chest. She leaned her head back turning her attention toward a gull that was wheeling above their heads. "Are we really friends like you said, Mr. James?"

"I hope so," James replied glancing at her. "I'd like to think we are."

Natasha didn't look at him, but her face lit up with a smile that rivaled the sunshine pouring over them.

Her obvious delight at the thought that they were friends made James smile too.

If only everything in life was as easy as making a child smile like that.

"Then you're my very first friend here. I had some friends in Boston, but I don't think I'll ever see them again," Natasha allowed.

James felt another tug at his heart with her frank admission, thinking of all that Natasha and Justine had lost when Natasha's father left them.

"You know. I'm betting that when you start school, you'll meet some new friends." The moment James said it, he knew that it sounded trite and almost insincere. Natasha didn't seem to notice, though.

"Mom says so too. But you know, making friends is hard work."

"I know it can be," James admitted. "But look at us. We've become friends just by getting to know each other little by little. You never know."

Natasha cocked her head to one side, pushed her hair back out of her eyes yet again, then nodded once. "Maybe. Can I ask you something else?"

"Fire away."

"Do you think that fish feel pain?"

"Do I think fish feel pain?" James repeated as if he hadn't heard her correctly. He hadn't been prepared for this quick shift in subject matter.

"Yes, that's what I asked," Natasha answered patiently.

James wrinkled his eyes in thought and puzzled over this for a second. "I don't really know, for sure," he answered. "Why do you ask?"

Natasha unfolded herself so that her legs were dangling from the bench once again. She crossed her arms in front of herself. "Well, I did what you said. I asked Mom about how to catch mackerel and all about it last night. We looked up stuff on the internet about them too."

"And?" James prompted.

"And I don't think I want to catch any fish after I learned about how, and I'm not even sure I ever want to eat fish again either." Natasha set her chin and tucked her arms in even tighter to herself.

"Oh. I see," James said. "You're worried about how it will hurt the fish when you catch them."

Natasha nodded. "I know it sounds dumb, but I never thought of it before. You know, how it would feel to be a fish that gets caught. I mean, don't you think it hurts when they bite the hook? Then you have to bash them on the head with a rock to kill them!" She unfolded her arms and reached up with one hand to rub her head. "That's gotta hurt bad. It's just plain mean, too."

James realized she was serious. He bit his lip, trying once again not to appear amused. He cleared his throat. "Well, first of all, the reason you bonk them on the head with a rock, or a little rubber mallet like I use, is because it knocks them out right away. I know it sounds mean, but really I think it's the most humane way to do it because just like that, they don't feel a thing."

Natasha was looking at him intently. "Mom told me that's what my grandfather does before he cleans them for Gran to cook," she said.

"That's right. Our fathers taught us to do it that way, and their fathers taught them. It's just the way it's done. Talking about it with you now though, I can understand why it sounds mean."

He smiled at her. "You know, Natasha, you certainly have a way of making me look at things differently."

Natasha looked concerned. "Is that all right?"

"Absolutely. I like it. It makes me think." James reached for the hat that was usually on his head, realized it wasn't there and dropped his hand to his lap. "My wife, Anna, had a way of doing that too." He paused. "She would've loved to have known you."

"I think I would've liked to know her too. My mom says she was super nice, and that she and my gran were friends."

"That's right. They were old friends. In fact, your gran was the first friend my wife ever had here in town."

"That's neat—like you being my first friend here. I bet Gran misses her. She doesn't spend time with people much, except Mom and me. She takes really good care of us. She makes the best cookies, too."

"I know she does," James agreed. "Sometimes Anna and Cora, your gran, would bake cookies at your house together for the church bake sales, then I got to be the lucky guy to taste test them when Anna brought some home." James grinned. "My favorites are the molasses raisin ones."

"I like her chocolate chip ones and the chocolate with white icing the best," Natasha said. "But you forgot to really answer my question."

"Oh, sorry. I got lost thinking about cookies for a minute. Let's see, you asked if I thought fish feel pain . . ." James scratched at his beard. "Well, I know that some folks believe that fish feel pain. But I also know that fish brains aren't the same as our brains. I think I remember something about them not having the same kind of pain receptors humans have. Maybe any discomfort they feel isn't like like the really hurting kind of pain we might feel, say like if you got a hook caught in your hand." He rubbed his index finger and thumb together. "Which I've done a few times, I might add. That hurts plenty, I can tell you. But personally, I don't think fish are able to think or feel like us. Does that make sense?"

Natasha nodded. "I looked it up; about their brains I mean. Like you said they have something in them that lets them know something feels different or uncomfortable. Still, even if they don't feel ouchy pain, it doesn't seem right to catch them for fun or to eat."

"Hmm. I can see why you'd say that. Can I tell you my thoughts about it?"

Natasha dipped her head. "Sure."

"Well, you have to remember that I'm a fisherman. It's all I've ever known to do. It's how my family has made their living for generations. So, I may be just a bit opinionated about fishing. But here's what I think." He paused a second. "Everyone has to eat."

Natasha snorted. "Maybe, but everyone doesn't have to eat fish."

James held up a hand. "Hold on. I'm not finished. Everyone has to eat. Remember our eagle friends up there?" He gestured toward the nest on the reach. "They go fishing and eat the fish just like that." He snapped his fingers. "There's nothing nice about it. They snatch it right out of the water and dig in. There isn't any stunning the mackerel on the head with a mallet first. They simply tear right into it. That poor fish that you're thinking about, is minding his own business and swoosh! All of a sudden, this huge scary bird dips their long, sharp talons down into the water, grabs him, and hauls him up to peck his insides out, guts and all."

Natasha giggled.

"Oh, so now it's funny, huh?" James grinned and raised an eyebrow at her.

"When you tell it like that it is." Natasha was belly laughing now, holding onto her side. James laughed out loud. He thought her laughter was one of the best sounds he'd heard lately.

"I'm glad you like my description," he said, smiling from ear to ear. "But seriously, all creatures need food to survive. You know food sources for all animals, including humans, is connected. I think of it like a big net with all kinds of things in it to choose from."

"I learned about the food web in science at school. That's what you mean right?"

"Ayup. That'd be it. The food web, huh? Way back when I went to school they called it a food chain. But I think web, or even net, like I call it, is a better description. Anyway, like you know, every living thing on the planet is part of that food web, from bugs, to fish, to eagles, to humans."

"Uh huh. And plants are part of a food web too. Some creatures only eat different plants."

"That's right. So, I think of it this way. Some animals eat just meat. Some eat just vegetables. You know some birds eat bugs. Other birds, like eagles, are not very discriminating. They catch and eat all kinds of fish and meat, even other birds sometimes. Some sea creatures, like shrimp and many whales, only eat organisms too tiny for us to see."

"Like Right Whales," Natasha interrupted. "I've been reading about them. They only eat microscopic copepods. They open their mouths and strain them through their baleen into their mouths. Like this." Natasha demonstrated by opening her lips to show her teeth clenched tight together." She continued talking, her voice muffled and slightly distorted behind her wall of teeth. "But the baleen isn't as hard and solid like my teeth. It has holes in it to let the tiny stuff through.

Other, bigger stuff just bounces off." She jerked her head and shoulders to the side almost falling off the bench.

"Whoa there." James reached out, but Natasha had recovered, wiggling back onto the bench. She dissolved in a fit of giggles. She had him smiling so wide that his cheeks hurt.

Natasha looked at him. "Can you imagine being a fish that gets run into by a whale mouth? You're just swimming along one minute and then, boing." She leaned sideways and waved both arms in the air, imitating a floundering fish. James couldn't help himself. Now he was laughing out loud at her antics.

"You get bonked right off course without any warning," Natasha continued. She snickered and shook her head once. "Crazy."

James slapped his knee. "I never looked at it like that—from a fish's viewpoint. Interesting."

Natasha shrugged. "I like to think about stuff in different ways. It's neat and I think it makes you realize things you didn't before."

"I believe you've got something there. That's a very good way to view the world," James said seriously. "I don't believe many people do that much, or at all."

"I know." Natasha nodded. "And grownups are the worst. Oh." She looked over at James wide-eyed. "Sorry. That didn't come out right."

"No, no." James waved his hand dismissing her apology. "It's fine. Grownups are the worst," he agreed. "Myself included. It seems we forget that we're not the only ones that matter—humans that is."

Natasha nodded again. She gave a relieved sigh. "What else were you going to tell me about the food web?"

"Oh, right. We got a bit sidetracked again, didn't we? Let's see," James rubbed his forehead. "So, there's this food web and everything on it is connected. Every bit of it. The neat thing is that unlike many animals, I can decide to eat anything I want from that web as long as it's edible for humans. And I do. I eat lots of different things. I can choose meats and grains and milk and fish and lobster. You get the idea. Some other folks choose not to eat any meat at all."

"Those are vegetarians," Natasha commented.

"Right. And that's just fine. It's their choice to eat what they want, just like it's your choice to eat what you want. As long as your mom says it's OK. You know you should always eat what your mom says to."

"You bet. I like all the stuff Mom and Gran make anyway. The only thing I never want to eat is mushrooms. But Mom doesn't make me eat them because she knows I can't stand them.

"Mushrooms, huh."

"Why in the world would you want to eat fungus?" Natasha flipped her hands up in the air in question. "And do you know where they grow those things?"

James chuckled. "I do and I have to tell you I'm not a big fan either, but I will eat them on pizza."

"Ugh. No way! Not even on pizza."

"I'll have to remember that," James said seriously. "But you get the idea. As humans we get to choose what we want to eat from our edible choices in the web. It's fine not to want to fish or hunt or gather whatever food you don't want to eat, for whatever reason. A lot of people won't eat lobster because they feed from the bottom and they eat a lot of stuff no self-respecting human would ever consider. But I happen to think lobster are one of the tastiest meals out there. I only eat the meat from their claws and tails. That meat is made by the nutrients in the stuff they eat. I don't directly eat any part that processes their meals, like their stomachs or intensities. Same with fish. I eat their meat, not their innards.

"Innards? That's a funny word."

"It's just a term for the insides that make the body work." James gestured from his throat to his stomach. "It's the organs that keep you alive, like your heart, lungs, stomach, and intestines."

"Oh. I get it."

"The point is, humans can choose their meals because our bodies let us eat a variety to stay alive and healthy. I don't feel bad about eating fish, because other animals eat it too. I never harvest what I'm not going to use either. If I'm not planning on eating it, or in the case of my lobstering business, selling it to other people so they can eat, then I feed it to other animals that like it. When I catch and clean a fish, I put the fish guts back in the ocean for other fish to eat. When I shell a lobster, I do the same thing. I put everything back into the ocean for other creatures' meals. Did you know that lobster eat their own shed shells, and the shed shells of other lobsters so they can make new strong ones?"

Natasha nodded. "I do. Mom told me about it."

"That's good," James said. "Well, I just figure I'm helping other creatures out when I put the parts of my seafood meals I can't use back into the sea. I've never been one to fish or hunt just for sport. If I harvest it, I try to do it in the most humane way possible, and I use every bit of it I can. I'm always thankful for the meal provided too," he added.

"Do you thank the fish before you kill them or eat them?" Natasha looked intently at James.

He shook his head. "I never thought of doing that. I just feel thankful inside. I suppose you could certainly tell a fish, or any other food you harvest, 'thank you' if you wanted to." James was bemused. "I'm sure there are folks out there who do just that." He shrugged. "I'm just glad I have food, and I get to choose what I want to eat. I like all the stuff on our food web. But cookies are the best."

"Mr. James!" Natasha giggled. "Cookies aren't technically part of our food web."

"Well, the stuff that makes them is and so they are part of *my* food web. So there."

Natasha grinned. "OK. I'll let you have that."

"Does any of what I said make sense?"

"Sure. I get it." She giggled again.

"What?"

"I was just thinking about us on the food web. There are some things that eat humans for their food too, or just bite us for a snack, like mosquitoes. You know no blood-sucking mosquito is ever going to ask me if it's OK to have dinner on my arm."

"Hah. That's true. But I can tell you it won't make it off me alive when it tries. And I won't be nice about it either."

That made Natasha giggle again. She slapped her arm at an imaginary mosquito. "Got it!"

"Just like that." James grinned at her. "All this talk of food has made me hungry." He stood up and stretch his arms skyward. "I think I'd better get on home. I've got to get ready for a lunch date with friends."

"Me too!" Natasha bounced off the bench. "I don't want to be late." She extended her arm toward James, her fist closed.

He looked at her quizzically.

"I'm trying to give you a fist bump. It's how my friends and I said hi and 'bye in school."

"Oh." James imitated Natasha extending his arm in the same way. She gently bumped his fist with hers. "See ya later."

"OK!" James replied.

Natasha turned on her heels and started jogging toward the road. She stopped suddenly and slapped her hand against her forehead. "Oops. I almost forgot. I rode my bike down here."

James looked around. He didn't see a sign of her old bike anywhere. "Where is it?"

"Over here," Natasha called, dragging it out from its hiding place behind the rocks. She climbed on the seat and waved back at James. "Mom and I will be over in a few for lunch and fishing." She turned forward aiming the nose of her bike toward the road.

James waved back at her. "See you soon." As Natasha pedaled away, James purposefully headed up the path toward home, feeling a whole lot better than he had an hour before.

Now he had to have that talk Sophia. On one hand he still felt he owed her an explanation for his ugly behavior, but on the other he felt she needed to know, and respect, his boundaries and wishes at home. Regardless, he had a feeling that the discussion he needed to have with her wasn't going to be near as pleasant as his visit with Natasha.

Fifty One

Tommy was trotting down the path as James was coming up.

"Hey. I was just coming down to find you."

"Everyone seems to be checking on me today," James remarked. "What made you think I'd be down at the cove?"

Tommy's eyebrows drew together in question.

James waved his hand. "Never mind."

"You were pretty worked up," Tommy said. "I figured you must be sitting on your bench. You good?"

"Ayup."

"Do you want me to go down to the store to grab the things you wanted for lunch? Justine and Natasha will be here in a little over an hour."

"That'll be fine, but not just yet. I want to talk to Sophia, and thinking about it, you should be there too. It applies to all of us."

"All right." Tommy turned and they walked the few steps back to the house together in silence.

Once inside James called out for his daughter. "Bean? Where are you?"

"I'm in the laundry closet," she called out. James heard the dryer door slam shut.

"Would you mind coming into the living room?"

"Be right there."

Tommy sat down on the sofa as his sister walked slowly into the room. Her eyes were a little swollen from crying, but that was the only sign that she'd been upset earlier. She was dressed for the day, her hair bound up in a messy bun, wrapped in scrunchy that matched the hot pink shirt she wore loosely tucked into her jean shorts.

"I see you got your clothes all set," James said. "You look very nice."

"Oh, Dad," a waterfall of words tumbled out of Sophia. "I'm so sorry I got into Mom's closet. It's just that she always let me go and pick stuff out to wear when I came home. She and I wear the same size. We shared clothes a lot. I didn't even stop to think that you wouldn't want me to wear her things or go into your room. I'm really, really sorry." She hung her head and James saw a single tear land on the floor.

He walked over to Sophia and put his hand under her chin. He gently lifted her face so she would look at him. "It's not entirely your fault. I never should have reacted the way I did. I don't know what came over me. I let frustration and . . . and I don't know what else, get the better of me. I apologize for the way I acted. It was completely uncalled for." He wiped the track of another tear off her cheek with his thumb. "Please don't cry."

Sophia sniffed and stepped back from James. She dug a tissue out of her shorts pocket, dabbed at her eyes, and blew her nose. "I seem to cry about a lot lately. I hate it."

"I think it's probably better to cry than to blow up like an idiot, the way I did," James remarked. "Tommy's counselor sure was right when he said everyone grieves differently."

"She," Tommy interjected.

"Huh?" James looked over at his son.

"She. My counselor is a woman."

"Oh. Sorry. I just assumed . . ."

"It's fine, Dad. I don't think I'd told you that."

"Regardless, I see now that she's right. Plus, I'm obviously having a rough time getting through some things." James gestured toward the couch. "Bean, would you mind sitting down?"

Sophia plopped onto the couch beside her brother.

"I think there are a couple things I need to talk to you both about. I think I should . . ." James began.

"Dad, you don't need to explain anything," Sophia interrupted. "I don't want you to have to talk about anything you don't want to. And I get that I violated your privacy. I was wrong. I never would have gone into your room, or Mom's closet, without asking when she was still here. I was out of line just waltzing in there. I should have asked you first." She shook her head. "I don't know what I was thinking. I'd be super mad if you went to my apartment and started going through things."

James opened his mouth, but Sophia wasn't done.

"And I never should have moved your stuff from the laundry closet. It's your house and your clothes. You can do whatever you want with them."

"Way to give Dad permission to do what he wants, Soph." Tommy remarked.

"Oh, geez. There I go again. I didn't mean it that way. I just meant . . ."

James held up his hands. "Enough,' he said firmly.

Both of his children looked at him and were quiet.

"Hey! That still works," James grinned.

Tommy chuckled. "And probably always will. After all, you are the dad."

James shook his head. "I don't know. Someday my dad magic might up and disappear. But seriously, Bean I know what you mean and thank you."

He crossed over and perched on the edge of his recliner. "But here's the thing. I want you both to know that I hope you come home often—as often as you want. I want you to come in like you never left and feel like this is still home, even though you move away and have families of your own someday that you bring to visit. The only thing I ask is that you respect that I live here all the time. You're both adults now, however that doesn't mean that a few house rules don't still exist. When you're home, I only ask that you respect my wishes, clean up after yourselves, and let me know if you're going out and when you might be back. So I don't worry. Most importantly, please respect my private spaces; even my laundry basket." He winked at Sophia. She bit her lip and ducked her head. "I'll do the same for you," James added. "Does that sound reasonable?"

"Sure," Tommy said.

"Yes, Dad. I won't go in your room again. I promise," Sophia vowed. "I really am sorry. I didn't mean to be disrespectful or to make you mad."

"I know, Honey. And I can't tell you how disgusted I am at myself for my reaction. Let's just go forward. I promise you I'll do my best to be less reactionary in the future." James shook his head. "I don't know what came over me. It's just. . .I can't stand to go in there or even see the door open. I realize it's irrational. I know that your mom is gone—up here." James pointed at his head. "But, . . ." He put his hands on his knees and looked up at the ceiling as a mist of sadness slid over him. He sighed and looked back down. "But my heart just isn't going along."

Fifty Two

"Tasha," Justine called up the stairs. "Are you ready to go?"

"I'm coming." A frowning Natasha clumped down the stairs holding a hairbrush in one hand and an elastic hair tie in the other. "Can you please fix my dumb hair? I keep trying, but I can't ever get all of it into the stupid ponytail right."

"Come here. I'll take care of it. Your hair never has liked to be tamed."

Natasha handed over the brush and turned her back to her mom. Justine ran the brush over Natasha's wild waves. "You have enough hair for three people."

"Ouch! Geez, Mom. I might have a lot of it, but I want to keep it!"

"Sorry, but you sure have some tangles going on back here."

"It's 'cause the wind whips it all around when I ride my bike," Natasha offered.

"Hmmm. We could braid it every day so it doesn't do that."

"But you're the one who does that, and you're not always here when I get up, and I don't know how. Besides how could I reach all the way down the back of my hair to do it?" Natasha sounded exasperated.

Justine made one more pass with the brush from Natasha's forehead back toward the crown of her head. Capturing the last wispy waves, she grasped it all together with her left hand, put the hairbrush handle in her mouth to hold it, then reached over her daughter's shoulder with her right hand to grab the elastic band Natasha held up for her. Justine slid the elastic over the ponytail looping it around three times. She pulled it tight, ran the brush through the entire ponytail twice, then turned Natasha around to face her.

"Don't you go being all grumpy with me," she admonished pointing the hairbrush at her scowling daughter. "I'm only trying to come up with a better solution. I can teach you how to braid without reaching all the way down your back. I do it all the time. Not only that, I'm sure Gran will help you if you ask nicely." She lightly swatted Natasha on the butt with brush, then handed it to her. "Now go put this away. We need to get a move on, or we'll be late. I'll meet you out front."

Natasha scampered up the stairs and was back down before Justine even made it out the door.

"That was fast. Ready?" Justine put her hand on the screen door.

"Not yet." Natasha was on her way into the kitchen. "I asked Gran to wrap up some of Mr. James's favorite cookies.

"Hold on. I've already got them right here." Justine patted the canvas bag looped over her arm. "Gran gave the package to me before she left to go grocery shopping. There are three different kinds of cookies in here and a loaf of banana bread too."

"Oh good! Let's go." Natasha pranced out into the yard toward the sidewalk.

"Whoa there, you wild pony you." She smiled at her daughter's exuberant antics. "I want to take a shortcut."

Natasha stopped short. "Shortcut? What shortcut?"

Justine smiled mysteriously and jerked her head toward the backyard. "Come on. I'll show you. I'm sure it's still there. I don't think anyone's used it since my friend Sarah's grandmom passed away the year after we graduated from high school."

"The abandoned yellow house next door? You knew the people that lived there?"

"I did. It was just Sarah's grandmom, Mrs. Dean. She was a widow. I heard that the house needs so much work now that no one can live in it. It's sad. I remember it used to be such a sweet place.

Justine led the way out into the back yard to the shed where Natasha's bike stayed when she wasn't on it. Then she walked along the far side of it. She ducked around the back of the building, then stopped in front of the zigzag hedge of arborvitae separating the back yard from the next yard over. Natasha was right on her heels.

"Let's see." Justine counted the tall shrubs as they passed them. "One, two, three, four. Here." She stopped. "There's a little extra space between these two. We go through this shrub and around to the right of the next one, and the path should be there. It runs through the forsythia hedges in Mrs. Dean's yard and along the little wooded area down toward the shore. I'm sure it's a little grown over, but it's pretty well shaded so I don't think it will be too bad. If it is we'll just go back and walk along the sidewalk."

"Way cool," Natasha said. "A secret passage."

Justine led the way around the two, tall bushes.

"These things are scratchy," Natasha complained pushing past the second one.

"They can be," Justine agreed. "Just go slow and push the little branches away from you." She stepped into a natural archway between the evergreen hedge and a dense, tangled row of brush.

It was shaded and cool in the tunnel. Bare branches wove in and out, basket-like on one side. There weren't any leaves on the side where Natasha and Justine stood, but about a foot inside the hedge a lush, deep green net reached out toward the sun in all directions. Natasha couldn't even see the yard through the leaves.

"What is this stuff?" Natasha asked, pushing aside a supple branch that poked at her side.

"Forsythia," Justine answered. "Just wait until springtime when they bloom. Every inch of them is covered with tiny yellow flowers. It's like a burst of sunshine."

"How come there's hardly any branches with leaves inside here?"

"Because no light can get through this far because the leaves are so thick out there on the outside. Every once in a while a branch or two will grow into the path between the hedges. Sarah and I started poking them back in on the bushes to keep the pathway open, like this." Justine demonstrated, bending a pencil-thin branch that had reached about a foot into the pathway back toward the main bush, weaving it in and out of other branches to hold it in place. "See? If you look around, you can see how we did that all along in here." She peered at the branch wall. "That's funny. Some of these have been cut away." She looked down at the path in front of them. "There are the cuttings right there. I guess some other kids must have found the shortcut and have been using it."

"That's kind of cool. Isn't it?"

"It is." Justine wrinkled her nose in thought. "But I can't think of any kids that live right around us. It's all just old-timers now, like my parents. Could be some summer kids going through at the far end past our backyard." She shrugged. "I suppose it's not like anyone would care since Mrs. Dean's house is empty now."

"We could just walk through her old backyard then. Right?" Natasha asked.

"Sure. But what's the fun in that when you have a hidden tunnel?" Justine continued down the path. "Come on."

"Where does this come out?" Natasha asked as she trotted along behind her mom.

"Right here," Justine said, pausing in front of a green curtain of arching forsythia branches. "I was worried we wouldn't be able to get through this end, but whoever has been using it has clipped away enough so we can get through easily." She gently pushed long draping branches to the side. "Here, you go first while I hold them."

Natasha slid past her mom. Justine came through behind her, then released the supple branches. They settled back into place.

"Wow. You can't even tell that there's a path behind there," Natasha said. "That's so cool."

Justine smiled down at her. "I thought you'd like it. This is where the hedge cuts the corner on Mrs. Dean's yard." Justine gestured to her left toward the house. "See how it turns right here and keeps going up the front part of her lawn? There's a gate somewhere along here to get into the yard, but I bet it's all overgrown and rotted now."

"That's kind of sad," Natasha remarked. "I bet it was a really neat yard. Now it's like no one even cares about it anymore."

"It was. Mrs. Dean had such pretty flowers too. I guess the gardens are all gone now," Justine mused. "So, do you know where we are?"

"Yup." Natasha grinned and spun around. "We're almost right across from Mr. James's house. I can see part of his yard from here." She pointed down the overgrown gravel driveway. A rusty chain with a weathered wooden placard swinging from its center looped across the end of the drive. On the other side of the placard Natasha knew there was faded black writing on it that whispered, "No Trespassing."

"Just past this driveway is as far as I've made it riding up the hill on my bike," she said as they walked along the drive.

"Really? Wow, that's impressive. I don't think I ever got that far before I had to walk my bike up."

"I'm gonna make it all the way to the top someday," Natasha declared. "It's a personal challenge."

"That's quite a challenge," Justine replied. "But, if anyone can do it, I know you can."

Natasha nodded. "Oh, I will. Just wait. I know I can do it if I practice."

Justine stopped and looked down at her daughter. "Just promise me you'll be super, super careful. I don't trust how some of these people drive down to the wharf. Folks don't pay much attention to where they're going sometimes. They might not even see you on that little bike."

"I promise. I stay as close to the edge of the road as I can. Plus I only go up and down the road on the right side, like you told me."

At the edge of the driveway they stepped over the chain and crossed the street. It was just a few yards more to the Edward's driveway entrance.

"Oh, look." Justine nodded toward a tall, thin man with reddish-brown hair carrying a brown paper grocery bag in both arms. He was walking toward the driveway on the opposite side of the road. "There's Tommy." She waved and the man shifted the bag to free one arm so he could wave back.

"Oh," Natasha said. "That's Mr. James's son, right?"

"Uh, huh."

They crossed to James's driveway and stopped. Tommy's long strides closed the last few yards between them in just seconds. He was grinning from ear to ear.

"Justine! It's so good to see you. It's been too long."

Justine returned his smile. "Hi Tommy. It's great to see you too."

Tommy looked over at Natasha. "You must be Natasha. It's a pleasure to finally meet you."

Natasha looked him up and down.

Her mother nudged her with an elbow.

Natasha looked up at her. Justine raised her eyebrows.

"Oh. Sorry. Nice to meet you too," Natasha said still eyeing him. "What's in the bag?"

"Natasha! Really."

Tommy chuckled. "It's fine," he said to Justine. "It's just part of our lunch. I'm starving by the way. What about you?"

"I can always eat," Natasha remarked.

"Well come on then," Tommy said leaning his head toward the house. "Let's get this party started."

Fifty Three

They hadn't even made it to the house before James was out the door to greet them.

"Hello, ladies. Welcome. I'm so glad you came over." He gave Justine a long hug. She returned it along with a warm smile.

"It's so good to be here, Mr. Edward," Justine said.

"James, Justine. Just James." He stood back to look at them. "You both look very pretty today."

"Mr. James," Natasha said, hands on her hips. "You act like you didn't know we were coming, and you didn't just see me a little while ago."

"Well it's the first time you've come to my house, and it's been a long time since your mama's been here. I'm excited," James replied sharing a fist bump with Natasha. "It's going to be a fun day." He held the screen door open. "Go on in."

"When are we going fishing?" Natasha asked.

"Whoa, there. Don't you want to eat first?" James followed them in, letting the screen door close on its own behind him.

"Well, sure. I guess so. But the tide is turning. Then the fish will start running in, right?"

James nodded. "Ayup, but it'll be a couple hours before fishing is at its best off the pier. The tide needs to swing in higher so the water's a bit deeper down there."

"Oh, OK." Natasha shrugged. "What's for lunch then?"

James and Tommy both chuckled.

"Natasha!" Justine shook her head at her daughter. "Really. Mind your manners." Her face was pink with embarrassment. "I'm sorry. She's just really excited."

James waved a hand. "It's perfectly fine. I'm hungry too. Tommy just came back from the store with supplies for sandwiches, and Sophia has made up a nice pasta salad for us." He looked around. "Where is she anyway?"

"I'm right here," Sophia said from just outside the screen door. Her arms were overflowing with a vivid collection of lilies. "Tommy, will you please let me in? I don't want to drop any of these. Hi, Justine!"

"Wow, those are gorgeous," Justine remarked as Sophia came into the kitchen.

"I had a thought that it would be nice to cut some from Mom's garden for the table." Sophia laid them gently on the kitchen island. "I think maybe I got a bit carried away." She turned toward Justine and held out her arms for a light hug.

"Wow, you look exactly the same," Sophia said, taking a step back. "You haven't changed a bit."

Justine laughed. "Thanks, I don't know about that. I sure feel like I'm different. But look at you! You were a sophomore in high school when I left and now . . ." Justine cocked her head. "You look so much like your mom. She was absolutely beautiful and, so are you." She fluttered a hand in the air. "Not that you weren't before, but now that you're older . . . Oh, geez, I sound like an idiot."

Sophia smiled. "It's fine. It really means a lot to me, that I look like Mom." She looked over at Natasha who was eyeing her with a slightly suspicious look. "You must be Natasha," she said to the girl.

"Uh, huh," Natasha answered folding her arms across her chest. "Everybody keeps saying that."

"Well, that's probably because we've known about you for years, but you're like a mystery girl because we haven't seen you until now," Sophia said. "It's so nice to finally meet you. And you look a lot like your mom, too."

"I hope so," Natasha grumbled. "I don't want to look like anyone else."

Sophia grinned. "Well, you definitely do. So no worries there." She gestured toward the flowers. "I better get them into water. Please make yourselves comfortable. Can I get anyone anything to drink?"

James was already in the refrigerator pulling out sodas and a pitcher of lemonade. Tommy and Justine moved over to the table. They were chatting like they'd just seen each other the day before instead of almost ten years prior. Natasha still stood in the middle of the kitchen looking around.

"What would you like to drink, Natasha?" James asked. "Don't you want to sit down?"

Natasha shook her head. "I guess lemonade. Mom doesn't want me to drink soda."

"You can today as long as it doesn't have caffeine in it," Justine remarked from across the room.

James held up the pitcher of lemonade and a can of ginger ale. "Here's your choices then, or water. What'll it be?"

"Umm, I think I still want lemonade."

"You got it." James poured the lemonade over ice into the glass on the counter, then handed it to Natasha.

"Thanks." Natasha accepted the glass from James and took a sip. "This is really good."

"Glad you like it. I just mixed it up. Now let's see about getting lunch on the table. We don't want to go fishing while we're hungry."

"Sounds good." Natasha watched James as he unloaded the bag Tommy had brought in. "Can I help?"

"Do you want to give me a hand with these flowers while Tommy and your mom talk?" Sophia asked. "Your mom and my brother have a lot of catching up to do. It's been a long time since we've seen her. You weren't even born yet the last time we were together."

"I'm almost ten," Natasha offered. "So, it's been more than ten years, because Mom said she hadn't come back here since before I was born."

"You're right. Wow. Ten years." Sophia shook her head. "It seems like a long time ago in some ways and not long at all in others."

"Um, can I help Mr. James instead?" Natasha asked. "Is that OK? I help my Gran make lunches all the time."

"Whatever works," Sophia said, gently poking lily stems into a vase she'd dug out of the cupboard. She held up a stem in each hand. "Hey, do you think it's ok to put orange and purple in the same bouquet?"

Natasha shrugged. "Beats me. Flowers are my mom's thing."

"Really?" Sophia asked.

"Yeah, she used to have a flower box on the fire escape at our apartment. Now she works at a farm." Natasha wrinkled her nose in thought. "I don't think they grow anything except vegetables there, though."

"My mom loved flower gardening, too." Sophia said. "These are from her garden."

Natasha nodded. "They're pretty." She looked at Sophia and opened her mouth like she wanted to say something else, but James broke in.

"So, if you want to help me, come on over here," he said. "You can put this lunchmeat and cheese out on a plate for me."

"I need to wash my hands first," Natasha said going to stand beside him.

"Good idea," James agreed. "You can do that right here. The pump bottle on the left is hand soap."

"Where's your cat, Mr. James?" Natasha asked as she stood on her tiptoes to turn on the water in the sink.

"Oh, she's around here somewhere." James opened the cupboard above his head and pulled out a serving plate. "She's probably asleep on the couch. That's where you'll usually find her if she's not in her window seat in here. You can go see if you want," he offered. "I can do this."

Natasha shook her head. "It's fine. I was just wondering."

"Just open a can of food. She'll come running," Sophia remarked pushing the last of the blooms into the vase. She slid the bouquet into the center of the island and started cleaning up the cuttings left behind.

James chuckled. "True. That cat loves food more than anything."

Sophia came up beside Natasha. "'Scuse me, please. I need to get to the trash can."

"Sure," Natasha moved slightly to the side.

Sophia threw away the cuttings, then reached over to the paper towel holder beside the sink. "Just give me a sec and I'll show you how to get Petunia wherever you want her. She can hear a cat food can opening a mile away."

"Really?"

Sophia snorted. "Oh, yeah. Just you watch." She wiped off her hands, tossed the paper towel into the trash, and walked over to the pantry. "I might not even have to open the can. Sometimes when she hears the pantry door open she hauls on in here." She stopped. "Hey, I have an idea. Come on over here, Natasha. Let's have you get the cat food out and open it. Then she'll come right to you."

"Really? All right!" Natasha scampered over to the pantry.

"If you open the door you'll see the cat food cans on the right, on the middle shelf," Sophia instructed. "Then we'll get her bowl off the mat, take it over to the island, open the can, and feed her. She'll be your best friend after that."

Sophia stood aside as Natasha did as she instructed. Sure enough, the minute she opened the pantry door and stepped in, Sophia heard the soft thump of Petunia's feet hitting the floor in the next room. "Here she comes," she whispered. "Do you see the cat food?"

"Got it," Natasha appeared, holding the can for Sophia to see. "I chose the ocean fish flavor for her."

"Perfect." Sophia grinned and pointed to the doorway. "Here she comes."

"Oh! Hi, pretty cat," Natasha crooned, crouching down. "Do you want some lunch?" She reached out a hand, but Petunia didn't come any closer.

Sophia retrieved the cat's bowl from the mat. "Bring that on over here and we'll put it in her bowl. She'll wind all around your legs while you're getting it ready. You can pet her while she's eating. She doesn't care."

"OK." Natasha walked over to Sophia, keeping her eyes on Petunia the whole time.

Sophia held out her hand for the can. "Don't you worry. She's not going anywhere as long as she thinks she's getting fed. Let me open that for you, the darn tops on these things will cut you to shreds if you're not used to them."

Natasha nodded as she handed the can to Sophia. "My mom cut herself really bad on the top of a soup can once. It was awful. There was blood everywhere."

The cat took a couple steps into the kitchen.

"Here she comes," Natasha whispered.

Sophia popped the can. Petunia trotted over to them. As promised, she began winding her way in and out of their legs.

"She's purring!"

"Oh yeah, she purrs most all the time. She's a pretty happy cat. Here take this on over to the mat by the door. Then you can sit down and pet Miss Fatty all you want while she's wolfing down her lunch."

"Here Kitty, Kitty," Natasha crooned as she crossed the room. Petunia didn't need any coaxing. She almost tripped the girl in her hurry to follow her. Natasha put the bowl on the mat and plopped down beside it. Petunia dug in like she hadn't eaten in days.

Sophia came over by them and knelt. "See, I told you. That cat eats every meal like it's her last."

Natasha tentatively reached out a hand.

"Go ahead, she'll let you pet her—like this." Sophia demonstrated by running her hand all the way down Petunia's back. Natasha mimicked Sophia's motion.

"You're so soft," she told Petunia. "I think you're the prettiest cat I've ever seen." Petunia kept right on eating, paying no attention to either of them.

Natasha continued to pet the cat. "Where did you get her?" She asked Sophia.

"She just showed up one day," Sophia explained. "My mom decided to keep her, so here she is."

"Look, Mom." Natasha glanced over at the table.

"I see. We've been watching ever since you got her food out," Justine said. "She's a beautiful cat and so friendly too. When are her kittens due?"

"Kittens?" James, Tommy, Sophia, and Natasha all asked in unison.

"What kittens?" James was frozen in mid motion on his way to place plates on the table.

"If I'm wrong, I'll skip lunch. But I'd be willing to bet that your cat is about to pop," Justine said laughing at the everyone's expressions.

"Dad, isn't she spayed?" Tommy asked.

"How would I know? She was your mom's cat. She handled all that kind of stuff."

"Oh, boy," Sophia remarked. "I thought for sure Mom would've had her fixed right away. I know she took her up to the vet after Petunia showed up here, because she told me they said she was about eight months old then."

"If she's going to have kittens can I have one?" Natasha asked.

"Uh, well, we're not even sure she's pregnant yet," James answered.

"Let's take a look at her," Justine said. She sat down on the floor by Natasha. Petunia had finished eating and was daintily cleaning her paws and face.

"Can I pick you up, pretty girl?" Justine asked slowly reaching for the cat. Petunia stopped grooming as Justine slid a hand under her belly and scooped her up. Justine stroked the cat's head as she curled up into a ball on her lap. Everyone could hear Petunia's contented, low rumbling purr.

"How can you tell if she's going to have kittens?" Natasha asked.

"Well, her belly is very tight and kind of round. It's not like if she was just a fat cat. Fat isn't so firm. Now that I know she's not afraid of me and she's comfortable, I'm going to turn her over to see if her nipples on her belly look like they're big and ready for babies to eat from them." Justine gently lifted the cat into her arms, turning her over so she could look at her stomach. "Oh yeah. She's going to have little ones all right, and I'd say in just a couple days. She's getting ready to make milk and nurse."

James scratched his cheek. "Well, how'd that happen?"

"I'm pretty sure you know the answer to that, Dad." Tommy quipped.

"Hah! Aren't you funny. But now I guess I know what she was up to when she was missing. I never thought about her not being fixed."

"Yay!" Natasha clapped her hands together. "Kittens! Mom, can I have one. Please?" She implored.

Justine looked from Natasha to James, then back to Natasha. "Oh, Honey. I'm not sure about that. At least not while we live at Gran's house."

James nodded in understanding.

"But, why? I'd take care of it and feed it and everything." Natasha looked like she was going to cry. Justine didn't look much happier.

James cleared his throat. "I don't think your grandfather likes cats much, Natasha. In fact, I know for certain that he doesn't. It wouldn't be a good idea for any cat to be anywhere around there."

Natasha looked at James and then at her mother. "How come? Why?"

Justine shook her head. "He just hates cats, that's all."

Tommy came over and knelt beside Justine. He reached out to pet the cat purring in her arms.

Sophia said, "Oh, I remember now . . ."

Justine frowned and shook her head in a silent plea.

"Wait a minute," James said. "I think I have a plan. If your mom approves that is," he said glancing at Natasha. "If Miss Petunia does indeed have kittens, you could choose one to be yours. And it can live here with Petunia and me until you and your mom move into a place of your own. I'll even take care of all the veterinary things it needs like vaccines and getting it fixed when the time comes."

"Really?" Natasha looked at her mom. "Can I have one then, Mom? Can I? Please, please, please?"

"Hold on, Tasha." Justine looked at James with concern. "Are you sure you want to do that?" She asked him. "That's a wonderful offer, but it's an awful lot to ask of you."

James brushed her concern off with a wave of his hand. "It's not much of anything. Besides, Natasha would have to agree to come and take care of feeding and all the other daily stuff. She'll have to be responsible for the little bugger."

"Oh. I will! I will! I promise!" Natasha was on her feet now, hands clasped together as she gazed earnestly at her mom. "Can I please, Mom? Please?"

Justine sighed, then smiled at her daughter. "If Mr. James says it's OK, then I guess it's fine."

"Yay!" Natasha clapped her hands together and began dancing around the room.

"But," Justine began. "You have to be a responsible cat mom and do everything to take the best care of it. I also think you should help Mr. James with some other chores, if he agrees, to help pay for the vet bills. Deal?"

"Yes! Deal! I will. I promise! I can't believe it! Oh, thank you!" She kneeled in front of Justine and gave her, and Petunia, still snuggled in Justine's arms, a swift hug. Then she gently stroked the cat's head.

"You're gonna be a mama, and I get to have one of your kittens for my very own!" She stood back up and skipped over to James.

"Thank you so, so much Mr. James. I promise I'll be a good cat mom like my mom says, and I'll take the very best care of it, and I'll help you with any chores you want."

"All right!" James exclaimed. "It's a deal!" He made a fist and held out his arm for a fist bump.

"Umm. Is it OK if I hug you?" Natasha asked seriously. "This is a way bigger deal than a fist bump."

"Oh." James cleared his throat, knelt, and opened his arms. Natasha flew into them, hugging him as tight as she could.

Fifty Four

"This is so nice," Justine said helping herself to a brownie from the plate Tommy brought to the table. "Lunch was delicious, and the company is even better."

She, Sophia, and Tommy had spent the past half hour eating and chatting, often running over each other's words with comments or laughter as they reminisced about their school years, and time spent with friends running about town.

Natasha had been mostly quiet, listening to the adults at the table as they shared their memories. James interjected comments every once in a while, but he too mainly listened to the banter. As he looked at the smiling faces of his children and their old friend his thoughts drifted back to times when he'd come in off the boat in the afternoon to find the same faces and maybe a couple more seated at this very table, in this very spot, talking, laughing, and wolfing down snacks that Anna had waiting for them. They'd been a few years younger then, but to him they were still the same kids in so many ways. He also recalled how it would only be a few minutes after he arrived that Justine would slip out the door to get home before her father had time to wonder where she might be. Cora always knew Justine's whereabouts, but if Homer had ever suspected his daughter was at the Edward's house it would not have boded well for the women in the Connor household. Now that Justine was all grown up James hoped that there wouldn't be any issue for the girls if Homer found out they were consorting with the enemy.

As if on cue Sophia said, "So, Dad says that you're living with your mom and dad right now."

Justine grimaced slightly, "Yes. But I'm working on getting us into a place of our own as fast as I can find one. If I can ever find something affordable. There doesn't seem to be much of anything to rent, affordable or not, anywhere in town or even close by."

"It's a problem," James remarked. "There's little to no affordable housing for families here on The Peninsula and the situation's only gotten worse over the years as folks buy up properties to make them summer homes. We're losing our young families because of it. They can't afford any place that does come up for sale. Plus, most anything out there for rent is a weekly vacation rental. The housing problem leads to an issue with labor for us lobstermen too. We can't find help because there's no places nearby for working folks to live."

Tommy shook his head. "You know, I haven't seen very many kids around this week." He paused in thought. "Well, that's not quite true. I've seen them, but they're all with adults I don't recognize and obviously on vacation. What I should say is that I haven't seen kids out in yards, or playing, or at the ball fields and basketball court like when we were kids."

"I see bigger kids sometimes at night when they're coming home from the pool," Natasha offered. "But I don't think there's really anybody my age around here. It's all old people." She stopped and covered her mouth with her hand for a second. "Oops. Sorry. That kinda came out wrong. I didn't mean it like that."

There was a light flurry of laughter.

"No worries," Sophia said smiling at her. "I think we all understand what you mean, and you're right. Most of the kids we grew up with left and didn't come back to live or work here." Her forehead wrinkled in thought. "I'm with Tommy. I don't think I've seen many youngsters in town. This time of year we were all out on our bikes or trotting around together every single hour of the day."

"We're becoming a shell of a community," James said. "In the summer we have lots of tourists come through. They might stay a few days. Of course the summer folks stay for a couple months. They hike, and sight-see, and buy stuff at the galleries and restaurants, but at the end of August everybody leaves. Then most all the shops and restaurants close except for the market at the corner and the General Store. I always wonder how they make enough money during the off-season to survive. There are hardly any of us left that live and work here year-round."

"Mom said that the congregation at the church is down to less than twenty people that attend regularly," Justine allowed. "I can remember when we were young you could barely find a seat in a pew on Sundays."

"That's telling for a lot of reasons," James remarked. "And not just that our population is dwindling."

"There's lots of old houses with no one living in them at all," Natasha observed. "I ride by at least four on my bike every day. Plus there's the house right across the road from here. The yellow house." She pointed toward the road. "Mom and I took the shortcut by that yard to get here."

Sophia nodded. "Mrs. Dean's. It's been empty ever since she passed away. It's so pretty, and there's a great view past the reach from her yard. I always loved that place."

"Me too," Justine agreed. "Sarah and I spent a lot of time there when we were kids. She's living in South Carolina now."

"That's a bit of a way from home," Tommy remarked.

"Yeah, but she's still on the water. She and her husband run a charter fishing business out of Myrtle Beach."

"See, another young person that left to find their fortune somewhere else," James said. "It's a shame, but I'm afraid we're a dying town. It started years ago when the sardine plant closed. What with all the challenges we fishermen are facing now I'm afraid we're headed toward the end of our way of life in our coastal villages, and I'm not the only one seeing it."

Sophia nodded. "That's a lot of what I'm researching and studying now for my Master's. But there are a plenty of people out there like me who are going to help fight to make sure that doesn't happen, Dad."

"Well, it's a fight. That's for sure." James sighed. "I just know I can't imagine any other way to live. What in the world would I do if I couldn't fish? I don't know anything else."

"Umm . . ." Natasha had been trying not to fidget in her seat too much. "Speaking of fishing, can we go soon?"

"Absolutely!" James exclaimed. "I'm sorry. You've been sitting there so patiently waiting for us to quit yammering on. If everyone's done eating we'll just clean up quickly and get right on with it." He put both hands on the table and pushed his chair away. "So, who's going to catch the most fish today?"

"I am of course," Sophia replied with a grin. "Who else?"

This was a game she and her father had played every time they went fishing together when she was younger. They tallied up the number of fish they caught each outing and kept a running total each year through the end of ice fishing season. They also kept track of the biggest and smallest fish that they pulled in, as well as a list of the strange things they snagged. At the end of the season Anna would come up with prizes she awarded them for each category.

Sophia turned to Natasha and explained all about it.

"That sounds like fun. Can I do that with you?" Natasha asked.

"I don't see why not," Sophia allowed. "Dad, what do you think? I don't want to change tradition. I think anyone who's going to fish with us should be in on the counts."

"But then I'll have even more competition," James complained in mock exasperation. "I may have to come up with some new strategies to give myself an advantage."

Sophia laughed at her father. "Oh, Dad. You know it's mostly luck. You won as much as I did. It'll be fun."

"Seriously I think it's a great idea. I'd like to keep on with it." James looked over at Tommy. "Are you going to come with us too, Son?"

"Why not?" Tommy asked. "I don't want to miss out on any of the fun. But I'm afraid I'll have to be a spectator this time. I don't have a fishing license or a fishing pole for that matter."

"Me either," Justine remarked. "I thought I'd just watch today, too."

"No 'just watching' today," James declared. "If you want to go fishing, we've got everything you could possibly need. Plus we can get you both your licenses right online, and print them off on Sophia's printer. Right, Bean?"

"Sure. It won't take but just a few minutes."

"I didn't know you need a license to fish," Natasha said. "Do I need one, too?"

"Nope. You're a small fry so you get to fish for free until you're sixteen," James assured her. "You're good to go."

Natasha clapped her hands together. "Yay! Mackerel for everybody for dinner!"

"You're already thinking about dinner? We just finished lunch." Justine shook her head in disbelief.

"I'm full right now. I just remember that Mr. James said we have to use every fish we catch today, so I was figuring with all of us fishing we'll be eating lots of mackerel tonight."

"Good point," Tommy said. "But I wouldn't count on a whole lot from me. I was never really any good at fishing. I left that to my dad and sister."

"You never really tried." Sophia smirked at her brother.

"True. But you never tried to draw fish like I can either," Tommy shot back with a grin. "And my fish don't stink like yours."

"Ooh, that hurts," Sophia put her hands over her heart. "Right here." They laughed at each other.

Justine snorted and Natasha dissolved in a fit of giggles.

"You guys are funny. But really, can we go now?" Natasha wiggled out of her chair and pushed it in until the back of it was snug against the table.

"You bet," James said as he carried his plate over to the sink. "Sophia, if you get Tommy and Justine all set up with their fishing licenses, Natasha and I will go out and grab the gear. We'll leave the rest of the cleaning up until later. The tide's on the way in and we have fish to catch!"

Fifty Five

"I got another one!" Natasha started reeling in the line on the fishing pole just like James had taught her about an hour earlier.

"Way to go, Tasha!" Justine exclaimed from the other side of the pier. "You're on a roll."

"She's a natural. Reminds me of you, Sophia, when you were about the same age." James smiled at his daughter and handed her his fishing pole. She grinned, taking one hand off her own pole to grab his so that she had a line in each hand.

"If one bites while I'm holding your line that means it's mine," she told James.

"Fair enough," he agreed.

He turned back toward Natasha. He leaned over to grab the line as she reeled it up onto the deck. A thin, silver fish about eight inches long flipped its tail and danced on the end of a diamond-shaped jig, making the line jerk.

"Hold on tight. This one's kinda feisty."

Natasha held onto the pole as tight and upright as she could while James grasped the fish with one hand. He gently backed the hook out of the side of the fish's mouth with the other. Then he slipped it into the five-gallon bucket by Natasha's feet. It was about three-quarters full of sea water and flashy mackerel.

Natasha peered into the bucket. "I think that's the biggest one yet," she declared. "This is awesome!"

"I think you're right. He's good-sized. Go ahead and add another mark to your tally," James directed. "I left the chalk right in the top of my tackle box."

Natasha retrieved the piece of chalk and made a hash mark under her initials on the wooden deck of the pier beside the bucket.

"That makes five for me," she announced. "You've caught three so far. Sophia has four. Tommy's only caught one. Mom hasn't caught any yet." She looked over at the other side of the pier where Justine and Tommy were standing side by side, their fishing lines dangling over the edge.

"Well, to be fair your mom has been helping Tommy remember how to fish, and I think they're doing more talking than they are fishing anyway." James chuckled. "Plus I've been helping you out a bit. So that means I'm not fishing up to my potential," he protested retrieving his pole from Sophia. "We'll just see when all is said and done who wins the count today!"

"I got another one," Tommy called out. "Watch out, Soph. I just might catch more than you."

"Fat chance," Sophia shot back. "And just look at that tiny little thing, it barely qualifies as a fish—more like a minnow!"

"Hey! That's not nice. No insulting the poor bugger. He just hasn't grown up yet. I'm gonna throw him back. He's not even close to keeper size." Tommy knelt and released it back into the water. "I still get to count him though."

"That's fair," James agreed. "We count what we catch, not what we keep. I know for a fact that we've thrown back more over the years than we ever ate."

A sharp screech rang out from the trees on the reach across the cove.

James turned and pointed. "Natasha, look. There's our eagle friend in the top of that fir by her nest."

"Cool! Mom, look!"

"I don't see it." Justine shaded her eyes with one hand, still holding onto her fishing pole with the other.

"There! At the top of the second biggest tree."

"Oh! There she is. I can see her white head now. Is that the same old nest? The one that was there when we were kids?"

"It is," Sophia answered. "It's too bad we can't leave some fish for Henrietta to get on the dock. It's so cool to see them come and pick them up."

"Henrietta?" Natasha asked. "That's her name?"

"Yup. Everybody down at the wharf knows her and her mate Henry. They raise their babies here every year. How many chicks hatched this season, Dad?"

"Two. I see the young'uns on the other side of the reach quite a bit when I steam in and out. They like to fish in the shallows over there."

"I wish we could give her have some of our fish, but I know it's illegal to feed them. I read about it on the Maine Natural Resources page after Mr. James and I saw them the first time," Natasha said with a sigh.

"You read a lot don't you?" Sophia asked.

"How else can you learn about all the cool stuff?"

"Exactly," Sophia agreed. "Unless you're lucky enough to experience things firsthand. I love to do research."

"Me too," Natasha said seriously. "It's way cool to find out about things you never knew about before. Especially things that are here around us and in the sea."

"What's your favorite thing to learn about?" Sophia asked.

"Pretty much anything, but the stars, the ocean, and sea animals are my very favorites," Natasha replied. "I especially like North Atlantic sea animals because we live here."

James smiled listening to Sophia and Natasha chat about their research interests and about the ocean in general. Natasha seemed to love sharing what she knew. And when Sophia offered up obscure facts about sea life in their own cove the child took it all in, asking questions when she wanted to know more.

"So you go to college and get to study all about the history of the sea?" Natasha asked, reeling in her line, then dropping it into the water again the way James had taught her.

"Kind of," Sophia answered. "What I work on now is the history and future of the North Atlantic fishing industries, particularly right here in the Gulf of Maine."

"I'm not sure what that means," Natasha said, wrinkling her nose.

"Well, I want to work someday where I make sure that we honor our history and how we make our living from lobstering and other seafood fisheries. I'm studying to find ways future generations of lobstermen can keep doing what their families have always done, but while taking care of our ocean in the best ways possible. That even includes the sea animals we don't fish for plus everything else in and about the ocean. Does that make sense?"

"I think so." Natasha started. "Oh wait, I got another fish!"

"Me too!" Sophia exclaimed reeling in her line. "They're really biting now."

James didn't have anyone to hand his fishing pole to with both girls reeling in their lines, so he wound his line all the way in and laid the pole on the deck before going to help Natasha.

"Will you teach me how to take the hook out this time?" Natasha asked. "I think I can do it."

"You bet," James said just as Justine sang out from behind them. "I finally got one! Mark one down for me!"

"At this rate, we'll be done with our catch in the next few minutes," James remarked reaching for Natasha's fishing pole. "Here you go. Let me hold your pole. Do you remember how I grabbed the fish before?"

Natasha nodded. "You started up near the top of its back and you pushed its fin down against its back with your hand."

"Right. That's because the dorsal fin on these buggers is sharp and will poke you but good if you're not careful. Go slowly, it takes some practice."

"Oh, Ouch!" Natasha shook her hand as she ran into the offensive fin James had just warned her about. "That hurt!"

"You all right?" James asked. "Do you want me to get it for you?"

Natasha set her chin. "No. I can do it. It just surprised me that's all."

"OK, give it another whirl. Make your hand into the shape of a 'c,' like this." James demonstrated with his free hand. "Then start right at the top of that fin and slide your hand down. It will smooth the fin against the fish's back."

Natasha bit her lip in concentration and mimicked the motion James had shown her.

"Got it," she proclaimed.

"Hold tight now. He's gonna try to wiggle right out of your hand."

"I've got it. I'm not letting go. No way."

"Good. Now take your other hand and grab the top of the hook between your thumb and first finger." James watched her carefully. "Yup, just like that. Now back that hook right out of his mouth. You might have to wiggle it a little when you hit the barb on the hook. Don't wiggle it too much, or you'll lose your grip."

"Got it. I got it!" Natasha was so excited she almost dropped the fish. She let go of the hook and ran over to the bucket where she gently released it into water with all the others. She looked at her hand. "I think I squeezed it too hard. I rubbed off some of the silver from its scales."

"You did just great," James assured her. "That gets on your hands even if you just touch them lightly. It flakes right off them. You couldn't have done any better."

"I did it. I really did." Natasha was all smiles.

"You certainly did. I'd say you are officially a fisherman now," James proclaimed.

"Um, excuse me," Sophia broke in. "I believe the correct title for Natasha would be fisherwoman; thank you very much."

"I stand corrected," James said with a smile at his daughter. "Fisherwoman it is. And a very good one at that."

Natasha clapped her hands together. "I'm official," she declared. "Mom, did you hear that? I'm an official fisherwoman."

"I never doubted it for a moment," Justine said over her shoulder. "You have it in your blood. You were meant for the sea. But I don't think you're only a fisherwoman. I still think you're a mermaid in disguise."

Natasha trotted over to retrieve her fishing pole. "I'll never tell," she said in mock seriousness. "By the way, that makes six for me, and I'm winning. Catch me if you can."

"I'll take that challenge," Sophia remarked as she reeled another in on her line. "This one should tie us up, I believe."

"Not for long," Natasha declared. "I got this. But that's a nice one, Soph. Look how fat he is."

"Game on," Sophia said. She raised a hand in the air. Natasha had to jump to slap her hand for a high-five and missed. Both of them burst out laughing.

As James watched and listened to the girls and their banter, he realized he hadn't stopped smiling for hours. He glanced over to where Tommy and Justine now sat together on the pier, legs dangling toward the water while they chatted. Their forgotten fishing poles lay on the dock. He gazed out past the reach to the horizon.

I sure hope you're seeing this. I know you must be. I just want you to know that I get it now. You always said I would someday. I only wish it'd been while you were here.

A puff of a breeze tickled past his face. James caught the light scent of vanilla and sugar cookie. He inhaled deeply and smiled. Out of the corner of his eye he saw his daughter tilt her head up. She sniffed at the air a couple times, then shook her head once lightly before turning her attention back to the fishing pole in her hand.

Fifty Six

"This was so fun, even if you did beat me for catching the most fish," Natasha remarked as she watched Sophia packing up the tackle box. "For sure I have to add this to my *Good Things About Here* list.

"You have a list for that?" Sophia asked. She closed the lid and fastened the latches.

"Yup. I like lists. I make them for a lot of stuff. They help keep me focused on the important things."

"My mom liked to make lists, too," Sophia said. "But mostly they were her 'to do' lists. I guess I kind of do the same thing in my daily journal."

"You should see Tasha's lists," Justine said. "They're amazing. They're works of art really. She illustrates them and everything. I like her tree one best. She has sketches of the leaves and even the barks of the different trees on it."

"That sounds so cool. I'd love to see it someday if you'd show it to me?"

Natasha shrugged, "Yeah, sure."

"I have something pretty neat to show you that you might want to add to one of your lists," Justine said. "That is if they're still there. Have you seen the sea stars under the wharf yet?"

"There are sea stars under here? Really?"

"There used to be tons of them living under here when we were kids. All different colors too, not just orange ones. Do you think they're still there?" Justine asked looking over at Sophia.

Sophia grinned. "I'm not sure, but I know how to find out. Let's go look."

"Dad," she called out to James. He and Tommy were chatting with a couple who had wandered down the hill a few minutes earlier. James excused himself and walked over to the girls.

"What, Bean?"

"I'm sorry. I didn't mean to interrupt you."

"It's fine. They were just asking about things to see and do in the area. Tommy's giving them a few pointers. They're headed toward the park."

"Oh. Well, I just wanted to let you know that the three of us are going to go look for sea stars down below. I didn't want you to think we just disappeared."

"OK. I'll have Tommy help me take everything up to the house while you explore. Just be careful getting down there, and watch out for glass and other crap that gets caught up in the rocks."

"We will. Promise."

"Come on," Justine said, leading the way. "I used to love to come down here to look for sea stars. Since the tide's coming in we'll have to hurry because they'll be under at least a couple feet of water. But there still should be a few near where the tide line is right now."

"We might find some in that big tide pool over there." Sophia motioned to her right. "You know, the one that's between here and the co-op."

"True. Let's check out under here first though," Justine answered. She sat down on a rectangular-shaped piece of granite about two and a half feet wide and six feet long. It was wedged at an angle, down into more granite pieces below it—like a slide. "I didn't really wear the right shoes for rock climbing," She said inching her way down the rock. "These little slip-on things have zero traction." When she reached the next slab of granite she looked up at Natasha. "Need a hand?"

"No, thanks. I've got it. My sneaks have great treads for climbing." Natasha didn't sit down like her mom. She took baby steps down the rock's face and then hopped off onto the rock beside Justine. "See?"

Sophia followed Natasha's lead easing herself down the slope on her feet. "Still, we need to be super careful. These rocks don't look like they could be slippery, but once you hit the high tide mark they can be super slick."

"OK," Natasha said. "I'll watch out."

Once they were all standing together on the rock below, Justine began to work her way toward the underside of the wharf picking her way along the surface of the granite chunks that lined the shoreline. Natasha followed her mother with Sophia a pace behind. Every few steps they had to get to the next rock by either hopping across spaces between them, or sitting down to slide along. In each crevice between, Natasha noticed small rocks, mussel shells, seaweed, lost bait bags, rope pieces and bits of other things, including plenty of glass, plastic, and other trash.

"It's a mess down here," she remarked. "Someone ought to clean this place up."

"You're right," Sophia agreed. "There's a group that used to do shore clean-up every spring. I don't know if they still do or not, but it sure needs it. These rocks catch a lot that washes up on the tide. It's a darn shame people can't throw stuff away correctly."

"These rocks are different than the other ones along the rest of the shore," Natasha observed. "They have sharper edges, and it looks like they got cut and put here on purpose the way they're all stacked up against each other."

"You're absolutely right about that," Justine said. She stepped onto the next slab and bent down, pointing at a shallow trough about an inch wide that extended from the top of the rock's surface down about a foot into the rock. "Look here. This is where they drilled to put a dynamite stick to split this piece away from a larger piece of ledge. They did this in the quarry up the road, then moved them all down here to create a barrier for erosion control that would be stable around and under the wharf. They keep the shore from shifting and washing out."

"Neat." Natasha leaned down and ran her finger down the groove. "It's really smooth."

"The drilling made it that way, but then the water running up, over, and back down over the years has helped too," Sophia said.

"Well," Natasha said straitening back up. "I guess the rocks they put here are doing their job because nothing much goes back out into the water when it gets caught in here, does it? But it still needs cleaning up."

"I agree. Tell you what," Sophia said. "If you'll come help me before I leave to go back to school in a couple days, we can come back down with some trash bags and pick stuff up." She glanced over Natasha's head. "If that's OK with you, Justine?"

"Absolutely. I think it's a great idea. I'll help too. We can even recruit Tommy. Maybe tomorrow after I get home from work?"

"Sure. I don't think we've got anything much planned for the next couple days."

"I'll check my schedule," Natasha said with a grin. "But it sounds fine to me."

Sophia laughed and shook her head. "Your daughter is something else, Justine."

"Don't I know it." Justine hopped down to the next rock. In a couple more leaps she was stepping onto an area of smooth sand at the edge of the side the wharf. "Come on. Let's find some sea stars. They should be holding onto the pilings and rocks right along here."

Natasha joined her mom, peering into the water that was around the nearest wharf piling. "I don't see anything but rocks and a little seaweed. Oh wait! There's a little crab." She pointed. "Do you see it?"

Justine and Sophia looked where Natasha pointed.

"I don't," Sophia said putting one hand on the wooden post. She leaned forward toward the water. "But I do see a sea star down there."

"Oh, I do too!" Justine exclaimed. "I'm so glad they're still here."

"What? Where?" Natasha squinted, looking hard into the crystal-clear water.

Sophia pointed straight down. "Right there. On top of that rock that's about as big as a softball. And there's a really tiny one beside it."

"Are you sure? I don't see anything except that ruffly seaweed and rocks. There's nothing orange down there at all."

"I see both of them now, Soph," Justine said. "That second one is tiny. Tasha, remember how I said the sea stars down here come in all kinds of colors? The big one is brownish-red, kind of rusty looking, and the tiny one is a muted, deep purple. You kind of have to trick you brain into looking for the shape instead of the color. They camouflage themselves really well."

Justine took a step forward and to the side. She knelt near the water's edge. "Come over this way. I think you'll be able to see better from here."

Natasha squatted down beside her mom.

"Now find the rock." Justine pointed to the water, about a foot in front of them. "About one o-clock. Like Soph said, the rock's softball-sized and almost perfectly round. Then look at the top of the rock carefully. You'll see it has a sea star right on the very center."

"I see it! I see it! I'd seen the rock already, but I thought that was just the colors of the rock on top. Oh look! It moved one of its legs a little."

Natasha pointed and wobbled forward from her crouching position. Sophia reached down and grabbed the back of her T-shirt. "Whoa, hang on there, Kiddo."

Natasha settled back on her heels. "Whew, that was close. Thanks."

"You bet. It's not deep enough to be a problem, but it's pretty cold water to take a bath in," Sophia remarked.

"Thanks, Soph," Justine stood up. "Do you see the little purple one beside the big one, Tasha?"

"I do now." Natasha pointed. "It's right down there, over to the left of it." Is that its baby?"

"Probably not," Sophia answered. "They don't hang around their parents when they're born. In fact, they aren't anywhere near their parents long before they hatch. The eggs get fertilized in the water and then settle to the sea floor. Those two are probably just buds—hanging out."

"Cool. But kind of sad for them too," Natasha said slowly.

"I'm pretty sure they don't have the same kinds of feelings we do. But I get what you're saying," Sophia agreed quietly. "It is kind of sad."

They were all quiet for a moment scanning the water. Justine crossed under the wharf to the other side. "Come over here, guys. There's a bunch of them here right at the edge of the water."

Natasha scampered over and crouched down again in the silty sand.

"See?"

"Wow, there are like seven, and they're all different colors too. There's even one that looks bright orange."

"I think I can reach one so you can hold it." Justine stretched out her arm out into the water. "Oof. The water sure is cold!" She picked up a mottled brown, star-shaped creature about three inches in diameter from the sea floor, gently prying one of its arms from the rock where it had attached itself.

"Put your hand in the water to get it wet, then hold it out to me."

Natasha did as Justine instructed.

"Here." She placed the sea star into her daughter's palm. "Just let it sit there. You don't want to touch it too much so you don't shock it or do anything to hurt it. You can softly touch its back to feel it. Like this." Justine ran a gentle finger over the back of the creature. Natasha mimicked her mom.

"It feels nubbly," she said. "Way cool." She got a strange look on her face.

"Is something wrong?" Justine asked smiling, her eyes crinkling at the edges as she watched Natasha's face.

"It feels like there are hundreds of little things tickling my whole hand," Natasha whispered. "It feels really weird."

Justine laughed. "Here. I'll show you why." She picked up the sea star and turned it over to reveal dozens of tiny suction cup-like feet. "It was trying to move on your hand. That's how it moves about or hangs on to things."

"I knew about their feet. I've seen pictures, but it's weird to feel it on my hand. Hey, look. You can see its mouth right in the middle. It sucks stuff up into that to eat."

"Yup." Justine looked up at Sophia who was standing next to them. She wasn't watching them, instead she was looking up at the underside of the wharf with her head cocked, listening.

"Sophia?"

Natasha looked up at the question in Justine's voice.

Sophia put a finger to her lips to indicate they should be quiet.

Justine placed the sea star gently back in the water where she'd found it and stood up next to her friend.

"What do you hear?" she whispered.

"Two trucks just came down and I think I heard your father's voice just now. He's giving my dad and Tommy crap."

"God, some things never change," Justine whispered back angrily. She put a protective arm around Natasha who was now standing beside her.

Sophia waved a hand at her. "Shh. I'm trying to hear what he's saying. Dad and Tommy haven't said a word yet, that I can tell. And I don't know who else is up there with them either. I don't recognize the voice at all."

There were a few words exchanged that weren't distinguishable, but the tone was obviously hostile. The next second there was no mistaking what was said and who was talking.

"So sorry to have interrupted such a touching scene—father and son fishing off the pier on a Sunday afternoon," a booming voice sneered. "Think you've got enough poles there to catch fish? Were you trying to scare them, so they just jumped up into your bucket, or did you steal all that gear from some little kids? You're a lousy lobsterman, so I doubt you could catch anything on your own."

"Yup, that's my father," Justine muttered, glaring up through the cracks of the wharf. "I bet he's already three sheets in, too. Sounds like it." She let go of Natasha's waist and turned as if she was going to start up the rocks toward the edge of the shore.

Sophia grabbed her arm. "Justine," she said softly. "Just stay put. We both know what will happen if he knows you're here. Just let my dad and Tommy handle it."

Justine shook Sophia's hand off her arm and glared at her.

Sophia leaned her head Natasha's way.

"Please. I know you're upset, but just let Dad deal with him."

Justine opened her mouth, closed it, sighed, and reached out for Natasha's hand. "You're right. Of course, you're right," she said her voice low and tight with anger. "I just hate it."

Justine's father was all but bellowing like a mad bull now. "How many fishies you got in that little bucket there? Probably not enough to feed anything a decent meal. If you made any kind of a good living like I do you wouldn't need to scrape the barrel to eat."

"Come off it, Homer." James retorted. "I've got stuff to do. I can't waste time while you play the hard ass. Let's go, Tommy. Leave 'em be. They're not worth messing up our day."

"You're the ones not worth a damn," Homer sneered. "Besides, Mr. High and Mighty, you never would fight like a real man. And you raised your artsy-fartsy little whelp to be just like you, didn't ya? No wonder your wife up and died. Why would she want to live with pansy-asses like you?"

Sophia and Justine both gasped at the same moment. There was the sound of scuffling, followed by a loud, long line of cursing as something—someone—tumbled down the gangplank from the wooden wharf to the aluminum deck.

"Wanna be next?" Tommy's obviously enraged voice floated down to them.

"Jesus. You're all crazy. I'm outta here," another voice exclaimed.

"Good plan," James called out. "And you might be more careful of the company you keep."

They heard a truck starting up, then speeding off, sending sand and dirt scattering onto the wooden deck above them.

A few seconds later Tommy's feet, and then the rest of him, appeared as he climbed down the rocks to the underside of the wharf. He peered down at them.

"I figured I'd find you right here." He shook his head. "Just like old times, eh? Stay put for a few minutes," he instructed.

"What happened?" Justine demanded.

"Oh, just a little misunderstanding with your father. We took care of it."

"Is Dad OK?" Sophia asked. She glanced sideways at Justine. "Sorry."

"Don't be. If my father is the one we heard hitting the ground, he deserved any of what he got." She looked down, took a deep breath, and then glanced up at Tommy. "He's not dead though, is he?"

Tommy chuckled. "I seriously doubt it. But Dad's down checking on him just to be sure. He's sauced enough I'll be surprised if he even knows what hit him."

"What did hit him?" Sophia asked an eyebrow raised.

"My fist—first," Tommy said. "But I only beat Dad by a split second. He got him good. Lifted him right off the ground. That's what knocked him over." Tommy rubbed the knuckles on his right hand. "I caught him by surprise, but I think my hand probably hurts more than his chin. I'll be right back. Let me see if Dad needs any help."

Justine glanced at Natasha who was staring wide-eyed and silent at Tommy's back as he climbed back up the rocks. She draped an arm over her daughter's shoulder.

"I know I've always told you never to hit anyone. But in this case, Tommy did what needed doing." She knelt and looked earnestly into Natasha's eyes. "I doubt it will teach my father anything, but sometimes the only way to deal with a drunk and a bully is to fight back. What he said was despicable. If I'd been up there, I'd have punched him myself. All of us have tried to ignore him and avoid him for years. This was a long time coming."

"Why are we hiding down here then?" Natasha asked. "Shouldn't we just go up there?"

"Well," Justine started and then stopped. She looked at Sophia and grimaced. "She has a point, you know."

Sophia shook her head. "No. Tommy's right. Your father doesn't know you're here. If he did, and then figured out you and Natasha are with us, who knows what he'd do? He's drunk and belligerent, and you were forbidden to be friends with us, remember?"

"Damn it. I'm so tired of all his bullshit. I'm sick of having to hide every time his drunk ass decides to play the big, bad bully over something from the past that only happened in his feeble mind," Justine protested. "I'm an adult for God's sake. He has no right to tell me what I can and can't do anymore!"

"Maybe not. But . . ."

"Please don't argue you guys," Natasha broke in. "Mom, remember what you told me? You said that if you fought with Gran over how he is, then he just wins. You said that since we had to be there the best thing to do was stay out of his way and ignore him. You said that bullies never change and if Gran stood up to him he'd just keep on and maybe even treat her worse, and that nothing would change until she decided to do something for herself and get out on her own. Isn't it the same for us?"

Justine looked at her daughter and Sophia for a long moment. "You're both right. It won't do me any good to confront him, and I don't want to add fuel to his fire."

A dull throb in her forehead was threatening to become a full-blown headache. She pressed the tips of her fingers on her temples, rubbing them in a circular motion. "God, Soph. I just want to be able to make it on my own—to give Natasha a good life. And, here I am, still hiding."

Tommy appeared again. "Come on. All clear. Let's go on up to the house."

"I wanted to look for more sea stars," Natasha complained.

"Oh, Honey, I'm sorry. We really should go now. But I promise I'll bring you back down to look again now that we know they're still here. Plus, we can go over to a place in the park where I'm sure there are more."

Natasha looked down in disappointment. "OK. As long as you promise."

"Cross my heart," Justine said making the motion of an 'X' over her chest. "Maybe we can even convince Sophia to come with us."

"You got it," Sophia agreed. "I wouldn't miss it. Plus then I can show you some other cool stuff in the water that I know about."

The girls scrambled up onto the rocks behind Tommy.

"Where's my father?" Justine asked, her hand on Natasha's back as they climbed over the rocks to the top of the shoreline. She knew her daughter would be doing her best to look around to see whatever she could if she didn't keep her focused on moving forward.

"Down on the dock passed out," Tommy answered. "There's no one else around. Nobody except that guy who came down with your dad saw what happened." He paused. "They were obviously on some mission. Anyway, Dad called Nate and asked him to come down so he could file a report to keep us honest. We were just defending ourselves, but the law might not see it that way. He's on his way. Dad also said it would be a good idea to tell our side because your father might try to cause more trouble once he wakes up."

"I doubt he'll remember enough to do anything," Justine remarked dryly. " Not if he's as drunk as usual. I honestly don't think he's ever sober anymore. He smells like booze all the time. But, I probably should text my mom to tell her at least a little of what's going on."

"Is she home?" Sophia asked. "We could run over to talk to her if she is."

"No. She's out shopping with another lady from church. Then they were going to visit some of the older folks from the congregation who are in the nursing home. She won't be back until late. I'll just text her to let her know that Dad's stinking drunk, and that she should call me before she heads home. It's not the first time we've tag-teamed to avoid him."

Tommy stopped at the head of the path to the house. He turned to look back at the girls. "Whatcha looking for, Miss Natasha?" She was trying to look over her shoulder toward the wharf for all she was worth.

"Uh, nothing," Natasha muttered.

Tommy chuckled. "It's OK. I'd be wanting to look too if I was you. But really there's nothing interesting going on that you don't already know about. And my dad's just down there standing over your grandfather who's taking a snooze on the deck by the punts." Tommy turned to head up the path. "And here comes Nate," he said as the black-on-black Balsam Cove patrol car cruised into the parking lot. "You all go on up. I'm going to head back down. We'll come home as soon as we're done with Nate and his reports."

"What about our fish?" Natasha asked. "Are they all right? Do you still have them? Shouldn't we clean them for dinner?"

"Yes, on all counts," Tommy answered. "We'll be up with them in no time. You can get everything set up on the patio table so we can take care of preparing them to cook when we get back. Sound like a deal?"

"Sure. We can do that. Right?" Natasha looked to Sophia and Justine for confirmation.

"Yup." Sophia said. "Follow me. I know just what to do."

Fifty Seven

"Now that we've got everything out can I go find Petunia while we wait for Mr. James and Tommy to bring up the fish?" Natasha asked peering around the doorway into the living room.

"Sure," Sophia answered. "If she's not in there, she's probably up in my room. It's the one on the left. She likes to sleep on my bed by the pillows."

"Are you sure you want Natasha in your room?" Justine asked.

Sophia shrugged. "I don't mind. There's nothing exciting up there; just my books and stuff."

"Geez, there's a whole lot of paintings in here," Natasha called out from the living room. "It looks kinda like a room in the art gallery my class went to on a field trip." She poked her head back around the corner. "Mom, you should see this. There are pictures of the whole town and the harbor and everything. They're really pretty."

Justine walked into the living room. "Soph, these are beautiful! Did Tommy do them? I don't remember him drawing stuff like this when we were in school."

"They're Mom's," Sophia said, joining Justine in front of a watercolor that looked through a rain-streaked window toward the sea. She cleared her throat to hide the lump in it that suddenly appeared as she thought of her mom sitting at the table watching through the rain for her dad to come in from his haul. "We. . . umm . . we found them in a trunk in the attic. It was quite the surprise. None of us knew that she'd made them."

Justine laid a hand on Sophia's arm. "She was an amazing woman in so many ways." She looked around the room. "What a treasure! What are you going to do with them now?"

"Well, Tommy had this great idea that we should make an exhibit and show them as a kind of memorial to Mom. Dad's not keen on a traditional service. Tommy's putting together the details to hang them down at the Arts Center. We can rent the space after the middle of September when whatever is in there now is done. We thought that since her art shows scenes from the town and community throughout her life, maybe everyone who knew her would enjoy seeing them."

Sophia walked over to the painting of the harbor depicting the end of the day with all the fishermen working on the wharf. "Like this one. Just look at everybody. It's fun to pick out who's in it or at least give it a guess. We thought it would be nice to remember her this way—kind of in her own words I guess."

"This has to be the best idea I've ever heard for a memorial." Justine gazed around the room trying to take them all in. "I could spend hours looking at them all."

"Me too," Natasha piped up. "They're awesome. But don't they need to be in frames? You know, like the ones at the art museum?"

"Uh huh," Sophia replied. "Tommy's taking care of all that. There are a few older ones in here that he says need a little restoration work too, just because they sat for years in the trunk."

"Oh! Look at this one!" Natasha exclaimed. "I can see Petunia sitting in the window. She's just a ball of fluff, but I know it's her because that's the kitchen window where her bed is."

Justine peered at the painting over Natasha's shoulder. "You're right. It *is* Petunia. Look at that window box outside though. What a gorgeous planting of ruby geraniums and German Ivy."

"Yeah that's pretty, but I think Petunia's prettier. I'm going to go upstairs now and find her." Natasha tapped her way up the stairs. The sound of her voice floated back down to them. "There you are, Pretty Cat."

Justine shook her head. "That poor cat is in for way more attention than she probably wants."

"Nah, she's an attention hog. It'll be nice for her." Sophia was studying the painting. "You know that flower box outside the kitchen window is in sad shape right now," she remarked. "Since Mom died, I bet it hasn't been watered or anything. I have no idea what she did to keep her boxes or gardens up. When I went out this morning to get flowers for the table I really had to work for them. I untangled all kinds of weeds just to get to the lilies in the back beds."

"You know I can help with that—weeding and keeping them up." Justine said thoughtfully. "I'd love to bring her gardens back to their glory. If that'd be all right with all of you," she added.

"Really? You'd want to do that?" Sophia raised an eyebrow. "I think that'd be great. I bet Dad and Tommy would too. I love the flowers, but I have absolutely zero knowledge about what to do for them. Not to mention I hate gardening and I'm not here enough to stay on top of it. I know for a fact that the guys have no clue about what to do with them either."

Justine smiled and shrugged. "It's what I do. Plants, I mean. I love them. They really ask for so little, just some tender care and cultivation. Then they give back so much. Do you really think your dad would let me work the flower beds here?"

"I can't see why not. We'll ask. I'm betting he'll jump at the idea. Fall's just around the corner, but so what? It'd be great to see the gardens neat and tidy for the rest of the season."

"I think it would be," Justine agreed. "Autumn is cold crop and mum season. It's one of the best times to put in pansies again and some autumn veggies too. Your mom and Mrs. Dean always had the best looking fall gardens in town. And right here, across from each other on the same street. I'd be so honored to be able to work on them." Justine took a deep breath, then exhaled slowly. "You know, I never could put in a garden over at our place. My father would just destroy it. He never even let Mom put a potted plant on the porch." She shook her head. "He's just a mean, miserable man."

"I'm sorry," Sophia murmured. "I can't even imagine how you must feel."

"You don't have anything to be sorry for. I'm the one who's sorry. I'm so embarrassed that I have to say that person is my father. I know I should feel bad because he's an alcoholic and it's a disease, but he's such a terrible person I can't even." She hung her head. "This makes twice now that your dad has had to step in and the law had to be called, all because of how my father acts. It's so humiliating. All I wanted to do was start over. Make a new life—a good life—for my daughter and me."

"Justine, listen. You're doing it. You really are. It just takes a little time to find out where you're headed that's all." Sophia turned and gave her friend a light hug. She stepped back. "I think one of the first things to do is find you and Natasha a place of your own. It's got to be so stressful living at your parent's place the way things are with your dad."

"Truth be told he's hardly even there," Justine answered. "He comes in late from the bar and leaves out early, even on days when he's not fishing. He's stumbling down drunk every night. He comes in, goes to his bedroom, and passes out. He's gone in the morning before Natasha and I are up. Then he does it all over. Wash, rinse, repeat. If we run into him he mostly ignores us. Sometimes I wonder if he even realizes we're around." She pursed her lips and shook her head. "You know, I keep waiting for the day that he hits someone with his truck driving home from the pub. I can't believe he doesn't get picked up for driving under the influence. Everybody knows he's out there like that."

"Yeah," Sophia agreed. "It sure doesn't seem right that he hasn't. But then again, no one is on duty after eight p.m.. Any calls get turned over to the county sheriff dispatch after that. There's no one patrolling, so unless someone calls on him . . ." She threw her hands up in the air. "Besides, it's only a couple miles from the pub to your place.

By the time they got an officer all the way out here your dad would have been home and passed out in bed for half an hour.'"

"True. Still I sure wish they'd get him. Maybe then he'd get some help."

"In all honestly, at this point, I don't think it would make a difference," Sophia said. "I mean, even if they took his license away for OUI he'd just drive anyway. Your dad isn't going to change a thing. He's who he is. He's been that way as long as we all can remember. I just can't imagine how your mom has lived with him, much less having any kind of intimate relationship . . ." Sophia's face flushed pink. "Oh! I'm sorry! I didn't mean to . . . I mean it's none of my business."

Justine slightly waved a hand and shook her head. "You're fine. Really. It's not like I haven't thought of that myself. But I'm sure there hasn't been anything even close to 'intimate' between my parents for years. There's no affection at all, and I'm positive sex is non-existent. It's been that way for a long time. Mom has never come right out and said so, but I'm pretty sure the drinking made him impotent. She moved her bedroom into the front parlor years ago under the excuse that my father snored too loud for her to sleep. It happened when I was pretty young, maybe thirteen or fourteen. I woke up to him yelling at her along the lines of about how it was all her fault, that she didn't do anything for him anymore. That next morning when I came downstairs Mom was asleep on the couch. Not too long after that she converted the front parlor into her own bedroom, complete with a locking doorknob." She paused staring off into space. "I've always tried to make sure I'm not around the house if he's home. Mom does the same. She'll go out to do things for the church and other stuff if he's anywhere nearby. Lately he rarely even shows up in time for meals. He comes in sauced just to fall into bed. They should have divorced years ago. She's only fifty-six and deserves so much better. He may be around a lot less these days, and they barely pass by each other, but she still takes care of everything to do with anything. She does his laundry, makes his meals, catches all his crap. She never says a thing about any of it. God forbid I should try to talk to her about him and how he treats her. She keeps going on with her routine like everything's hunky-dory and normal. I just don't get it."

"I'd guess maybe because it's all she knows," Sophia mused. "The first couple years I was at school one of my friends that shares my apartment had a boyfriend who was an addict. He was abusive like your father. She thought it was normal because she grew up with that kind of behavior. He acted out in the same ways her own father did. Then one day he went from screaming and yelling to hitting her. That's when she finally broke it off and got some counseling help. She told me once that even though she knew that her boyfriend was abusive, she'd convinced herself it was fine, that she didn't deserve any better because of how she was raised. Laura's father acted toward her mother the same way Laura's boyfriend treated her. It's a terrible cycle, but anything else seems scary or foreign to someone who has only lived in that kind of relationship."

Justine stared at Sophia. "Oh my God," she said dropping her head into her hands. "What have I been doing? And I've dragged my daughter right along with me."

"Whoa. Hang on. I wasn't talking about you."

"But you are," Justine protested. "Even if you didn't realize it, you are! And you are so right. I did the same thing, except for the alcoholic part. Kason, Natasha's father, had a lot of the same personality traits and behaviors as my dad. I always was making excuses to myself that he acted the way did because he was so busy and stressed with school and his residency and all."

"Oh. . .. But you're done with him, right?"

Justine nodded. "Oh yeah. But I'm not the one who finished it. I was living in a fairy-tale of what would happen once he finished school and became a doctor. I'm not sure I ever would've been honest enough with myself to leave him. Then I ran right back into the same environment by coming back here."

"Well, I'm not sure you had a choice about at least some of what's happened lately," Sophia said. "I mean, I don't really know anything about what you went through, but Dad did mention that you'd basically become homeless. The only logical choice was to come back home, right?"

Justine sighed. "That's what I thought anyway. I didn't want us to end up living in a shelter. Besides, there wasn't any room in one for the two of us. I checked. On top of that I was terrified they'd try to take Natasha away if we didn't have a place to live. I may be a lousy judge of men, but I'd like to think I'm a good mother."

"No worries there," Sophia said smiling. "From what I've seen you're a stellar mom. Your relationship with Natasha seems awesome. She's a great kid."

"Thanks. That really means a lot. She is one amazing little human even though we challenge each other all the time. I wouldn't trade being her mom for anything. But you're right, we were about to be homeless. The apartment lease was up. I couldn't afford it or anywhere else in Boston. When I called Mom in a panic she told me to pack up the car and come back regardless of what my father had said in the past. She said this would always be my home, and she wanted us to be here. She told me my father wouldn't turn us out even if he pretended he wanted to. She was right about that part. He's just a bully. A weak, drunk, pathetic bully. But he sure knows how to make life feel rotten. And most of being back doesn't seem like home to me."

"Justine, you may see your father as weak and pathetic. But he does whatever he wants. And the way he's always treated your mom—the way he treated you as a child whenever you didn't do exactly as he wanted—really is abusive and controlling."

Justine looked away toward the window. "I know you're right. When I met Kason I never thought that he might be anything like my father. But . . .he was." She chewed on her bottom lip, thinking. "Even though he wasn't a drinker and rarely raised his voice, the way he treated me was very much like my father treats my mother. He always seemed ashamed of me in public, not good enough except when he wanted something, but sweet and wonderful as long as things went perfectly his way. So I always tried to do exactly what he wanted. I thought that would make him love me. I was head-over-heels from the minute he asked me out. He was charming and attentive. I was sure I'd found 'the one.' When I got pregnant he wasn't thrilled, but we moved in together and I was certain we'd marry someday, after he finished his degree. He was disappointed when he found out we were having a girl, but I thought that would change once she was born.

"Tasha's a brilliant child. I thought he'd be thrilled with that. But he hated that she was different in other ways. He never was mean to her, but he didn't interact with her like a loving father would either. She was simply—there. I dropped everything for him. Everything. And in the end, I was just convenient to have, to take care of him while he was in the States. We truly meant nothing to him." Justine looked at Sophia. "Do you know in the 10 years we were together I never met any of his family? I mean, sure, they're all over in Sri Lanka, but I never even spoke to them on the phone or on video chat or anything. Not a word. He went back and forth to see them over the years. But he always said it was too expensive for all of us to go, and that he'd take us there as soon as he was done with his studies. That's when I thought we'd get married. I was so naive and stupid."

Sophia was silent, just letting Justine talk it all out.

"Geez, listen to me," Justine lightly smacked the palm of her hand against her forehead. "I've said way too much. You don't need to know any of this. What is wrong with me? I'm so sorry."

"Would you stop already?" Sophia demanded. "I don't mind at all. I was just thinking that life is so complicated. You know? When you're young you think you've got it all figured out and then, poof! Things go in a totally different direction than you ever imagined, and you get knocked on your ass." She looked down and scuffed the toe of her shoe against an imaginary spot on the floor. I learned that the hard way these past few months." She looked up at Justine. "I guess we all have."

Justine nodded. "Yes, but . . .

The screen door squeaked opened.

Tommy called out. "Hey, where are you guys? I've got fish out here, and I 'm not cleaning them without help."

"On our way. We were just looking at Mom's paintings," Sophia replied.

"Well, make it snappy. Dad's putting the gear away. Everything's all good. We'll fill you in when you come out." The door slammed shut as he retreated.

Justine put a hand on Sophia's arm. "Thank you for listening," she said softly.

"Anytime," Sophia replied smiling. "I'm glad you trusted me to talk to. Sometimes we just need a good friend's ear."

Justine linked her arm through Sophia's as they started toward the back door. "I'll return the favor, anytime. Promise. Oh, wait!" Justine stopped mid-step dropping her arm from Sophia's. "I almost forgot about Tasha. She'll have my hide if I don't go get her. I'm surprised she didn't come running when she heard Tommy."

Sophia cocked her head listening. "Maybe she doesn't know they're back. I don't hear her talking to Petunia anymore. I wonder if she fell asleep."

"That would be a first," Justine remarked. "Sometimes I'd swear that kid doesn't ever sleep. She's afraid she'll miss something."

"Well come on. Let's see." Sophia led the way up the stairs.

They peeked into the room. The late afternoon sunshine, filtered through white linen curtains, bathed the matching comforter on the bed in a warm yellow glow. Natasha was curled up on her side smack in the middle wrapped around Petunia who was wound in a ball between the child's knees and chest. The cat opened one eye, then closed it again, dismissing their presence.

"Well," Justine murmured.

"That's a picture if I ever saw one," Sophia whispered. She slid her phone out of her back pocket and quickly snapped a couple photos.

"I hate to wake her," Justine whispered back.

"Then don't." Sophia pulled the door toward them until it was almost closed. "Let her be." They turned and tip-toed down the stairs. "We can get started and you can check on her every so often. She won't freak out if she wakes up and has to come look for you will she?"

Justine shook her head. "I doubt it. She's pretty independent. Besides, she knows we planned to clean the fish out on the patio. She'll find us."

"Good enough." Sophia slid through the screen door and held it open for Justine to follow. "Anyways, that will give Dad and Tommy time to tell us all about what happened without little ears hearing the sordid details."

Justine hung her head. "Ugh. Different day, same drunken song."

Fifty Eight

Natasha still hadn't appeared by the time James and Tommy had related the last of the details from their run-in with Homer.

The mackerel were cleaned. The leavings had been thrown back in the bucket of sea water to take down to the harbor—an offering to the other creatures who would benefit from an easy dinner.

"I'd like to take Natasha with me when I dump this," James said. "We talked about it this morning."

"I can't believe she's slept this long," Justine remarked, looking toward the house. "I don't think she's taken an afternoon nap in years. I should go check on her."

"Don't wake her. We can take these guts down when she gets up." James wrinkled his nose. "As long as it's soon. Before long they'll stink even more than they do now."

Sophia picked up the tray of fish. "We should get this inside and get cooking. I was thinking of pan frying them in seasoned olive oil like Mom used to."

"That sounds so good. My mom only makes patties out of them, because that's the only way my father will eat it. He dictates just about everything over there." She shook her head. "I still can't believe that he tried to accuse the police chief of harassment and threw a punch at him. He's really lost it."

"Any addiction can destroy your mind, that's a fact," James said as he rolled up the newspapers they'd used to protect the table. "Young as I was when my father died, I remember how unhinged he was when he was drinking. It's a terrible sickness, being a slave to alcohol. At least Homer's out of the picture for the next twenty-four hours as he sleeps it off at the county lockup. That should dry him out for a little bit. Calm things down. Assaulting an officer, whether you're drunk or not, is a serious charge. They might let him sit there a bit before a judge sees him."

"Nate didn't say as much," Tommy remarked, "But he kind of indicated he felt we were acting in self-defense. He said he'd come by and get formal statements from us a little later."

"Why didn't he make a report right away?" Sophia demanded.

"He started one, but he needs to put it all together. That will take a while. Homer didn't even know we were there and probably won't remember a thing about the whole afternoon. Nate told us to go up top out of sight when he started to come 'round. Then the darn fool tried to start a fight with Nate after the paramedics got there to check him out. He had no idea how he ended up on the dock. I imagine he thinks he just passed out."

"Well he does that enough. So why not?" Justine said bitterly, her jaw set and angry. "I guess I'd better let Mom know."

James nodded. "Good idea. I was going to go talk to her before we came home, explain what happened, but Tommy said you'd mentioned she was gone shopping for the afternoon. Since your father is in lockup for the night, why don't you ask her to come over here and join us for supper. There's no reason for her to be home alone, and we have plenty."

Justine bit her lower lip. "That would be nice. If she'll come."

"I bet she might. She used to come over and visit with Anna sometimes during the day when we were all out to haul. The ladies kept an eye out so that when they saw the *Sea Gold* coming in Cora could scoot on home, ahead of your father. There's no one around to say a word to Homer about her being here. I seriously doubt anyone would say anything anyway, considering."

Justine reached in the pocket of her sundress for her phone. "I'm at a point where I really don't care if he finds out, or what anyone has to say about anything." She tossed her head. "I'm going to figure out some way to deal with all this. It's gone on way too long."

James smiled gently at her. "I agree that his behavior has gone on way too long, but you don't need to try to figure things out all on your own. I think the time has long passed for some accountability. Nate and I talked a little bit about that today. Since he took over in March there's been more than a few things he's trying to crack down on. He's not one to let things go the way they have in the past. There won't be any more good-old-boys club antics, or turning blind eyes because 'it's just the way it is.' It won't be like the past fifteen years that old Hanson was chief." James lifted the bundle of rolled-up newspaper with both hands. "I'm going to throw this stuff out, go in, and wash up. Then we can get cooking. Please tell Cora we all really hope she'll join us."

Justine dialed her mom's number as she walked away from the patio and down the driveway. She stopped on the side of the drive next to one of the trees, her back to them. Tommy watched her for a few moments while she talked into the phone. Her stance was stiff and unyielding. Every so often she gestured with an arm as if to emphasize her part of the conversation.

"That's one ticked off woman," he remarked to Sophia as they walked to the house. He opened the door for her.

"Yup. She's pretty worked up, but who could blame her?"

"Do you think her mom will come over?"

Sophia set the tray down on the counter and walked to the pantry. She shrugged. "I dunno, but I hope so. Justine's right. This stupid nonsense of Homer forbidding them to be friends with us and dictating where they can and can't go has got to stop. It's all so stupid. Plus, it's just empowered him over the years. I'd like to give him a few pieces of my own mind."

Tommy nodded. "Ditto."

Sophia glanced sideways at her brother and grinned. "I think you gave it a pretty good start already. I'm impressed. I didn't think you had it in you."

Tommy raised an eyebrow. "Maybe you don't know me as well as you think. You have to admit we've pretty much gone in different directions since I left home for college. It's been a few years."

"Maybe you're right," Sophia admitted. "It's sure been nice spending time with you again. I've missed being around my big brother."

"Don't tell anyone. It'll blow my new cover as a tough guy. But I miss you just as much. We need to do better than a phone call every couple weeks."

Sophia nodded. "For sure, and we need to come home together more." She set the cornmeal and olive oil she'd retrieved from the pantry on the counter. "Can you grab me the eggs and milk please?"

"Hey," Natasha wandered into the kitchen rubbing at her eyes. "Where's my mom and Mr. James? Can we clean the fish now?"

Hey, yourself," Tommy answered. "Your mom is right outside calling your gran, and my dad is washing up. We already cleaned the fish while you were resting."

"Oh."

Her crestfallen look made Tommy glance at Sophia in concern. She widened her eyes and lifted her shoulders slightly in response. He looked back at Natasha. "Don't worry. There will be plenty of other times for you to help. My dad saved the best part for you anyway—taking the innards down to the wharf to feed the other fish. He was waiting for you to wake up to do that."

Natasha still looked unhappy.

Tommy kneeled in front of her. "I'm sorry. You look disappointed. Would it help if you cook the fish with us? I think your gran might be coming over for supper, too."

"I guess," Natasha said rubbing her eyes again. "Have you seen Petunia? I woke up and she was gone."

"She's right behind you," James said on his way toward them through the living room. "She came to see me when I came in. I fed her dinner already," he added. "I was hoping it would keep her from underfoot while we made supper, but I have my doubts."

"Oh there you are, Pretty Cat," Natasha crooned. She kneeled to pet Petunia who was winding in and out of her legs. "Did you have a good nap with me?"

James leaned on the door frame. "I see Petunia has decided you're her new best friend," he remarked.

"I just love her! I can't wait for her kittens to come." Natasha plopped down on the floor. "They're going to be so beautiful. Just like you," she said pulling Petunia onto her lap.

Sophia poked Tommy's side gently with her elbow, "I think the cat trumps the fish," she whispered. "We're off the hook."

"You might be right—at least for now," he murmured back.

"Right about what?" Justine asked through the screen door.

"Miss Petunia having Natasha wrapped right around her little paw," Sophia replied. "Did you get hold of your mom?"

"Yup. I gave her the down and dirty. It took a little convincing, but Mom says she'd love to come have supper with us. She just got home and has to put stuff away. Plus, she wants to bring some things over to contribute to dinner. So I told her I'd run over to help. Then we can walk back over together. Tasha, do you want to come with me?"

Natasha kept petting the cat without looking up. "Can I just stay here?"

"It's fine that she stays if it's all right with you," James offered. "Or you can come down to the wharf with me if you want, Natasha. I'm going to dump the chum over the edge there and see what might come looking for their supper."

Natasha gently removed Petunia from her lap and set her on the floor. She got up and walked over to the door. "I want to go with Mr. James," she said through the screen. "Can I, Mom? I didn't get to help clean the fish. So can I go?"

"Sure. Have fun. I won't be long anyway. Sophia, is there anything in particular I should grab?"

"I think we have everything we need right here," Sophia answered. "I'm going to bread and season the filets. That'll take me a bit. We can start frying them as soon as you get back."

"Sounds like a plan. Back in a few."

"Hey, did we write down the fishing counts?" Natasha asked. "We have to do that because we need to keep track all year. Plus, I got the biggest one today and I'm gonna win most fish next time."

"Uh-oh. I didn't" Sophia replied. "With all that happened I didn't get a chance to. I bet our tally marks are still there, though. Maybe you could take a picture of them while you're down at the wharf, Dad. I'll hunt up a notebook to keep them in."

"Your mom's little tally book is in the top drawer of the buffet on the left. Same as always." James said. "It hasn't been opened since the last time you and I went fishing. If you agree, I think it's fine to just continue on with it."

Sophia tilted her head and then nodded. "Why not? It seems like we should. We can get it out after supper, just like we used to."

"Mr. James, you don't even need to take a picture unless you just want to. I know all the counts for everybody. It's like a picture in my head. I like numbers so I always remember them exactly right."

"Do you now?" James raised an eyebrow. "I suppose I shouldn't be a bit surprised. I might just take that picture though, to keep just so we have it as a photo memory for the first time we all went fishing together."

"So that means we really will go fishing together again?"

"Absolutely."

"Tomorrow?"

Sophia and Tommy both chuckled. James smiled down at the girl's earnest face.

"Maybe not tomorrow, but soon. I promise. I hope all of us get to do lots of other fun things together too." He put his hand on her shoulder, "For now, let's go see who's hungry down in the sea."

"Maybe even a shark?"

James winked at Tommy and Sophia. "Maybe. You never know what might show up down there."

Fifty Nine

Natasha

This was one of the greatest days ever. Maybe even *The Best*. The very, very best thing is that Petunia Cat is going to have babies, and I get to have one for my very own! She'll have to live at Mr. James's because for some reason my grandfather hates cats and won't allow one around here at all. I asked Mom why, but she said I didn't need to know, and she didn't want to talk about it. That made me want to know more than ever. But she told me that was the end of it. When she says that I know. I better. Just. Stop. I don't want to do anything to make her to change her mind about letting me have my own kitten. I can't wait! I hope Petunia has them soon. Mom says she figures within the next few days. Mr. James said I can come over every day to check on her and when she has them, he'll call us right away.

After Tommy and Sophia leave, he'll have to go out lobstering most every day, so I hope Petunia will be OK while he's not home. Mom says she'll be just fine, that we like to think that animals need us a whole lot more than they really do, and that cats don't want an audience for having their babies. Still, I wish I could be there with her. I think she really likes me. She purrs all the time when I pet her. If I stop she puts her paw on my hand like she wants me to keep going. She's the best cat. I wonder what her kittens are going to look like. Mom said my guess is as good as anyone's because nobody knows who, or where, the daddy cat is. Petunia and her kittens are kinda like Mom and me that way. I mean we know who my dad is and where he went, but he's like across oceans away, and no one here knows him. It really doesn't matter though, because we are doing just fine. Mom and I don't need anyone but us. Well, maybe that's not exactly true. I think it'd be lonely sometimes if it was just the two of us and no Gran or Mr. James or Tommy or Sophia. If we weren't all here there wouldn't be *Best Days* like today, and that would stink.

Fishing was more fun than I ever imagined, and the fried mackerel was so good. We caught a whole bucket full. I came in second in my very first fishing count contest! Sophia had five more than me and Mr. James had only one less than I did, but I have to be honest and say he probably would've beat me too if he hadn't had to help me learn how. I caught the biggest one though, so I won that category today. Mr. James said I was a true fisherwoman, and Sophia says that she knows it won't be long before I can beat her hands down. She teased me and said that now that my mom told her I'm a mermaid in disguise, she knows I can just sing songs to the fish and they'll jump right onto my hook, so that gives me an unfair advantage. That made me laugh. She's nice. I like her. She teases me a little, but it's not mean at all, and I get it. Plus, I can tease her back. That's pretty cool.

I didn't get to learn how to clean the fish with Mr. James because somehow I fell asleep up on Sophia's bed with Petunia and missed the whole thing. It turned out OK though, because Mr. James promised that we'll get to go fishing again lots of times. He says I probably won't like cleaning fish much anyway. We'll see.

I still got to go down to the cove with him to put the guts back in the water to feed other fish. The minute we dumped the bucket into the water off the edge of the floating deck the water churned all up because the fish found it and started chowing down. Mr. James called it a 'feeding frenzy' because of the craziness of the fish thrashing around trying to get some. We didn't see any sharks though, like when they throw chum over the sides of a boat on the shark shows on TV. Mr. James said that there are some sharks in the water here. He sees them when he's out on his boat sometimes. He told me about nurse sharks that are super big, and how one time one came right alongside the *Salty Lady,* and it was as long as the boat! I asked if he'd ever seen a great white shark out there, but he said he hadn't, yet. He told me how they usually like warmer waters and never used to be in our part of the sea, but the past few years he's heard of a few sightings around Maine. He said he figures more will come up into the Gulf since the water is warming.

I told him I knew that was right because the Gulf of Maine is the fastest warming body of water in the world. It is getting warmer faster than ninety-nine percent of the global oceans and scientists say climate changes will only make it worse. Mr. James said that the sea warming causes a whole lot of issues for all sea life and us humans, too. He said that even the mackerel population is down, but that may be just because they've been fished too much. He told me they were thinking of putting limits on how much fisherwomen like me could catch. He said they were thinking only twenty at a time would be legal. I said that I couldn't ever eat twenty fish by myself anyway, unless they were super tiny. That made him laugh. I told him that I wouldn't have thought their population numbers were going down from how easy they were to catch and from watching hundreds of them trying to eat the chum we dumped in the water. But I also know that just because we see some right here, doesn't mean they are everywhere they used to be. I also said how I think it seems weird that fish will eat the same fish as themselves. But I guess that's just proof of part of what we talked about in the morning, about fish and their brains. They just see it as food, not as one of their friends who is smaller than them swimming around in the water, or maybe on the end of a hook.

Now I want to find out more about how different kinds of animals' brains work and how much they know and feel. I never really thought a lot about it before. Maybe I'll see if there's a book at the library for that when Gran and I go on Tuesday.

Oh, another super neat thing from today was that Mom and Sophia showed me how to find sea stars right here under the wharf! I didn't know they lived right here by the shore. Now that I know how to look for them in the water I bet I can find more. Maybe there are even some down on my beach. I'm going to look tomorrow.

You know what else? Everybody felt really good most all day. It was the first time I've seen Mr. James really smile a lot. A couple of times he got that look he gets when he's remembering. But he didn't look as sad to me as before.

Today also was the happiest I've seen Mom since we left Boston, except for that little bit where my grandfather started the fight. But Tommy and Mr. James took care of that and called the cops and everything. I wanted to know more about what happened, but Mom said it was something for her and the other adults to handle. She told me all I needed to know was that it was all going to work out. She said maybe my grandfather might get some help with his drinking problem because they'd taken him to jail for fighting, and he couldn't get booze in there.

I figured out enough about what's been going on, but I'm not going to tell her that because she worries that I know too much. I'm not stupid just because I'm young. I hear a lot more than they think I do. I think my grandfather should have to stay in jail until he gets smart and stops all his bad behavior, but I won't say that to her because it just makes her feel bad about us being here.

When Mom tucked me in to bed tonight, she said it was time for some things to change, and she was going to make sure they did. I asked her if that meant we'd have to move again, but she said even when we move, she's going to find a place so we we'll still be in town or close by. I don't know how she thinks she's going to do that because I keep hearing the grownups talk about how there are no houses for families, even though there's so many places that no one seems to live in around here. I know Mom means what she says though. I trust her. She always makes sure to take care of us, no matter what.

The next most surprising thing today, after finding out Petunia was going to have babies, was that Gran came over to supper at Mr.

James's even though Mom had told me before that she was sure Gran probably would never go over there because of how much my grandfather hates Mr. James. I just don't understand grownups most of the time. But I'm super glad Gran came over. She and Mr. James talked a little about Miss Anna and how much they missed her. She wasn't surprised to see all of Miss Anna's art like everyone else seemed to be. She told Mr. James that she'd found out a few years back that Miss Anna was drawing and painting, but she figured if Miss Anna wanted folks to know she'd tell them herself.

When they were all talking about things they remembered about her, sometimes it felt a little sad. But no one cried, so I guess you could say it was mostly happy kinds of memories. Everybody sure loved her a lot.

It's not like when Mom remembers something about my dad or has something to say about him. That's a whole different kind of remembering. Mostly, if she has anything to say about him it's not much of anything good, or it's about how mad she is at him. I don't get all of it, but I heard Mom tell Gran when we first got here that my dad never planned to stay with us. She said something about us being 'convenient." I'm not sure what that even means. I think if I asked Mom she'd just get upset and tell me that it was too complicated for me to understand, but I bet I would get it if someone would just explain it to me. It didn't seem like things were too bad when we were all a family. I mean there were sometimes when Mom and Dad had disagreements, but there was hardly ever any drama or yelling. He wasn't there much. He was always at the university or working at the hospital. We didn't do a lot of things together, but it was nice when we did. I mean, he wasn't like Mom and me—we're a team. But he still was nice to me. I remember he used to pat me on the head whenever he went to work and came back. He never really hugged me, but he talked to me and read things to me sometimes. And it's not like I'm a real huggy person anyway. I mostly just like my own space. But he's still my dad, you know? I really want to know why he went away. I mean when he left for that last trip, he didn't even tell Mom he was going or that he wasn't coming back. He just . . . left.

I still think it was my fault even though Mom says it wasn't. I know I was in the way and aggravated him sometimes—actually a lot. A couple days before he left on his trip I said at dinner that I wanted some new shoes; pink high tops with sparkly laces, that I'd seen at the store where Mom worked. He got mad and said that I always wanted stuff I didn't need, and he wasn't going to pay for unnecessary American consumer-something-or-other. I don't remember exactly the words, but he always was saying mean stuff about Americans which I don't get at all, because we are Americans and live in America. Maybe that's why he left. Maybe he didn't like America any more.

I don't know. It just hurts my head to think about it. Besides, I'm too tired to think any more about anything right now.

Today mostly was a really good day. One of the best ever. And I'm going to have a kitten soon—maybe as soon as tomorrow.

Sixty

"Mr. James?" Natasha was leaning over the handlebars of her bike, watching James as he re-painted the forest green trim around the front door of the house.

James dipped his brush into the can, then slid the brush gently against the inside edge of it to remove the paint from one side. "Uh huh?"

"How come you had to scrape the old paint first and wash the wood before you started putting on the new paint?"

"Well," James said as he meticulously slid the brush along the edge of the trim board. "It makes the new paint stick better. If I just slapped up another coat over top of the cracking, dirty stuff, before long it would flake right off."

Natasha wrinkled her nose. "That makes sense I guess. This way you won't have to paint it again real soon, right? It looks like a lot of work to me."

James chuckled. "It is, but I don't mind. I like making the old girl look fresh and new again."

"Why do you call the house an 'old girl?'"

James dipped the paintbrush back into the can. He shrugged. "I dunno. That's just what she is."

"Like boats are ladies too?"

James chuckled. "I guess."

"Have you talked to Sophia and Tommy? How are they? When are they coming back?"

"I talked to Sophia on the phone Friday, and I'm going to touch base with Tommy today. They're both fine. Sophia is planning to come up next Thursday afternoon for the weekend. Last I knew Tommy will be here that Saturday morning. You're full of questions today aren't you? Any particular reason you ask?"

"Not really. I just wanted to know," she sighed. "And I miss them."

"Ah, me too," James said. He moved the can to the opposite side of the step and dipped the brush in.

"My turn now," he remarked casually. "How's school going?" He already knew the answer to this, at least from Justine's point of view. In the few weeks since Tommy and Sophia had returned to their own lives, Justine had started to make a habit of coming by a couple of afternoons each week after work to tidy up Anna's flower beds. James thought it was a wonderful idea for her to come and "play in the gardens" as she called it. He wasn't sure how much it was play. It sure looked like work to him. But he told her to do whatever she wanted. He also said he'd be happy to buy any new plants or whatever else she might want for them.

Anna had loved her gardens. James knew he could find her out in them more often than not throughout the warmer months. Even in the winter she'd put greens and decorations in the window boxes to keep them looking sharp. She'd always been a little disappointed that Sophia didn't have a love of plants and gardening like she did. James figured Anna would be thrilled if she knew Justine was giving the flower beds some loving care. Not only that, in some strange way, it made James feel like part of Anna was still present in the living things that she'd planted and tended. At least he could remember her there whenever he looked at the blooms. He had an ulterior motive too. Justine and Natasha coming by gave him a chance to keep an eye on the girls. He was more than a little concerned about the ongoing situation over at the Connor residence. Justine had reported that Homer had simply reappeared at the house without a word the afternoon after James's and Tommy's run-in with him at the wharf. She said he acted like nothing out of the ordinary had ever happened. He still hadn't said a thing to either his wife or his daughter, and they weren't going to breathe one word to him. She said he'd been mostly absent since then. James knew this already because he'd been fishing every possible day himself, and Homer was always coming and going from the cove just about the same time he was. The most interesting thing was that Homer either didn't remember any of what had happened, or was simply choosing to ignore it. He never even looked James's way, which was exactly how it had been for years. Nate had been by to update James on the situation. They all agreed it was better just to leave Tommy and James out of it, unless Homer had something to say about the altercation. There still was the mystery about the other guy that had come down with Homer and then taken off. James hadn't ever seen him around, and no one else had mentioned a new sternman in the area. Nate said that he hadn't seen anyone matching the description the Edward men had given of the man either. Nate's take on it was that Homer had hired him as a third man and that the incident had scared him off. He'd probably realized he didn't want any part of Homer's antics. James figured that was as good a guess as any, so long as the guy didn't reappear and start running his mouth so that Homer suddenly remembered what happened. That would just open the can of worms right wide.

With Justine coming by regularly, she and James chatted quite a bit. One of their favorite subjects was Natasha. The afternoon before, while Natasha had been shopping at the market with Cora, Justine was weeding Anna's front flower bed. She was preparing it, and the window boxes, for a fall display of mums and gourds. This was the same afternoon that James noticed the trim around the doors and windows was in need of a touch-up.

Justine told him that everything seemed to be going fairly well for Natasha at school, but she was still a little worried. It was a completely different environment than the inner-city, primary school she'd attended in Boston. Now James was curious if Natasha might have anything to allow.

Natasha shifted slightly on the seat of her bike before she answered James. "School's OK."

James smiled to himself at her non-committal answer, thinking of how he never got much else from his own children when he asked the same question. "That's all? Just, OK?" he asked. "Do you like your teachers? Have you met some of the local kids?"

"Yeah. My teachers are fine. I know some of the kids now. They're pretty nice. Did you know that there are only fourteen kids in my grade? Not only that, but it's the most kids in any grade in the whole school. It's crazy how small the school is."

"That must make it a little easier to get to know your classmates." James had been crouching down to paint the last few inches of trim near the step. He stood and stretched both arms toward the sky. He leaned down to pick up the can of paint so he could move to the next spot needing attention. "Excuse me, but I need to get right in front of you so I can get to the window."

"Oh. Sure." Tasha sat up straighter on her bike, grasped the handlebars and moved her feet on the ground backing up the bike to give him room to navigate. "I'm not in the regular classroom a lot. That kind of stinks because everybody knew right away that I was in specials, and then it's harder to get to know anyone. Plus, other kids think I'm weird because I learn different stuff than they do in the regular class. This one boy said that I was too stupid to be in class with them. He called me "Special Ed" and told me I should go back to the hole I crawled out of."

James turned to look at his young friend. He tried to keep his face neutral, but his blood was boiling. Justine had briefly mentioned that there had been an issue with a boy and some name-calling the first day. She said that Natasha had told her that another girl stuck up for her, and the teacher had been made aware. But she hadn't told him exactly what had been said. "I'm so sorry that happened," he said carefully. "But you do know that what he said is just mean and not even remotely true, right?"

Natasha waved a hand to the side. "Oh, I know I'm not stupid. And I know I'm different. I'm used to hearing dumb stuff like that. Mom says it doesn't take any kind of brain to be a mean person who says awful stuff, so it just makes them look ignorant." She grinned. "Besides Maddie stuck up for me. She's a lot like me and super smart. We're in math and science specials together. She's pretty deaf. She wears these big hearing aids, and she talks a little different. But she reads lips really well. Anyway, she saw what Jake said to me—that's the mean boy's name —and went right up to him. She told him to shut his big, stupid, mouth and leave me alone, and that if he ever said anything else like that she'd tell her dad to have a talk with his dad. I asked her later why it mattered if her dad talked to his dad. Maddie told me that her dad is Jake's dad's boss, and he wouldn't put up with anybody, or anybody's kid, making fun of kids like us." She shrugged. "I guess that means something, because Jake's just ignored me since then."

James raised an eyebrow. He scratched at his beard with his free hand. "Hmm, I think I know who you're talking about. I don't know Maddie or Jake, but I do know their fathers. Is Maddie's last name Bailey?"

Natasha nodded. "Uh huh. Maddie Bailey."

"Her dad, Stan, owns the *Maddie Sue*. Jake's father is Matt Stout and he's Stan's sternman. They've been fishing together out of Bunker's Harbor since they were just a few years older than you. Their fathers are lobstermen too. I know both families back at least a couple generations. I bet your friend Maddie is right. I can't see anyone from either of those families putting up with that kind of behavior. It's too bad one of their youngsters acts that way."

"Mom said the same thing. I guess she went to school with Maddie's mom and dad, and Jake's dad too. Mom said she doesn't know Jake's mom. She's from somewhere else." Natasha paused and wrinkled her nose. "Mom said it different though. She said she's 'from away.' Anyway, Maddie told me that Jake's mom and dad are getting a divorce, so Jake and his little brother live with just their dad now."

"Well, I don't know about any of that. But I'm really sorry that young Jake said those things to you."

"Yeah, I'm not a fan," Natasha remarked. "Boys are dumb anyway."

"You just remember that in a few more years," James remarked turning back to the window trim.

"Remember what?"

"Never mind. It was good of Maddie to stand by you. It sounds like you might become good friends."

"We already are," Natasha declared. "She likes a lot of the same things I do, and we think a lot alike. We talk about lots of stuff, all the time. Mrs. Brandt, our math specials teacher, always has to tell us to be quiet and get to work." Natasha paused. "Umm, can you not tell Mom that part?"

"What part?" James teased, his back still to Natasha where she couldn't see his big grin.

"The part where Mrs. Brandt has to tell us to stop talking. Mom knows everything else."

"Ah. Your secret's safe with me. But maybe you might want to listen to your teacher, eh?"

Natasha sighed, "I know. It's just so neat to have a friend my age that's like me."

"I bet it is," James agreed.

"Besides, I'm learning ASL. That's American Sign Language," Natasha added. "Maddie already knows it. Then we can sign stuff to each other, and no one can tell us to be quiet 'cause they won't hear a thing."

James had a tough time not laughing aloud at that logic. He was trying to think of an appropriate response, but Natasha was already onto the next topic.

"Is it all right if I go in to see Petunia and the kittens?"

"Sure. Just remember, don't pick them up since a grownup isn't in there to help. They're wiggly and unsteady since their eyes aren't open yet. You can pet them all you want though. Have you picked out your new baby cat yet?"

"Not yet. It's too hard. I love them all."

James glanced at Natasha. He smiled at her hopeful face. "Well, we can't keep all five of them. That's a fact. But you have about seven more weeks to decide which one to call your own."

His phone rang the distinctive tone that told him Sophia was calling. He stepped back from the window and reached into his pocket with his free hand to answer it. "It's Sophia," he said to Natasha. Still holding the paintbrush, he poked at the button with his pinky finger. "Hi, Bean. Hold on just a sec, let me put this brush down."

"OK. I'm gonna go in. Tell her I said, 'Hi,'" Natasha instructed as she started to pedal her bike down the front walk to go around to the driveway to the back door. "Tell her I'm going in to check on the kittens and I can't wait to see her."

"I will," James called after her retreating back. He put the brush across the top of the paint can, wiped his hand on the leg of his work pants, then put the phone back up to his ear.

"Hey, Dad. I heard her. Please tell her I said, 'Hi, back' next time you see her. She's a sweetie. What are you painting?"

"I'm just freshening up the trim on the front of the house. A little busy work, that's all. I wasn't expecting a call from you today. Everything OK?"

"Everything is great. I have an idea I want to talk to you about. I already ran it by Tommy, and he thinks it's a great plan. But you have to promise to hear me out, OK? Just let me tell you all about it before you say anything."

Sixty One

"I want to go to work with you on the boat, as your sternman. And I've..."

James interrupted. "Listen, Bean we've already been over this. I'm not saying that I don't want you to work with me. Not at all. I'd absolutely love it. But what about your classes and your own future career? You can't quit."

"Who said anything about leaving school?" Sophia demanded, her tone sharp and irritated. "Dad, I asked you to listen to me all the way to the end. You could at least let me finish before you try to shoot me down, again. And by the way, I get to decide what my career looks like. Tommy was right. He said it was going to be next to impossible to talk with you about this, especially over the phone."

James felt a flash of anger at her words. "That's not fair. I'm only looking out for you."

"Come on, Dad. You're not even listening. Let me talk first. Then you can tell me what you think. But please, at least give me the respect of hearing me out. I'm a grown woman for God's sake. I think I might just know a little bit more than you give me credit for."

James sighed and sat down on the front step. "OK. I apologize. Go ahead. I'm listening."

"Thanks." James heard his daughter take a deep breath and exhale. "Like I was saying, I want to move home and come to work for you on the boat. I finally decided on the focus for my Master's thesis. All the ongoing hoopla about new regulations to preserve the Right Whale population has got me right riled up. Maine already has the most, and best, regulated seafood fishing industries in the world. Plus, it's all absolutely ludicrous since there aren't even any Right Whales in Maine fishing waters anymore, and there hasn't been one that has been entanglement in Maine lobster gear since two thousand four. I'm starting to think this is some kind of backhanded excuse to regulate the industry out of the water and shut us down. The truth is that it has wide-reaching impact with very little base in scientific evidence.

I love the whales. I want them to rebound and thrive. But there must be solutions that work for saving sea life, the whole ocean itself, and the fishing industries. I really need to be out there in the thick of it day-in and day-out. I need to get it right in order to do my thesis, and my career, justice." She briefly paused for a breath. "You still there?"

"Yup, go on. I'm listening. You sound pretty charged up."

"I am! You should be too. So should anyone who has any stake in lobstering or sea harvesting in Maine at any level."

"Oh, believe me. I am. That's all that's been talked about down on the dock, out on the water, on the radios, and around town for the past couple years. It's a damn mess for sure. The fishing industry's already in a bind and this makes it worse. I just don't know what an old guy like me can do to stop corporate interests and big money."

"I know. But there *are* some things we can do, if we all pull together. It takes numbers for sure. I really believe I can be in a position to advocate and help do something about it. Lobstering's been our past, our legacy as a family, for one hundred plus years. As you know it's the same for many families up and down the Maine coast. We need it to stay our future. If corporate greed succeeds in driving the lobsterman out of business, what's left? Towns will simply shrivel up and die. There isn't much else out there for folks to do to make a living. And most of the stinking reports and recommendations are all based on absolutely zero evidence that the whales are being harmed in any way by *our* fishing gear. There are no documented entanglements in Maine gear in the past nineteen years. Not to mention that with the break-away rope we use now, if a Right Whale hit a line, it'd get right through it.

The focus needs to be on global solutions, not targeting one gulf and one fishing industry. These outfits on the other side of the country trying to tell us how to save our own sea and sea life have no idea about all the preservation efforts and rules already in place."

She stopped to catch her breath. "Sorry, I know I'm preaching to the choir, but I finally figured out what I really want to work with. I'm in a great position with the research I've already done, plus the ability to be right there working in the field. My advisor agrees with me and loves my plan. She's already signed off on my thesis intent. I've talked with both my profs. I can do my Tuesday class remotely. It starts at six and goes a couple hours. It's more of a round-table discussion between the professor and six of us degree candidates than it is a traditional class. We discuss things that have to do with current research, marine commerce, and how our own work is going. We hardly ever meet on campus anyway. We just Zoom in together. So, it doesn't matter where I am, physically. My prof said he doesn't care where I sign in from, as long as I show up online every week. So, that's not an issue."

Sophia paused for another breath. "I have to be in my other class on Thursday mornings. But if I you're OK with it, I will take Thursdays off and just drive down here to campus for the day. I can do my weekly check-in with my advisor at the same time. She's fine with that. Next semester is my last one before graduation. I basically have the same set-up, only I've managed to get everything scheduled on Thursdays from January to May. It's only a two-hour drive. I'll be done by early afternoon and back home in time for supper. So, I just need Thursdays off for the next eight months. I can work the rest of the week. I figured I'd move back this weekend and get started with you next week."

"Can I talk yet?" James interjected.

Sophia gave a short laugh. "Hang on. Not yet, please. First, let me tell you answers to the things I think you probably want to know. One: I already talked to my boss at work here. I explained what I want to do, that you need help too, and I want to move home. I told him I'd work out two weeks' notice, but he said he's got a couple other students begging for hours, so I could just finish this week and he's perfectly fine with that. Two: We haven't signed the lease yet for the next year on the apartment here. It's due October first with the rent. Stephanie and Julie don't have any problem with me not renewing along with them. Fact is, Steph and her boyfriend Tim just got engaged and they want to move in together, so the timing is perfect for them. I offered to pay my October share for such short notice, but they said they're all set. Julie graduates in December so she'll be leaving then, and the lovebirds can have the whole place to themselves. Three: I don't have a whole lot of stuff down here. No furniture or anything. I think I can get most of it in my car the first trip up, but I can keep anything here in a closet and get it next Thursday when I drive down for class." Sophia stopped talking for a split second. "So? What do you think?"

James cleared his throat before carefully choosing his words. "I think you didn't call me to ask me about any of it. You just wanted to tell me what you're doing," he said dryly.

There was silence on the other end of the line. "Are you mad?" Sophia finally asked. "Do you not want me to come home?"

"No, no. That's not it. I can hear you've definitely worked through this, and you know what you want to do. Truth-be-told I'm thrilled that you're excited about doing something with your degree that could really make a difference. "And," James cleared his throat again. "Selfishly, I love that I could have you working with me. But are you sure you really want to do this? Will you be able to do your research and schoolwork and work on the boat full-time too? I mean, you only work two days a week right now, and it's not near as physical as being out on the boat."

"I'm sure," Sophia said firmly without any hesitation. "I study at night anyway. We're in most days from hauling by three. I'll do my research and writing after that. Plus, we'll pull the boat out from late November until April, and I graduate next May. I'll have five whole months over the winter just working part-time repairing traps and stuff with you while working on my studies. It will be the perfect setting for me to finish my thesis writing."

"Hmm," James grumbled. "I suppose I can't argue with your plan. It seems you've really thought this through."

"Don't sound so excited, Dad."

"Oh, I am. I just hope that you aren't giving up what you want just to come and help me. I don't want you to regret what you're doing."

"Dad," Sophia sounded exasperated. "How many times do I have to tell you that I want to take over the boat someday. I want to continue the family business. But I want to do more. I want to be a voice, an advocate, for our industry. The best way I can do that is to be out there, right in it every day, instead of being stuck in some office pretending I know what's going on."

"OK. OK. I'm just checking. I don't want you to resent any part of the job, or me, down the line because you cut your college experience short."

Sophia snorted. "I've had enough of the 'college experience.' I want to come home and get to work. Real work. There's a lot to be done."

"I don't disagree with you there," James said. "But I do have one question, Bean."

"Yeah?"

"Should we convert Tommy's room upstairs into two rooms? Like for a bathroom and maybe a study area for you? I'd think you'd want more personal space than what's up there."

"Oh! I forgot to tell you what I thought about that. What if I cleaned out the old studio apartment above the garage that you and Mom stayed in when you were first married? That way I could totally have my own space, and you can have yours. No offense, but I really don't want to live with you full-time, Dad."

James laughed. "No offense taken. I really don't want to live with you full-time either, Bean. I kinda like my own space. I'm pretty set in my ways. But that place has been used for garage storage for over twenty-five years. It won't be any easy task to clean it out. Plus, the kitchen and bathroom definitely need updating."

"It can't be any more work than if we were to try to convert Tommy's old room into a bathroom. And I know how to clean out stuff. I think it will be fun to make my own place up there."

"Well, OK then. I say let's do it!"

"Really? You're really all right with it?" Sophia sounded amazed.

James paused. He was impressed, not only how Sophia really had thought through what she wanted to do, but how she had presented it to him. "I'm really all right with it. You've covered everything. What did you expect me to say? That I don't want my daughter to come home and go into business with me? I'm going to have the best sternman in the state. You definitely have worked through this. You're on a path to accomplish what you want. You know, I'll always do my best to support you and your decisions no matter what they are. But selfishly, I can't wait to have you home for good. Do you want me to take Saturday off to come down to help you move your stuff?"

"Yay! No thanks. I don't need any help. I'm going to finish packing up stuff and load what I can into my car. My last day of work is Wednesday. Class is over before noon on Thursday. So I'll stop on my way home and bring something for supper Thursday night. Sound good?"

"Sounds like a plan," James agreed. "I'll get up in that space above the garage today, to see how bad it looks. I'm sure it's a mess. I imagine you'll have to stay in your old room for at least a couple weeks until we fix up the apartment the way you want it. You sure took me by surprise. Now I can't wait to have you here!"

"Awesome! I'll try to stay out from underfoot. I promise."

James chuckled, "I bet I'll be more in your way than you'll be in mine. I promise I'll try to stay out from underfoot too."

"Hah! I better run. I have to work this afternoon. Love you so much, Dad. I can't wait to move home."

"Love you too, Bean. Be safe. See you in four days!"

James heard the line disconnect on Sophia's end. He took the phone from his ear and stared at it. He felt like he'd been rolled over by a pop-up summer storm and he wasn't sure what had hit him. He took off his ball cap, then glanced up at the early afternoon sky as the light dimmed. Wispy clouds meandered across the sun, half-filtering its light before bursting out in full force when the clouds passed by.

Hey Anna. Our girl's coming home. To stay. Can you believe it?

A murmur of a breeze ruffled his hair and tickled the back of his neck. He smiled, wiped his forearm across his forehead, then settled his cap back on his head. *I know. I know. Quit standing around and get back to work. There are things to be done.*

Sixty Two

James opened the box and grabbed a third slice of the pizza Sophia had picked up on her way home.

"This is really good. I don't think I've had pizza from Pat's in over a year."

"Really? I know you like their food. You and Mom used to go there for supper quite a bit when you went to town."

James shrugged. "I don't do a lot of things the same way I guess, it just being me now."

"I can understand that. It'll be a little weird not having the same roomies that I've lived with for the past four and a half years around me all the time." She smiled at James. "But hey, now you're stuck with me. Lucky you!"

James shook his head and grinned back at her. "You are too much. I don't think I'll ever consider myself 'stuck' with my favorite daughter."

"Hah. You have to say that since I'm the only one. Now I have nowhere else to go either. So you really are stuck."

"Doesn't feel that way. You'll always be my favorite girl." James took another bite. "You know, we may have to pick up a pizza once in a while. I do love this stuff."

"The perfect meal. Bread, meat, cheese . . . ." Sophia raised her glass. "And a cold beer to share. What's not to love?"

"Your mom would disagree unless we added vegetables," James chuckled.

"No veggies on my pizza," Sophia protested. "That would be sacrilege."

"Deal," James said raising his beer can in salute. "No veggies on our pizza. Do you want to go look at the apartment after we're done?"

"Sure. There's still plenty of daylight left. I figured I wouldn't unload the car until tomorrow. I thought I could use Tommy's room to store some of my stuff until I can unpack it into the new place. I don't want to put it up in the apartment until it's ready. And I don't think I can put much of it in my room and still be able to move in there."

"That sounds fine," James agreed. He got up to throw his paper plate from dinner into the trash can. "I better stop. If I eat one more piece I might explode."

"Me too. Cold pizza for breakfast!"

"We can do better. I was thinking I'd take you with me to Milbridge and go out for breakfast in the morning. I need to make a run to the Marine Supply for a few things—one of which is a proper survival suit for my partner and sternman."

Sophia grinned. "That sounds awesome. But do we have to go at the crack of dawn? I was hoping to sleep in until seven at least."

"Sure." James scratched at his beard. "I know I've got a few more things to add to my list, too. I'll have to think on it though because they escape me at the moment."

Sophia got from the table. She threw her plate and napkin away. "Ready if you are to see the apartment. What should I expect? You didn't tell me how bad, or good, you found it when you checked it out."

James headed toward the door. "Well I guess you'll just have to see for yourself."

They had just stepped out the door when Natasha on her bike came barreling around the corner of the driveway toward them.

"Sophia! You're back! Mom said you were coming home today. Yay!"

"I think someone else is glad you're home," James observed.

"It seems that way. Hi Tasha! What's up?" She asked as the young girl braked to a hard stop by the walkway.

Natasha hopped off her bike and laid it down in the grass. "I really came over to see the kittens like I do every night after supper," she said seriously. Then she bobbed her head and giggled. "But I was kinda hoping you were here already and you are!"

Sophia laughed. "So I am. And I'm here to stay."

"I know! It's so exciting. Mr. James, did she go look at the apartment yet?"

"Not yet. Do you want to come see it with us?" He turned to Sophia. "Is that all right with you?"

"Why not," Sophia said. "The more the merrier. Who knows what we'll find up there."

Natasha giggled again. Sophia raised an eyebrow. "OK, you two. What's going on here?"

"What?" James asked in mock innocence as he led the way to the side of the garage.

"Wow. The steps look great, Dad. I love the green paint. But you didn't have to repaint them just for me."

"Well, actually I did. If you look closely you'll see that it's a brand-new staircase. The old one wasn't exactly safe anymore after all these years."

"That's almost a lie, Mr. James," Natasha accused. "They weren't safe at all." She turned to glare at him, her hands on her hips. "You fell right through the second step when you tried to go up there the first time. Don't forget. I saw you do it."

"Really? Did you get hurt, Dad?"

He took his hat off and leaned his head toward her to show a bruise and some scratch marks on the left side of his forehead. "My pride got hurt more than anything, but I did bump my head on the side of the garage." He plopped his hat back down. "They looked sound enough, but I didn't think to test them."

"Holy! You could have broken something. I'm glad the garage caught you."

"Me too. But it was even luckier that I was able to get someone out here to replace the whole dad-gummed thing on Tuesday. It was all too rotten to save. Two local kids who just started a carpentry business were finishing up a shed over at the Carter's place. I remembered seeing their trailer over there. So I went by to talk with them Monday after I fell through the step. They came right over the next morning. By noon we had new stairs. They worked so quickly and did such a good job that I hired them to take care of a few other things that needed doing around here. They've been working right steady while I've been out to haul the past two days."

James winked at Natasha. "Tattle Tale," he complained with a grin.

"Well, she should know," Natasha protested frowning. "Now that she's home she can look out for you when I'm not around. You were being dangerous, not checking it first. Even Mom said so."

"I'm only kidding. You're absolutely right, and I'm really glad you were here." James looked at Sophia. "Miss Natasha made me sit right down. Then she went and got Justine and the first aid kit. But I really was fine. It's just a little bump."

"People get concussions by bumping their head," Natasha said, her hands still on her hips. "And concussions are bad news. You know that. You always have to be careful about head injuries."

Sophia was biting her lips trying for all she was worth to not laugh out loud at the two of them. She cleared her throat. "You both crack me up. But I'm so glad you were here, Tasha. Thank you for looking out for my dad."

"Well somebody has too. Sometimes I don't think he pays such good attention to stuff."

"Sometimes I think you know too much for your own good." He held out his hand to Natasha for a fist bump which she delivered with a smile. "Or maybe it's you know too much for my own good."

"Hah! You're so funny, Mr. James. Can we go see the apartment now?"

"You bet." James started up the stairs. "This time I'll try to stay upright." He picked his hand up from the railing and rubbed his fingers together. "Just be careful of the new paint. It's only been on here since this morning. I think it's dry enough though. It doesn't feel tacky to me. So let's go see what we see up there."

Sixty Three

James stopped for a second on the landing at the top of the stairs. He turned to the girls as they stepped up beside him. "I had them make the landing a little longer. You'll be able to put a chair and little table out here now so you can sit and watch the harbor."

"That's awesome, Dad. It'll make it easier to get things cleaned out and get my stuff up here too."

"Out was easy," Natasha muttered.

"What's that?" Sophia asked looking over at her.

James shook his head at Natasha behind Sophia's head.

Natasha waved a hand. "Uh. Nothing. Really."

"OK, Ready to take a look? You've been up here before, Bean."

"Oh yeah. But when I was a little kid. You and Mom were always putting things in storage up here. I remember it being piled high with all kinds of old stuff."

James nodded. "That's true. After we moved into the big house it did become storage. Once it was mostly full, we finally stopped adding things. Then we forgot about most of it. It's interesting what you think you need to keep for another day. Then you never touch it again. Most of what we put in here was old yard and garage stuff that should have just been tossed to begin with."

He stepped into the room. Sophia stopped in the doorway and peered in. The early evening sun through the two west facing windows cast a soft pink glow across the space.

"But it's almost empty," she said in surprise entering the room. "You cleaned it out already."

"Ayup. I had the boys take most of it away. I just stood up here and said if it was to stay or go."

"You really didn't keep much at all, Mr. James. Except for the furniture that's still here. Look Soph, we found this table and chairs in the bedroom. Mr. James said it was your mom's and his first kitchen table. It's an antique."

"It's beautiful," Sophia murmured.

"Here's a little something to make it even prettier," Justine said coming through the open door. She held a large vase full of bright orange lilies and black-eyed Susans that she set on the center of the table before turning to give Sophia a hug. "Welcome home."

"Thanks. I'm so glad to be back, for good."

"Well, what do you think?" Justine asked surveying the room. "Your dad really cracked the whip to get this place all cleaned out and scrubbed up."

"It's amazing. I can't believe you made this happen in four days, Dad."

"I had a lot of help, and it's not done by any means. We still need to update the plumbing in the bathroom. The kitchenette could use new cabinets, and we'll need to buy a fridge and a range for you. You'll want to repaint everything too. That hasn't been done since your mom and I got married."

"I can help with the painting," Justine offered. "I have all weekend free if you want to get started on it. Or I can help any day next week after work."

"Me too," piped up Natasha. "I can paint."

Sophia walked over to the bathroom and looked in. "Dad, I don't think we need to update anything in here. I love the retro fixtures."

James peered over her shoulder. "They could qualify as 'retro,' I guess. I wouldn't have thought that rose colored porcelain would be something you'd like."

"Actually, I love it, and the linoleum with the roses on it looks like it's brand new."

"Your mom picked out that sheet linoleum, and the pink fixtures, at a salvage place. She loved anything floral, that's a fact."

"I want to keep it all. Do we need to replace any pipes though?"

James shook his head. "Amazingly enough the copper is still all good, even though they've been shut off for years."

"Your old dresser is still up here, too," Sophia remarked traveling into the tiny bedroom. "I can just move my bed up here from my old room. I can't believe you got everything cleaned out so fast."

"I wanted to make it so you could just get going on making it your own space," James said. "Natasha and Justine helped me out the past three days. They're ruthless when it comes to throwing things out and cleaning up."

"That's what I was saying on the way up. I almost spoiled the surprise," Natasha admitted. "Out was easy. We just tossed everything to get thrown away over the railing of the new landing. Then the worker guys put it into their trailer and took it away. I liked that part. I didn't like the cleaning part so much."

"You never like the cleaning part much," Justine allowed with a smile. "But you did a lot anyway."

"Thank you all so much." Sophia came back out into the main room. She gestured around the room. "I just can't believe how great it all looks. What a gift. We can put a coat of paint on the walls and then I can start moving all my stuff in."

"I bet you'll want to pick up a few things you don't already have, like curtains and housekeeping stuff," Justine observed. "A girls' shopping day would be a whole lot of fun."

Sophia clapped her hands together. "You're on. We'll make a whole day of it when we go."

"I know one thing you really, really, need up here," Natasha said.

"Yeah? What's that?"

"A kitten. You need a kitten. And we have four left that you can choose from."

"A kitten?"

"Our young kitten whisperer has been lobbying for all Petunia's babies to have homes close by," James explained. "She was on a mission to keep them all, but we compromised. The agreement is we'll work to find very good homes where she can possibly visit them."

"Is that so?" Sophia exchanged an amused look with Justine.

"I'm afraid it is," Justine replied. "It took quite a bit of negotiation and a promise that we will consider keeping two of them for ourselves." She help up a hand as Natasha opened her mouth to speak. "*If* we find our own place to live before they're all spoken for."

"Yeah, I don't think that's gonna happen," Natasha remarked glumly. "But I can hope, right?"

"Good attitude," James said ruffling her hair.

"But you could have two up here, Soph." Natasha suggested. "If you have two, they won't be lonely while you're out working on the boat."

Sophia laughed. "Well, first I'd have to ask my landlord if I can even have one cat. Second, I'm not sure how lonely a single cat would get. I mean Petunia doesn't seem concerned being alone in the house when she's there by herself all day."

"I already asked Mr. James and he said it's up to you what pets you might want. Except that you can't have anything very big. Two cats are small. Right?" She asked hopefully.

Sophia held up hand. "Whoa there, you little tornado. I just got here. I'll have to think about it for a while."

Natasha looked down at the floor. "Oh. OK." Then she looked up at Sophia with a little grin and a twinkle in her eye. "You have a few more weeks before they can leave their mom, but you don't want to wait too long because someone else might snatch up the ones that are your favorites."

Sophia shook her head laughing along with James at Natasha's persistence. "You're a tough salesperson, you know that?"

"Pushy and bossy would be better adjectives," Justine sighed. "Give it up, Tasha. You've made your pitch. Now let's not hear about it again."

"At least not for today," James interjected. "I'm sure Sophia needs time to think about it. There's a lot of responsibility that comes with taking care of a pet."

"But I'm gonna help her too," Natasha protested. "I have to be here anyway to take care of Grumble and Petunia."

"You named your kitten Grumble? Does that mean you picked out the one we're keeping?" Justine asked. "Which one is it?"

"The all orange one that I was calling Marmalade until you told me he was a boy."

"You know, Marmalade could be a boy's name too."

"I guess. But I like Grumble better for his name because when he purrs it sounds like he's grumbling."

"I thought you wanted a girl like Petunia," James said. "What changed your mind?"

Natasha shrugged. "I just love Grumble most. That's all."

"Well, I think that's a fine reason to choose him then."

"I bet he's a cutie," Sophia remarked. "I haven't even seen them yet. Dad and I sat down to eat as soon as I got here so the pizza wouldn't get cold. So I haven't had time to check them out."

Justine put a hand on Natasha's shoulder. "I'm sorry. We both barged right in, didn't we? We should run on home and leave you two to your evening."

"But I haven't fed Petunia yet, and I want to play with Grumble," Natasha protested looking up at her mother. "Plus I have to tell Sophia all about each kitten when she meets them so she can pick when she decides she wants them."

Justine shook her head. "I said that was enough, Miss Pushy Pants. If you don't lay off, Sophia might decide she doesn't want to think about it at all."

Natasha hung her head, "OK. I'm sorry, Soph. I just love them so much I want to be sure they get the best homes. You would be such a good cat mom. I just know it."

"It's fine. I totally understand. I promise you I'll seriously consider it," Sophia reassured her. "I want to meet them for sure. Where are they anyway?"

"She had them in the closet in the downstairs bedroom," Natasha answered.

"Really." Sophia turned to her father, her head tilted slightly to one side as she studied his face.

He shrugged. "She kept going over to the door one night meowing and scratching at it. I finally gave up and let her in so I could get some sleep. The next morning I went in to find her, and we had kittens."

"She has a big comfy bed of fluffy towels that Mr. James made her in the corner of the closet. We keep a bowl of water in there by her too because Mama cats need to drink a lot of water all day to make enough milk for the babies. She still comes out into the kitchen to eat though."

"Ah. I see." Sophia put a hand on Natasha's shoulder. "Well don't you worry. You can take me in to see them in a little while. I'd just like to do a couple other things first. I want to make a list of stuff I need to get to remodel in here. I'd love all your suggestions, especially since you're going to help me do the work. Plus, I bought fudge ripple ice cream on my way home. Who wants some?"

"Me. Me. Me! But I need to go feed Petunia and check on the babies first. I'll meet you guys inside." Natasha skipped out of the room and onto the landing.

"I'm right behind you," James said. "I think I want some tea with dessert. Anyone else?"

"I'd love a cup," Justine said.

Sophia shook her head. "No tea for me, thanks. I'd rather have coffee. I'll make some decaf when I come in. I won't be too long. I just want to look around a little more, think about what I might want to do paint-wise and stuff." She glanced at Justine. "I'd love your opinion on colors and how to set up the kitchenette."

"Sure! I can do that. It'll be fun."

"You girls take your time. There's no hurry. I'll put the kettle on. Natasha will be tied up with the kittens for a bit. She has a specific routine she goes through every time she comes to take care of them. If you're still up here when she's done, I'm sure she'll come find you." James left them standing in the middle of the room.

"Natasha's certainly taking her duties with the kittens seriously," Sophia observed.

"Oh yeah. When Tasha makes a promise it's iron clad. It doesn't hurt that she's head-over-heels for them either. They're about all she talks about right now."

Justine walked toward the corner of the large room on the same side of the door. "You've got a blank palette here. What do you think you want to do to make it home?"

Sophia shook her head. "I'm not sure. I suppose we should start with getting some kitchen cabinets. I could've sworn there were some before, but I really don't remember because I was just a kid."

"You're right. There was at one point." Justine pointed to faint gray lines on the paint on both sides of the window. "You can see the marks on the wall where the cabinets hung. But this was all that was here when we started cleaning out."

"I'll need at least a couple for sure, with a countertop on either side for working space. I want a full-size range too. I love to cook." Sophia put a hand on her hip, studying the corner. "What do you think about some open shelves on either side of the sink, instead of closed in cupboards?"

Justine nodded. "That would sure keep the corner looking more open. The room will seem bigger that way. I think some simple, white, base cupboards would be great on either side of the sink too. That'd make a nice little corner kitchen area without taking away much floor space."

"I like that idea a lot. Where will I put the fridge and stove? Do I want them on the same wall or apart like in Dad's kitchen? He's got that big island in there so he can lay things out and prep on it. My original thought was to have something similar. I was thinking the bar height would be great for seating on one side of it too; like a little breakfast bar. But this space is too small to plop a kitchen island in the middle. Then after seeing Mom and Dad's table, I just knew that it had to stay."

"It is a beautiful piece and sentimental too," Justine agreed. She tapped her index finger on her chin. "Hey. I think I know a way to do sort of what you originally thought. What if you put the range on the side by the door at the end of the cupboards? It looks like that's where it was anyway." Justine pointed to the lower wall. "The propane inlet is right there. "Then you could put your fridge at the end of the other cupboard. That is if you only put one cupboard section on that side. Then you could get a kitchen island cart on wheels that you keep on the other side of the fridge, right by the bedroom door. I've seen some pretty ones that even have drop leafs so you can make the top nice and big. You could even use it as a table if you want."

Sophia swept her gaze from the open outside door around around the kitchen area to the bedroom door. "I really think that would work," she said slowly as a smile came over her face. "I love it! And if I only put one cupboard and countertop on either side of the sink cabinet, then I could also store the island beside the stove if I want."

"True. What are you going to do about the cabinet the sink's set in? It's hand-crafted. I don't know if there were ever any doors on it. I don't see any screw holes or anything where hinges would've been."

"I think it's perfect. I'll find some cute curtains to put over the front, like all those retro farmhouse kitchen designs that are so popular." Sophia leaned over the sink to look out the kitchen window. "I'll match whatever I choose for curtains with ones for this window. I'm thinking a blue buffalo check."

"That would be sweet. Fresh too."

Sophia was silent, staring out the window.

"You OK?" Justine asked coming to stand beside her.

Sophia shook her head. "Yeah. I'm fine. I was just looking over toward the point, thinking how far you could see from up here, and I saw this weird flashing light out past the reach."

"Maybe it was the sun catching a buoy or something."

"No. The sun is way too low now for it to be that. Plus, there isn't any buoy out there. It was a weird greenish color, not like any natural light, and in some kind of sequence. Look! There it is again. Two o'clock about a fourth of the way into the channel past the reach off the tip of the point. See it?"

Justine squinted looking toward the area Sophia pointed. "I don't see a thing but water. Wait! Yes, I do. I see it now. Is it a distress signal from a boat?"

"I don't see any boat out there and it's not any distress signal or pattern of flashes I recognize. Plus, it's way low in the water. Like it's floating." Sophia reached in her pocket for her phone. "Keep an eye out. I'm going to text Dad to bring the binoculars up. Maybe we can see what it is."

"I don't see it anymore," Justine remarked.

"There was about thirty seconds between the flashes before. We'll keep looking. Dad's on his way."

By the time James arrived, binoculars in hand, the girls still hadn't seen any more flashes of the green light. They all took turns looking through the binoculars to try and discover the source with no luck.

"That is so weird," Sophia said handing the binoculars to James. "I swear, Dad. We both saw it. It was a funky series of bright green flashes, kind of neon, maybe eight or ten in the sequence, but all short blips, not Morse Code. It wasn't big or anything. I think the only reason I noticed it was because the sun had dipped below the tree line on the reach right then."

"I believe you, Bean. But who's to say what it was? It's certainly not the first time someone's seen a strange, unexplainable something out on the water. It may even be some kind of research float from the science center over in the park. I don't see a thing now. It's possible that whatever it is has rotated around, so the blinking light isn't facing this way. Plus, there's just enough chop out there to conceal anything that's low-lying in the water."

"Huh, I didn't think about the research center having anything out there. Since it's at the edge of the point that could be an explanation for sure," Sophia agreed.

James scanned the top of the sea one last time.

"Are you guys coming in?" Natasha's voice floated up to them from the yard below. "I'm ready for ice cream."

"On our way," Sophia called back. "Hey, Dad. Justine and I think we have a couple pretty good ideas for the kitchen area with you. We'll tell you all about them."

"And go see kittens," Justine reminded her as they started down the steps. "We probably should do that first or we'll get no peace, you know."

Sophia chuckled. "I'm sure."

"What about you, Dad?"

James shut the door as he stepped out onto the landing. "Right behind you. You go on ahead and see the babies. I need to reheat the kettle anyway."

"OK." Sophia reached the bottom of the steps. She waited for Justine to join her. "Hey, when do you get off work tomorrow? I was thinking about going into Bangor to look for a kitchen island."

"I can be here a little after three, after I pick up Tasha at school."

The girl's voices faded around the corner of the garage. James was about a third of the way down the steps when the distant sound of a boat's motor caught his ear. It was a powerful high-pitched whine—not the low thrum of a fishing boat's motor. On a whim he stopped where he was, turned toward the water, and raised the binoculars to his eyes. A long sleek, black speedboat was racing toward the point from behind the reach. James followed it with the binoculars as it slowed and swung around with its nose facing out toward the open ocean. It came to a near stop when it was parallel to the shore near where Sophia had said she'd seen the mysterious flashing light. A passenger, his back to James, stood up and leaned over the water, then stood up again. Even from the back, the man's arm motions indicated to James that the guy was pulling a rope up from the bottom of the sea. Curiosity mounted in James. There wasn't any sign of a buoy or anything to mark a lobster trap and James would be willing to bet that no one in a boat like that would be out fishing for anything anyway. In less than a minute the man leaned back over the water again and carefully hauled something out of the water. When he turned to place the object on the floor of the speedboat, James got a good look at a squarish lump about the size of a cement block tied to black rope, wrapped up in something else that was black—possibly plastic, James thought. The passenger sat back down as the boat throttled forward, speeding off toward open water. The whole operation took less than two minutes and in the fading light no one would've noticed at all, unless they were really looking.

James lowered the binoculars and started back down the stairs, deep in thought. He was pretty sure he recognized that boat even if he couldn't tell exactly who was in it. What to say, if anything and to whom, were the questions. James couldn't prove what he'd just seen, or what he thought it might be. He had no idea what they'd pulled up, even though he felt he had a pretty good inkling. There was no law that said you couldn't drop something into the sea and retrieve it later. No, he decided. The best thing was just to keep it to himself. He was certain this wasn't the first time something like this had gone on, and it wouldn't be the last.

James strode toward the house. Hand on the screen door handle, he turned to scan the inner harbor. The lobster boats bobbed gently against their moorings in the rosy dusk of early twilight. All seemed peaceful and calm, but James's gut was tugging at him with worrisome tension over the scene he'd just witnessed. He shook his head. *No, I still think it's better to leave well enough alone—for now anyway. But make no mistake. I'll be watching you Riley McCord. Count on that.*

Sixty Four

The timer on Sophia's brand-new range beeped insistently. She reached to turn it off, then opened the oven door to check on the pan of lasagna that had been baking for the past hour. The sauce was bubbling near the edges. The mozzarella cheese had melted and browned to golden perfection. She grabbed the green and blue, sea star patterned oven mitts she'd purchased just that morning and pulled the steaming pan from the oven placing it on the waiting trivet on the countertop.

"That smells divine," Justine said from the other side of the room where she was setting the table. "I didn't know I was hungry, but I think I'm starving now."

"I hope Tommy gets here soon," Sophia remarked. "He said he was in Ellsworth almost forty-five minutes ago. I wonder what's keeping him?"

"I bet he stopped at the store to grab some hanging wire for the pictures. When I talked with him right after he left he mentioned he'd forgotten to bring what he had at his place. He said he was going to stop somewhere to pick supplies up. I thought he'd finished getting the pictures ready to hang when he was here last weekend. But I guess not," Justine mused. "I'm sure he'll be here any minute."

Sophia sighed. "Well, I guess we can always start without him. I don't want dinner to get cold. I was just hoping I'd be able to give him the grand tour before we ate."

"If my overly helpful daughter doesn't get to it first you mean," Justine said wryly. "Seriously, don't worry though. That huge lasagna is going to be piping hot for at least another half hour. We still need to put the garlic bread in anyway," Justine reminded her. "Besides, James and Tasha are sitting out on the patio waiting to pounce on Tommy to drag him up here the minute he pulls in. You'll have plenty of time."

"He's here. He's here." Natasha's voice sang out from the bottom of the stairs.

Sophia crossed to the living room space opposite the kitchen. She looked out the window toward the driveway. "I don't see his car," she said. "Wait, it's just turning in now. How did she know?"

Justine laughed. "I bet instead of sitting with your dad, she rode her bike down to the corner and has been watching for Tommy to turn up Main Street. That'd be just like her."

"Here they come." Sophia went over to the screen door as three pairs of feet started clomping up the stairs.

"Just wait until you see," Natasha was proclaiming. "You won't believe everything we've done this week."

Sophia grinned over at Justine who threw her hands up in the air. "See? It's inevitable. Even if she only helped a little after school."

Sophia held open the door as the group arrived at the landing. She swept her hand dramatically toward the room. "Come on in. Welcome to my humble abode."

Tommy stepped through, followed by Natasha, and then James. He handed a bottle of white wine to his sister. "Happy housewarming. I stopped to get this for you. That's why it took me a few minutes longer. I wanted it to be cold. Dad has the rest of my present."

"Here it is." James held up a bag. "Where should I put it?"

"Right there on the chair is fine, Dad. Thanks, Tommy. I can't wait to open it."

"You'll want to do that before dinner," he instructed. "Wow, it looks like an entirely different place in here." He scanned the room, turning around to look at everything. "I can't believe what you got done in less than a week!"

"I had a whole lot of help," Sophia allowed. "It was definitely a team effort."

"And some very late nights," Justine added. "They delivered the stove and installed it just this morning. We finished the final touches on everything else this afternoon."

"Yeah and while they were painting and putting things where they go, I got to help Mr. James take the lobsters over to the co-op. Then we cleaned up and organized the stuff on the *Salty Lady* to get ready to go out again tomorrow," Natasha said. She wrinkled her nose. "Mr. James said that if I ever want to be a lobsterwoman like Sophia, I have to start with learning the basic stuff about the boat. He says keeping her clean and ship-shape is the number one rule."

"That's what Dad's always said," Tommy agreed. He grinned at James. "Maybe that's why I never wanted to become a fisherman. I really don't like boat cleaning."

James looked up at the ceiling. "Hmm, that's not how I remember it. I don't think that your theory holds much water, Son."

Tommy chuckled. "You're probably right. Seriously though, I bet Dad's boat is the cleanest one in the harbor. She certainly is the prettiest."

"I just love the *Salty Lady*," Natasha gushed. "Someday I'm going to have a boat just like her."

"I totally believe you," Sophia said.

"Me too," Tommy agreed. "You seem to do whatever you set your mind to."

Natasha nodded emphatically. "Yup. I'm gonna. Come on. I'll show you everything we did in here."

"Oh no you don't," Justine admonished. "You need to stay right here with me and help get dinner on the table. You let Sophia do the tour. It's her house, remember?"

Tasha looked crestfallen. "Oh, right. I forgot. Sorry."

James chuckled. "Tell you what. We'll both help your mom get the rest of dinner set while Sophia shows off the place. Sound like a plan? And while we're doing that you can tell your mom all about our idea we had for tomorrow afternoon once Sophia and I are in from hauling. That is, as long as Sophia has time. She might have to work on school stuff."

"I guess. Sure," Natasha conceded.

"I'm free tomorrow after work," Sophia offered. "I wanted to be able to spend time with everyone at least one day over the weekend. I do have stuff to take care of Sunday for school, though." She looped her arm around Tommy's. "Come on. You've got to see my setup in the bedroom. Justine helped me put together a neat study area where I can look out and see the cove."

"All righty now. How can we help?" James asked Justine.

A few minutes later they were all at the table and Tommy was pouring the wine into the glasses he'd bought to celebrate Sophia's new apartment. He'd even brought a bottle of sparkling cider for Natasha so she could join in.

"There," he said setting the now half-empty bottle at the center of the table. He picked up his glass. "Here's to Sophia's shiny new digs, and to us all being together to celebrate."

"Hear, hear," James agreed raising his own glass.

"Aren't you supposed to clink them together when you toast?" Natasha asked. "That's how they always do it on TV."

"We can," Sophia said, "Gently, though. OK? We don't want to break my first real wine glasses." She reached over to gently touch her glass to Natasha's. "Cheers, Little Mermaid."

Natasha turned and touched her glass gently to her mother's. "Cheers, everybody," she said before she took a drink and set her glass down by her plate. She rubbed her nose. "This cider stuff is good, but the bubbles tickle. Now can we eat? I'm starving and I don't have all night. The weekend is finally here and I still have lots of stuff to do, like feed the kittens and make the plan for tomorrow afternoon."

Sixty Five

Natasha watched out the door as Justine washed out a thermos, preparing it for the coffee that was brewing in James's kitchen.

"I'm going to go up on Sophia's stairs so I can see the cove better. They should be coming in anytime now. Or I could just ride down and wait on the wharf, so I can help when they get back. Lots of other boats are already in."

"Patience." Justine tucked some paper plates and napkins against the inner edge of the picnic basket on the counter. "It's just now two thirty. Tommy still needs to get back from the store with meat from the deli for sandwiches and some other stuff to go in the cooler. James said they'd be back in about three, and he told us to be ready to leave by three-thirty . They'll be right on time I'm sure."

"Well, I'm going to go watch from Sophia's anyway."

"Hmm, hmm." Justine was looking around the kitchen. "Say, where did you put the bag with the cookies and chips we brought over?"

"What? I didn't bring any bag. I thought you had everything. I rode my bike and met you here, remember?"

"Oh," Justine said. "I could've sworn I asked you to grab it. I guess I just thought I had." She pressed the palm of her hand against her forehead and rubbed it. "I'm kind of tired. This week's been pretty busy. I'm worn right out."

"That's why Mr. James thought it would be good for us to go on a picnic today. He thought everyone could use a break away from all the work, especially since they're going to set up the art show for Miss Anna next week."

"I think that next week will be tough for all of them," Justine allowed. "You and I will have to be very understanding, and let them have all the time alone they need to have."

"Mr. James said he's letting Tommy take over the whole thing, and he'll just do what Tommy asks him too. Setting up the art show, I mean."

"That's good, because Tommy is the expert. He'll make the exhibit perfect. But it still all has to do with publicly saying good-bye to Miss Anna. That's going to be very emotional and hard."

"Oh. Well, Mr. James is my friend and so are Sophia and Tommy. So I want to be sure I'm around to help them if they need me. I think I understand how sad they're going to be. They'll need us."

Justine went over to her daughter and gave her shoulders a hug. "That's very sweet, Honey. And we'll be available if they need or want us to be. Let's not worry about that today though. Today we're just going to let James take us on a fun picnic to his mystery destination."

"It's not a mystery to me," Natasha said. "But I made a promise not to tell, so I won't."

Justine smoothed a stray strand of hair from her daughter's temple, tucking it back behind Natasha's ear. "Would you mind riding over and getting that bag from Gran for me?"

"Can I put it on my handlebars? It can't be too heavy, or I can't steer right."

"It's just got some cookies, a bag of chips, and a bag of pretzels in it. So it's not heavy. I'll text her to let her know you're on your way."

"OK. Be right back." Natasha pushed the door open and ran to her bike. As she pedaled out she almost collided with Tommy who was just walking into the drive. She waved and kept on going.

"Where ya headed in such a hurry?" he called after her.

"I'm running back to Gran's for some things. Be right back."

Tommy was still shaking his head when he got into the kitchen. He set the reuseable cloth bag on the counter. "That kid of yours has enough energy for all of us."

"Attitude too," Justine remarked dryly. She started to pull things out of the bag. "If we had one iota of her spunk we must've driven our parents half out of their minds."

"I guess," Tommy said. "But Natasha doesn't seem to make you nuts. I know I'm still getting to know her and all, but the way she is just makes me smile all the time. Of course," he allowed as he opened the refrigerator. "I don't have to live with her either."

"For the most part she's pretty good. We do have our moments. She certainly knows her mind. Sometimes it's hard to get her to see that maybe she might not know everything she thinks she does."

Tommy walked back over the island his arms loaded with bread and other fixings for sandwiches. "I think that was probably true for all of us—maybe even still is sometimes."

Justine smiled. "You're right. God knows I'm guilty of it. Sometimes I keep on doing things just out of plain stubbornness even when I know deep down it's going to bite me later."

"Yeah. Guilty as charged. Truth is that's the main reason I stayed in Boston after school—besides the great job offer. Mom told me that someday I'd discover where I truly belonged. I thought I'd only find work in a city gallery or museum. I thought if I settled down anywhere else, like here, that meant I wouldn't be able to work in art and would have to give it up like Mom did. But I've done that anyway. I've given up my own art. Instead I'm curating and showing others' work. I'm an administrator. I haven't picked up a sketch pad or paint brush in at least two years. After working with Mom's renditions, seeing the reflection of how she viewed her life in them—all the vibrancy and joy—I'm questioning that I'm doing what I really want. I'm not even sure where I should be."

Justine searched his face. "I thought you loved your job?"

Tommy grimaced. "I think I loved the idea of the importance of the job more than the job itself. I do mostly office and administrative work now. I don't work with the art itself much at all. It's a glorified front office position. I rarely put my hands on any of the pieces. The past few weeks as I went through Mom's work in detail, cleaning, preserving, framing, even restoring tiny areas on a few, made me realize how much I love that end of the art world—actually working with the pieces themselves. There's an undeniable intimacy that links you to the artist when you become involved in their interpretations of life. There's something . . .," He leaned his hands on the counter and shook his head. "I feel like I'm babbling. I don't know if I'm making any sense at all."

"No. I think I get exactly what you're saying. It's like how I feel when I have my hands in the dirt in the gardens. It feeds my soul."

"Yes," Tommy said staring out the window. "That's it. It feeds my soul. I love the connection. I feel it here." He made a fist and placed it right below his rib cage. "Like in the center of who I am."

"I get it. I really do."

"I feel such a bond with Mom through her work. At first, I could hardly get through just cleaning a piece without bawling my eyes out. But after a while I was able to really see them, to think about her life and our world here, through her eyes. She truly had a way of capturing the essence of Balsam Cove and the people who make it home. I came to realize what she meant when she told me I'd find where I belonged someday. It's not just a place, it's our connection to it. It's the landscape and everyone surrounding us. It's everything."

Justine had stopped making sandwiches. She was just watching him as he spoke.

Tommy looked away from the window. "Like I said, I haven't picked up a sketchbook or a paintbrush for at least two and a half years, ever since I took the promotion. I've given up my own art, my own questioning and interpretations of the world, and of life, for a job that keeps me in offices and galleries putting together displays for other people to enjoy. I took my position, and myself, so seriously thinking that I had to be there all the time because no one else could do what I do—so much so that I didn't even come home when my mom was dying. I didn't even come!" He looked over at Justine. His face was drawn with grief. "I've been seeing a therapist for weeks and I still can't deal with that. I put a job before coming to be with my own mom and my family. I buried my head in the sand and believed that she was going to get better. I convinced myself that I would see her when I'd finished setting up the show, and everything would be just the way it always had been."

"Tommy," she said gently. "You can't beat yourself up for the rest of your life over that. I know your mom would agree with me. Sophia told me that Anna was adamant that you not be told she was as sick as she was. She was certain you'd found the perfect job that you wanted. She knew that if you left for an extended time in the critical part of that project you were doing the institute would replace you on it, and you'd most likely not have a chance like that again." She shook her head. "You know, she made Sophia promise not to tell you even when she was near to the end. She told her that there was no need for you to come to watch her die—to lose your life's dream because of her. Sophia and I have talked a lot about your mom's cancer and her passing, and how it's affected all of you."

Tommy stared at her. "I didn't know Mom told her that. I mean, Mom made me promise not to come home, but I didn't know she made Sophia promise not to interfere." He shook his head. "That was so wrong to put Soph in that position. Mom had to know that she'd never go against her wishes or a promise. She was always doing everything she could to be closer with Mom. It was almost competitive between us."

Justine nodded. "You and your mom always had that artist bond. But Sophia is your dad's girl. Still, she really craved a closer maternal connection. She wants to be the kind of person your mom was, and she's struggled with that. It's hard for her. She feels terribly guilty about promising Anna such a ridiculous thing. Regardless of her intention, your mom's thinking was a bit selfish too. I feel that in some way Anna was living a part of her interrupted dreams though your career." She bit her lip. "If you feel like I'm out of line, please stop me. But Sophia told me about the baby and your parent's love story."

"That sister of mine!" He shook his head. "Dad asked us not to tell anyone."

"Don't worry. I'll never breathe a word to anyone except to the two of you. But a girl's gotta have a trusted friend to keep secrets and talk with about girl-stuff. Sophia and I have found we are a lot alike in many ways. We're becoming pretty great friends." She smiled and tilted her head slightly. "Anyway, I was saying I think that while your mom found a great love and made her home here, I bet part of her always wondered and longed for what might have been if she'd not had to leave New York that one summer. I know exactly what that might have felt like for her; struggling with her parents, having to quit art school, and all that. When she had you, and you became an artist and then pursued art school in the city, you were finishing what she had left behind. I wonder, whether she realized it or not, if she was living that part of her young life over, vicariously through you."

"Huh. I never thought of any of that," Tommy said.

"Of course you didn't. Why would you?" She grinned at him. "Besides, you're a guy. You just don't think about stuff like we women do."

"You don't have to be sexist about it you know."

"Oh, don't be . . ."

The screen door opened. Natasha ran though the room. It banged shut behind her.

"Natasha!" Justine exclaimed. There was no answer. "Natasha! Get back in here. What are you thinking banging into the house like that?"

"I have . . . to hide Grumble . . . and Petunia and all the kittens." Natasha howled.

Sixty Six

Tommy looked at Justine in alarm. They both moved at the same time toward the sound of Natasha calling out to the kittens between sobs.

"Where is she?" Tommy asked as they entered James's bedroom.

"In the closet," Justine answered. She got down on the floor and crawled toward the back. Natasha was sitting on the floor with Petunia and every single kitten scooped up into her lap. Tears were streaming down her little face as she tried to contain the squirming mass.

"Honey, what's wrong? What's happened?"

"He said he's going to come find them, to kill them," Natasha sobbed. "He's going to put them in a bag with rocks and drown them all like he did to your cat. He said he should drown me too because I'm a screwed-up, half-something! Then he ran over my bike and it's all broken to bits! I hate him! I hate him so much!" A fresh torrent of sobs erupted from the child.

Justine was furious. She could hardly speak. She moved closer to Natasha. Petunia took the opportunity to escape, scooting along the side wall of the closet and out past Tommy. Justine reached out for her daughter. Her voice was tight and low. "Tasha. Look at me."

Natasha looked up at her and took a shuddered gulp of air. Even in the dim closet light, Justine could see the absolute fear and misery in her daughter's face.

"I'm so sorry he said all those things. He's a terrible, miserable person and a liar! None of what he said is true. None of it! I promise you. Not one single thing he said means anything at all."

"But he said he was going to kill the kittens and he ran over my bike!" Natasha's sobbing began again.

"Honey, listen to me. It's going to be all right. No one is going to let him near the kittens or you ever again. I promise."

"That's absolutely right," Tommy growled. "I can promise you that neither one of you is going near that excuse for a human ever again. Not as long as I'm around."

"He smashed my bike," Natasha sobbed. "It was mine, and he broke it all to bits."

"Honey, I'll get you a new bike," Justine tried to console her.

"I don't want a new bike! I want mine!"

"Natasha! Justine! Are you here?" Cora's voice rang out into the house.

"We're all back here, Mrs. Connor," Tommy called out from where he was crouched in the doorway of the closet. "Come on back."

Cora appeared, gasping for air. "Is she all right? Is she hurt? That bastard almost ran her over with his truck because he wanted to destroy her bike."

"Justine, she's not injured, is she?" Tommy demanded in alarm.

"Are you hurt anywhere, Honey?" Justine was trying to see in the dim light of the single bulb in the closet.

Natasha shook her head, tears still running down her cheeks. She sniffled and tried to rub her face on her sleeve, her lap and arms still full of squirming, mewing, fluffy balls. "Just my knee where I fell on Mrs. Dean's driveway when I was running."

"I think she's all right," Justine said over her shoulder.

"She may not be banged up badly, but she's not all right," Tommy said through gritted teeth. He held one clenched fist with the other, massaging it as he fought the urge to go find Homer to beat him senseless. He turned to Cora who was standing behind him just outside the closet doorway. She was bent over, still trying to catch her breath. "Did you see it? Did hear what he said to her?"

Cora stood upright. She nodded. "I did all right," she sputtered. "This is the final straw. I'm done with that miserable son-of-a," she began to cough.

Tommy went to Cora and took her arm. "I think you better sit down." He led her to the edge of James's bed and pushed a pile of clothes out of the way so she could sit.

"I'll get you a glass of water," Tommy said as Cora coughed again.

She waved her arm. "I'm fine," she said clearing her throat. "I'm just not used to running anywhere." She stood up.

"Your face is awful red," Tommy remarked. "Maybe you should just sit down for a few minutes."

Cora glared at Tommy. "I want to see Natasha. Right now."

Tommy held up his hands. "OK. Sorry, I was just worried that's all."

"Oh, Thomas," Cora touched his arm. "I'm sorry. I'm just so angry. I didn't mean for it to sound that way at all."

Tommy nodded. "It's fine. I understand."

"I'm not sure you do, Deah. But thank you."

Cora went to the closet door. "Natasha, I want to talk to you, please. Will you come out or should I come in?"

"I'm not coming out," Natasha declared. "I'm staying in here with Grumble and the other kittens. No one can ever make me come out."

Cora sighed. "OK. I'm coming in then. You best make some room because that corner looks awfully small for three people."

"What is going on?" James appeared in the doorway. "We saw Cora running across the road as we were mooring the boat. I left Sophia to finish up so I could see why she was in such a sure-fire hurry. Why is everyone in my closet?"

"It's not a picnic. I can tell you that," Tommy said grimly. "Hang on. I'll fill you in with what I know." He peered into the closet. "Are you ladies all right in there?"

"We're getting there," Justine replied. "We got the waterworks stopped. We'll be out in a few minutes."

"I told you I'm not leaving the kittens!" Natasha howled.

"OK, Honey. You can stay here as long as you want to," Justine agreed. "Please don't cry. No one is going to hurt the kittens or Petunia."

"All right." Tommy said. "I'm going to fill Dad in with the little I know. We'll be in the kitchen if you need us." He turned to James who was standing in the middle of the room looking concerned and completely confused.

"What in the world?"

Tommy just shook his head. "I'd like to make fish bait out of a certain cretin right about now," he said lowly. "This is the last straw. Something's got to be done."

"Homer."

"Oh yeah." Tommy walked out into the hallway. James followed. "I've only heard part of what happened. But it's enough to make me not care about serving jail time."

Natasha's wavering voice called out, "Mr. James?"

"I'm right here, Little One. What is it?" James responded turning back into the bedroom.

"Would you please find Petunia, feed her supper, and give her some extra treats. I think I made her upset, and I know she's hungry."

"You bet."

"Thanks. Oh and Mr. James?"

"Yes?"

"Do you know how to fix bikes?"

Sixty Seven

"I appreciate the concern and the offer, but I'm not leaving my house," Cora stated firmly. "If I do, he'll go on the offensive and it will be bad—worse than it already is. He came roaring in today in a mood. I guess Natasha had dropped her bike at the edge of driveway by the sidewalk because she was just running in to pick up the cookies and chips for your picnic. I'd just asked her how the kittens were doing. She was telling me all about their eyes being open now and how Grumble purrs all the time when she picks him up. Homer must've heard her say 'my kitten Grumble.' That was all it took for him to go off like a rocket and say every cruel thing he could. Then he stormed out of the kitchen. Natasha ran after him before I had time to say a word or stop her. By time I got to the door he'd run over her bike and backed up to do it again. Natasha was trying to pick up the mangled thing. She barely jumped out of the way! I don't know if he even saw she was there. I'm horrified to think that he might have seen her and then backed up trying to hit her." She took a deep breath and looked around the table her eyes glittering with unshed tears. "I never would have forgiven myself if she'd been hurt more than she is. It's awful enough he verbally attacked her and she's got a skinned knee from falling." She looked down, gripping the now cool mug of coffee she had yet to take a sip from even harder than before. "I've been thinking of what I want to do for a long time. This was the very last straw. Homer Connor can be an ass to me all he wants, but I will never, ever again allow him to threaten or hurt my daughter and my granddaughter. I never should have put up with any of it." She looked over at Justine who was seated next to her. "I should have left with you when you were just a tyke. I'm so sorry."

"Mom," Justine reached out and laid a hand on her mother's arm.

Cora shook her head staring into her mug. "He'll show up later like nothing ever happened, and that will be that. But, this time he's crossed the line. I'm done. I just have to keep pretending for a little while longer—at least until I get into town and see the lawyer. Until then I can make myself busy and scarce like usual."

She looked toward the kitchen window where jaunty red and orange mums could be seen through the glass in their window box, basking in the late afternoon sun. "Anna was helping me to set things in motion before she left us. I just didn't have the gumption to do it on my own. But then I've never had the catalyst to make it happen, I guess. Now I do." She looked over the group at the table, her eyes resting on Justine. She put her hand over the her daughter's and looked her square in the eyes. "Now, I want you to listen to me. You and Natasha are not coming back to that house until he's gone for good. It may take a few weeks before he's gone, but I'll pay for a hotel for you both. I've been squirreling away money for years now, just waiting until the time was right for me to do what I wanted. I have enough."

"There's no need for that," James said.

"James, I mean what I say."

"I'm not trying to change your mind or tell you what to do, Cora. I understand perfectly what you're saying. But just like I offered before, the girls can stay here as long as they need to. There's no cost involved. Save your money for the other things that need doing."

"I don't need anyone telling me what to do, either." Justine glared across the table. "I can take care of my daughter just fine."

"Whoa there. No one said you couldn't," Tommy interjected. "I think we all just need to take a breath and calm down. We're all angry at the same person, but we're starting to take it out on each other."

James nodded. "Agreed. We're on the same side. We love you and Natasha, Justine. We only want to help."

"I know." Justine sighed. "We love you all too. Tommy's right. I'm just so mad I can't see straight."

"I get it." James rose from the table. "I'm going to check on Natasha; make sure she and her kittens are fine. I'll be right back."

"It'll be a while before she comes out of that closet," Justine said grimly. "She doesn't react well to situations like this. When I had to tell her that her father wasn't coming back home, she barricaded herself in her room for almost twenty-four hours. That was after she tried to run away. The only thing that got her out was that she got hungry."

"Well, she hasn't had any supper yet, so maybe we won't have to wait all night," Tommy offered hopefully. "And her being holed up in there has given us some time to talk without her hearing us and upsetting her all over again. Plus, maybe if she knows she'll be staying here for a while and close to the babies that will keep her happier, too."

Justine frowned at him. "Give it up, Tommy. I appreciate it, but the answer is no. And, Mom, I'm not taking your money. I have a little bit saved up. I'll think of something."

"Look, Justine," Sophia said. "I know you don't want to be told what to do—that you want to take care of everything yourself. I'm right there with you. But I'm also with your mom, Dad. and Tommy on this. Staying here is a good solution. You need a safe place. We have room. It's only temporary until we can find a place of your own for you and Natasha. And we will," she declared. "Natasha can have Tommy's room. You can have my old room. Since I got the new bed for my place, it's still all set up the way it was. Tommy will be fine with bunking on my couch while he's home. It's not like you both aren't here more than at your mom's place anyway since we hang out all the time now. It makes perfect sense."

Justine rubbed her temples with both hands. The dull throbbing in her head was threatening to become a full-blown headache. "It does make sense when you put it that way, Soph. But I still don't want to leave you alone over there, Mom," Justine protested.

"Listen, I've been alone over there for many years, in a manner-of-speaking," Cora replied with a sad smile. "Your father's current supposed issue is not with me. He'll leave me alone as long as I just keep on doing what I do. I doubt he'll even realize that you girls aren't around for a few days. By then it won't matter. I know how to avoid him. I've never meant enough to him for him to be all that concerned with what I do. He's on his way out. He just needs to think nothing's changed until I get everything in place legally. That should only take a couple days at most."

"I hope it's as easy as you think, Mom," Justine said shaking her head. "But he's a loose cannon and I think he's getting much worse."

"A couple days, Justine. That's all. Just a couple days. Then you and Natasha will be able to come back to stay, if you want to. I'd love to have you both live with me as long as you like, but I know you'd like your own place. You might find something of your own sooner rather than later. Please, trust me on this."

"It's not that I don't trust you, Mom. I'm just worried about you."

"I know, Sweetie. I do. But I know what I need to do, and I'm going to make it happen first thing."

"It'll be Monday before any offices in town will be open," Tommy reminded them. "Are you sure you'll be all right until then?"

Cora nodded. "Absolutely. I have church. Then the ladies and I go visit our nursing home friends. On the way home we take ourselves out to supper at Helen's. By time I get here, he'll be at that stinkin' bar. Monday morning I'll leave his lunch out for him to take as always. Then I'll call the lawyer, borrow a car from one of my friends, and get right to town to take care of business."

"We can get you to town Monday that's no issue. I'm more worried about tonight," James said coming back into the room. "Natasha's fine," he added. "She's singing some kitty song that she made me learn and sing with her."

Justine laughed. "'Soft Kitty.' I showed her a YouTube clip from a TV show I used to watch."

"Ah," James poured a cup of coffee and held out the pot. "Anyone else?"

"Can I put mine in the microwave?" Cora asked. "I swear I never drink a whole mug before I have to reheat it six times."

"I've got it," Tommy offered.

"Well," James said settling himself back into his chair. "What's the verdict?"

Justine grimaced. "I hate to impose, but what you all say makes sense. If you truly don't mind, Tasha and I will bunk here for a few days."

"We get to have a sleepover?"

"Well, another country heard from," Cora remarked as Natasha came to stand between her chair and Justine's. Cora put an arm around Natasha's waist and hugged her lightly. "I love you so, so much," she said, looking up at her granddaughter. "I'm terribly sorry about everything that happened."

Natasha's red and swollen eyes teared up again. "I didn't do anything wrong! Why is he so mean? Are you sure he doesn't know the kittens are here?"

"I'm absolutely sure. We didn't ever say a word about where the kittens live. He'll never know. I promise," Cora vowed. "No one will ever tell him."

"Still, I'm not leaving them alone. Ever!" Natasha swiped at a single tear that escaped to run down her cheek."

"Well, that might not work out so well," James chuckled. "You still have to go to school. Besides, you can't stay holed up in the closet all day, every day, But, how about this? If you and your mom come stay with us then you can spend most of your time here."

"Really?" Natasha looked to Justine for confirmation. "Could we really come to live here, not just stay for a sleepover?"

Justine sighed. "Yes. Everyone says it's the best thing to do, and I agree. However," she cautioned, "It's only until we find our own place."

"But that might take a long time, right?"

"It doesn't matter how long it takes," James interjected. "You're going to take over Tommy's room. Your mom will stay across the hall in Sophia's old room. Our home is your home for as long as you need." James directed this last comment toward Justine with a smile. "How does that sound? It's a good plan, and selfishly, I know I'll sleep a lot better at night knowing you girls are safely tucked in here."

Natasha looked from James to Justine and back again. She didn't think that her mom looked any too happy about the idea. "I want to do it, Mom. Can we? I want to stay here. I want to be with the kittens. I don't want to go back over there to live anymore. Please don't make me." Natasha's voice was starting to rise in both pitch and volume.

"Slow down, Tasha," Justine said gently. "We're going to stay here. That's already been decided."

"But what about my stuff in my room and what about Gran? Is she going to live here too?"

"I'm going to be staying right where I always do, in my own little room in my own little house," Cora said giving Natasha's waist another quick squeeze. "I'll be just fine."

"Oh. But I'll miss you."

"Don't you worry. I'll be visiting back and forth. I promise."

"Can I have my stuff from my old room?"

"I'll go over and get what we need after a bit," Justine said.

"OK." Natasha was chewing on her lip. She looked like she might start crying again. Cora thought it was a good time to change the subject.

"I thought you were in singing to your kitties?"

"I was, but Mr. James put them right to sleep when he sang with me and he promised me he won't let anyone in the door except us. So now I can come out here. Are we gonna eat? Our picnic plans got all spoiled, and now I'm starving." A wave of laughter erupted. Natasha looked around the table at them all.

"What's so funny? Why are you laughing? Did I miss supper?"

"No, not at all," Tommy said seriously. "It's definitely past time to eat and we're just happy you decided to join us."

Sixty Eight

Natasha

I'm so tired. It's the second night here. And I still. Can't. Sleep. I miss my room at Gran's. It is super nice here with all of us, and I love that I get to be with Petunia and the kittens to keep an eye on them. Mom and Sophia went over to Gran's and got some of our stuff right away, so I have most of my clothes, and my journal, and my lists, and my school stuff for tomorrow. But I'm used to having to go through Mom's room to get to the little stairs up to my room that's almost like a secret room because it's in the attic. Mr. James's house has an attic too, but it's not finished out with a bedroom like at Gran's. My room there is higher up than here. There is a cool dormer window here where you can sit and read and stuff and look out the window. But I can't lie in bed and watch the stars or just sit up to see the ocean. I could see all the way across the cove from my room at Gran's. I can barely see the water at all here because you have to look through the leaves of the great big maple tree in the yard. It's right in the way of the view. Tommy says once the leaves fall you can see the water just fine. But that's still a long time from now, and I really need to see the stars and the ocean. I can't explain why. I just do. Plus, for right now I'm not supposed to go down to the wharf at all. So I can't even visit the ocean during the day.

Mom says it's better if we keep a low profile. That means stay out of sight. She says that if my grandfather figures out that we're over here it will be bad news. She even drove our car up to the farm so no one would see it around. Sophia is letting her borrow her car to take me to school and then go to work in the morning. Mom told me that Gran is going to see a lawyer in the next few days, and that she's going to get a divorce, and that once all that is started things will be better. I don't see how. Every kid I ever knew at my old school whose parents divorced—and there were plenty of them—go through all kinds of rotten stuff. It makes the kids nuts. Like that boy Jake at my new school. Maybe he's such a butthead because his parents have split up.

You know, thinking about it, I'm kind of in the same situation as those kids. I mean my mom and dad weren't married. But it's a lot like a divorce anyway because they lived together the whole time I've been alive. The only different thing about a kid whose parents get divorced is that they usually still get to see and do stuff with both their parents. Most of them don't have their dad just up and disappear.

It doesn't matter, I'm too tired to even think about it right now. Everything is just swirling around in my head and making no sense. Mom thinks I never really sleep, but that's not true and now I really, really wish I could shut my brain off. I'm literally gonna be useless at school tomorrow if I don't get some rest.

Maybe if I got dressed and went out into the yard I could at least look up at the stars and find Jupiter, which I can't even see from in here. Tonight is the night that Jupiter is in opposition to the sun and closest to Earth as it's been in fifty-nine years! That's a long time—even longer than Gran and Mr. James have been alive. It won't be this close again for one hundred seven more years. So, this is a once in a lifetime thing. With all the drama from the past two days I totally forgot to tell Mom and Mr. James about it. Still, I could go look for it myself. I can just put on my shoes and leave my pajamas on. It's not like anyone will care if I'm in the yard dressed in my jammies looking up at the stars. I think that will help me feel better. Besides no one said I couldn't.

Sixty Nine

Natasha opened the door to the room as quietly as she could, just enough to slip through, and tiptoed down the stairs. She was still in her pajamas, but she'd put on her socks and tennis shoes and pulled on a hoodie sweatshirt over her pajama top. The late September nights were getting chilly, and she hated feeling cold. The hallway light wasn't on, but the soft glow from a light in the living room was enough to see clearly to navigate the stairs. She paused briefly as she stepped into the hallway. She could hear the steady stream of the shower running in the bathroom at the end of the hall. To her right, the door to James's room was open to allow Petunia to come and go. Natasha had turned off the closet light a couple hours before she went to bed so that the kittens and Petunia could go to bed too. So it was still and mostly dark. Only a sliver of light shone into the room. It illuminated a path toward the bed. Natasha could make out the mountain of clothes and other things still covering it. The pile had been there since they'd pulled it all out of the closet to make room when Petunia had decided that was the place to have her babies. She thought for a second about going to check on the kittens again, but decided not to disturb them.

She walked past the couch and the side table that held the lamp, then into the kitchen. James hadn't closed up the house yet for the night. The early fall crickets' chorus wafted through the screen door. Natasha pushed it open. She made her way out into the yard, halfway between the house and Sophia's place. There, she stopped to gaze up at the night.

The sky was an inky, blue-black. The sun had set hours before, a little past six, and it was the night of the new moon so the stars seemed especially bright. Natasha figured it had to be at least ten o'clock now. Everything was quiet. It didn't take her any time at all to spot Jupiter toward the southeast. From there she found the constellations Pisces and Pegasus above it. She took a deep breath and exhaled. This was so much better. This was history—stellar, planetary history—definitely something to write about in her journal. She'd have to remember to tell her mom about Jupiter tomorrow. It would still be close and fun to find, just not as close as tonight. Tonight, she was the only one who saw it from her own private, real-life observatory. She knew that wasn't quite true, but it was neat to pretend she was the only human seeing it. She thought if only she could go down to the water that would make it perfect. She'd never been on the wharf after dark. She'd only looked at the ocean at night through her window.

A thought popped into her head. She just could go down the path to be a little closer to the water. It technically was still part of the yard. No one would see her. Mr. James had told her that he owned the land all the way to about ten feet from the shore edge where it became town property. So if she just went down the path to the end she'd be able to be closer to the water and still be in the yard. Brilliant!

She scurried out past the shed and garage toward the path between the beach roses. Even though it was dark, she was able to see well enough to navigate without issue. She was standing at the path's entrance across from the cove in twenty seconds flat. There was no light on the wharf. There was an old light post, but as far as Natasha could tell it hadn't worked all summer long. At least she'd never seen it on when she looked out her window. The boats murmured to each other from their moorings as the water lapped against the wharf pilings in time with the crickets' sad end-of-summer tune. She turned her face toward the reach. She could almost taste the salty tang of the water on the slightly chilled breeze that ruffled her hair. Her entire body relaxed. She closed her eyes and sighed. This was perfect. But she knew she better go up and get back inside. Even though it was perfectly clear right now, she'd heard Mr. James telling Sophia that there would be a storm rolling in overnight. She thought maybe the breeze had picked up a little bit just since she'd come outside. It felt cooler. Plus, it was pretty late. Soon everyone would be in bed. She knew she wouldn't get locked out because Mr. James never locked the door. He'd told her that when she first started taking care of Petunia and her babies. Still, she didn't want to wake anybody up, or have to explain why she was outside, when she was supposed to be in bed already asleep for hours.

She turned to go. Glancing up the hill, she saw that the kitchen light in Sophia's apartment was still on. She figured Sophia was studying like she did every night, and Tommy was probably working on Miss Anna's stuff. It was nice to see the light on. It felt good knowing they were there. Natasha realized she finally was ready to go in and actually sleep.

She turned toward the water and took one step forward for a last glance at the stars and the silhouette of the reach on the sea. Then, just as she turned to go back up the path, she caught a shadow of movement to her right, near the side of the road, so close to her that she could hear something breathing heavily, like it had been running.

Seventy

Natasha froze in her tracks. She held her own breath. A man was slinking along the side of the rose hedge that wrapped around the Edward's property close to the road. Her heart pounded in her chest so hard that she was sure the man would hear it, even if he didn't see her yet. Although she wanted to run with every fiber in her being, she managed to stay stock still hoping he wouldn't discover her. She watched him leave the cover of the hedge and cross quickly to the edge of the wharf. He glanced around. She realized with relief that he hadn't seen her. But as she watched him, all of a sudden she knew who he was. Even in the darkness there was no mistaking the form of her grandfather. She knew that shape and how he moved. She'd watched him leave out to haul in the shadows just before dawn so many times.

Now, apparently satisfied no one was watching him, he began moving again, scurrying along the top of the wharf, down the gangplank, and onto the floating dock where the punts were tied. She couldn't see the dock from where she was standing, but she knew he was on it because there was a ripple of water that pushed against the rocks on the shore as the dock dipped under his weight.

She let her breath out. Before she realized what she was doing curiosity had overtaken her and she was crouched by the edge of the wharf trying to peer under it toward the dock to see what Homer was doing. She couldn't make out much of anything except she heard the dipping of oars into the water. At first she thought Homer was taking a punt out, but then she realized there were other men talking to him so that meant that someone had just rowed in. She stayed crouched low and still, listening.

"You have it?"

"Of course I have it."

"Hand it over then." Natasha recognized Homer's growling demand.

"I get the cash first. Like always."

There was a clunk like an oar hit the dock.

"Jesus, be careful would ya," someone hissed. "Why don't you just announce we're here."

"Nervous much? Just shut up. There's no one around. This town rolls up and dies by eight every night."

"Who the hell is with you? That's not Tucker."

"New hire. Tucker disappeared on us a few days ago."

"Huh," Homer grunted.

"We're too far away for me to reach out to grab it," A voice complained.

"I can't reach any farther over to you or I'll fall in," Homer retorted.

"You could except you're too damn drunk to stand up straight on dry land, much less down here."

"Screw you. You want it or not? Bossman won't be happy if you don't get his cash," Homer taunted.

"No less happy than if your end man doesn't get his product."

"Well, I'm not swimmin' out to ya so . . ."

"Would you two just shut up? Get this boat close enough that I can step onto the dock. Hurry up. Someone's gonna call the cops and we'll all be sunk."

Homer barked out a short laugh. "This dumbass doesn't know we've got no cops around here after six p.m.. And there's no one living anywhere near that has the balls to call in a damn thing to nobody. Let's get this over with. I want to get to bed sometime tonight."

The water moved in another hard swell against the rocks, so Natasha knew someone else had stepped onto the dock.

"OK, here's the stuff. Hey! Give me that!"

"I don't take orders from you. You want it, you can sashay your happy ass up top and get it." Homer sneered.

There was a dull thump not far from Natasha's head. Something about the size of a shoebox slid off the side of the wharf and dropped to the rocks, just below where she was crouched. Her heart dropped. There was no way she wasn't going to be discovered.

"What the hell is wrong with you! It's all the way over on the rocks now."

"Well, go get it."

"There was muttering; words Natasha couldn't make out as someone scrambled up the gangway onto the wharf.

"Oh no you don't, old man," someone said. "You're not going anywhere. You stay right there until we've got that money. You've already got your product."

"I don't think you'll be telling anyone where to stay or go," Homer growled. "Now or ever."

A gunshot rang out.

"Holy shit! Are you fucking crazy?!" The man on the wharf yelled. Then there were sounds of scuffling. Another shot rang out.

Natasha screamed. Her ears were ringing. In her terror she could only think that she needed to run. She needed to go somewhere they couldn't find her.

RUN! RUN! RUN! Her brain commanded.

She found her feet and scrambled to cross the road. A third shot rang out. Terrified, she screamed again. She tried to think. She had to hide! She had to get somewhere, anywhere, where no one would find her. She knew her screaming had exposed her. The men would be looking for her. She had to get away before they came after her and killed her! Right then her feet took over. They knew right where to go.

Seventy One

Sophia and Tommy both flew to the window at the sound of the first shot.

"What the hell?" Tommy barked.

"That was a gunshot, right?" Sophia asked her hands gripping the edges of the sink as she tried to see outside into the dark. Just then the second shot reported. A girl screamed and then screamed again.

"Yes! I'm calling 9-1-1. For God's sake, get out of the window!" Tommy ordered.

A third shot rang out. The screaming stopped. Silence.

Suddenly Justine's frantic voice cried out in the night. "Natasha! Natasha! Where are you? Natasha!"

"Dear God!" Sophia gasped.

They flew to the door and down the steps. Justine, barefoot in her pajamas was racing toward them. James, fresh from the shower in just a T-shirt and sweatpants was hot on her heels.

"I heard a loud bang in my sleep. Natasha was screaming! It woke me up and then I heard another shot. She's not in her room! I can't find her!" Justine babbled, sobbing. "She's not in her room! Natasha!"

James was already halfway to the wharf. "Call 9-1-1! Get them down here. Now!"

"Done!" Tommy caught up with him just as two black SUV's came roaring down the road with blue and red lights flashing through their grills. A spotlight shone on them. They both put an arm up to deflect the light that was blinding them.

"Stop right there!" a male voice commanded. "Hands up!"

The doors of the SUVs opened and bodies started pouring out toward them.

Sophia and Justine came running up behind James and Tommy.

"Stop! Hands up! All of you!" ordered the man in front of the rest.

"My daughter's out here. She's nine years old!" Justine was hysterical. "She may have been shot! We have to find her!"

Four men dressed all in black, guns drawn, approached.

"Stand down. It's the Edward clan and Connor's daughter," one of them ordered. "You three go find Donovan and Turner and anyone else down there," he continued. "Jackson and his men are in pursuit of Connor. I'll stay here and help these folks."

"We can't stay here! We have to find Natasha!" Justine sobbed.

"We will, Ma'am, I promise. Just give me a couple seconds to get more help on the way." His radio crackled. A distant voice came through. "Medics needed. We've got Turner—shoulder wound. Donovan is down. No sign of anyone else here."

The man reached a hand toward the radio strapped to his shoulder. "Roger. Medics on way. Hawkins stay with Turner. Everyone else searches for the girl."

"OK," he said turning to the group. "If she's out here we'll find her."

James was off before the officer could even finish his sentence. "Bring a light, a good one!" He yelled over his shoulder. "If she ran, I know where she might be."

A vision clear as a morning sunrise had come into James's head. He didn't know why or how, but it was there. He could see Natasha kneeling in the sand against a huge basalt boulder. He realized that it was the rock formation she'd told him about, the one she called "Black Whale" that was on the tiny, secluded, crescent beach to the left of the wharf. It was the same place she often waved to him from as he rounded the edge of the reach coming in from hauling.

James scrambled as quickly as he could down the rocks by the hidden beach. "Natasha," he called out over and over. "It's me, Mr. James. I'm here. It's safe now. You can come out. Natasha, where are you?"

He fished into his sweatpants pocket for his phone and turned its flashlight on trying to pick up any sign of Natasha, but the tiny beam immediately got swallowed up in the night. It was barely bright enough for him to see a couple of feet in front of him as he eased his way as quickly as he dared over the rocks onto the beach. The slight breeze from earlier had picked up, pushing rolling whitecaps one after the other onto the shore along the rising tide. The waves crashed into the rocks, water filling the crevices between, before rushing out again. They covered and carried the sound of his voice out with them. He knew Natasha would never hear him unless he was right at her, so he called out for her as loud as he could again and again. He moved along the edge of the beach toward the half-submerged, whale-shaped, basalt boulder Natasha had confided was her favorite spot to hide from the world. As he got closer to the rock formation, when the waves broke, water rolled up onto the sand dousing his bare feet and ankles in near frigid water. He continued to yell out Natasha's name, holding up his phone, shining it around looking for any sign of her. It was futile. A distant flash of lightning far out over the water, followed seconds later by a low rumble unsettled his gut even more into a feeling of near panic. Something brushed against his ankles as the water rushed over them, then bumped him on the way back out. It didn't feel like any animal. It was more like a *something* than a *someone.* He shown his light down to see a child-sized tennis shoe upside down, racing away from him on the receding wave, its laces trailing behind like they were reaching for the shore.

Dear God, NO!

Desperate now to reach the outcropping just a few feet away he kept moving. His feet were raw and felt like ice. The sand shifted and pulled away under them as the water rolled in and out, making it impossible to move quickly. He could barely keep his footing.

"Dad? Dad?" He heard Sophia's panicked voice calling to him.

Her voice was so faint he wasn't sure he wasn't imagining it. A beam of bright light swept the area lighting up the beach to his left side. It swept back over, just missing him before it swung back the other way. "Dad? Are you out there? Where are you?"

A male voice rang out. "Mr. Edward. Can you hear us? We don't see you."

"I'm over here," James hollered back toward the source of the light.

The beam swept back over the area. It missed landing on James by just a foot or so this time.

"James, Natasha, where are you?" This time James recognized Justine's distressed cry joining Sophia's.

"Here. Over here," he turned and yelled again toward the light. His voice was getting hoarse. There was no way they would hear him. He began waving his arms wildly above his head. Then he turned back toward the rocks, with only his phone to light his way, waving his other arm high as he stumbled along, hoping that the movement would catch in the spotlight. He called out for Natasha with every breath, fear turning toward terror as each second passed with no response. He came to the basalt boulders as lightning flashed again, closer this time. A wave splashed up and over the rocks drenching him from head to toe. The spotlight swept by him, swung back, then stopped illuminating him and the rocks.

"I've got him! James, hold on! We're coming."

The light starting bobbing closer. James put a hand on the rock trying to steady himself. "Natasha! Natasha! Where are you?" Frantic, he strained to see any sign of her. He couldn't bear the thought of what he might find. He was immersed to his knees, soaked to the skin, and his feet were beginning to numb.

He slid his hand along the smooth rock as he waded toward the rounded, outermost edge of the boulder straining to find any sign of Natasha.

There! There she was! He could see her lodged in between the smooth basalt and a sharp ledge of granite, half submerged in the frigid sea. A wave rolled in and broke over the child. She disappeared under the water.

"Natasha!" James cried out.

The swell washed back out, exposing her head and shoulders once more.

"I've got her! I've got her!" He yelled wading toward her, "Get that light over here!"

"We see you!"

"Hang on, Little One. Hang on. I'm here. I've got you." He reached her just as another wave came sliding up to them.

He could see her looking at him through the tangled mess of hair on her face. Relief washed over him as he realized she was alive and still alert. She said something, but he couldn't make it out.

"Hold your breath," he commanded. "Here comes another wave." This one didn't quite wash over her head before it rolled back out toward the sea. He leaned over her, his chest next to her head. He put an arm around her back and leaned close to her ear so he wouldn't have to yell. "I'm going to pick you up, now."

"I'm stuck," she croaked out. "I lost my shoe."

"I know. It's OK. I've got you."

The beam from the light came close and stayed still. "Right behind you, sir. How can I help?"

"Just keep that light right there," James hollered over his shoulder. "Her foot's wedged between the rocks. Every time the surf rolls out, it pulls it tighter into the crevice. When the next wave comes in I need to work with the water; try to ease her foot in toward me."

"Can you tell if she's injured anywhere else?"

"No clue."

Now that he had another light, James ditched his phone. He needed both his arms and all his strength. He turned his head and put his mouth up to the tangled wet mess of hair that covered Natasha's ear.

"Natasha, listen to me. This might hurt a little bit, but maybe not. I'm so sorry if it does. I'm going to push and pull on your foot to get it free."

Natasha didn't answer.

"Natasha?" He looked down at her. Her eyes were closed, but he could see she was still breathing.

Dear God, please.

"Honey, if you can hear me, hold your breath, NOW," he ordered. He heard the next wave pushing toward the shore. With one arm around Natasha's back, her head cradled agains his chest, James tried to dislodge her foot from the rock's grasp with his other hand. He gently pushed down and then tugged on her ankle, following the wave's direction. At first there was no give at all. He wiggled his hand slightly as the water rushed in over them. Suddenly he almost fell over as her foot came loose from the rock. The water broke on the rocks around them and slid back by. He scooped his left arm up under Natasha's knees and stumbled to stand.

Strong arms behind him, steadied and help right him.

"I can take her," the man offered.

"No," James shook his head. "No. Thank you."

"All right. I've got you, Sir. Great work. Let's get you out of here. You both need medical attention. I've already had my men call for assistance. I'm right behind you." He shone the light ahead of James to light the way.

James stumbled up the beach praying every step of the way on feet that were rapidly losing any of the little feeling they had left in them. There was no way he was letting anyone else take Natasha from his arms.

It seemed like miles to the house even though it was only a couple hundred yards. Climbing over the rocks up to the road without falling took every bit of will and strength he could muster. Every so often he felt the young man behind him who was lighting their way put a steadying hand on his back or elbow as he lurched along. He finally reached the road and strode out toward the path to the house ignoring the stinging pain in his feet.

"I'm taking her up to my house to get her out of her wet clothes and start warming her. Send the ambulance there."

"Yes, Sir. I'll direct them now."

James heard the officer talk briefly into his radio as they reached the head of the path.

"Mr. James."

James glanced down at the limp child clutched tight to his chest thinking he must have imagined hearing her whisper.

"Mr. James."

He saw her lips barely move. He stopped and bent his head down. He put his cheek against her forehead, wet strands of her dark hair against his beard. "I'm here. We're all right here. We'll get you warmed up and dry in no time."

"I know." Natasha coughed. "I have to tell you something," she sputtered, her voice distant and small.

"Shh. It's OK. You can tell me later."

"No. Now." She frowned and struggled in his arms.

"Be still, Little Mermaid. We're almost home and help is on the way."

James lifted his head and hugged her tighter willing any warmth he had into her soaking, chilled body. He reached the top of the path in a few more steps heading toward the house. Justine and Tommy came running up to them from behind. Tommy ran to the door and held it open.

"Is she OK? Is she still . . ."

"She's going to be just fine," James said firmly, as they stepped into the kitchen, willing it to be so with every fiber of his being. "She's going to be all right."

Tears were streaming down Justine's face. She reached out and laid a hand on her daughter's head. "Oh," she choked out.

Natasha was limp again in James's arms. Her breath was shallow, but even.

Tommy had briefly disappeared, but now came back into the kitchen with a bunch of blankets in his arms. "I got these from the back of the couch and the linen closet. I'll go find more," he said. "The ambulance should be here any minute now."

"Good. But we need to get her into the living room. Move that coffee table to the side and lay those blankets on the rug. Then grab a throw pillow for under her head," James instructed.

Tommy and Justine moved into action. Seconds later James knelt, gently laying Natasha down onto the pallet of blankets.

"All right, Mama. Let's get her out of this wet stuff—every bit of it." James said loosening Natasha's remaining tennis shoe. He took it off and peeled her socks from her feet, tossing them to the side. He rose and hurried into his room to grab the big quilt from his bed. Justine was stripping away the rest of Natasha's clothing.

"Check her over carefully for any signs of wounds," James instructed. "God knows what happened down there."

"She looks fine," Justine sobbed. "She's just so cold."

"You lie down right with her, Justine. I'm going to roll her onto her side and you wrap yourself right around her, give her as much contact as you can to warm her. Don't rub at her skin, just keep your warmth against her. Try not to press against her chest at all. She swallowed a bit of water and I'm sure breathed a bit in. That's right. Just like that."

Tommy and James wrapped the edges of the blankets on the floor up around both of them. They folded the quilt and laid it on top tucking it in like a cocoon around them so only their heads were visible. Then Tommy draped two blankets he'd grabbed from upstairs over that. James laid a gentle hand on on top of Justine's head, then against Natasha's pale, cold cheek.

Dear Lord, please. Please let her live. Please.

He gently tugged at the blankets just a bit to be sure Natasha was completely covered. Only her nose and mouth were free. A single tear rolled down Justine's cheek. James knelt down and kissed the side of her forehead.

"Everything will be fine," he vowed. "More help will be here soon. You just keep her warm. I wish I had the survival blanket off the boat," he said. "But this will have to do." He straightened up, looking around. "Where's Sophia?"

"She went to get Cora right after you found Natasha."

"Good." James nodded.

Tommy kneeled by Justine who was doing her best to keep Natasha warm. She was beginning to shiver herself. Her head was tucked down into the blanket against her daughter's neck. Tommy adjusted the quilt around them again, trying to keep every bit of warmth that he could inside the cocoon of blankets.

"Dad, you've got to get out of that wet stuff, too." Tommy looked over his father. "Your pajamas are soaked and your feet are beat to hell."

James waved a hand at him. "I'm fine. I'll take care of that once the ambulance gets here and I know Natasha is being treated." He shuffled to the window peering out into the darkness. "Where the hell are they?" The knot in the pit of his stomach was tightening. They needed to get Natasha where she could be properly evaluated and treated, and soon.

He looked at his son seeing the same question in his eyes. He turned back to the window as he saw a flash of red lights out of the corner of his eye. A small wave of relief and hope washed over him. "Here they come. They just turned the corner," he said heading toward the door. "Justine, help is almost here. You stay right like you are until they get in here and take over."

Seventy Two

The doors to the emergency room waiting area swished open as James approached the entrance. He could see Tommy, Sophia, and Cora huddled together talking quietly. Since James's phone was floating out in the ocean somewhere, Sophia had left her phone with her dad. Tommy had already updated James via text as far as Natasha's condition. She was suffering from hypothermia, but it looked like she was going to pull through just fine. They were waiting on x-rays of her lungs to be sure she hadn't aspirated any seawater. If she had that could cause pneumonia. Surprisingly enough there were no broken bones and very few contusions, except for on her ankle that had been caught in the rocks. She was in a warming bed with heated IV fluids dripping into her veins. They were planning to move her to Pediatric ICU as soon as they had a bed ready. James knew enough to know Natasha wasn't completely out of the woods yet. Still, she had everything going for her right now. That, along with faith, would have to do.

On the other hand, the news James now had to deliver to the group wasn't going to be pleasant. He wasn't looking forward to the conversation one bit.

"Hey, Dad." Tommy stood up. "We're just waiting for now. No one but Justine can be in emergency, but once they take her up to the floor, we can each visit for a couple minutes one-by-one."

"Good. That's all good." James suddenly felt like the walls were closing in on him. He sat down next to Sophia, across from Tommy and Cora. He clasped his hands together and stared at the floor as his throat tightened. He felt like he was about to start bawling.

"Are you all right, Dad?" Sophia asked, reaching out to touch his arm.

James nodded. He patted her hand. "I'll be fine." He cleared his throat. "I'll admit I don't think I've ever been so scared for someone my entire life. I was terrified of what I would find when I got to her. It's a miracle she's not in worse shape than she is."

"What happened down there? Did you find out?" Tommy asked.

"Quite a bit of it," James said slowly. "I guess all that I'm allowed to know. Nate and Agent Campbell came up and got me right after you all headed to the hospital. I had to give a statement, of course. Then they filled me in. I'll tell you all about it in a while."

He looked over at Cora. Her head was bowed, hands clasped together in her lap. She was small in stature already, but she was so pale and withdrawn that she seemed even more slight than usual. James knew she was silently praying for her granddaughter with every ounce of her heart and soul.

"Cora. Would you please take a walk with me? I need to talk with you alone."

She looked up at him, startled. "Oh. Sure."

James stood up and offered her his hand. She let him help her up. He took her elbow.

Tommy and Sophia looked at them questioningly.

"We'll be back in a few minutes. I'll tell you everything then. I just need to talk to Cora alone first."

James guided her down the hallway toward the main hospital. It was after midnight now. There was no one except the two of them in the corridor. He stopped and turned to face Cora.

She looked up at him. "I have this feeling that you're going to tell me that Homer was involved in all this. Aren't you?"

James nodded. "I'm sorry, Cora. He was the one that started the shooting."

"What? What in God's name was he doing down there? What was he into?"

"Drugs," James said grimly. "He's been delivering drugs that are run in from across the border. He was making an exchange tonight. Natasha stumbled across the latest drop off. She was in the wrong place at the wrong time."

"She could have been killed," Cora whispered. Her eyes widened. "She could have been killed!"

James nodded. "The luckiest thing, besides that the shots missed her, is that the two men who came in to make the exchange tonight were planted DEA agents that have been undercover here for months. They never would have fired at Natasha or anywhere near her. Unfortunately, Homer was . . . .Hell, I don't know what he was. He shot and killed one agent and badly wounded the other."

Cora was staring at him like he was speaking a language she couldn't comprehend. She turned and grabbed the railing that lined the hallway with both hands.

"I'm sorry. This is so much to take in. We should find a place to sit down."

"No. I'm fine," Cora said. "It's just . . .it's just . . ."

"Unbelievable," James finished for her. "I know. I'm still trying to wrap my head around it all."

"Is the officer that's wounded going to live?"

"Yes. He took a bullet to the shoulder. I'm sure he's in surgery in Bangor by now. They took him there, straightaway."

"Where is Homer? Did they catch him? Is he in jail?"

"They got him. He fled through Dean's yard to your place through some hidden passage in the hedges. He got in his truck and high-tailed it toward Milbridge. He was apparently drunk and most likely high on whatever drugs he's been peddling. He ended up wrapping his truck around a tree on Route One, just this side of Steuben. He missed the curve by the fire station."

"Is he dead?"

James shook his head. "I have no idea how bad he is. He was still alive when they found him. They life-flighted him to Bangor." He took a deep breath. "I'm so sorry."

Cora pursed her lips and shook her head. She looked up at James. There were no tears. All he could see was fire in her eyes. "Don't you be sorry, James Edward. God forgive me, but that man deserves whatever he gets. He is not the person we knew years ago. He's become a sick monster. I hope he lives, and I pray he goes to prison and pays for all the terrible things he's done. And I hope I never have to lay eyes on him again."

James held her gaze. "I hear you, Cora. I'm right there with you." He sighed. "There are a couple other things you should know. I really hate to tell you, but I'm sure they'll be rumors everywhere in town before it's done."

"Well, I don't know that it could be much worse than what it is, so you better just say it," Cora stated firmly. She drew up all five-foot-two of herself, waiting.

James searched her face. Neither piece of information was anything he wanted to relay, and he was afraid what he had to tell her was going to send her right over the edge. But he also knew it was best if she heard it from him. "I'm really sorry I'm the one to tell you this. Truly I am. But I found out tonight that Homer also has been fooling around with some woman from Jonesport. I didn't recognize the name, but the agents said it's been going on at least since they started watching him. I guess about year or so ago."

Cora barked out a short, angry laugh. She waved a dismissive hand toward James. "That's not news. I already know all about that. Don't forget this town knows everyone's business before they do. She's Diane something-or-other. That's nothing. She's been around for a couple years hanging onto his arm every night down there at that stinkin' bar. Truth is I'd been hoping he'd decide to actually take up with her for good and leave. That would've made my life easier by far."

James looked down at her in amazement. "I guess I should've known that wouldn't come as a surprise to you. There's been muttering on the wharf for a long time about it, along with about a dozen other supposed affairs everyone loves to speculate about. I never paid any mind to it. I figured it was just idle talk, like most of the gossip." James took a deep breath. "But, Cora," He took his hat off and rubbed at his forehead before settling it back down. "What I'm going to tell you next is the worst of all of this. I think we should find a place to sit down."

"Good Lord. Get on with it, James. I already told you, there's not much worse you could tell me. I'm already madder than a crab in a trap. I can handle whatever it is."

"This woman he was running around with was one of the leaders of a big drug ring the feds busted up tonight. They've been funneling drugs in and moving them all over the state. Homer was their go-between, the person that made the exchanges. They said he's been doing that for at least a couple years."

Cora's eyes narrowed, her mouth tightened in anger. "That sorry bastard."

James nodded. "But the worst thing is that the agent who is wounded says that he watched Homer shoot directly at Natasha."

Cora gasped.

James closed his eyes and shook his head quickly as if to rid himself of the mental image. "Cora, he wanted to kill her. They both saw her run in in front of the wharf and across the road. The agent said even in the dark they could see that it was a child. Homer yelled something about getting rid of the nosy brat. Then he shot right at her. That was the third shot we all heard. That's how the agent got wounded. He lunged at Homer to try to disarm him because he took aim at Natasha as she ran away."

Cora was staring at James, eyes wide in disbelief. She swayed slightly. James reached out and grasped her elbow to steady her.

"Are you sure? He tried to kill her? His own granddaughter? Oh, my Lord!" There was a catch in her voice. James was certain now she was going to start crying. He fished his handkerchief out of his pants pocket with his free hand and held it out to her.

Cora waved it away. She stepped back releasing herself from his hold on her elbow. "I'm not going to cry. I'm too damn furious." She took a deep breath. "That man is pure evil. God forgive me. I could kill him myself for what he's done. I hope he rots in hell."

"I know. I feel the same." James agreed grimly. "But the authorities have him now. It's up to them to handle it, if he survives. Something went terribly wrong in him a long time ago."

"I know. He's not been the man I married, or I thought I married, for so many years now. Oh James, this never would have happened if I'd left long ago when I first should have. Now my granddaughter is fighting to live, a man has died, and another one is injured. I contributed to all of this."

James took a deep breath. "Cora, that's ridiculous and you know it. None of this, I repeat, none of this, is your fault. You couldn't have had any control over any of it any more than you can make the tides turn."

Cora was shaking her head. "No James. I have some responsibility here. Make no excuses. I'm done making excuses. For years I was so sure the man I loved was still in there somewhere. Later I was just too weak to do anything about it. It was easier to just keep on. I'll spend the rest of my life trying to make it right. I should have divorced him years ago and made a better life for my daughter and granddaughter."

"And for you," James reminded her.

Cora smiled sadly up at James. "You know, your Anna always told me that. She told me all the time that I was sacrificing my own life and happiness by staying." She shrugged. "I knew she was right, but I just didn't have what it took to strike out on my own—to start all over again. Then when I finally decide that I have to do it, regardless of how scared I am, the world falls apart before I can even start."

"But, Cora, you can still do that now. It's not too late to start again." James paused. "As long as we're still here it's not too late for any of us."

Cora shook her head. She looked at the floor, then back up at James. She sighed. "Well, I guess we'll find out. I'd say *that* road has appeared in no uncertain terms."

James's pants pocket buzzed. He reached in to grab Sophia's phone and scanned the message on the screen. "Tommy says they've taken Natasha upstairs. They'll meet us up there." He hit the thumbs up sign to reply, then slid the phone back into his pocket.

"Will you be all right?" He asked.

"I'll be fine," Cora said staring straight ahead, lips pursed. She looked over at James. "I'll be just fine," she repeated firmly. "But only God can help Homer Connor if I ever have to lay eyes on him again. And James," she said as they started walking toward the elevator.

"Yes?"

"I think we should just keep all this between us for right now. I'll tell Justine myself when the time is right. I want her to be able to focus on Natasha and nothing else. If she asks anything about Homer, I'll tell her. But only if she asks."

James nodded. "Agreed." He pushed the button beside the elevator doors. "Now, let's go see if they'll let us in to visit that little mermaid of ours. I'm sure you want to hug the stuffing out of her as much as I do; probably more."

Seventy Three

They'd been sitting in the waiting room outside the pediatric ward for over an hour when Justine finally appeared. Sheer exhaustion etched her face.

They all stood up at once as she came toward them.

"How is she?" Tommy asked tentatively.

"Gaining. Her body temperature is near normal again. She's been awake off and on. They just took her off the oxygen because her blood levels are perfect. I don't know how, but her chest x-rays are completely clear. They're going to keep her in critical care for the next twenty-four hours to keep a close eye on her. Then we'll see how it goes."

Cora walked over to Justine. She didn't say anything as she held her tight. Justine clung to her mother for a long moment before letting go.

"They'll let one other person in there with me for five minutes at a time if you want to go see her," she said. "But we have to space it out so she can rest."

"Cora, you go right ahead. I think the rest of us can wait until tomorrow to see her," James suggested.

Justine shook her head. "She's been asking for you, James, every time she wakes up. She's very insistent. I think you need to see her first. She won't rest until you do. Then Mom can come in. Sorry, Mom."

"Oh." James looked at Cora questioningly. She smiled gently at him. "It's fine James. Go on. I'll go next."

James followed Justine. She pressed the button on the side of the wall and spoke into the intercom to be let into the ward.

"I don't know how to thank you," she said turning to him in the hallway as the doors swished shut behind them. "You saved her life." Her eyes filled with tears. "I'll owe you the rest of mine."

James folded her into his arms, resting his chin against the top of her head as she laid it on his chest. She was shaking all over. "Honey, you don't owe me anything. If anything, I owe your little one for showing me that I still have a life, and a purpose, on this earth. Just a short time ago I was wondering why I was still here—how I was going to go on. Then she blew into my world. She promptly took my old-geezer, self-centered way of life and fed it to the fish."

Justine stepped back and wiped away a tear that had slipped down her cheek. "You make it sound like that's a good thing."

"You have no clue," James said. "I have a whole new perspective—on so many things. Plus, she brought you back home and back into our lives. Now I can't imagine not having you and Natasha right here. And Sophia is home for good and Tommy is coming to visit more and more."

Justine gave James a little smile. "You're so good to Natasha—to us. She loves you so much."

James hugged her shoulders. "She's one special little mermaid. I love her right to pieces. It tears me apart to think that we almost lost her."

"Me too. I can't even . . ." She began walking down the hall. James fell into step with her. "I do know we better get you in there or she's liable to get up to search for you herself. She already tried to get out of bed to find you when she first woke up."

They reached the room just as a young man in scrubs came out.

"There you are. I was just going to get her some ginger ale. She woke up again asking for a Mr. James. She also said she's hungry, but the doctor doesn't want her to eat anything just yet."

"Well, I'd say that's a pretty good indication she's feeling a bit better," James remarked as they entered the room and went to the side of Natasha's bed. A bag of fluid dripped down a line taped in place on her left hand that was wrapped to a board to keep it straight. Multi-colored lines ran across the monitor beside the IV pole. An oxygen tent was pulled back and tied back like window curtains on either side of the bed.

It suddenly hit James that the last time he'd been in a room much like this one, Anna had been the one lying there. He took a deep breath and exhaled as he felt the walls begin to close in around him for the second time that night.

"I think she's out cold again," Justine said.

"Hmmm?" It took a minute for James to register that she was talking to him. "Oh. I'm sure. It would be good if she slept right through."

"Mr. James. Is that you?" Natasha's eyes were closed. Her voice sounded tiny and distant.

"I'm here. Right here." James leaned over Natasha. She reached out her hand patting the covers of the bed trying to find him. He laid his hand on top of hers and squeezed it to let her know he was there. His throat closed up tight. His eyes began to burn. His entire hand swallowed hers up. He thought of how they'd almost lost her. A wave of fear, and then grief, flowed through him even though he knew now that she was going to pull through just fine.

Natasha opened her eyes. She looked up at him, but her gaze was distant. "I have to tell you." She closed her eyes and frowned.

James squeezed her hand again. "It's OK. Just rest. Whatever it is can wait until you feel better."

"No. I have to tell you now so I don't forget," she said slowly, carefully. "She told me right before she left, when we heard you coming to get me. She stayed with me the whole time."

James glanced over at Justine by his side. She looked as confused as he felt. He looked back down at Natasha's face that was just starting to show signs of a little color in her cheeks. She appeared to be asleep again.

She wriggled in the bed and whispered, "I promised."

"Who?" Justine asked. "Tasha, who did you promise?"

"Miss Anna." Natasha whispered again.

James started. He was sure he hadn't heard her correctly.

"Miss Anna?" Justine looked alarmed now.

James thought he saw Natasha nod her head once, but then he wasn't sure because the movement was so slight.

Natasha's voice was stronger, almost a normal volume. "She sat on the rocks by me the whole time tonight down at my beach. She said I would be fine; that Mr. James would come to get me unstuck. She told me when to hold my breath every time before the waves started coming over my head. She told me a story too, about when you and Sophia and Tommy were little. But I don't remember it right now." Her words trailed off.

James squeezed her hand. He felt unsteady and slightly sick to his stomach. "Just go to sleep Little One. You need to rest." He straightened up, still holding onto Natasha's hand.

"She must have been hallucinating because she was hypothermic," he said softly to Justine. "We've all talking about Anna quite a bit the past few days while we've been getting ready for her art exhibit."

"No! I saw her. She was there. Right with me. She helped me," Natasha protested. She coughed weakly, frowned, and took a breath. "I promised her I would tell you exactly the words."

Natasha opened her eyes. They were clear and bright as she peered up at James. When she spoke her voice was soft, calm and sure. "She said to tell you, 'Stay safe, Love.'" Natasha smiled at him, closed her eyes, and drifted off to sleep.

The world blurred and slid away from James. Something tore deep within him. He needed air, but could only manage to draw a shallow, ragged breath. His eyes burned and filled—brimming with hot anguish. Still holding tight to Natasha's hand, he knelt on the floor, laid his forehead against the bed, and wept.

Seventy Four

Epilogue

"Come on, Mr. James. "You're holding up progress."

"Where in the world did you hear that?" James asked as he ambled along behind the youngster down the driveway toward the freshly painted, sunshine yellow house across the road from his own home. He stopped briefly, deliberately stalling to give the others time to put their gifts for Natasha under the Christmas tree.

"Gran says it all the time when I get distracted and I forget what I'm supposed to be doing," Natasha replied, facing him as she skipped backwards toward the porch. "Come on! I can't wait for you to see your Christmas present I got you!"

"A present for me? Christmas is supposed to be for kids."

"Hah! That's not true. Everybody gets Christmas and Christmas wishes," Natasha retorted. "Mom says so."

"Now it's wishes, huh? I thought that your only Christmas wish was that you got to move into your new house," James said. "Was there more?"

"Well, I guess that's still the biggest part of it. But there are a couple other things under the tree now too. I had some secret wishes. We haven't opened anything except our stockings. Mom and Soph said we had to wait for you before we could. They said we had to all be together."

"I see," he remarked, stopping to look up. "Will you just look at that sky. I wonder if we'll get to see any sun at all today." He knelt on one knee, pretending to tie the laces on his boots.

"Come on slowpoke! Mom's gonna make you take your boots off inside anyway." Natasha was already standing at the front door waiting for him.

"OK. OK. I'm moving," James said. He stepped up onto the porch. "Do I have to knock before I go in?"

"Don't be silly." Natasha opened the door wide. "Merry Christmas! Welcome to the Sunflower House!"

She was watching his face to see his reaction. The girls had decided three days earlier as they'd begun moving their belongings into the newly renovated house that they weren't going to let James see the results of their labors until Christmas morning. As hard as they'd been at it, James was certain it was going to be beautiful.

"Wow! Just look at that tree!" He exclaimed stepping in front of Natasha, blocking her view. "It's gorgeous! I can't believe all the stuff under it that Santa must've just left."

"What do you mean?" Natasha shut the door and moved around in front of him.

"OHHHH! Oh! Wow! Look at all the presents!" She glanced back at James, her eyes wide with wonder. She stared back at the Christmas tree and the multitude of brightly wrapped boxes and packages cascading from under it. "But none of that was there when I came to get you. Look! There's a bike. There's a new bike!" She ran over to where a bicycle sporting a huge iridescent purple bow on its handlebars was partially concealed by the tree and other presents. "Is it for me?"

"I don't know anyone else in this house that would want a blue bike with mermaids on it. Do you?" Justine asked pushing through the swinging door that led into the kitchen. Cora, Sophia, and Tommy were right behind her. They were all smiling for everything they were worth.

"Surprised?" Justine asked.

"Oh, yeah! I can't believe it! We were supposed to be surprising Mr. James. But, wow!"

"Oh, I'm still surprised." James said looking around. "You girls have made this old place just shine. It's absolutely amazing."

"None of it would have happened if not for you, Dad. You helped us buy the house, after all."

James waved Sophia's words away. "It's a good investment. You ladies have done all the work to bring her back to life. I'm just glad I thought to find out if they wanted to sell it. It sat empty for way too long. A house needs to be lived in to be a home."

"Do you want the grand tour?" Justine asked handing him a cup of coffee.

James shook his head. He took a sip from the steaming mug, then looked over at Natasha who was inspecting every detail of her new bike. "Not right yet. There's plenty of time for that. I think we better let our little mermaid open her presents now, or she'll start riding that bike in the house terrorizing the cats."

Tommy laughed. "Those teenage kittens are pretty laid back. I bet they'd ride with her in that basket."

"It's so beautiful," Natasha gushed. "I can't wait to tell Maddie. Can I call her?"

Justine shook her head. "Not right now. I'm sure she's doing Christmas with her family. Besides, you'll see her tomorrow when you go to the movies together."

"That sounds fun," James remarked. "That was something we used to do when we were young; go to see a movie the day after Christmas."

"I can't wait," Natasha said. "Maddie's grandpa takes her every year. It's like a tradition. He asked Gran and me if we wanted to come too."

James looked over at Cora. "I see," he said winking at her.

Cora's face flushed pink. She shook a finger at him. "James Edward, don't you start."

"What?" James held up the palms of his hands. "I wasn't going to say a word. Except that I think it's wonderful."

"Me too," Natasha agreed. "I love movies and I've never been to the theatre in Bangor. Mom, can I at least go ride my bike later, after we open the other presents. Can I?"

"Umm, probably not. I think we'll have to put your bike away for another day." Justine pointed toward the window. "Look outside."

Natasha scampered over. "Snow! It's snowing! Mr. James, come see. It looks just like a painting." She leaned her elbows on the windowsill and cupped her chin in her hands. "Now it's an absolutely perfect Christmas."

James went to stand behind Natasha watching the huge fluffy flakes of Christmas snow drifting down. He looked out over the yard and beyond, to the sea past the reach.

I just bet you had something to do with this too, my Anna. We miss you so. Merry Christmas, my love.

The others had come up behind them to watch out the window. The sky darkened to a deeper, silver-gray as the storm moved in. The lawn was quickly becoming a sea of white. When James shifted his gaze slightly, everyone inside the room appeared reflected in the window against the backdrop of the multi-colored tree lights—a dreamlike portrait.

A fleeting wisp of something caressed his cheek. He closed his eyes, basking in the faint scent of vanilla and sugar cookie that surrounded him. Beside him, a little hand stole into his. James opened his eyes to look down at Natasha still intently watching out the window. He wrapped his fingers around hers giving her hand a gentle squeeze, holding it firm in his own.

Together they watched the snow whisper down from the woolen sky. The yard was fully blanketed in white now. Christmas lights looped along the newly-repaired picket fence shimmered through frosty, white lace. Beyond the fence, through the gate, past the rocky beach, snowflakes drifted, then swirled together on a breeze before slipping into the frothy, winter sea.

Natasha's
Good Things About Here List

1) The Ocean
2) My Bike
3) The Ocean
4) The Stars Here
5) Gran's Pancakes and Mochas
6) My Attic Room
7) Super Interesting Rocks
8) My Very Own Beach
9) Bald Eagles
10) Long Walks by the Ocean with Mom
11) Mr. James - My First New Friend
12) The Library Reading Room
13) Petunia Cat
14) Fishing
15) Petunia'a Kittens (Especially Grumble)
16) My Friend Maddie
17) Our Awesome New House
18) My Mermaid Christmas Present Bike
19) Our New Big Family
20) It's Home

Acknowledgements

A special thanks to my bestest friend and critical reader, Lydia Pryor, who loves and supports me even when she's convinced I'm a cracked nut.

****

Many thanks to dearest friend and fellow author, sidney woods, for checking in on my process, progress, and me, almost daily.
My writerly sanity would have flown long ago if not for you.

****

Hugs and love to the rest of our long-time writing group whose support and encouragement keeps me plowing forward:
You all inspire me every day.

****

Additional gratitude to: dear friend, reader, and constructive cheerleader, Ellen Lancaster; sweet pal, Maureen Schauerte who read and reread the umpteenth draft and loved the story so much she asked for more; and my lobstermen family, friends, and neighbors, for taking the time to share with me some insights about their lives and livelihood.

****

Much love, respect, and thanks to my very first proofreader—the brave woman who told the school librarian when I was in first grade that yes, I was allowed to check out and read the book on the history of the Roman Empire. She always let me be who I am. Thank you, Mom.

****

Most importantly, my whole heart and gratitude for the unwavering support of my incredible husband Brian who listened to and loved this story first, and to our amazing children and grandchildren.
I love you all as big as the moon and as high as the stars.
You are my world.

www.ingramcontent.com/pod-product-compliance
Lightning Source LLC
LaVergne TN
LVHW010306070526
838199LV00065B/5451